THE WEIGHT OF THE WISHING STONE

SILVETTICA

Published by Silvettica | 2025

For more information, visit: **http://www.authorkevincox.com**

THE WEIGHT OF THE WISHING STONE

FATES OF GALANOR 1

KEVIN COX

CHAPTER 1

THE CITY OF Tathara teetered between revelry and ruin. Its massive stone walls, worn by time but still formidable, rose defiantly against the encroaching darkness, perhaps the last bastion of hope for the Kingdom of Elenior. As the hour of dread approached, the cacophony of merriment energized the air. Streets, usually quiet at night, now vibrated with the frenetic energy of those seeking solace from their fears.

Rykan wandered to a quiet spot alone where he could watch the crowds of people laughing and cheering from a distance. The water of the cool marble fountain behind him trickled calmly as his mind raged with worry and doubt. Faces blended together as people passed by, some familiar, others strange. Underneath the festivities, Rykan felt the pulse of Tathara's fear. Some masked their fears with brave faces, while others seemed oblivious to the coming storm. Throughout the night, nobles raised their cups skyward with hollow cheers, soldiers clanked their swords against shields in feigned confidence, and minstrels played tunes that strayed dangerously close to the edges of despair.

Three of the brightest stars clustered together in the clear skies above. Rumors had circulated of a rare convergence, a celestial event that only occurred once every few centuries, warning of times of chaos. Legends spoke of heroes born from such moments, stories painted in broad strokes of courage, honor, and triumph over encroaching darkness.

Rykan often dreamed of times like these from books of history and myth, how he might face such trials. He wished to be someone

who made a difference in the world, who others respected and revered. As a boy, he had longed to follow in the footsteps of his father and stand among the ranks of Tathara's famed Crimson Shield, his deeds immortalized in the lore of the city. But now, with the shadow of the Iron Flood upon them, those dreams twisted into doubt.

The impending siege by the Iron Flood, led by their charismatic yet ruthless leader, Vatreus, had been proclaimed a tactical blunder. Tathara's commanders boasted of a decisive victory, confident it would end Vatreus and his dreaded army. Though the walls of the city were often touted as unbreachable, Rykan sensed something beneath the boasts: a tangled thread of desperation. A fear that this night wasn't a celebration of assured victory, but one that could be their last.

Footsteps sounded against cobblestones, louder and closer.

"Rykan! Come to the tavern with us! The captain's splurged on ale!" Daveth's voice broke through his contemplation, each word jolting Rykan further from his spiraling thoughts.

His friends Daveth and Brant appeared beside him, their hands clapping onto his shoulders, grounding him. Brant, with his golden hair and ivory skin, and Daveth, a Lith with white hair, sunlit skin, and pointed forked ears, guided him toward the tavern's warmth.

As they pushed through the tavern's heavy wooden door, a wave of laughter and the rich aroma of spiced ale and roasted meat greeted them. Anticipation and stories of old battles resonated in the thick air of the packed room. Daveth led the way, elbowing through the crowd, as Rykan and Brant followed, the weight of the night momentarily lifted by the promise of camaraderie.

Laughter and shouts filled the tavern as soldiers, some still donning pieces of armor, regaled each other with tales of valor and made bold predictions about the morrow's battle. Waitresses in swirling skirts wove through the boisterous crowd with ease, balancing trays laden with drinks.

Rykan and his friends found a spot at one of the long wooden tables, its surface sticky with spilled ale. He took a deep breath, letting the sounds and scents of the tavern wash over him, if only for a moment. Here, among friends, the impending siege seemed a distant worry, replaced by brotherhood and the fleeting comfort of shared stories and laughter.

"Get one for Rykan too!" bellowed a nearby soldier, raising his mug in a hearty salute.

In the corner, a bard plucked at a lute, his notes weaving through the air, while a woman's clear voice lifted in song above the din.

The crowded area around the musicians had transformed into dance, where young and old people spun and clapped, their movements as exuberant as the music. Their laughter mingled with the melodies, creating a sound that pulsed with life.

A waitress approached with a welcoming smile, her eyes crinkling at the edges. She handed him a frothing mug of ale, the foam kissing the brim. Rykan took a deep sip, the rich, earthy taste keeping his focus on their surroundings. His gaze wandered across the tavern, taking in the familiar faces of those he might never see again.

A loud horn blew, a piercing sound that cut through the noise of the tavern. Silence crept over the crowd as the captain rose from his seat. The woman stopped singing, but the lute player continued his tune. Dancers wound down their movements and shuffled back to their seats.

"Warriors of Tathara, citizens," Captain Mirell began as he raised his mug in salute. "Tonight, we gather within the shadow of these walls that have guarded us since the dawn of Elenior. As the Crimson Shield of our forefathers gleams beneath the starlit sky, let us raise our cups to the eve of victory!"

The tavern erupted in shouts and applause. Rykan took another sip of ale as he watched the others' expressions. Unlike those outside, he couldn't find any hint of doubt or fear in their faces. How did they find such courage in times like these? How could they be so sure of themselves? He worried that they could read the doubt in him, the anxiety and fear. Would they think him a coward?

"Tomorrow, we will meet the Iron Flood," continued the captain. "This enemy has only known victory in battle. They have seen others crumble at their feet, but they have not seen the strength of Tathara's heart nor the depth of our resolve."

More cheers rang out through the crowd. Even Daveth and Brant put down their mugs long enough to join in the shouts.

"Tonight, let your hearts be light, for more than any armor, it is the courage in your laughter and the bond in your songs that fortify our spirits."

Rykan felt as though the captain was speaking to him directly, as if he knew the cloudy thoughts in his head.

"Let us toast to the valor that runs in our veins, to the ties that bind us to each other, and to this sacred ground that has protected us for years. May the shouts of victory resound through the mountains of Galanor, carried on the winds that whisper the blessings of our ancestors."

As the captain's voice climbed to a crescendo, everyone in the tavern rose in anticipation. "To the unbreakable spirit of Tathara!" he bellowed, his tankard thrust high.

A resonant cheer reverberated through the air, making the very stones of the tavern seem to thrum with energy. Even Rykan found himself drawn into the collective fervor, his voice blending with the chorus. It was as if an electrifying current of unity coursed through the crowd, binding every heart and soul in the room.

Rykan downed his ale as the chattering, dancing, and singing resumed. Another group of soldiers entered the already crowded tavern, men from another company. He began to feel a bit uncomfortable. All these experienced soldiers made him even less confident in his own skills.

He turned his attention to the citizens. It amazed him how the whole city had come together. People from every station had come to support them. They knew how important this night was to show appreciation to those defending Tathara and to help take their anxious minds off the coming battle. In turn, he and the other soldiers had to do whatever they could to defend and preserve this city. Rykan couldn't imagine another like it in all of Galanor.

"See that girl over there?" Brant nodded toward a table where a pair of soldiers sat with a few women.

As Rykan's eyes searched, one stood out among the others—a girl about their age with long brown hair. Their eyes met for a moment, and Rykan quickly turned away, afraid she would think he was staring.

"She keeps looking over here," Brant said, a sly smile playing on his lips. "I think she's looking at you."

"No, she's not," Rykan replied, trying to sound indifferent.

"Go ask her to dance," Daveth urged, leaning closer to make his point.

Rykan glanced at her again, noticing her eyes dart back toward their table. "She's only looking over here because you guys are staring at her," he muttered.

"You're going into battle tomorrow and you aren't even brave enough to ask a girl to dance?" Brant chuckled, his laughter light but teasing.

"You just want me to make a fool of myself by going over there," Rykan said, shaking his head.

"If you don't ask her, I will," Daveth declared, pushing his chair back and starting to stand.

Rykan's chest tightened as he watched Daveth rise. If this girl really was looking at him, the thought of Daveth intervening was unbearable. He didn't want his friend to steal the moment that might have been meant for him alone.

Rising from his chair, he squared his shoulders. "She was looking at me. I'll go ask her."

The brown-haired girl bore a look of panic when she noticed Rykan walking toward her table. She seemed as though she wanted to hide. His newfound confidence faded, but something told him to keep going, stay the course, no matter what. He silently rehearsed what he should say when he got there, words echoing in his head. But planning never worked for him.

Rykan tried to clear his mind and allow the words to come when they were needed, fresh and spontaneous.

"Dance?" he asked.

Then he narrowed his eyes, wondering why that was the only thing to come out of his mouth. A brief look of confusion, followed by blankness, crossed the girl's face, as if she were waiting for him to say more. He almost started over, in an attempt to turn his question into a full sentence, as people normally do. But he decided to let it stand. After all, it was simple and direct. The fewer words he used, the better.

Once the others at the table realized that was the extent of his proposition, they turned to the girl, waiting for her answer.

She blinked, her initial panic giving way to a tentative smile.

"Sure," she said, her voice steady but soft. She stood up, smoothing her dress with a quick motion, and extended her hand toward him. "Let's dance."

The others at the table exchanged amused glances before she took Rykan's hand, leading him toward the open floor. Her light touch contrasted with her firm grip, and her eyes met his with a mix of curiosity and something else he couldn't quite place.

As they reached the center of the room, the music shifted to a slower, more melodic tune. Rykan placed his hand on her waist, feeling the warmth of her body through the fabric of her dress. She rested her hand on his shoulder, and they began to sway to the rhythm, their movements tentative at first, then gradually more fluid.

The room around them faded, the sounds of talking and laughter dimming to a distant murmur. The girl's eyes softened. She appeared calmer now, making him feel more at ease. He realized he didn't even know her name.

"I'm Rykan," he said, trying to keep the awkward silence at bay.

"Isara," she replied with a small smile. "Nice to meet you, Rykan."

Rykan's earlier nerves began to melt away, replaced by a sense of unexpected peace. He could feel the eyes of his friends on him, but for once, he didn't care. This moment was his.

"I can't believe you're all going to battle tomorrow," she said, breaking the silence. Her voice trembled slightly, betraying her fear. "This whole thing scares me. I never thought anything like this would happen. I can't imagine what it must be like for you."

"I can't believe it either," Rykan admitted, his eyes scanning the room before returning to her face. "But I've seen these men fight. They're the best in all of Galanor. And we'll be defending the greatest city. There's no better motivation than that."

Isara looked down briefly, her grip on his shoulder tightening slightly. "I hope you're right," she said. She lifted her gaze to meet his, her eyes earnest. "I know we just met, but … I'd hate to see something happen to you. I'll be praying for all of you."

"Thank you," he said softly, touched by her concern. "That means a lot."

She hesitated, then asked, "What do you plan to do? Once this is over with?"

Rykan took a deep breath, glancing at the ceiling as if searching for answers there.

"I once wanted to be one of the Crimson Shield," he said. "But I don't think I'm cut out for that. I've always wanted to be part of something that will last in Tathara long past my lifetime. Like helping to build something like the Archive of Ages."

Isara's eyes lit up with interest. "Yes, your name would be recorded in history," she said. She paused, then added with a touch of self-deprecation, "I just work at Windham Bakery, my father's business. My name won't be remembered by anyone."

Rykan shook his head, a smile tugging at the corners of his mouth. "It will if you make your bakery the best Galanor has ever seen," he said with a lighthearted, encouraging tone.

She chuckled, the sound light and musical. "I suppose that is something to strive for."

The song ended, and they stopped dancing, but stayed standing close to each other. Around them, the tavern's lively atmosphere bustled, but Rykan felt a connection between them. At the very least, he had found a new friend, someone who understood the weight of the times they were living through.

"Thank you for the dance," she said.

"Thank you," Rykan replied, his heart beating a little faster. "Maybe we'll see each other again, after … everything."

Isara nodded, her eyes hopeful. "I'd like that."

They parted, and Rykan made his way back to his friends. He couldn't help but feel a glimmer of hope amid the looming darkness. For the first time in a while, the future didn't seem entirely bleak.

"He's smiling," said Brant as Rykan returned to the table. "I guess that went well."

"Yeah, I think so," Rykan said, dropping into his seat.

Daveth got up from the table. "I'm going to find someone to dance with."

"Me too," said Brant. "If I die tomorrow, I need to make this a night to remember."

Leaning back in his chair, Rykan watched them step through the crowd. Dancing with Isara had opened his eyes to the many people in Tathara he had never met, people he might connect with if he only took the time. It wasn't the only thing missing in his life, but it was definitely something. A connection with someone who understood him, who supported him through the highs and lows. Someone he could encourage and uplift, who found happiness just in his presence. They could share each other's victories and bolster each other after their defeats.

"There he is!" shouted a familiar voice from across the tavern, startling him out of his thoughts.

Rykan glanced up to find his parents entering the room. His father had a commanding presence Rykan wished he shared, drawing nods of respect from the other patrons. His mother smiled warmly as she made her way through the crowd.

Though Rykan had grown up in Tathara, he had been born in the Candasara Isles. His parents often reminisced about the warm welcome they had received from the Tatharans. Others had found themselves here for one reason or another. Though a human city, Tathara was also home to some Kren with their ridged foreheads, Liths with their forked ears, and Anvir with their sharp horns. They all lived together harmoniously, and Rykan never felt out of place as an islander.

Captain Mirell greeted his parents. Rykan could see their mouths moving but couldn't hear anything they said. After a few moments, the three of them made their way over to where Rykan was sitting.

"How are you feeling, soldier?" asked the captain.

"Good, sir," Rykan replied.

"You have a good look about you, lad. Your father here is one of the best swordsmen I know." The captain turned to his father and smiled. "If you're half as capable as him, you have nothing to fear." Captain Mirell eyed Rykan with an amused grin. "Before my first battle, I was so nervous I couldn't stop shaking. You've already surpassed me in that regard." Captain Mirell clapped Rykan on the shoulder. "Even though you'll be on the front lines with the other swordsmen, you won't be in front of the main gate. That's where the attack will come. But we've prepared a bit of a trap. The most you'll have to do is cut off their escape once they attempt to retreat. We're going to make certain this is the last anyone hears of the Iron Flood."

"I can do that, sir," said Rykan, trying to sound brave.

"A battle like this will make a man out of you," his father added, pride evident in his voice. "You'll have no problem making your own fortune around here after this."

"Where will you be, Father? During the battle, I mean?" Rykan asked.

"My company will cover the eastern gate," his father said. "With the river there, it's unlikely the Iron Flood will come that way, but we'll be ready for anything."

"So you won't be in any danger?" Rykan asked with a hint of relief.

"I'll likely miss out on most of the battle," his father said with a reassuring smile. "But remember, son, the true challenge of any warrior isn't just in how he wields his sword, but in how he holds his ground when the tides of battle turn. Like a tree in a storm, you must stand firm, absorb the shock, and adapt."

"And when you see the enemy, don't hesitate," the captain interjected. "Show them no mercy, because you will get none from them."

His father wrapped his arms around Rykan, bringing him into a tight hug. "If you think all this revelry is something, wait till you see the celebration tomorrow."

It had been a while since his father had hugged him like that. With the dangers that loomed ahead, it felt comforting and terrifying all at once.

"This storm will be over soon, Rykan." His mother leaned up, kissed his cheek, and gave him a warm embrace. "We'll all be back home before you know it, just like nothing ever happened."

As they left, the captain moved to the center of the tavern. "Down your drinks, men. We're marching back to the barracks. Get some rest for tomorrow. We'll celebrate all night after the battle."

Rykan finished the rest of his ale and found a place at the back of the line where the soldiers were forming up. He spotted Daveth and Brant as they joined the group and moved out of his place to go with them.

"Don't do anything foolish once the fighting starts, lads," Daveth said to Rykan and Brant. "Make sure we're still alive so we can meet back here tomorrow."

"What about the Dreadstorm?" Brant asked. "Some of the refugees say just one of them has the strength of ten men."

"Stories often grow in the telling, Brant," Daveth said. "Especially after a defeat. People need a way to explain why they lost."

Rykan smirked, nudging Brant playfully with an elbow. "If you see any, let Daveth deal with them."

When they made it to the barracks, Rykan, Brant, and Daveth entered and were directed to their assigned beds by a stern-faced quartermaster. Rows of sturdy, wooden beds, each with a straw-stuffed mattress and covered in thick, woollen blankets, filled the barracks. At the foot of each bed sat a small cedar chest for personal belongings. Rough, woven rugs lay beside the beds to ward off the chill of the stone floor.

Rykan approached the bed temporarily marked with his name on a small parchment tag tied to the bedpost with twine. On the chest at the foot of the bed lay a sheathed sword. He picked it up and drew the blade from the sheath, admiring the gleam of the pristine metal. This was his own sword, brand new and untested. With a flick of his wrist, he twirled the hilt, spinning the blade into an upright defensive position. The sword caught the dim light of the barracks, reflecting a sharp, almost hopeful glint. This sword would soon bear nicks and scratches, the marks of its first stories to tell.

CHAPTER 2

THE SCENT OF dew-damp earth and the smoky remnants of last night's fire tinged the crisp morning air. A horn's call jolted Rykan, and he and the other soldiers scrambled to their feet. He quickly wrestled into his leather jerkin, its stiff folds resisting him as he tugged it over his linen tunic. He strapped on his pauldrons, bracers, and boots and finally buckled his belt and sword. While some soldiers dashed out the door, he noticed Brant and Daveth still standing near him, but nearly ready.

Brant finished and headed outside with the others, leaving Rykan and Daveth behind. Just as Rykan was about to follow, he remembered his knife. His father had given him a boot knife for his birthday, a gift Rykan initially thought too small for anyone but a kid. However, he didn't want to seem unappreciative. His father insisted he keep it on him at all times, so Rykan decided it would be best to have it with him to show he had carried it into battle. After rummaging through his clothes in the wooden chest, he found the knife still in its tiny sheath and slipped it inside his right boot.

Stepping outside, Rykan joined the neatly forming ranks, each soldier's armor glistening with the pale light of dawn. He straightened his back, his stance rigid as the sergeant began his inspection. Rykan's heart raced, and he could feel a bead of sweat trickling down his back.

The sergeant approached Rykan and looked over his armor, tugging on the pauldrons to make sure they were secure. He grabbed Rykan's arm, forcing him to bend his elbow slightly to correct his position as he held the sword.

"You know the rules," said the sergeant. "Last one in formation gets relay duty."

"Yes, sir," Rykan replied, catching himself before he could sigh in frustration.

Relay duty meant running back and forth, often delivering messages through the most dangerous sites of battle.

Captain Mirell led the company through the gatehouse passage where the commander and the ranks of the Crimson Shield had taken up position. They would serve as the last line of defense if the Iron Flood breached the main gate. The gate opened, and the company followed the captain outside. Knights in silver plate armor already stood at attention in their places among the swordsmen of the other companies in the front rows. The captain took up position behind them near a postern gate, somewhat hidden by vines that grew along the side of the walls to the left of the main gate. He waved Rykan over to him.

"I don't think we'll need a message runner," Captain Mirell said. "But keep close."

"Yes, sir," Rykan replied, trying to calm his nerves. Behind him, spearmen took their places, and above, archers found spots along the battlements and towers.

After hours of tense waiting, Rykan began to relax. Soldiers around him joked and laughed, momentarily giving him hope that the Iron Flood had reconsidered their attack. But that hope faded quickly as a plume of dust appeared on the horizon.

"Form up!" shouted the captain.

The soldiers quickly realigned, watching the dust clouds intently.

The first line of ridgebacks appeared, and Rykan saw the riders in black armor carrying banners with a symbol resembling two three-pronged blades. The ridgebacks stopped some distance away, surrounded by foot soldiers.

"Draw swords!" yelled the captain.

Rykan's heart raced as he unsheathed his sword. He scanned the defenses for Daveth and Brant, but he couldn't find them in the crowd.

"Look at their numbers," one Tatharan soldier remarked. "They don't have nearly enough to break through our defenses."

A low bellow sounded from a horn among the Iron Flood, and the soldiers started toward the city. The ridgebacks trotted forward, matching the speed of the running soldiers.

"Take aim!" shouted one of the captains from the tower. "Fire!"

Arrows rained down, felling a few, but their armor mostly held strong. The Iron Flood soldiers marched on as the cavalry charged toward the main gate.

"We need spears up front!" yelled Captain Mirell.

The spearmen moved forward between the columns of swordsmen, and the swordsmen drew back. The captain remained in his place by the postern gate, and Rykan stayed by the captain's side, his pulse quickening. The smell of blood and sweat overpowered his senses, and fear threatened to cloud his mind.

Whistling arrows from Iron Flood archers targeted the battlements, some of them raining down near Rykan. The ground shook as the cavalry clashed with the spearmen. Ridgebacks collapsed, men were trampled, and dust filled the air.

"Form the line!" Captain Mirell ordered.

The remaining spearmen moved to replace the fallen as a second wave of ridgebacks charged. The Iron Flood foot soldiers attacked the spearmen, focusing on the gate. Rykan stood close to the captain, unable to make sense of the chaotic melee. The Tatharan swordsmen on either side of the gate began closing in, like two great arms surrounding the Iron Flood troops that concentrated on the main gate.

Suddenly, the postern gate burst open, and a panting boy stood holding it.

"Sir! The eastern gate is under attack!" the messenger boy said. "Captain Oswin needs any men you can spare!"

A chilling metallic screech drew Rykan's attention back to the main gate. Two Iron Flood soldiers in black armor were cutting down everyone in their path. Their eyes burned with blue flames through T-shaped visors. Taller than most men, they wielded swords surrounded by blue fire, slicing through spears and swords with ease. They bore all the hallmarks of the Dreadstorm, the elite warriors of the Iron Flood, feared for their supernatural strength and mercilessness.

"I can't spare anyone until the gate is secure!" Captain Mirell responded as a salvo of arrows bounced high above them off the walls. "Tell the commander what's happening!"

"I already have, sir," said the boy. "The eastern gate is being overrun!"

The Dreadstorm Knights cleared out swaths of Tatharan swordsmen and spearmen while the captain stared blankly ahead. The archers above focused their arrows on the Knights, but most of their projectiles deflected off the metal armor.

"I'll send soldiers over as soon as I can," said the captain.

"Yes, sir," the boy replied, slamming the gate shut.

"Bring those two down!" the captain yelled.

An arrow had made it through the armor of one of the Dreadstorm Knights, wounding him. But he continued clearing a path, allowing Iron Flood troops to carry a battering ram to the gate behind him. The captain grabbed hold of Rykan's shoulder and lifted his hand to place a sealed scroll inside.

"This is the king's seal," said Captain Mirell. "Find some way to Rowanar. Remind them of their oath to the king, call for their aid. Tell them we need reinforcements."

"Yes, sir," Rykan said.

He could feel his breathing coming in rapid bursts. Fortunately, he knew the way to Rowanar. It was probably the closest town to Tathara, and his uncle lived there.

"Tathara is counting on you, lad." Captain Mirell said, handing him the key to the city gate.

Rykan rushed to the lock and turned the key, opening the gate and then slamming it shut behind him. Two archers drew their bows when he entered the city but quickly recognized that he was not Iron Flood. He ran toward the gatehouse as archers fired volleys over the walls and Crimson Shield troops leaned against the eastern gate to reinforce it.

Before he reached the main road through the city, a loud crunching sound split the air as the battering ram penetrated the wooden part of the gate. Iron Flood troops burst through the opening while others continued to hack at the gate, widening the breach. The Crimson Shield engaged the Iron Flood soldiers who poured in.

Rykan changed course, heading into the small streets of the residential district, his mind racing with thoughts of the battle raging behind him and the crucial mission ahead. He sprinted through the labyrinthine alleyways, darting behind houses and shops, weaving through cramped, grubby spaces where once-forbidden childhood laughter still echoed defiantly in his memories. These were the secret realms of his youth, places where gleeful rebellion dismissed the rules. Many a time, he had ventured into these nooks, oblivious to the warnings, seeking the thrill of forbidden adventures hidden within the folds of the everyday.

The sound of booms and hammering filled the streets, a harsh reminder of the present danger. No time for nostalgia now. This network of pathways would serve his escape. He crawled into one of the larger drainage openings and lowered himself to the bottom. The rough and misshapen stone blocks down here made it a more difficult path to traverse than the streets above. Every step jolted. Every stone wobbled. Fortunately, this marked the drier stretch of the season, with little rain to speak of in recent times. Otherwise, the flow of water would have submerged this entire system of tunnels. Luck, for once, seemed to be on his side.

Drainage slots on streets provided the only light in the tunnels. Rykan slowed his pace, taking care where he stepped in the dark. Darkness could hide a thousand threats. He could hear cries and murmurs of terror above him as people filed out into the streets, awaiting their fate. Echoes of fear bounced off the walls, mixing with the pounding of his heart.

The tunnels slanted more dramatically downward as he continued toward the eastern gate. Downward, always downward. Into the depths, into the unknown. Rykan made his way into an open area where a network of drainage tunnels merged. At last, he spotted the pipe that led under the outer walls and out into the river. A glimmer of hope, the way out.

Others assembled in hiding down here. He couldn't understand their whispered words, but they didn't pay him any mind. Faces blurred by the dim light, shadows of fear and desperation. Rykan crawled around the perimeter of the chamber, hoping to avoid their notice. Invisible, just another shadow.

He reached a pipe with a heavy grate covering it, designed to prevent intruders from sneaking into the city. The metal bars were thick and rusted, but they were bolted securely to the stone. Rykan's heart pounded while he considered what to do next, knowing that time was of the essence.

Kneeling down, he examined the bolts. They were old, but the rust had not weakened them enough to break by hand. Rykan reached for his sword, then slid it carefully under the edge of the grate. Using the flat of the blade, he tried to pry the grate upward, but it wouldn't budge. He would have to loosen the bolts first.

Realizing he needed more precision, Rykan reached into his boot and pulled out the knife his father had given him. He wedged the blade into the crevice between the first bolt and the stone, using it as a lever. With a grunt, he twisted the knife, applying as much force as he could muster. The first bolt resisted, then slowly began to turn. Sweat dripped down his forehead as he worked, every sound of the battle in the distance urging him to move faster.

Once the bolt loosened, he used his sword again, prying it further until the bolt finally fell free and clattered to the ground. Rykan repeated the process with the remaining bolts, using the knife to loosen them and the sword for extra leverage. His hands began to shake from exertion and nerves. Each bolt took precious minutes to loosen, but right now, whether they knew it or not, everyone in Tathara was counting on him. At last, the final bolt fell free, and he grabbed the grate with both hands, pulling it aside.

Rykan took a deep breath, trying to steady himself. He tucked the knife back into his boot and sheathed his sword, feeling a new sense of purpose. Then he ducked into the pipe, crawling through the dark tunnel as quickly as he could. He could see nothing ahead but a small point of light. A beacon, a promise of freedom. Water pockets left over from the last rain soaked the knees of his pants. Cold seeped through, a reminder of the urgency of his mission. For a while, it felt as though the light ahead was not getting any closer. Rykan came to a stop in despair, fearful that he would never make it to the end.

This storm will be over soon. His mother's words played in his head. Starting up again, he crawled on his forearms and knees. He stopped looking ahead, focusing only on his movements, repeating the bodily mechanics of propelling himself forward. One step at a time, one crawl closer to freedom. Focus on the now, survive the moment.

As Rykan reached the end of the pipe, the sun's warmth touched him. With no room to turn around, he carefully slid headfirst into the water.

The calm currents on the city's east side had provided him and his friends with many joyful swimming sessions during childhood. Although he normally sought any excuse to dive into these waters, he had never imagined that one day it would serve a real purpose. Freedom, finally within reach.

His feet found solid ground again, and he made his way onto the riverbank. Drenched, he moved toward a grassy field and the forest ahead, each step forward a small victory.

"Tathara has fallen under my dominion," declared a commanding voice.

A striking figure emerged before a line of Tatharan soldiers. Clad in black linens edged with gold and adorned with intricately decorated armor, his presence was imposing. Long black hair cascaded over a metal mask that obscured most of his face. His dark robe fluttered like a spectral flame around his legs.

Unlike the Dreadstorm, whose eyes pulsed with blue energy, the masked man's eyes blazed with an intense, almost blinding, blue light that seemed to pierce through the soul. His pointed ears, like that of a Lith or Anvir, added to his uncommon appearance. He carried an oversized sword that outmatched his height, as if it had been forged for a giant. The blade burned with the same eerie blue fire. He gripped it like one would a walking stick, leaving scorch marks on the ground, as if the earth itself recoiled from its presence.

"Discard your arms and yield to the inevitable ascendancy of the Iron Flood."

"It's Vatreus! Seize him!" The Tatharan defenders, spurred by defiance, charged forward.

The man, now clearly identified as Vatreus, the Imperion of the Iron Flood, extended his hand. He made the Tatharan soldiers stop in their tracks with some kind of debilitating force. As arrows hurled toward him, Vatreus lifted his hand, stopping them mid-flight and flinging them back toward the archers who had fired them. Extending his long blade, he used some sort of wind force to pull soldiers toward him. While some anchored themselves against this force, three of them found themselves skewered on the masked man's long blade.

Rykan, hidden by the trees, watched in horror as Vatreus decimated the Tatharan forces.

"Vatreus! Vatreus!" the Iron Flood troops chanted triumphantly. Their voices rose in unison while the man finished off the Tatharan soldiers.

Another group of Tatharan cavalry and soldiers arrived and entered the battle. The Iron Flood troops engaged them as they swarmed around Vatreus. Rykan caught sight of his father among the group of soldiers.

Rykan dashed across the field toward him, hoping to warn him of Vatreus's power. As he neared, his father turned.

"Rykan? You need to get back to the main gate!"

"Father, he's too strong!" Rykan shouted, his voice lost among the clash of steel and the cries of wounded men.

His father and the others continued their advance toward Vatreus. An unseen force slowed their progress, but they pressed on. Vatreus engaged them one by one, blue fire trailing in arcs as he cut them down with his huge blade. Rykan tried to move in to help but ran into the invisible barrier Vatreus was using against them. Struggling, he pushed forward, but even his full strength only allowed him to move in slow motion.

His father fought through the repulsion, raising his blade to strike Vatreus. Suddenly, the force vanished, and Rykan fell forward as his over-compensated effort abruptly met no resistance. He glanced up just in time to see Vatreus using his power to pull his father onto the point of his sword, stabbing him through the chest.

Rykan screamed, but no sound escaped his lips. As he watched, Vatreus, with a mere hand gesture, sent his father reeling backward with a burst of invisible force. The dark warrior then turned his chilling focus toward the city.

His arm extended in a slow, deliberate motion toward the ancient stone walls of the city. The air around him seemed to hum with power, a visible tremor in the atmosphere, as if the very essence of the air was bending to his will. The heavy chains of the drawbridge creaked and groaned under an unseen power, their links straining against the force until, with a sharp, metallic wail, they snapped. The drawbridge crashed down with a thunderous impact, the wood splintering against the cobblestone road with echoes that rang like the tolling of a bell.

Dust and debris rose in a cloud as the bridge settled, forming an ominous pathway for the Iron Flood. The river, previously a barrier, bore witness to the onslaught when the first of Vatreus's troops began to pour across. The sound of their boots on the wood was like the drumbeat of war, relentless and unyielding.

Driven by a surge of adrenaline, Rykan rushed to his father's side, his fear drowned out by seething rage. As he ran, two Iron Flood soldiers converged on him, their swords gleaming menacingly. With a reckless disregard for his own safety, Rykan aggressively thrust his sword at the first soldier. His blade plunged deep into the soldier's armor, crumpling it enough to penetrate. Rykan's momentum carried him forward, and he twisted away just in time to evade the second soldier's blade. He retaliated with a swift, vicious slash, cutting deep into the soldier's side and bringing him down.

Breathing heavily, overtaken by pain and fatigue, Rykan staggered and fell to his knees. The grass beneath him was slick with blood—the first he had ever spilled. It felt nothing like he had imagined. There was no triumph here, only horror and exhaustion.

Rykan dropped his sword and crawled across the grass, reaching desperately for his father.

"Rykan … you must go …" his father gasped, his voice weak but urgent. "Find safety … live for us … for your mother … please."

His father's eyes blurred into a blank stare as he expelled his final breath. The world around Rykan shattered, feeling unreal, like a nightmare from which he couldn't wake. Before he could regain his bearings, someone grabbed him by the tunic and hauled him to his feet.

Iron Flood soldiers prodded him with spears, forcing him to walk ahead of them. Stumbling as he tried to keep his balance, Rykan was ushered to a group of other Tatharans, mostly citizens who had likely tried to flee the city. They looked frightened and confused, most of them older than Rykan. But as he scanned the group, his eyes locked onto a familiar face—Brant.

His friend, face marked by the strain of recent horrors, offered a nod of grim recognition. Relief surged through Rykan, a brief spark in the encroaching gloom, but the stark realization of their shared plight quickly smothered it. The Iron Flood soldiers continued to poke them with spears, herding them toward a row of ridgeback-drawn carriages.

CHAPTER 3

ONE OF THE Iron Flood soldiers searched Rykan's clothing, finding the sealed scroll he had tucked away under his jerkin.

"The king's seal," said one of the soldiers as he unwound the scroll. "There's nothing written," the soldier muttered.

Rykan froze, his breath hitching. He clenched his fists at his sides, but his eyes betrayed him, darting between the soldier and the parchment. Captain Mirell hadn't had time to write anything. Perhaps he knew that Rowanar would listen to a verbal message from someone holding a scroll with the king's seal on it.

The soldier rolled the parchment up, and then slapped Rykan across the face with it. "What was the message on this?"

"There wasn't any message," Rykan said. "I just found it in the city."

"You're lying," said the soldier, hitting Rykan across the face with the scroll again. The soldier pulled him by the tunic, shoving him ahead. "Whatever it was, it doesn't much matter now, does it?"

Rykan noticed a strange woman observing the procession of Tatharans with intense scrutiny. Dark, flowing robes that seemed to absorb the light encompassed her body. Her bald scalp and pallid skin made her a ghostly figure against the backdrop of the Iron Flood's camp. Her eyes, glowing an eerie blue reminiscent of Vatreus's own, held a chilling stillness.

From beneath the shadows of her robes, she extended her hands—one notably gnarled and twisted, as if sculpted by darker forces. With a disturbing grace, she gestured toward the group of beleaguered citizens. An invisible force gripped them. Brant and others were hoisted into the air as if by spectral hands, their bodies rigid with shock and disbelief. Suspended momentarily, they were then unceremoniously dropped onto the bed of a waiting carriage, the impact echoing with a series of harsh thuds.

The woman repeated this unnatural act on the others, placing more of them into the carts. Rykan struggled futilely against the invisible bonds of her power as he found himself carried over to one of the carts. When he felt the pressure leave his body, he braced for impact, and then collided with two others, who hastily shoved him aside.

The soldiers of the Iron Flood tied ropes around the feet of those in the cart, tying them to chains that wrapped around the floor of the carriage. When they came over to Rykan, one of the soldiers ran a rope across his lap, knotting it and pulling it taut.

Once the hairless woman settled beside the driver in the lead cart, which also held Brant, the ridgebacks began their slow, ominous march. They passed through the city gates, leaving Tathara behind. Rykan felt pangs of regret when he realized he had failed everyone. The air smelled of blood as the carriage traversed a battlefield littered with the remains of the defenders of Tathara. Though his heart dreaded the sight, Rykan's eyes scanned the lifeless faces in search of anyone else he knew. With his father gone and the city in shambles, it felt as though he may as well be one of them. So many, only recently starting their own lives, had been thrust into this battle. So many dreams shattered, so much potential wasted.

Dark armored soldiers roamed the battlefield in search of more corpses to add to the piles. Carrion birds circled overhead, heralding the gruesome feast.

Above, arcs of sunshimmers crisscrossed the sky, a familiar yet awe-inspiring sight. This atmospheric phenomenon formed walls of prismatic colors, cascading down to the horizon like radiant rainfall. Cherished by the people of Galanor, sunshimmers bathed the sky in ever-changing hues, a spectacle that appeared almost daily in several variations. Now, Rykan looked upon them, blind to their splendor. Funny how the prospect of dying could dull even the world's most breathtaking sights.

Some of Rykan's fellow captives eyed each other silently as the cart carried them across the ravaged land. One of the older men constantly fidgeted, while one of the women rocked back and forth in her seat. A younger woman tugged at her curly black hair. The carriage made its way from the war-torn fields into a landscape of rolling hills covered with thick green grass.

After some time, the soldiers stopped to rest the ridgebacks, grudgingly untying a few prisoners at a time to relieve themselves under heavy watch. Any sign of delay earned a sharp shove or muttered curse before they were tied back up, their bonds tighter than before. As they traversed a particularly rough patch of road, the cart jolted violently, launching Rykan a few inches into the air. Landing with a thud, Rykan looked over the edge of the cart. Two soldiers eyed him with grim expressions, causing him to straighten up against the wooden divider at his back. Once they passed the ruins of Old Neberin, Rykan realized he had never been this far from home.

The caravan halted at dusk, the weary ridgebacks snorting as the soldiers unhitched and fed them. The captors tossed small pieces of stale bread to the prisoners, along with just enough water to wet their tongues. Rykan barely slept. His mind raced with worry about what awaited him and his mother. He couldn't help but think of Brant in the other cart, wondering how his friend was holding up and how they had both ended up in this predicament. And Daveth—what had become of him?

Only now did the reality of his father's death begin to bear down on him. As the others slept, the tears came rushing through, and he cried silently in the dark, his body shaking with the effort of stifling his sobs.

At first light, they resumed their journey, winding into a rocky valley scattered with tufts of yellow grass and trees with orange leaves. With little else to do, Rykan watched the other captives. The older girl across from him often whispered to herself. Rykan strained to hear her words, but he could not quite make them out. Perhaps she was reciting prayers.

Rykan's legs had gone numb and prickly from sitting too long, yet he resisted the urge to stretch them fully, afraid of drawing the soldiers' ire. He occasionally shifted slightly, trying to restore circulation, but the other captives' stares made him cautious about moving too much, until he remembered the knife in his boot.

"What are they going to do with us?" whispered a girl seated next to him, who appeared a little younger than him with curly brown hair.

He had been gazing at the distant mountains, but her voice snapped him out of his reverie.

"What?" Rykan turned toward her, his expression blank.

"You don't think they'll kill us, do you?" the girl asked, quietly.

Rykan only shrugged in response, not trusting himself to speak.

"We should welcome death," interjected a man who appeared slightly older than Rykan. "Our long sleep will be over, and we'll wake up in the Everdream."

As the others talked, Rykan bent over, pretending to scratch an itch on his foot, but instead reaching into his boot and pulling out the small blade, keeping it hidden in his palm.

"My mother told me there is no Everdream," the girl whispered back, her voice filled with fear. "She said that, when you die, you go to sleep but never wake up again."

Rykan shook his head, trying to inject some logic into the fear-laden conversation. "If they were going to kill us, why would they bother taking us this far out?"

"Who are you? You don't look Tatharan," the girl asked, eyeing him curiously.

"What do you mean?" Rykan's brow furrowed.

"You look like one of the refugees from the islands," she explained, somewhat apologetically.

Rykan hadn't often considered his heritage, but it was true that his skin was a shade darker than most other humans in Tathara, who had ivory or sunlit skin. His parents had fled their island home shortly after his birth.

"I've lived in Tathara since I was a baby," he clarified. "I don't remember living anywhere else."

"Oh, I didn't mean it like that," she said quickly, a hint of regret in her tone. "I wondered if the Iron Flood had taken other cities. If you live in Tathara, you're the same as any of us."

"How far from Tathara are we?" another captive, a blond girl, chimed in anxiously.

"I think we're heading toward the edges of Elenior," said the older boy. "Toward Nordravin."

"Keep quiet back there!" barked one of the soldiers, causing them all to flinch and fall silent.

During three days of mindless riding and three nights of restless sleep, Rykan slowly worked the small blade against the ropes around his feet, only working on one rope at a time when he knew no one was looking. They traveled through a rocky forest, passing a patrol of Iron Flood soldiers. One of the Dreadstorm Knights, with blue fire burning from his eyes through the slot of his helmet, walked up to the front of the cart ahead as it slowed. Why would the Iron Flood guard a road out here in the middle of nowhere?

"Velkar, I was beginning to think you had deserted your station," the powerful, bald woman commanding the patrol said, her voice carrying a feigned reprimand.

"Never," replied the Knight, his voice resonating with a metallic echo from within his helmet. He shifted his stance, the armor plates clinking softly. "You should know me better than that, Amera."

"Any activity?" Amera asked, her eyes scanning the horizon as if searching for any sign of trouble.

"Haven't seen anyone out here in days," Velkar responded, his gaze following a bird flying overhead. "Not since the last caravan came through."

"I'll see you on the way back," Amera said with a nod, signaling the drivers to get the ridgebacks moving again.

She turned, her cloak swirling around her as she walked to her ridgeback.

Velkar stood by the carts as they started up again, smacking the captives as they moved by. Rykan leaned forward, attempting to avoid the Dreadstorm's hand, but Velkar pulled him back, giving him a punch in the back of his head with his fist. Rykan's vision blurred out of focus after the blow, and he rubbed his head to try and regain his bearings.

As nightfall approached, they moved out of the forest into a ravine through a vast mountain range. The ravine was carved through the mountains as if rivers had run through here at some point in the past. The cart took them along the crooked road, into a maze of ravines and canyons. Hitting uneven ground, the cart leaned sideways for a stretch before they returned to a flatter road.

Rykan sliced through the last rope around his ankles but resisted moving his feet, out of fear of revealing that he had partially freed himself. One of the wheels struck something in the road, jolting everyone in the cart. With the momentary distraction, Rykan went ahead and cut through the rope that crossed his lap. Once they stopped to rest the ridgebacks, Rykan waited for the right moment. As the occupants of the cart began to close their eyes, he focused on the Iron Flood soldiers.

Both soldiers jumped down from the cart, and then walked around and stretched their legs. One of them took a blanket and reclined on the ground to get some sleep, while the other paced around. Once this soldier had moved away, Rykan rolled backward off the cart onto the hard dirt below. He lay there, stunned by the impact, unsure if he should move. He rolled into a divot between the sloped path and the stone side of the mountain, hoping he would remain hidden once daylight came.

He awoke to see the ridgebacks and carts getting further away. It appeared that the guards hadn't noticed he was missing. Keeping a safe distance, Rykan jogged along behind them. He may have failed to get to Rowanar, but maybe he could help Brant and the other Tatharans escape. After a while, the soldiers jumped off the carts, gathering the captives up. They marched through a narrow gorge and came to a path that led up the mountain.

Rykan climbed the slope on the other side of the ravine, hoping to find a vantage point where he could see what they were doing. Reaching a ledge that was high enough, Rykan watched as they gathered on a plateau. Amera, the bald woman, stood in front of a massive gate of iron embedded into the mountainside. He crept slowly along the edge, getting a little closer for a better view around the rocks. One of the soldiers was leading a young blond girl away from the other captives.

The menacing gate had rows of spikes running down its surface. From the outer edges to the center, jagged, tooth-like protrusions jutted out. The drivers and soldiers took places on either side of the gate, kneeling in reverence. The gate lay flush against the rock of the mountain, its edges melding perfectly with the stone around it. Not a single crack or seam betrayed how it might open, as if it had been carved from the mountain itself—an impenetrable barrier that seemed more a part of the landscape than a passage through it. The lower right corner held the only imperfection, appearing peeled back, bent, or warped—perhaps by intense heat. This opening was the only glimpse into the hollow darkness that lay beyond.

"Come to me!" Amera commanded, and the blond girl was drawn by an unseen force, her feet dragging across the dust of the ground, to the woman's side.

Even from a distance, Rykan could discern the girl's heaving shoulders as her breaths grew shallow and rapid.

Amera's smile widened as she glanced at the soldiers. With a rough shove, she pushed the trembling girl forward, forcing her to stand near the jagged, twisted corner of the iron gate. Stepping back, Amera folded her arms, a grim satisfaction settling over her features as a suffocating tension thickened the air around them.

Everyone's focus converged on the gate when a guttural and ominous rumble, like the growl of some ancient and malevolent beast, reverberated through the ground beneath them. A faint yet unsettling blue glow began to seep from the contorted metal, growing in intensity and eeriness with each passing second.

The girl stood, barely keeping her footing as the vibrations intensified. The blue radiance flared brighter and sharper, until sheer terror forced her to stagger back abruptly. She clearly wanted to flee but struggled to move, Amera's invisible force holding her in place. Within the eerie, pulsating blue glow, ethereal ribbons of shadows began to slither with grotesque, unnatural movements. Suddenly, an enormous, clawed hand materialized near the gap in the gate. Its claw snaked through the opening, grabbing the girl and yanking her into the pitch-dark abyss beyond. Her piercing scream tore through the air before abruptly silencing. The undulating vibration continued to ripple through the air, and the once-intense light inside slowly subsided, leaving only a lingering sense of dread.

"Flesh … blood …" an otherworldly voice whispered from the other side of the gate, the words carrying an eerie resonance. It was a voice that seemed to crawl beneath the skin, a spectral chant that echoed with a sinister hunger. "Blood and flesh …" It spoke the words as if it relished the sound of them.

Rykan burst from the ledge, sprinting down the mountain as fast as his legs could carry him.

Behind him, the voice continued to chant in a malevolent whisper. "Bleeding veins, pulsing life. Skin to peel, bones to slice …"

The words hung in the air like a horrific incantation, each syllable sending shivers down the spine. The harrowing scene he had just witnessed replayed in his mind, leaving him bewildered and unable to make sense of what had transpired. As he ran from the terrible iron gate, he couldn't stop the sounds and images from playing over and over in his head.

CHAPTER 4

BREATHING IN THE refreshing embrace of the forest breeze, Selaina halted her steps just short of the muddied banks of the brook. Her mother's words echoed in her mind like a cautionary lullaby. *Never venture beyond the stream.* She had been told this countless times. For beyond the safety of the forest surrounding their cabin home stretched a realm of darkness and suffering. Her mother called it the wicked world.

Navigating along the meandering waters, Selaina caught sight of her reflection in the surface of the still shallows. She expected to see her hair shaped just right and everything in place. Something, however, was amiss. One of her feather earrings was gone. Brushing her long white locks away, she examined her ear but found no sign of the missing earring. It frustrated her when things were out of sorts, she wanted everything to be perfect. With a huff, she lamented losing it. Jeth, who had long been a family friend, had made the earrings for her. He seemed to enjoy crafting them, though he never wore earrings himself. Perhaps the shape of his ears deterred him. Where Selaina's and her mother's were long with a delicate separation, making them forked into two points at the top, Jeth's were oval-shaped and smooth.

Following the edges of the brook, Selaina searched for an easier spot to fill the deep bucket she was carrying. Through the trees, she noticed Jeth sitting in a leisurely manner by the pond the brook fed into. He looked utterly at peace, with a fishing pole propped beside him, supported by a stone, as he leaned back against a grassy knoll.

"Must be nice having such easy chores," Selaina called out, a playful smirk on her face.

Jeth sat up straight, looking around to see where the voice had come from. He shaded his eyes with his hand and grinned when he spotted her.

"This is very important work," he replied. "Much more difficult than it looks."

"We could trade chores," she said, adjusting her grip on the bucket. "I'll do the fishing and you can fetch water."

Jeth chuckled, shaking his head. "I'm already too far along," he said, leaning back again. "Once I start something, I can't stop until it's finished."

Dipping the wooden bucket into the water, Selaina filled it a little more than halfway, to the point where it wasn't too heavy to carry. She straightened up, watching the ripples dance across the pond's surface.

"You could at least hold the pole," she said, raising an eyebrow. "Look like you're doing something."

"If you think it will help," he said with a laugh. "I'll consider it."

He reached over and picked up the fishing pole, giving her a mock-serious nod as he held it upright.

Selaina shook her head, smiling as she made her way back to the brook, the pail of water sloshing gently with each step.

"Such dedication," she teased, glancing back at Jeth, who gave her a cheeky salute with the fishing pole.

She smiled as she made her way back up the hill, being careful not to spill any water. Concentrating on the water in the bucket, she nearly stepped on the sweetsprouts Jeth had planted. Carefully, she walked around the leafy pods, which were just beginning to bloom. She stood for a moment, admiring the perfectly measured rows of sweetsprouts, each nearly the same size.

"Take that water outside, would you? I forgot to water the bunnets earlier," her mother said as Selaina entered the house, her voice muffled by the sound of bubbling stew.

Selaina set the bucket on the kitchen table, wiping a stray drop of water off her forehead.

"You don't need it to cook?" she asked, glancing at the simmering pot.

"Not yet," her mother replied, stirring the stew with a wooden spoon. "When you're done with that, go back and get some more."

Selaina nodded, picking up the bucket again. "Jeth is at the pond fishing," she said with a hint of a smile. "Though he's doing more relaxing than anything else."

"He's been chopping up wood all day," her mother said in a softer tone. "Let him relax a little."

Selaina paused at the door, glancing back at her mother. She saw the weariness in her eyes, the lines etched from years of hard work. With a sigh, she stepped outside again, the cool breeze a welcome contrast to the warmth of the kitchen. She walked toward the garden, the smell of earth and growing things filling her senses as she poured the water over the bunnets, watching as the soil eagerly soaked it up.

She noticed Nibbles and Snickers, two of the fleecehorns, at the fence watching her.

"Did you need something?" Selaina asked the fleecehorns in a higher-pitched voice than she normally used.

Once she had used up all the water, Selaina headed toward the fleecehorn pen. She ran her hands over their heads, feeling the coarse fur beneath her fingers. Their feed trough was still mostly full, but the water bin was empty.

"Oh, you drank all the water. Don't worry, I'll fetch you some."

She went back to the brook, filled the bucket with water, and returned to pour it into the fleecehorns' bin. As soon as the water hit the bin, the rest of the fleecehorns came over, nudging each other to get a drink. Selaina smiled at their eagerness before heading back to the brook for yet another bucket of water for her mother.

Setting the full bucket on the kitchen table, she asked, "Anything else?"

"Not right now. I'm almost done with this," her mother replied, sitting with a pile of freshly picked beans in her lap. She popped open each pod, extracting the beans and placing them into a container. "Go finish the rest of your chores."

Selaina nodded, though she had already finished her chores for the day. Taking her mother's words as permission to do as she pleased, she ventured into the deeper part of the forest. The songs of birds guided her, their melodies leading her to where the brook curved in a half-circle, carving a crooked path through the soft rock. She breathed in the cool, damp air, feeling a sense of peace and freedom in the embrace of the trees.

Preparing to leap, Selaina steadied herself on a large stone, her eyes fixed on the opposite bank. She carefully measured the distance, her focus narrowing to the path ahead. With a graceful bend of her knees, she sprang over the babbling stream, landing lightly on a bed of leaves on the far side.

Selaina was not one to disobey her mother's rules, but this particular temptation sometimes proved irresistible. Having combed through the vicinity surrounding their cabin countless times, her curiosity for the mysteries hidden within the deeper woods on the other side of the brook had grown insatiable. With each secret journey, the twinge of guilt that had initially accompanied her adventures had all but faded. After all, she rationalized, her explorations had never ventured too far past the stream, and therefore, she convinced herself, there was no true danger.

The treetops resonated with the chattering rebuke of birds, as if scolding Selaina for intruding upon their domain. Undeterred by their avian complaints, she quickened her pace, drawn toward the special place she had discovered. It had become her cherished sanctuary, a hidden realm entirely her own. Even Jeth, who she usually confided in, remained unaware of her clandestine refuge.

No longer needing to follow the marks she had put on the trees, she pressed ahead until she could see faint blue light reflected on the leaves. As she ventured onward, the grass gradually receded, revealing a small stone hill that rested slightly above her head. This corner of the forest was unlike any other she had encountered. Here, branches arched in graceful curves, vines wove simple yet symmetrical patterns with each other that soon spiraled into bewildering complexity. Each blade of grass on the ground and strip of bark on the trees held an arrangement that defied the natural world. It lacked the haphazardness that characterized the rest of the forest.

As she climbed the hill, Selaina could already feel the familiar tingle on her skin. At the hill's summit, she knelt before the fractured stone where the faint blue glow seeped through narrow cracks, flickering like distant starlight caught beneath the surface. The light seemed almost alive, pulsing with an energy she couldn't fully comprehend, as if it were part of something much larger than herself. When she stretched out her hand, the glow responded, wrapping her in warmth that wasn't just physical but visceral, deep within her bones. It hummed faintly, a primal rhythm that seemed to echo the heartbeat of life itself.

Selaina closed her eyes, allowing the sensation to wash over her. It was as though she could feel the breath of every living thing, every glimmer of life, connected to her in ways she couldn't understand. If only she could see them or speak to them. Perhaps one day, she would be able to convince her mother they were not the only good people in the wicked world, and she would allow Selaina to leave the forest to find them. Her mother would understand, if only she could feel this light. But Selaina could not tell her mother about it, not yet. Revealing she had gone beyond the stream would result in her mother forbidding her from making these excursions altogether. If she were ever to reveal this place, she would have to wait for the right time.

But underneath these ambitious thoughts, Selaina knew it was only a dream. An amazing idea she clung to. That somewhere out there was the hope of a purpose beyond her daily chores. Deep down, she knew her place was here and always would be.

Seated atop the hill, Selaina reveled in the cool caress of the breeze, her eyes following the graceful arcs of birds as they darted from one tree to another. The sunlight filtered through the interwoven branches, painting her skin with its gentle warmth. In the midst of this enchanting landscape, where trees of varying sizes and species stood sentinel, where tall grasses swayed in harmony, and where blossoms burst into bloom, Selaina felt a stirring deep within her. The foxes, rabbits, and warthogs pursued their daily quests for sustenance, oblivious to the environment around them. Yet, for Selaina, it was nothing short of magic.

The brown and white spotted bunny she often saw scampered among the inhabitants of this serene forest. She frequently spotted him as he hopped gracefully through a mossy clearing nestled at the base of the hill. The desire to approach him, to observe him up close, was strong, but she understood that any sudden movement would send him darting away. The rabbit nibbled cautiously on the vibrant green grass, his tiny mouth moving swiftly as he twitched his head, ever watchful of sounds and movements in his surroundings. Clearly, the little rabbit harbored a deep nervousness, a wariness of the world around him. This cautiousness had kept him alive thus far.

Amid the forest's breathtaking beauty, Selaina had borne witness to the raw violence it concealed. She had observed the cruel realities of nature, as foxes and coyotes launched ruthless attacks on rabbits and other small creatures, ultimately consuming them. That kind of thing must happen to people in the wicked world. But the creatures of the forest were not evil, Jeth had told her. They had no sense of good and evil and acted according to their nature. Though some used others for food, they all had great respect for each other, Jeth said. They all knew their place in the endless cycle of life and death. He said that it had to be this way, the old making room for the new.

Jeth had introduced her to the art of hunting on many occasions, imparting the skill of stealthily maneuvering through the swaying grass to catch elk by surprise. He had patiently shown her how to wield a bow, and she had even taken the lives of a few animals herself. Though Selaina didn't relish the act of killing, she understood its grim necessity for their survival. Strangely, each hunt made her feel more attuned to the wild, as if she were becoming more a part of nature, rather than an outsider observing it.

The shadows grew long, and Selaina knew her mother would be putting food on the table. If she didn't get back to the cabin soon, Jeth would come looking for her. She stood and carefully stepped down the hill, the slope near the bottom forcing her to run to keep her footing. As she hurried back toward the brook, the crunching of dried leaves behind her grabbed her attention.

The noise stopped when she turned around. Expecting to see one of the forest creatures, she instead saw nothing. Knowing she could not afford to be seen past the stream, she ignored the sound and continued on her way. Not long after she started again, she heard the sound again, louder this time. It was too heavy to be a rabbit or even a warthog, but it didn't have the galloping pattern of an elk.

Selaina came to an abrupt halt, her gaze drawn back in an instant. A person, a man, stood beneath the looming shadows cast by the towering eldum trees. He stood tall, eyes locking onto hers. For a fleeting moment, she thought it was Jeth, and her heart sank into her stomach, knowing he had caught her beyond the stream. Yet, as she strained her eyes, peering into the shadows, a new fear began to materialize. It was not Jeth.

Her pulse raced as she stood paralyzed, staring at the man.

"I didn't mean to intrude," the man called out, stepping forward slowly. "I seem to be lost. Do you know where I could find shelter? Do you live here in the forest?"

Images flashed before her eyes, too quick to fully grasp. She'd experienced this before—once with her mother, and once with Jeth—their recent thoughts flickering in her mind like fleeting echoes. But it had only been those two times, and she never understood what to make of it. This time felt different, more unsettling. It wasn't just the flashes. It was the man behind them. He wasn't from the world she knew. She was seeing the thoughts of someone from the wicked world beyond the forest.

Among the visions, Selaina saw a little girl, her eyes conveying a profound sadness. She could sense a bond the man felt with this girl, the love he felt for her. Yet, darker threads interwove with the affection. A surge of rage, more potent than any she had known, flowed through her, while the bloodied and bruised faces of both men and women flickered like a candle teetering on the brink of extinguishment. The man before her was dangerous.

CHAPTER 5

WITH ADRENALINE COURSING through her veins, Selaina made a swift turn and broke into a sprint. She wove through the thickets of trees and underbrush, her footsteps marked by a rhythmic pounding on the forest floor. In her ears, the ragged cadence of her breath resonated, accompanying her relentless dash.

The brook, which normally seemed so close, now felt a hundred miles away. As Selaina's breaths grew labored and the winding path of the brook drew nearer, her eyes scoured the bank for the familiar spot where she could safely make her leap. She eased her pace as she neared the soft earth at the water's edge, stealing another quick, anxious look behind her. To her immense relief, there was no sign of the man. He had not pursued her.

Nevertheless, Selaina wasn't willing to take any chances. Without hesitation, she vaulted over the flowing water, her landing less graceful than usual, but she managed to regain her balance and continue her desperate sprint. When she reached the haven of the cabin, she finally allowed herself to exhale a shuddering breath of relief.

She entered the kitchen area, and her mother stood leaning over the table, kneading dough. Her mother's white hair had a streak of black running through it. As her mother grew old, her hair would all turn black, and one day Selaina's would too. Though her mother dreaded it, Selaina always thought black hair would be pretty on her. Jeth's hair, on the other hand, was a shade between both, a dark sort of gray.

Two small steaks of some animal she couldn't quite identify lay on the hearth, cooking on wooden planks over the open flame.

"What have you gotten yourself into?" her mother asked as she continued shaping the dough.

The question worried Selaina. Did her mother know she had crossed the stream?

"What do you mean?" she asked.

"Your face is blood red," her mother said. "And you're huffing and puffing like you've been racing the wind itself."

Selaina hadn't realized she was still breathing heavily from running from the strange man.

"I saw it was getting dark."

She knew she should probably mention seeing another person in the woods, but he hadn't been that close to the cabin, and if she said anything, her mother and Jeth would never let her walk anywhere in the woods alone again. Aside from that, they may figure out she had gone past the brook.

"Everything is almost ready now," said her mother. "Why can't you get here in time to help out a little?"

"Sorry, Mama," Selaina said. "I'll try to get back sooner next time."

"It would be nice," her mother said. "Did you do your chores?"

"Yes, Mama," Selaina said. "I fetched water for the garden, fed the fleecehorns, washed the clothes—"

"And then wasted most of your time wandering around in the woods," said her mother.

"It's not a waste of time," said Selaina. "One must have something to look forward to, once the work is done."

"You remember everything Jeth says but never listen to a word I tell you. The satisfaction of a job well done is what you look forward to. And what is so interesting in those woods?" asked her mother. "You used to keep me company."

"You told me, after we pass on from this world, that we become spirits of the forest," said Selaina. "I like to walk around in the trees. It helps me think. I like to imagine our ancestors there, whispering their wisdom through the leaves."

"What is there to think about?" asked her mother. "You sound just like—" Her mother's voice trailed off, and she stared ahead without completing her thought.

"Just like what?" asked Selaina.

"I just don't see what there is to think about, other than keeping the farm going," her mother said.

"You should come with me sometime, Mama," said Selaina. "There are some amazing places in the forest."

Her mother sighed as she cut the loaf of bread into slices. "Maybe if you helped me more, I would have time to think."

"Is there anything I can do to help now?" Selaina said.

"I already have everything ready for tonight's dinner," said her mother. "Why don't you go help Jeth with the fish?"

Selaina went back outside, moving through the trees downhill. The brook curved through the forest much closer on this side of the cabin. She found Jeth scrubbing one of the fish he had caught in the stream that ran over the edge of a group of rocks.

"What brings you out here?" Jeth asked without turning around.

He could always tell it was her by the sound of her steps.

"I came to help."

"Well, have at it," he said, nodding toward the bucket of fish sitting beside him.

Selaina grabbed one of the smaller fish and took the knife sticking in the ground. Poking the knife into the fish's belly, she moved the blade along the underside until she had made a small incision.

"How long have you and Mama lived here now?" she asked.

"I can't even remember, it's been a while," Jeth said as he held one of the fish under the flowing water, cleaning the rest of the bloody residue. "How old are you now?"

"Seventeen years, according to Mama," Selaina said, putting her fingers into the fish and pulling out the insides.

"Has it been that long?" Jeth lifted his head and stared out at the forest. He threw his fish into another bucket with the other cleaned fish. "You came along soon after we came here."

"More than seventeen years ..." Selaina said under her breath as she continued removing the organs of the fish, letting them plop into the flowing water. "Is there anything you miss about the wicked world?"

"Some things, I suppose," said Jeth, grabbing another fish from one of the buckets.

Selaina began stripping off the scales of the fish with the blade. "Like what?"

"Good friends, wild stories." He grabbed her hand and took the fish from her. "You're cutting good meat off with the scales."

Selaina flushed slightly, embarrassed by her mistake, and handed him the fish. "I'll gut, you scale."

"Deal," he said as he continued with the fish he had taken from her.

Selaina took a new fish from the bucket. Her sharp knife sliced through its belly. "What kind of stories did they tell?"

Jeth paused for a moment and then spoke. "I told you the one about the Sky Serpents, didn't I?"

She nodded, shifting the slippery fish to avoid dropping it. "Yes, but it's been a while," she said. "Tell me again."

Jeth's voice dropped slightly, and he slowed his cadence as he always did when telling a story. "According to the legend, there were once three celestial beings: Auronia, Verantis, and Zaryneth," he said. "They dwelled in the unseen realms, with mortals never knowing they looked down on them."

Selaina nodded, her hands moving automatically as she listened.

"Though they were not allowed to intervene in the affairs of mortals, they became fascinated by them and grew to love them," Jeth continued, glancing at Selaina as if to ensure she was following. "They obeyed their station, never interfering, until one day, a great danger befell the land. These celestial beings found themselves facing a great burden. Should they disobey and help the mortals, or should they stand by and allow tragedy to befall them?"

Selaina's hands stilled for a moment, and her brow tightened as she imagined the celestial beings' dilemma.

Jeth threw another cleaned fish into the bucket. "The celestials disobeyed, granting some mortals their power to fight off the danger and survive."

"Did the mortals survive?" Selaina asked quietly.

"They did, but the disobedience of these three celestials had to be punished. They were cursed with physical forms, transformed into Sky Serpents, given wings but no hands, which stripped them of their ability to shape the land. Banished from the hidden realms forever, they now roam the skies."

"Has anyone ever seen them?" Selaina's eyes widened, her imagination painting vivid pictures of the serpents soaring through the skies.

"Some say they have," said Jeth, "at the top of a great mountain when the sun is low. But there is no way to know for certain." He paused, wiping his hands on a rag as he looked off down the stream. "Reminds me of something I once heard: 'True strength lies not in seeking to change the river's course but in becoming the water itself—adaptable, enduring, and essential to all life.'"

Selaina resumed her work, the legend swirling in her mind like the water around her fingers.

"Did this really happen or is it just a story?" she asked, allowing her awe to reach her face.

Jeth shrugged, his eyes twinkling. "Who's to say? But it makes for a good story, doesn't it?"

"If it's only a story, what's the point?" Selaina asked, puzzled.

"That it is important to respect and obey those in authority, even if you don't understand their reasons," Jeth said, his tone changing. "Or there may be consequences, like the serpents faced."

"But didn't they do the right thing?" Selaina pressed. "They helped people fight against the danger."

"Often, wickedness comes disguised as benevolence," he said. "Sometimes, we must comply, even when our instincts urge us to act differently."

Selaina felt her face growing warm as she thought about crossing the brook against her mother's wishes. For a moment, she wondered if Jeth knew.

Changing the subject slightly, she said, "There must be some good in the wicked world." "It can't all be wicked, can it?"

Jeth slowed down, distracted. "Where did you get an idea like that?"

Selaina deposited the innards of the next fish into the water while she gazed up at the first star of the evening. "I don't know. I have this image in my head of tall houses and ground like a quilt made of hard blocks with many people walking about."

"Nonsense." Jeth's tone grew more serious. "You were born here in the forest. Be thankful you've never had to live in the wicked world. Don't let your mother hear you talk like that. You are a good person. Your mother is good too. That is all that matters."

She found it odd that such an innocent question had evoked such a hard response. Either way, she dared not bring it up again. She focused her attention on the fish, and they both worked silently until they were finished.

Selaina opened the door, turning to see her mother absent from the kitchen. Checking the hallway, she saw her mother's shadow in the candlelight. She made her way toward her mother's bedroom and found her staring at a scrap of paper. When her mother realized she was there, she quickly threw it back into a drawer and slammed it shut.

"Bread is on the table, go on and sit down."

Selaina had noticed her mother looking at items from that drawer before. When she had asked about it, she was met with anger in response. Her mother seemed to have different reactions each time Selaina had seen her open it. Sometimes anger, sometimes frustration, other times sadness.

Without hesitation, Selaina went back into the kitchen as Jeth came through the doorway. He placed each fish on a thin block of pinathy wood that sat on the hearth. He found a container of herbs and spices, and then sprinkled some over each fish. Selaina pulled out the wooden chair she always sat in. Jeth had built it just for her when she was younger. It was a bit too small for her now, but she hadn't stopped using it.

Her mother came into the kitchen and collapsed into the chair beside her, taking a moment of rest. As they waited for the fish to cook, Selaina took a knife and cut two slices of bread for each of them. She took a ceramic jar and dug the knife into the raddleberry jam. Then she spread the jam onto each piece of bread.

"I saw my favorite bunny again today." Selaina passed her mother one of the slices of bread.

"What?" her mother asked as she took the bread.

Selaina bit into her piece of bread. The jam gushed into her mouth, making her realize she had not spread it well.

"The rabbit with the brown and white spots."

"How do you know it was the same one?" her mother asked. "There are many brown and white rabbits."

"Not like this one," Selaina said between chews. "This bunny has particular spots."

"Is this what you do all day?" her mother said. "Watch rabbits?"

"What else is there to do around here?" said Selaina. "I finished all my chores."

"If you don't have enough to do, you should take on a little more work," said her mother. "There's always something that needs doing around here."

Selaina slammed her bread onto her plate, mostly slapping her palm onto the table. "I don't need more work." She glanced at Jeth as he turned back toward the fish on the hearth. "I enjoy being outside in the forest. The sounds are peaceful. I like watching the animals."

"She has a curious mind," said Jeth. "Maybe it's time to do more of her lessons, like she used to."

"What did I tell you about taking her side?" said her mother.

"I wasn't taking her side," said Jeth. "It was only a suggestion."

"She's learning everything she needs to know," said her mother. "As long as she can keep the house and the farm going, she will be just fine."

Once the fish were ready, Jeth placed one on each of their plates. Selaina couldn't wait to dig in. The wood Jeth had cooked them on gave the fish a nice smoky flavor. After they had all finished, Selaina heated a container of water on the hearth until it was nice and hot. She took their plates and washed them in the hot water, scrubbing them with something her mother mixed together with adjas leaves.

She looked out of the window at the flat darkness that surrounded the house. Nothing of the forest around them remained, except for the birds that called out in the night. The darkness outside had never frightened her before, but now, the mere thought of the stranger lurking somewhere out there was overwhelming. Perhaps she should have told them about it, about seeing the man in the woods.

Her mother gave her a quick kiss on the cheek, and Jeth wrapped her up in the safety of his big arms, giving her a nice warm hug. After closing the shutters, her mother used the kitchen candle to light the lanterns in their bedrooms. Once the lanterns were aglow, she returned to the kitchen and blew out the candle, leaving only the soft light from the bedrooms to illuminate the hallway. Jeth and her mother retired to their separate rooms as Selaina went to her own.

Figurines Jeth had carved for her lined the only shelf in her room. Some were fairly accurate, while others were not so great at representing the animals they were supposed to be. Selaina picked one from the shelf, one of her favorites. Though she had never actually seen a wolf, Jeth had told her a lot about them. They could be dangerous predators, but they were also loyal and would fiercely protect their pack. She set the piece back onto the shelf.

Selaina settled into her bed, wrapping the bed sheets around her like a cocoon. The day's events replayed in her head as she extinguished the flame in her lantern. Her thoughts kept returning to the enigmatic man in the woods. The flashes persisted, refusing to fade. The violence, the rage—undeniably, he was a resident of the wicked world. Yet, there lingered something more.

She couldn't shake off the echoes of love she had sensed in his heart, especially for his young daughter. It was a peculiar emotion, distinct from the warmth she felt for her own mother or for Jeth. The wicked man's love for his daughter seemed fearful, more desperate. Selaina hoped he had moved along, far away from the forest and back into the deep recesses of the wicked world.

CHAPTER 6

A GENTLE GLOW SPILLED through the shutters, painting Selaina's room in hues of soft gold. She unwrapped herself from the sheets, sliding her feet off the edge of the bed. In the kitchen, she took a bowl of a concoction her mother had made from some fragrant herbs and discarded animal fats.

A wide streak of golden bands beamed across the sky between the trees above the cabin. Her mother called it skyfire, while Jeth referred to this effect as sunshimmer. Selaina used both, calling the bands and arcs skyfire, while dubbing the vertical walls of sparkling colors sunshimmer.

Her bathing spot was ahead, upstream from where they cleaned the fish. Making sure Jeth and her mother were out of sight, she took off her shoes and stepped into the stream. The smooth pebbles along the bottom felt good to her feet, much better than the slimy mud. Once submerged in the water, she removed her clothes and began scrubbing them against some abrasive stones.

Selaina poured a bit of the thick liquid from the bowl onto her clothes, and then diligently scrubbed her woven tunic and leggings. After she squeezed out the foamy residue, her garments were sufficiently cleansed. While her mother and Jeth permitted her this private section of the brook for bathing, Selaina remained vigilant. Ensuring the solitude of her surroundings, she briefly leaned out of the water to hang her wet clothes on a nearby limb.

Sniffing her hands, Selaina savored the fleeting flowery fragrance before pouring out more of the thick liquid. With a deliberate touch, she lathered it onto her skin. The sudden rustling of leaves nearby seized her attention. As she strained to listen, the cacophony of birds and insects in the forest surged, filling her surroundings with a natural symphony. Yet, amid this vibrant chorus, the haunting images of the strange man she had seen in the woods the day before intruded upon her thoughts once more.

If he were to find her now, she'd be left with no option but to forsake her drying clothes and hastily make her way back to the house as she was. Mentioning the strange man would then be unavoidable, and the privilege of bathing alone in this tranquil spot might become a luxury of the past.

Crunching leaves echoed once more, drawing nearer. Involuntarily, Selaina drew a quick breath, holding it as the sound intensified. Footsteps approached, their pace quickening. Silently, Selaina glided toward the bank of the stream, and then extricated herself from the water. She turned back as the noise manifested just on the other side of the brook.

A majestic elk emerged, its long antlers standing proudly above its head. Selaina exhaled in relief and hurried back into the water. She locked eyes with the elk for a moment before it gracefully retreated into the recesses of the underbrush.

After putting on her damp clothes, Selaina started on her chores for the day. At the house, she took a large ceramic container from the kitchen and went back to the stream. She filled it and then splashed water around the garden, making sure to hydrate the plants just enough, but not too much.

In the pantry at the back of the house, she took a handful of grain from a cloth sack. Then she headed toward the fleecehorn pen. Her mother was already there, milking the fleecehorns.

"Good morning," Selaina said, her voice cheerful as she filled the fleecehorns' trough with grain and their bucket with water.

The fleecehorns bleated happily, crowding around the trough.

Her mother glanced up. "Good morning, dear. One of these days, I need to show you how to do this," she said, returning her focus to the rhythm of milking.

Selaina watched the steady stream of milk flow into the pail, mesmerized for a moment.

"They're used to you," she replied. "I don't think they'd want me doing that." She reached out to stroke Clover's head, the fleecehorn leaning into her touch with a contented sigh.

Milking seemed like a strange and difficult task, and not one Selaina looked forward to taking over in the future.

As the sun moved toward the other side of the sky, Selaina completed her chores and eagerly anticipated spending the remaining hours in the forest. Stepping toward the edge of the trees, however, the memory of the strange intruder from the day before disrupted her thoughts. A dilemma presented itself. Should she avoid the woods today or continue with her cherished ritual of visiting her secret enchanted place?

Selaina decided to take a different route, once she crossed the brook. If she circled around the area where she'd encountered the man, hopefully she would not run into him again. Keeping a watchful eye on the surrounding trees, Selaina decided the man must be long gone by now. He had surely only been passing through, not realizing he was in their territory. If he had moved too close to the cabin, Jeth would have forced him away.

With no sign of the man, Selaina's fear began to subside. By the time she arrived in the enchanted part of the forest, the sun had moved closer to the horizon than she'd expected. The longer path had stolen some of her time.

She moved straight for the hill, foregoing her usual time watching the animals in the area. The surrounding trees bent and curved into mind-bending patterns, each forming an intricate relationship with the others around them. Upon reaching the summit, Selaina extended her hand into the warm, azure glow. As the light vibrated over her hand, she discerned elaborate swirling patterns of luminance, each layer more infinitely complex than the last.

She sensed love and goodness, but this time, there was something more. Selaina felt the goodness retreat from an encroachment of darkness and despair. The once-beautiful order of nature succumbed, replaced by meticulously ordered patterns spiraling ceaselessly into an abyss. Faces flashed in rapid succession, accompanied by violent images that sought to challenge her resolve. As much beauty and love as there was in the world beyond, there was just as much ugliness and hate.

Selaina drew her hand back. Her mother was right. The world beyond the forest was indeed wicked. The good out there needed a way out of these places of evil. But could such a thing be done? Even if it could, who would ever be willing to enter that darkness to bring light to the innocent?

An eerie familiarity echoed, as if she had traversed this path countless times before. Yet, no tangible memory accompanied the sensation—only a lingering feeling, a whisper of an elusive truth. A voice rang out, again and again, *we seek a vessel…* The feeling began to fade, but she knew whatever it was, whatever she might attempt to solve in this unfathomable puzzle of endless mechanisms and meticulously structured arrangements, it would always end in failure. Though somewhere within that mesmerizing luminosity lay an answer she sought, an enigma that slipped through her grasp with every endeavor.

The forest around her snapped back into her senses. Songs of birds and insects began again, as if they had been waiting for her return. Selaina climbed slowly down the hill. Something about the forest had changed. No longer did the wind guide her motions, caressing her hair. Instead, it seemed to resist her. The shadows of the forest stretched further than before, and the harmony of sound became dissonant. An uneasiness filled her stomach as she returned to the brook.

When Selaina finally made it back to the cabin, finding everything so quiet surprised her. As she entered the kitchen, her mother was not there preparing the next day's bread. Nothing was being heated on the hearth. Selaina couldn't remember the last time she had returned home before her mother began cooking.

The late afternoon sun showed that Selaina had not come home early. It was her mother who was late. Could she have had some problems with her chores? Maybe one of the fleecehorns had gotten loose.

"Mama!" Selaina called out, stepping into the dark hallway.

None of the candles had been lit. Peeking into the opening to her mother's bedroom, the tightness in her stomach increased. Selaina walked into the room, her weight making the boards creak. Her foot kicked something as she moved further in, making a hollow thump.

Dim light shone through the window onto the bedside cabinet. Selaina carefully made her way to the cabinet until she reached the lantern. Opening the drawer in the cabinet, Selaina found flint and steel and used it to throw sparks onto the char cloth inside the lantern.

The room bathed in a new light, unveiling scattered piles of discarded items strewn across the floor—books, clothing, and delicate pieces of broken ceramic pottery among them. It struck Selaina as peculiar. Her mother was meticulous about tidiness, and the sight of such disarray, especially on the floor, was unsettling. Selaina noticed the drawer, which her mother only opened when she thought she was alone, was now left open.

This might be Selaina's only chance to see what was inside. But the heavy feeling in her stomach had now reached her chest. All she wanted at this moment was to find her mother and know that everything was as it should be. She picked up the lantern, and then hurried through the other rooms, intent on finding some kind of sign, something that made sense.

Jeth's room was also in disarray. The bookshelf had fallen over, most of its contents spilled out onto the floor. His bed had been moved and his clothes scattered about.

Selaina's room was in the same condition. The few clothes she had were unfolded and thrown around the room in the messiest way possible. The animal carvings Jeth had made for her lay scattered everywhere. She knelt and began picking them up off the floor, but the feeling of concern had grown into fear.

Selaina rushed out the door of the cabin and made her way past the fleecehorn pens. They were all still there, moving about as if everything was normal. The sun sank behind the trees as she followed the path down to the stream.

A sigh of relief escaped her throat when she saw Jeth by the water.

"Jeth!" she called out, her voice filled with anticipation as she ran to him.

Suddenly, she stopped in her tracks. There was something off about the manner in which he sat, something awkward and unnatural. Her heart pounded harder, a sense of dread creeping in.

Selaina quickened her pace again, her breath coming in short, sharp gasps. As she drew closer, the unsettling scene became clearer. Jeth wasn't sitting. He was lying on the rocks, his legs submerged in the flowing water.

"Jeth!" she shouted once more, her voice echoing eerily through the silent woods.

Standing over him, a chilling numbness began to envelop her thoughts.

Nothing made sense. He appeared as though he were merely asleep, but there was no response, no sign of life. She nudged his shoulder gently, her fingers trembling. His head rolled lifelessly to the other side, his eyes staring blankly into the distance.

Then she noticed the red stains all over the rocks. Blood had pooled underneath him, some dried and some still sticky. The realization hit her like a punch to the gut. In her mind, she understood, but her heart refused to accept it. Jeth lay stiff yet limp, like one of the dead elks they had hunted together.

Selaina sank to the ground beside him, her legs giving way as the sun dipped behind the trees and cast long shadows over the scene. Tears streamed down her face, her sobs breaking the heavy silence. She reached out to touch Jeth's cold hand, her own shaking uncontrollably. The weight of the moment crushed her, leaving her feeling small and vulnerable. She was alone, truly alone, for the first time in her life.

With no sign of her mother and no idea what to do, Selaina felt utterly lost. Where could she go? As darkness began to cloak the forest, every corner seemed fraught with danger. The once-familiar woods had transformed, closing in around her—the wicked world encircling its unsuspecting prey.

CHAPTER 7

Rykan's breath tore through his lungs, each inhale a battle, as though he had never ceased his wild dash. The craggy mountain walls, studded with stones and sparse shrubs, closed in around him. Silence obscured his surroundings, harshly reminding him of his solitary plight far from the faint buzz of civilization. Hunger clawed at his belly, and thirst scraped his throat raw like sandpaper.

He had traced the elusive tracks of ridgebacks and the deeper ruts left by cart wheels across the wild. But now, against the unforgiving rock, these clues dissolved into nothingness. He crouched, his fingers brushing the ground in vain, trying to pick up any sign of their path. Logic might have counseled patience, urged him to wait out the caravan's departure. He could hide, he could bide his time, and when they left, he could follow their trail. But logic was often a stranger to Rykan.

Waiting felt wrong, like surrendering to fear. With no clear destination, he forced himself to choose a direction, trusting only his instincts. The haunting crunch of bone, images of people being dragged under the gate, and that voice—ominous and chilling—drove him onward. He had to move. He had to act.

The weight of his failures bore down on him relentlessly. Despite his attempts to shove it aside, guilt gnawed at his soul. He had failed to prevent his father's death, failed to reach Rowanar to call for reinforcements, and failed to save Brant and the other captives from a horrible fate. What would a real hero have done? How could anyone willingly face that terrible thing behind the gate?

Choosing a path he hoped would lead him to Rowanar, Rykan tried to maintain a brisk pace, careful not to exhaust himself. The landscape offered little change, and he barely noticed the mountain walls in relation to his turbulent thoughts. Each step was a risk, a gamble in a game where the rules kept changing.

Shadows stretched long and twisted as he trudged up the cliff's narrow path. Legs screaming, Rykan's pace started to drag. Something about today made every step weigh more. Then, he spotted a leafless tree, stark against the dusky sky and lifeless, yet standing defiant. Not rotten, no—sucked dry, like the last drop of water had been wrenched from its core. Odd, standing there among the vibrant yellows and fiery oranges splashed across the mountainside.

Drawn to it, almost against his will, Rykan felt the tickle of alarm as the hairs on his arms stood on end. He circled the withered tree, and there it was—a black knot hole, but not just any. It glowed an eerie red, calling, beckoning. He leaned in, his curiosity elevating.

Inside a chaotic storm, a maelstrom of dizzying shapes, something danced in the shadows. Eyes? Were those eyes? Staring across some vast cosmic abyss? Stars burst, gases swirled, and forms pulsed—life and decay in a relentless cycle. His stomach churned, the world tilting. Too much, too wild. He staggered back, the tree's frantic heart beating behind him.

A dream came upon his waking eyes, a vision of a woman with black hair asleep on a bed made from twisting roots and vines. She was about his mother's age, perhaps a little older. In her mind, she spoke into a dark corner of a hollow tree. Behind her, a wooden shelf filled with trinkets concealed a deep red flame that burned without end.

"Nociferon, my lord, you visit me in dreams? I have waited long for another task to prove my loyalty and strengthen the gifts you have bestowed upon me," she said.

"Beware the child of silver snow," said a voice that echoed maddeningly from all sides, making the rest of its words unintelligible. After a moment, the reverberation dissipated, and its voice became clear again.

"From the shadows she shall rise,
In search of wishes, truth, and lies.
The child of silver snow must know,
The secret path where few dare go."

"Tell us where the Wishing Stone rests,
Reveal its place, where stars have blessed.
Where fate and time in silence meet,
The child shall wake what lies asleep."

Rykan felt himself snared in the claws of madness, this chaotic nightmare pulling him into suffocating oblivion. With all his will, he tore himself out of the vision and found himself back in front of the barren tree. Stumbling away, he regretted ever approaching it, feeling as though it had somehow imparted a kind of corruption onto him.

Hurriedly leaving the area, he sought respite on a nearby ledge. The sun dipped, a slow, fiery descent into night. The dark crept in, and with it, a calm. Under a red shrub tree, Rykan let the night embrace him, the chaos of the day settling into the stillness of twilight.

The first star of the evening made its appearance, twinkling high above the land in the direction he had been heading. Perhaps it was a sign of a city out there, waiting for him underneath the star. Tomorrow, he would find it.

After pulling up some of the tall grass, he fashioned a soft place to lay his head. Through the leaves above him, he gazed up at the stars and the blue and green colors of the aurora. All he could think about was his mother, wondering, hoping that she was well. If nothing else, it kept his mind off the thing behind the gate.

A howl sounded in the distance. Soon, another joined it. Rykan shivered. He had rarely slept outside like this. Only twice that he could recall. Both times had occurred when he had traveled with his mother to visit his uncle in Rowanar. Strong, capable men who could protect them had accompanied them. He had never traveled alone.

Maybe he could still get to Rowanar in time to save Tathara. He had to try. Perhaps his uncle would know what to do. If only he could find his way out of these mountains.

With all the strange noises around him, Rykan found it difficult to sleep. But it was more than that. He had the strange feeling that someone nearby was watching him. Rykan dozed off a few times but always awakened soon after. He both welcomed and dreaded the approaching dawn. Lying in the grass, he slept another hour before the light started shining too brightly for him to stay asleep.

Brushing the grass off his clothes, Rykan resumed his journey. His stomach growled for food and his throat ached for water. He was determined to find some form of civilization. Just as he was about to press on, something at the base of a nearby shrub tree caught his eye. A bow, weathered and old, leaned against the tree, accompanied by a quiver brimming with arrows. Had that been there last night? It must have been too dark to see.

Rykan picked up the bow and tested the string—it was surprisingly taut and in good working condition. Why would anyone abandon such a useful weapon? he wondered, slinging it over his shoulder and securing the quiver on his back.

The possibility that the bow's owner might be nearby nagged at him, heightening his sense of unease. Rykan already felt as though unseen eyes were watching him. He kept his eyes peeled for any sign of movement as he ventured forward.

"Anyone out there?" he called softly, his footsteps quieting as he strained to hear a reply. Hearing nothing, he shouted louder, "Hello!"

If someone was careless enough to leave the bow behind, he should be its new owner. Although Rykan had never really used one before, he understood the mechanics. Perhaps he could hunt a slow-moving animal and prepare a meal. At the very least, having the bow bolstered his confidence. It was not just a tool for hunting—it was a means of protection against potential threats.

After trekking a considerable distance over the mountains, Rykan spotted a large bird landing on a tree branch ahead. Awkwardly, he reached for an arrow from the quiver on his back, fumbling before ultimately deciding to remove it entirely. With a moment's hesitation, he grasped an arrow, dropped the quiver to the ground, and nocked the arrow onto the bowstring. Tentatively pulling back, he aimed at the bird and released. The arrow tumbled end over end, landing harmlessly in the grass, far short of its target. Rykan retrieved the misfired arrow as the bird took flight and disappeared into the sky.

He slung the bow over his shoulder and grabbed the quiver. It wasn't his weapon of choice, but it might be useful later. For now, there was no time to practice. He'd have to rely on his sword instead.

As the sun reached its zenith, Rykan spotted a heap in the grass ahead.

A pronghorn lay motionless, its hoofed legs stiff and extended. The absence of insects or scavengers around the carcass suggested it had died only recently. A small patch of dried blood on its side marked where something sharp had pierced its chest.

Where there was prey, there had to be a hunter. Searching as far as he could see, Rykan found no signs of anyone around. Maybe another pronghorn had impaled it. Either way, the meat could sustain him for a week.

After taking his boot knife out, he sawed into the pronghorn's side, trying to quarter it the way he had seen the butchers in the market do. It was a lot messier than he expected, and the knife wasn't big enough to slice like he needed.

He finally gave up, wiping off the blade and placing it back into his boot. Edible plants were his best hope with the tools he had to hand. With no feasible way to utilize the pronghorn, Rykan reluctantly continued his journey. The terrain shifted under his feet, from grassy knolls to a downward slope of loose dirt marked by small channels and grooves—signs that water occasionally carved through this area. Hope swelled within him. Water often meant civilization was near.

Quickening his pace, Rykan descended into the basin. But the dry grass beneath his boots dashed his hopes for water. He rubbed his cramping stomach, his shadow elongating as the sun dipped toward the horizon. A chill ran through him, sparked by the cooling air or perhaps the dread of another solitary night.

Suddenly, a voice cut through the silence. "You're hopeless, lad." Rykan whirled around to find a man standing there, effortlessly tossing the dead pronghorn onto the ground. "Did nobody teach you anything?"

Startled, Rykan reached for an arrow but hesitated as the bearded man with copper-shaded skin knelt and began to clear the dirt and pebbles away from a spot on the ground. Caught between fleeing and a desire to know what this man was doing, Rykan watched, transfixed.

The man looked up from his task. "Find us some tinder," he instructed, his tone making it clear there was no time to waste.

Rykan's jaw tightened at the order. "You've been following me? Who are you?" he demanded.

"Name's Garrick," the stranger replied, not looking up. "I've been trying to help you."

"This bow must be yours then." Rykan removed the bow from his shoulder. "I don't need your help."

"The wilderness is no place for the untested," Garrick said, meeting Rykan's gaze briefly before returning to his work.

Rykan continued watching Garrick, unsure what to make of him.

"Listen, there's no shame in not knowing what you were never taught," Garrick said, his tone gentler. "If you want to help, gather some tinder, and I'll teach you what I can."

Rykan hesitated, then strode toward the nearest tree, searching for any dried, fallen branches. After finding some broken into small pieces, he carried what he could back to Garrick. Dropping his handful in the dirt, Rykan waited, eyes on Garrick for approval.

As he stood there, a voice within urged him to move on. He wasn't beholden to this stranger's commands. After all, he didn't even know who this man was. Yet, despite his reservations, Rykan found something oddly endearing about Garrick. His gruff demeanor and few terse words resonated with Rykan.

After Garrick kindled the fire into a steady blaze, Rykan watched intently as the man drew a knife and expertly slit the pronghorn's belly. With fluid motions, he removed the organs, then skillfully used the blade to separate and peel back the skin. Rykan found parts of the process unsettling, yet he couldn't tear his eyes away, eager to learn every detail.

Once he'd quartered the carcass, Garrick selected a large branch, skewered a piece of the meat, and held it over the flames. He rotated it slowly, ensuring it roasted evenly. The aroma of the cooking meat filled the air, and Rykan's first bite showed him how he had once taken food for granted.

"To live in the wilds, you must earn its respect," Garrick said between bites as they sat by the flickering fire in the encroaching darkness. "I take it you didn't come all the way out here by choice."

Rykan swallowed the tender, smoky meat and hesitated. "The Iron Flood," he began, his voice trembling slightly. "They—"

"They took you to the gate," Garrick interjected, his voice low and knowing.

Memories flashed through Rykan's mind—the terrible vision of a giant clawed hand, the horrid voice echoing. A lump formed in his throat, choking him.

"How did you get away?" Garrick asked.

The slight change in topic allowed Rykan's memories to switch to something else. He knocked his hand against his boot. "They didn't take my boot knife."

A slight grin emerged on Garrick's face. "Resourceful. I like that. You've got some fight in you, even if you're not much of a hunter."

Rykan nodded, looking up at the stars to avoid the man's gaze. He didn't want to dwell on what could have happened if he had not escaped.

"Did you see it?" Garrick pressed. "The thing behind the gate?"

Rykan's heart raced as he thought about the giant clawed hand grabbing the girl and dragging her underneath the bent corner of the gate. He didn't want to talk about it, refusing to answer the question. But with every passing moment, his curiosity continued to get the better of him.

"How do you know about that?" he asked.

"I say this with regret, but I was once a soldier with the Iron Flood," said Garrick.

Rykan paused his chewing, standing up straight over the man sitting in the grass. "My father was murdered by the Iron Flood!" he fumed, kicking loose rocks and dirt toward Garrick. "I don't need your help!"

"Whoa, whoa, whoa," said Garrick. "I'm on your side, lad. Once I saw what they were doing, I left."

"Why would anyone ever join Vatreus!" shouted Rykan. "You should all be rotting in a dungeon for the rest of your miserable lives!"

"I'm truly sorry about your father," Garrick said, his voice sincere. "Sit down, and I'll explain. If you've ever studied history, you know that every war has two sides, and each believes wholeheartedly that they are right."

Rykan remained standing. "Go ahead then, explain."

"Very well," Garrick said, taking another bite and chewing slowly, as if using the time to gather his thoughts. "I knew Vatreus early on, before he lost his way. He was always a bit of an outsider, hated by some just for being a Lith. I guess that's what first drew me to him—I was a bit of an outsider myself. There was something about him, a power within that no one could explain. I heard he'd been through a lot as a boy, surviving things that would have broken most. Maybe it was everything he'd overcome that gave him that strength.

"Vatreus wanted to unite people from all walks of life, to end the injustices and conflicts that plagued the kingdoms of Galanor. He wasn't quiet about his ideas either. He spoke passionately about a better world. He had plans. The more he spoke, the more people listened. They saw in him a leader who could bring about real change. But somewhere along the way, his vision twisted, and his methods grew darker."

"He wanted to end conflicts?" Rykan huffed. "By starting a war?"

"It's ironic, no doubt about it," said Garrick. "But it didn't start like that at all. His passion was contagious. Listeners became followers, and for some, that passion turned to zeal. They began to demand more aggressive action. As Vatreus's power grew, it only worsened. People started calling him Zhal Evurah."

"Zhal Evurah? What's that?" Rykan sat down, his anger fading as curiosity replaced it.

"It means 'The Whisper Beyond the Stars,'" Garrick explained. "Some ancient prophecy. Legend has it that, whenever the world teeters on the brink of disaster, a person of great destiny will emerge, sent by the immortal realm of Archeinor to restore balance and right the wrongs of our time. It has been over a thousand years since anyone has seen a Zhal Evurah.

"After witnessing what Vatreus could do, I started to believe. We were tired of being dragged into petty disputes among the nobility. Good men dying in battle, because a king's nephew was insulted. Cities devastated by wars over a neighboring lord who refused to marry someone's daughter. Vatreus promised we could change that—he claimed that, together, we could reshape the world."

Rykan frowned as the anger seeped back in. "The Iron Flood invaded my city unprovoked. They killed many good people. Vatreus murdered my father. How is that supposed to save the world?"

"When Vatreus first took action, Barathal surrendered without a fight when they witnessed his power, just as he had predicted. They believed Vatreus had been sent by Archeinor, and they joined the Iron Flood. That's how it was supposed to go."

"But not everyone believed," said Rykan, tapping his fingers on his knee.

"Not everyone did, no," Garrick repeated. "Some said he did not bear a certain mark of the chosen. They didn't surrender."

"Why are you out here then?" Rykan challenged.

"I was assigned to the caravans, same one you probably rode on the way here," said Garrick. "The first time I saw that … thing drag a boy under the gate, I was done. I deserted them, hid here in the wilderness."

"You should be out there fighting him," said Rykan.

"He's grown too powerful now," said Garrick. "He's even shared some of that power among his captains, the ones he calls the Dreadstorm Knights. His army is large enough now to sweep across Galanor on multiple fronts."

"So why do they feed people to whatever is behind that gate?" asked Rykan.

"I didn't stay around long enough to find out," said Garrick, his voice dropping to a whisper. "But I dread to think what would happen if that gate were ever opened fully." He glanced at the remainder of the cooked meat. "Let's finish up. It's about time to shut down for the night."

Rykan nodded, his mind racing with the implications of their conversation as he chewed the last of his meal. Even with everything on his mind, sleep came quickly. The wilderness felt much safer with this stranger around.

⤜∞⤛

The sounds of Garrick burying the remains of the fire under the loose soil startled Rykan awake. He brushed debris from his hair and sat up.

"There's a cave a few miles from here," said Garrick, pausing in his task. "If you've nowhere to go, you can stay as long as you need."

Rykan stretched, feeling the stiffness in his limbs, and gazed toward the horizon, painted with the first light of dawn.

"Where are you going?" he asked, his voice still thick with sleep.

Garrick chuckled. "I'm going back to the cave. No point going anywhere else. Once the Iron Flood sweeps across the world, the wilds will be the only free air left to breathe."

"I'm going to Rowanar," Rykan declared, rising to his feet and dusting off his tunic. He squinted against the rising sun. "If there's any chance of saving Tathara, I have to try."

"The capital of Elenior. I wouldn't have guessed you were from there," Garrick mused, looking Rykan over as if seeing him for the first time.

Anticipating the next question, Rykan volunteered, "I was born in Peranda, one of the Candasara Isles. We fled to the mainland when I was very young."

"I've heard many were killed when the volcano erupted," Garrick noted with a somber tone. "You've been close to death most of your life."

"I try not to think about it," Rykan admitted, staring at the ground.

"Tathara was one of the more peaceful cities I've seen. But now sanctuaries have become battlefields. Come with me." Garrick straightened, facing Rykan squarely. "I'll teach you to live off the land."

"You might've given up, but I'm not done yet," Rykan retorted, starting to walk ahead under the shadow of the mountains. "Maybe if you had tried stopping this mess earlier, we wouldn't be in this situation. You should be out there getting every city, every kingdom, to fight back against the Iron Flood. Stay in your cave if you want, but I'm heading to Rowanar."

"Then you should know that you're heading in the wrong direction," Garrick called after him, a hint of frustration in his voice. "You'll end up in Wekenwild going that way."

Rykan stopped abruptly, then turned back with a skeptical look. "Wekenwild?" he echoed, confused. "I've never heard of any such place."

"Wekenwild is an enchanted forest," Garrick explained, "a place from which no one ever returns."

Adjusting his direction slightly, Rykan continued on.

"Rowanar is that way." Garrick pointed to Rykan's left.

Rykan shrugged nonchalantly. "The most direct way isn't always the best way." He corrected his course to appear as if he had known the right direction all along.

As he walked away, Rykan felt torn. He wanted to prove he could manage on his own, but he also acknowledged he needed help.

"You forgot the bow," Garrick yelled out.

"That's your bow," Rykan called back over his shoulder. "I'm much better with a sword anyway."

"Ah, a fellow swordsman," Garrick remarked, causing Rykan to slow his pace slightly. "But a good soldier must be familiar with many weapons, including a bow. Not many animals you can hunt with a sword."

Rykan ignored the comment and continued walking toward the tree line with bold steps.

"How many soldiers in Rowanar?" Garrick asked, still following him.

"I'm not sure, a few hundred I imagine," Rykan shouted back.

"I suppose it's a start," Garrick said, his voice closer than expected.

Glancing back, Rykan saw Garrick closing the distance between them. Though he said nothing, he felt a bit of relief that he wouldn't be alone.

CHAPTER 8

SUNLIGHT CASCADED INTO the room as Selaina lay ensconced in the bed. Despite the passing hours since dawn, she clung tightly to the sheet, navigating a tumultuous sea of emotions from sorrow to fear. Inhaling a staggered breath, she resisted the idea of confronting the outside world once more. Her resolve insisted on remaining cocooned in the bed until the world itself dissolved around her and pulled her into oblivion. Amid the ache of missing her mother and the horror of Jeth's fate, Selaina found herself grappling with a more immediate struggle—her own well-being.

A relentless internal tug-of-war unfolded as her mind grappled with conflicting emotions. Doubts about her ability to persevere waged war against a persistent glimmer of hope desperately seeking something positive to grasp onto. Yet the overwhelming weight of sadness swiftly quelled each attempt at optimism.

After a few more hours passed, logic began to win out. She couldn't lie here forever. Things had to be done. The fleecehorns had to be fed. She couldn't let them go hungry. And the crops, she would need to water them in case it didn't rain.

As much as she would like to go about the day's chores and pretend nothing was wrong, she had to address something first. She couldn't leave Jeth lying in the stream. When their fleecehorns had died in the past, Jeth always buried them in the dirt. Partly to prevent the odor from attracting scavengers to the cabin. But Jeth had spoken of it as a way to honor the animals as part of the family. He believed it allowed them a peaceful transition into the Netherwood, where their former bodies became one with the mortal forest, rather than being consumed by insects and animals.

After more than an hour of digging with the tiling shovel and rolling Jeth's body from the brook into the grave she had made nearby, Selaina finally collapsed against one of the trees, utterly exhausted. She let her sore arms rest limply at her sides, her breath coming in slow, ragged gasps. Closing her eyes, she whispered a prayer, hoping Jeth would find his way among the spirits of the Netherwood.

With no sign of her mother yet, she could only conclude the worst. Most everything that had happened the day before seemed like any other. The only thing out of the ordinary was the man she had seen in the woods.

A chill went through her as fears flowed like streams through her veins. Perhaps if she had told Jeth about seeing the strange man in the woods, he would have been on his guard. Maybe Jeth would still be alive, and maybe her mother would still be here. What if this was all her fault?

That couldn't be. She was good. The strange man came from the wicked world. He had to be the only one to blame. But why did she feel so wrong?

With little remaining daylight, Selaina mustered the will to get to her feet. She put the rest of the grass and carrots her mother had gathered near the fleecehorn pens into their feeding troughs. As she made her way back inside the house, the pain in her stomach became too great to ignore.

Lighting one of the candles in the kitchen, Selaina swept her gaze across the cluttered space. Ceramic pots and wooden spoons lay haphazardly on the surface where her mother prepared food. A chair near the table had tipped over. The table, where she expected to find the last loaf of bread her mother had made, was bare. A frown creased her brow, and she moved further into the kitchen, her eyes narrowing at the disarray.

The loaf of bread lay on the floor, surrounded by crumbs. The cutting knife her mother often used was also on the wooden floor, its blade glinting ominously in the candlelight. Selaina's heart tightened with irritation.

Selaina reached down to pick up the loaf of bread. As she placed it back onto the table, she noticed four long scratches on the wooden surface. As she slid her index finger along the crooked grooves, an image flashed into her head. Before the vision vanished, she saw two men grabbing her mother. When she touched the marks on the table again, a quick picture of her mother's fingers digging into the table as the men pulled her away flashed through her mind.

Selaina recoiled, slumping over the table. A wave of dread washed over her as the images kept repeating in her mind. Who were these men? Where had they taken her mother and why? Why would they kill Jeth?

The cabin grew dark. She sat, leaning her head on the table. She couldn't get the images out of her head. Having neglected to light a candle before nightfall, she couldn't see anything in the darkness. Selaina held her head in her hands as thoughts of Jeth and her mother tormented her. She didn't want to be here anymore, the dark silence of death seemed more appealing than this.

Her head throbbed, the pressure of pent-up sadness threatening to burst forth. She had held it back, fearing it might consume her if released. But she could no longer restrain it. The sweet agony of sorrow poured out in torrents. As she let go, a part of her never wanted it to end. She realized it was more than mere grief. Emotions long suppressed followed in its wake. Feelings she didn't fully understand flowed from her, overwhelming and raw. Selaina wanted everything out now. Revisiting every painful memory, she wrung out her pain as one might squeeze a soiled cloth.

With the morning sun streaming into the kitchen, Selaina lifted her head from the table. The scratches on its surface greeted her, like a lingering echo of the vision from the previous evening. The thought that her mother might still be alive persisted. Standing up, she smoothed out the wrinkles in her clothes. If her mother was out there, Selaina knew she had to find her.

In Jeth's room, she found his hunting bow and a quiver nearly filled with arrows. Carrying them on her shoulder, she went through the drawers of his chest, searching for anything that could be useful. After initially finding nothing but clothing, Selaina at last discovered one of his knives and placed it under her belt. Moving on to his desk, she found nothing of interest except for a book. The cover had clouds and mountains with one standing tall above the rest. It depicted three snake-like creatures flying around the top of the tallest mountain. It reminded her of the story Jeth had told her of the Sky Serpents. There were words, but Selaina had never learned to read. Thumbing through the pages, she came across several pieces of artwork, some with the three serpents and others of the mountain.

After wrapping the book in cloth, she placed it inside one of Jeth's leather bags. Perhaps she could learn to read it, and in the meantime, she enjoyed the pictures. It made a nice keepsake, something to remember Jeth by.

Chills crept down her spine as she moved from Jeth's room into her mother's. Searching for anything her mother kept that might be useful in finding her, Selaina combed through every drawer in the room. After finding mostly old, tattered clothes her mother occasionally wore, she spotted something shimmery at the bottom of the stack.

Selaina pulled it out from under the other clothes, allowing it to unfurl. It was a lovely silver dress. She had never seen her mother wear it, neither had she ever seen anything like it before. How would such a thing be made? With its soft reflective material, the dress had to be something from the wicked world. There was nothing like this cloth in the forest. Selaina put the dress back into the drawer.

Selaina's eyes moved to the open drawer that was normally locked. Though she had already made up her mind, she sat on the bed trying to settle the guilt she felt. If there was ever a time that searching through her mother's private table was justified, this had to be it.

The drawer contained a few small carvings of wolves, like the one Jeth had made for her. Selaina's eyes lit up when she found sets of earrings made of gold and silver. They were intricately detailed, holding large gemstones. Unable to resist, Selaina removed her feather-and-wood earring, which was still missing its match, and replaced it with two silver ones containing a blue gemstone.

After moving some of the items aside, she uncovered a small, framed picture—a painting crafted by a more skilled hand than those adorning the walls. It was a painting of her mother. She was much younger in this depiction, her hair still fully white. White flowers surrounded her mother as she sat in a chair with her hands cradled in front of her. Selaina wiped the droplets from her eyes. This gave her a way to see her mother again, if only as an illusion.

The most unexpected thing in the drawer was a second painting, this one of a man who also had white hair. He had a pleasant smile on his face and appeared to be a good person. Why did her mother never mention him?

Placing the picture of her mother in the bag made it a little bulkier, but it was small enough to easily fit. As she reached the doorway, Selaina took one final look at the interior of the cabin. It was all she had ever known.

She envisioned Jeth seated in the main room, deftly carving a block of wood. Her mother, detailing a piece of pottery she had made, while scents of leaves brewed on the hearth for a comforting pot of tea. Selaina had never realized how much she cherished those moments until now. If only she could return to them again, she would savor them as much as they truly deserved. But some things can never be revisited. Life was forcing her to leave them behind.

Selaina said goodbye to Nibbles, Snickers, and the rest of the fleece-horns, stroking each one's fur. When she opened the gate, a few of them trotted out while the rest of them stayed inside, munching on the grass in the pen. She hoped they wouldn't go too far. Maybe they would come back when she and her mother returned home. There was plenty of grass and wheat for them near the cabin, as long as they didn't eat it all before it had a chance to regrow.

Drawing a deep breath, she braced herself against the unknown, moving off toward the forest. Boundless uncertainties awaited her, both exciting and frightening. This moment, long dreamed of, was unfolding under circumstances she had never desired. Life's cruel irony, it seemed, allowed her only one wish at a time, demanding pain, death, and sorrow as its currency.

Passing near the hill where the blue light seeped through the cracks in the stone, Selaina paused, her gaze lingering for a moment. She had always felt something special here, a quiet pulse in the earth, like the forest was alive in ways she couldn't quite understand. She would miss this area she had claimed as her own. The thought of the spotted rabbit and all the other creatures of the forest tugged at her heart. She would miss them too. Hopeful that one day she could return here with her mother, Selaina continued deeper into the woods.

Pushing through fields of weeds, between tall skinny trees, and over small rocky hills, Selaina heard the splashing of water ahead. As she pushed between two crooked trees, her eyes widened as she found the end of the woods. The largest body of water she had ever seen lay before her. Its waters lapped against rocks and a small sandy shore to her left.

The lake stretched out wide and far, to a distant shoreline on the horizon. It appeared as though the forest was completely surrounded by water, separating it from the wicked world. But if her mother and Jeth had come here, there had to be a way to cross it.

Selaina trekked around the shoreline, over the sandy beaches, and around trees standing near the water's edge. Small cliffs rose in certain places, giving her a chance at a better view. After walking for a while, though, she was unable to find a path that would allow anyone to cross.

Selaina spotted something floating near the shore with a large white bird perched on it and moved in for a closer look. The bird flapped its wings when she approached, cautiously eyeing her every move. Whatever it was appeared to be made of wood. Patches of moss and algae grew along its surface. As Selaina drew closer, she noticed a rope attached to it, the other end tied to a nearby tree.

The bird leaped from its perch into the bottom of the object, causing it to move in the water. Even with the bird's weight, it remained on the surface of the water. A memory flashed across Selaina's mind. Jeth had told her once about boats that carried people across vast bodies of water. Selaina crept to the water's edge and took the rope in her hands. She pulled the boat toward her, making the bird take flight and leave the area. If only she could fly, she could get across this water to the other shore easily.

After pulling the boat onto the shore, Selaina stepped inside and sat on the moss-covered seat. The water continued to lap against the side of the boat, but the craft didn't move. It had settled on the sand.

She took a long wooden tool with a flat end from the bottom and tried to push the boat back into the water but was unsuccessful. After some trial and error, Selaina realized she would have to exit the boat and push it back into the water as she boarded it.

With a running start, she slid the boat along the sand and out into the deeper water, splashing along beside it. Selaina jumped on, nearly landing on her face in the bottom of the small boat. After settling herself, she took the tool again, trying to push against the land under the water to thrust the boat forward. The tool could not reach the bottom. Selaina continued to feel for something to use to thrust the boat forward but discovered the water itself provided enough resistance to do so. After turning the boat around, she realized she would have to paddle a bit on each side of the boat to keep it straight. Now she was moving. Her journey had begun with her heading toward the hazy shores of the wicked world.

CHAPTER 9

RYKAN MAINTAINED A brisk pace as he and Garrick descended the rugged hillside, moving toward the vibrant yellow valley that unfurled below them. They dodged stark black rocks that jutted out from the verdant grass, weaving through the towering weeds. Above, the sky boasted a splendid, broad arc of pink sunshimmer, painting the horizon in strokes of celestial magic. Garrick slowed, directing Rykan's attention toward a nearby hill. A gathering of brown creatures clustered together, indulging in the dark green grass that adorned a particular patch. Not far from them, a shepherd sat in the comforting shade of a tree, using a large stick to trace lazy patterns in the dirt.

Garrick changed direction, walking toward tis other hill as he raised his arm to get the man's attention. The shepherd pushed himself up, leaning against the tree trunk while he watched their approach.

"Good day," Garrick said as he stopped before reaching the tree's shade. "Your flock is well mannered, especially for balkorns."

The animals, resembling woolly beasts with thick, curling horns, seemed imposing even as they knelt to graze.

The shepherd nodded to Garrick and Rykan. "As long as they have ripe grass below and blue skies above, they are content in these hills."

Rykan, puzzled by the distance Garrick kept from the shepherd, scanned their surroundings, his instincts tingling with the thrill of the unknown.

"What's that you are marking there?" Garrick asked.

The dirt at the shepherd's feet drew Rykan's attention. He had carved circles with lines tracing to each other in the soil.

The shepherd glanced at the markings before lifting his head back to Garrick. "The mischievous stars, Auronia, Verantis, and Zaryneth are converging," he said. "The sign that the Wishing Stone has reappeared."

Rykan's thoughts drifted back to the vivid, disorienting vision he had recently experienced. He remembered the eerie red glow of the tree's knot hole, the chaotic swirl of stars and forms that had seemed to pulse with life and decay. The words of the vision echoed in his mind, "Tell us where the Wishing Stone rests, reveal its place, where stars have blessed." The voice from the vision, maddening and cryptic, had spoken of the Wishing Stone and the child of silver snow, a warning wrapped in riddles.

"Auronia, Verantis, and Zaryneth… those names sound familiar," Rykan murmured, his mind still tangled with the vision's unsettling clarity. He looked up, focused now on the shepherd. "Aren't those the Sky Serpents of Kylinshan?" His fingers drummed rhythmically on the back of his neck as he awaited the shepherd's answer.

"Of course," said the shepherd. "They were once celestials but now wander the skies, following their own paths. They come together only for this event."

Garrick took the bags he was carrying off his shoulder and laid them in the grass. "When was the last time that happened?"

"It was three hundred twenty-seven years ago," said the shepherd. "I mark this ground to track them. Once they form the triangle, they will call the Wishing Stone from the hidden realm."

Rubbing the thick hairs on his chin, Garrick shook his head side to side. "Don't tell me you're going to try and find it?"

The shepherd spoke with a firm voice, his weathered face reflecting the weight of his words. "To meddle with forces beyond our reach is to walk a path shadowed by peril. Like the river that carves the valley, power shapes the wielder in unseen ways. Should fate ever lead me to such a stone, it would not be to wield its might but to ensure it lies undisturbed, sparing others from the burden of its allure."

"You are a wise man, Shepherd. My companion and I are passing through, on the way to Rowanar," Garrick said. "What would you consider the fastest road?"

Rykan wanted to move underneath the shady tree and get out of the sun for a moment but stayed with Garrick.

The shepherd turned, gazing across the valley. "The pass ahead would be the quickest road," he said as he glanced back at Garrick, "but perhaps not the safest. There are rumors of travelers ambushed by bandits. You may be better off going through the foothills."

"Bandits?" Garrick pressed his lips together. "How many?"

The shepherd spread out his hands. "Some have said as many as ten, some say less." He glanced at Rykan. "Either way, more than the two of you could handle."

Garrick squinted as he surveyed the horizon. "Thank you, we'll be on our way then."

The shepherd lowered himself to the ground, resuming his seated position as he watched over the balkorns. "Peaceful journey."

Garrick picked up his things and started off down the hill. Rykan took another glance at the shepherd before following Garrick down into the valley. He moved across the grassy meadows, heading toward the foothills.

Rykan quickened his pace, walking alongside Garrick. "We need to take the fastest way."

"You heard the shepherd." Garrick maintained his speed as their feet brushed through the thick grass. "Too many bandits."

Frowning, Rykan shot back, "We're going all the way around because of some rumors? Even the numbers in these reports don't match up."

Garrick sighed. "Shepherds know this valley better than anyone. If they say there are bandits, it's wise to listen."

"We must get to Rowanar immediately," Rykan insisted. "If we have to risk a few bandits, so be it."

"Those words would only come from someone who has never been ambushed by bandits," Garrick said. "Very well, I'm not interested in walking any further than I have to."

More balkorns gathered in the middle of the valley, drinking from pools of water that had collected in the lower pockets. Tall grass protruded through the water's surface as the wind traced its hands along it, making ripples.

"Tell me about the Wishing Stone," Rykan said as they moved into the widest part of the valley.

Garrick snorted and spat on the ground. "It's a myth that's been going around for centuries."

"Well, what's the myth?" Rykan turned to see Garrick's expression. "Does it grant any wish you want?"

Garrick seemed surprisingly uninterested. "You're asking the wrong person," he said. "Myths, prophecies, legends, what use are they? They only lead men to follow people like Vatreus."

"If I found a Stone like that, I would wish for the Iron Flood to be ended," said Rykan. "For the world to go back to the way it was."

"The way it was?" asked Garrick. "That's it? If things had been good, there would be no Iron Flood. At least have some imagination. What about riches? Fair maidens?"

"Well, what would you wish for?" asked Rykan, a bit put off by Garrick's remark.

"I'm done with any crusades to save the world, so I suppose I would wish to be the wealthiest man in all of Galanor," said Garrick, plucking a blade of grass as they walked.

"I thought you wanted maidens. Do you value riches over companionship?" asked Rykan, growing bolder with his words. "That's a bit selfish, don't you think?"

"If I've learned anything the last few years, it's that people don't always want what you think they want. All I can know is what I want. With riches comes everything else," Garrick replied, his gaze following the swaying grass, "including fair maidens."

"But not love?" Rykan questioned, looking sideways at Garrick. "That seems a bit hollow."

"Love often is." Garrick sighed, his eyes aiming at the horizon. "You seldom find another soul who is truly devoted to you all the way to the end."

"What good is all the wealth in the world," Rykan countered, pausing to adjust his pack, "if you have no love to share it with?"

"Plenty." Garrick chuckled, waving his hand at the expansive valley around them. "I could hire a caravan, travel the world. There's lots of wondrous things out there I'll probably never see. Would be quite an adventure."

"If that's what you truly want." Rykan pressed on, stepping through a thicker patch of grass. "Why wouldn't you simply wish for that? What need would you have of riches?"

"I suppose because riches make everything easier," Garrick explained, his steps slowing as they approached a steeper incline. "I could wish for the means to see the world or I could have riches that take care of all the little details that accompany it."

Rykan was determined to out-reason him, to find a detail he didn't have an answer for. "If everything is easy, where's the adventure?"

"It wouldn't all be easy, lad," said Garrick. "Only the bothersome logistics. Gold wouldn't make much difference in the wilderness."

Rykan rolled his eyes as he slowed, allowing Garrick to move ahead. Clouds covered the sun, dimming the valley as they moved ahead. The walls of the foothills narrowed as they made their way to the pass. Hard sand and rock replaced the tall grass and continued on through the rest of the valley.

For days, he had done little more than walk since he left that horrid gate. He was growing weary. Hopefully, it wasn't much farther until they reached Rowanar and his uncle. It would be nice to see a familiar face again.

As he increased his pace to keep up with Garrick, a tapping sound from above caught Rykan's attention. A stone cascaded down the rocky hill, loosing pebbles and rocks along the way. They clattered into a bed of gray sand at the bottom.

Garrick stopped, lifting his hand as a gesture for Rykan to hold. The cliffs grew silent as he waited as if something were about to happen.

A chill came over Rykan when he noticed concern in Garrick's eyes. Men dressed in gray and wearing masks over their faces left their hiding places behind large boulders and stones. Wielding knives, swords, and crossbows, they moved in behind Rykan and Garrick, blocking the way back to the open valley.

Garrick dropped his bag, his bow, and his quiver and unsheathed a long sword. Grabbing Rykan's hand, he pulled him back behind him. Rykan's heart felt as though it would beat through the skin of his chest as the bandits crept toward them.

"Care to dance?" Garrick asked as he twirled his blade, taking a deep breath before suddenly charging the bandits.

As one of the swordsmen raised his blade, Garrick thrust his sword into him. Quickly removing his blade from the torso of the swordsman, Garrick leaped away from a swing at his head. Reaching behind his attacker, he slashed the blade across the man's back. Rykan ran into the fray, picking up one of the bandits' fallen swords.

Rykan engaged the dagger-wielding bandit, and the bowman fired his arrow. The arrow whistled by him as Rykan evaded the dagger strikes, sidestepping to use the bandit as cover from the bowman. Rykan attacked, cutting down the bandit. After quickly grabbing one of the daggers, Garrick flung it at the bowman. The dagger narrowly missed the bowman as he fumbled to load his crossbow with another arrow.

Garrick drew back his hand, ready to throw the other dagger while Rykan closed in. The bowman dropped his crossbow and fled into the valley. While keeping an eye on the runner, Garrick struck a final blow into each of the three who lay on the ground. They had appeared to be dead already, but now they surely were.

Trying to settle his shaking body, Rykan hesitated to move when Garrick picked up his belongings and hoisted them over his shoulder.

"The shepherd was right," Garrick said as he patted Rykan's shoulder. "There were bandits in the pass. Keep a sharp eye out."

He walked ahead as if nothing had changed. But for Rykan, everything had changed. He was taken aback by how little remorse Garrick had. He had inflicted pain and death and seemed to feel nothing. Rykan hadn't pictured heroism this way, the reality of blood and pain. He wondered how he could have any use in war if he had not the stomach to inflict death on his enemies.

Garrick continued on the path between the cliffs as Rykan stood still, uncertain where to go from here. But when Garrick glanced back, Rykan felt a bit of relief. Gazing up at his face, Rykan caught sight of his wry smile. There was a kindness in his eyes. He thought about how Garrick had helped him, a stranger in the wilderness. Garrick wasn't a monster. Garrick had a kind heart with the spirit of a lion. He had only shown danger to those with ill intent.

CHAPTER 10

HAVING MADE IT to shore, Selaina felt her boots squelch into the soft, wet dirt, each step sinking slightly deeper than she intended. Layers of misty fog rose just above the ground. Thick patches gathered around large puddles scattered about this new land. She ventured forward into the forest, a labyrinth of twisted trees that cloaked the path ahead in mystery and shadow.

Sounds of unseen creatures throughout the rotting woods played in harmony with the silence. Shadows created strange shapes, playing tricks on her imagination. This was nothing like the forest she had once walked in the latter part of each day. Here, a spectral murmur replaced the rustling of leaves, as if dark entities conversed in hushed tones beyond her perception. The distant hooting of an owl, unnaturally prolonged into ghostly wails, sent shivers down her spine. Frogs croaked all around her in some kind of distorted laughter. The murky forest itself seemed alive.

The gnarled branches of trees reached out, clawing at her with skeletal fingers. Occasional splashes in the water hinted at creatures lurking beyond her sight. This truly was the wicked world.

Her feet continued to sink further into the mud, the ground sucking at her boots with greedy, clinging cold. She tried to find more solid footing, veering slightly off her intended path, only to encounter thick, spongy moss that offered no respite from the pervasive dampness. Every sense was on full alert as she came to the edge of a lagoon. Selaina made her way around it, but she couldn't shake the feeling that something out there was watching her every move.

After reaching the end of the lagoon, Selaina began circling it, hoping to quickly get back on track. The trees on the far side were stark silhouettes against the deepening gloom. Out of the corner of her eye, a dark shape flickered—an elusive shadow moving against the backdrop of trees. Her heart lurched, and she froze, every sense heightened.

Staring into the rows of tangled thickets, she saw nothing. After a tense few moments, she mustered the courage to continue, her steps hesitant. Yet, her eyes compulsively darted back to the clump of trees with every rustle and whisper carried by the wind. Another shadow twitched in her peripheral vision, vanishing as soon as she tried to focus on it. An unfamiliar fear spread slowly through her veins, urging her on—a primal warning that, if she stopped, the sinister wilderness might swallow her whole.

Once she made her way to the other side of the lagoon, Selaina resumed her original course. Suddenly, a peculiar object caught her eye, slanted oddly between two trees. When she faced it directly, it snapped upright and vanished into the tree's silhouette like a mirage dissolving under scrutiny. Her skin prickled, and she forced her feet to move toward it, her gaze locked on the spot where it had been.

Another shadow shifted behind a different tree. She halted, scanning the surrounding woods. Nearby, something that resembled a head peeked from behind a trunk. The moment she turned toward it, it snapped back, hidden once again.

The air grew thick with a strange, metallic scent mixing with the earthy aroma of damp foliage. Selaina's heart pounded, resonating with the eerie silence that fell over the area. As she approached another tree, a shadowy figure ducked behind it. Changing her direction, Selaina attempted to side-step the mysterious figures but found more of the shadow people moving swiftly to hide behind the trees. Her panic escalated. Turning back the way she'd come, she started to run, but shadows swirled around her. The tree branches reached for her with their gnarled fingers, blurring the line between the natural and the supernatural. Her breaths came in ragged gasps, her heart hammering against her chest as if trying to escape. The world spun around her, disorienting her further. Each step felt more desperate than the last.

"Fear not, wanderer." The voice of a woman spoke calmly nearby.

"They will bring no harm to you. They are only the Nadrok, watchers from the deep."

Selaina couldn't speak. She tried to take slower, deeper breaths, but it was taking time to calm herself down. Somehow, the sudden appearance of a new voice did not startle her more.

"Does this murky swamp filled with shadows stir a chill within your bones?" asked the woman. "Only those with discerning eyes can fathom the beguiling allure of this place. Not all life craves the caress of sunlight, my dear, for in darkness there is beauty, a clandestine realm where life finds its own silent bloom." Though she lived in the wicked world, the woman spoke pleasantly, filling Selaina with a sense of calm.

Standing before Selaina, the woman wore dark, ragged clothing that blended into the gloom. Gray streaked through her black, stringy, unkempt hair. As she moved, small white sticks hanging around her neck jangled with a hollow sound, like a macabre melody that accompanied her every step. Dark red, violet, and blue jewels worn around her wrists occasionally caught the gloomy light.

As Selaina met her amber-colored eyes, a sudden vision flashed through her mind—a vivid montage of the woman's recent memories. Selaina saw her running through green marshy fields as the sun began to rise. She felt her pain when she rubbed a salve on her burnt skin. Her fatigue as she stepped over the feathery wings of birds scattered on a wooden floor gave Selaina an unsettling feeling that crept down her spine.

"I supposed it is what I should have expected of this world." Breathing more easily now, Selaina felt her heart slow. "Why do they watch?"

"No one truly knows," said the woman. "They have been here since the dawn of this world, watching over sacred lands. Their presence is a rarity to behold. You, my dear, should count yourself among the favored."

Selaina wasn't sure what to make of the visions she had seen from the woman. "Their presence is unnerving," she said. "I don't like being watched. Are they guarding something here? Making sure I don't disturb some dark secret?"

"They are simply part of the swamps of Ravendrith," said the woman. "Like the insects, reptiles, you, and me."

"Is there anywhere I can go away from them?" Selaina asked.

"Come with me," said the woman. "I know a place that will keep you away from their gaze."

She gently took Selaina's hand and softly urged her to follow her through the swamp. Fearful doubts crept into Selaina's mind. She wasn't sure she wanted to be near this woman, but so far, she had seemed nice. Selaina realized, if she were to have any chance of finding her mother, she would have to talk to people in the wicked world.

Following the woman through the marsh, Selaina passed the nearby Nadrok, standing unnaturally between the trees. Leaning sideways, almost completely parallel to the ground, they remained, only moving to hide if Selaina looked directly at them.

Trying to ignore the Nadrok as much as she could, Selaina followed the woman further into the swamp. They came upon a set of enormous, gnarled roots that protruded through some eroded soil before snaking back into the ground. The clearing fog revealed the mammoth base of an old oak tree. As wide as ten people at least, the old tree trunk appeared to have broken off about twenty feet from the ground. Selaina could hardly imagine how tall the tree must have been once.

At the base of the ancient tree, a small red door stood out against the gnarled bark. Above it, several strands of twine were attached to the rib bones of some small creature, creating a morbid wind chime that chattered with the breeze. The woman gently pushed open the door, revealing the hollow interior of the giant tree.

As Selaina stepped inside, the musty scent of damp wood and rich earth mixed with a faint, unidentifiable herbal aroma that seemed to seep from the walls themselves to envelop her. The cool and slightly humid air clung to her skin as she moved further in. The dim light filtered through tiny cracks in the bark, casting soft patterns on the ground. Roots intertwined with the floor, making it feel like stepping into the heart of the forest itself.

In the far corner of the hollow, a quaint bed suitable for a single person was nestled against the curving bark wall. Scattered across the wood-grain pattern cast by the light onto the earthen floor were tufts of feathers, like those Selaina had seen in her vision. Cobwebs clung to the corners of the ceiling, and a layer of dust covered the small shelf brimming with old, leather-bound books, each spine creased from years of use. Another shelf, cluttered with odd plants and mysterious, covered objects, caught Selaina's eye. She squinted at the strange assortment, recognizing some herbs but puzzled by others. Selaina wrinkled her nose at the sight and hugged her arms to her chest, resisting the urge to sweep away the cobwebs and tidy the place up.

Near the center of the room, an oddly shaped table that resembled a drop of water at the moment of release from a surface, caught her eye. The floor around it showed signs of decay, with patches of rotted wood replaced by soil and where embers glowed warmly in a nest of firewood. Above this primitive hearth, a kettle made from the large shell of a tortoise hung suspended, filled with a dark brown liquid that emitted a rich, earthy aroma.

The woman moved gracefully toward the bark wall and pulled down a black curtain, dimming the streaks of light that pierced through the cracks.

"Please, sit, rest," she invited in a gentle voice, retrieving a wooden spoon from the table to stir the simmering liquid in the tortoise shell. "I am Elowen."

Selaina introduced herself and chose a seat on a circular cut of a tree trunk placed conveniently in front of the table. As she settled in, she glanced around the hollow interior, searching for a way to break the uncomfortable silence.

"I've never seen a house inside a tree before," she remarked, her voice echoing slightly in the wooden chamber.

With a slight smile, Selaina removed her hood, unleashing her white hair to cascade down her shoulders. Elowen paused her stirring and moved closer with a slow, measured step that seemed too quiet for the earthen floor. As she stood just behind Selaina, her presence felt imposing despite her gentle touch. Elowen's fingers delicately traced through Selaina's hair, sending a slight shiver down her spine.

"Such radiant tresses, like silver snow," Elowen mused in a whisper that lingered in the air a moment too long. "And those ears. You must be a Lith."

"What do you mean by Lith?" Selaina's brow furrowed with piqued interest.

"Do you not call yourselves Liths?" Elowen asked, returning to the kettle to adjust the flame beneath it, ensuring the brew would simmer gently as they talked.

"My mother told me little of the wicked world," Selaina replied cautiously.

"Wicked world?" Elowen echoed, a frown creasing her brow as she added a pinch of dried herbs to the kettle, the aroma subtly beginning to fill the space. "You speak of this place?"

"Yes, this dark forest, with these creatures you call Nadrok, who watch from the shadows," Selaina explained.

"This is my home," Elowen stated firmly, her tone indicating a slight hurt, as she stirred the contents of the kettle. "And you call it wicked?"

"Not yours in particular," Selaina hurried to clarify. "I meant no offense. It's just that everyone who lives in these woods—"

"I have seen no one in Ravendrith for many years," Elowen interjected, her expression thoughtful as she tasted the brew with a small wooden spoon. "Which leads me to wonder, what would bring one of the Lith to a place like this?"

The image of her mother being dragged away from the kitchen table flashed through Selaina's mind again, reigniting her urgency. "I'm looking for my mother," she said. "Two men took her while I was away from the house."

Elowen paused, her expression unreadable in the dim light of the hollow. "What makes you think she was brought here?" she asked slowly.

"She isn't in our forest. She must have been brought here," Selaina replied, with hope and desperation. "She has to be somewhere close."

"There are many places outside of Ravendrith, my dear," Elowen cautioned, her tone hinting at the vastness of the unknown. "Without more to go on, there's no telling where she might have been taken."

Confusion clouded Selaina's thoughts. "How far does this world stretch?"

"This land sprawls for many miles," Elowen explained, gesturing vaguely with her hand. "It weaves here and there in all directions and fades into other lands that stretch even further."

"The world is that big?" Selaina's voice held awe and a growing realization of her daunting task.

Elowen chuckled softly, a sound that seemed to hold more knowledge than it let on. "Not very well traveled, are you? Or is this some kind of mischief you are playing?"

Selaina studied Elowen's expressions intently, searching for any clue to what prompted her sudden question. "Mischief? No, nothing like that."

"People come to Ravendrith driven by many legends and tales," Elowen said, her eyes narrowing slightly as if trying to read Selaina's thoughts. "Some come seeking answers, others for relics buried within these woods. What drives you, I wonder?"

"All I am concerned about is finding my mother," Selaina responded. "If you think I'm intruding, then I'll leave."

"No, please, my dear." Elowen quickly softened, her voice turning sweet again. "Join me. I am making us a pot of tea—my special brew."

Despite the invitation, Selaina felt a growing urge to depart. The sudden shift in Elowen's demeanor made her uneasy. If she wasn't going to learn anything about her mother here, there was no point in staying.

"I should be going."

"Where do you plan to go?" Elowen inquired, casually stirring the tea again, adding another pinch of something from a jar on a nearby shelf.

"I don't know," Selaina admitted, trying to disguise the resignation in her voice. "I suppose I will walk in whatever direction my feet take me."

Elowen tasted the brew from the wooden spoon. "Not a prudent course, my dear." After she grabbed another jar, she sprinkled powder into the liquid, then turned back to Selaina with a serious look. "Begin by departing Ravendrith and take the winding road of Elmwyn Trail. It will lead you to the town of Silvaren."

"What will I find there?" Selaina asked, with curiosity and apprehension.

"A quaint and snug haven," Elowen remarked, adding some small branches of wood to the crackling fire. "Radiant, unlike this dim abode. It's teeming with lively souls, a place that should suit you well."

"How many people reside there?" Selaina's voice was cautious. She wanted to avoid as many people as possible in this wicked world.

Elowen retrieved something from a diminutive wooden bowl, which looked like dark grains of sand, and gently sprinkled it into the bubbling kettle. "A typical hamlet, I suppose, boasting around a hundred or so souls."

"A hundred?" The number made Selaina's head reel.

How would she remain unnoticed in such a crowded place? Yet, the more she thought about it, the more she realized it could be beneficial.

Among so many, there surely had to be someone who had seen her mother. She watched Elowen stir the kettle briefly before the woman came over to join her at the table.

"You prefer smaller company," Elowen observed with a knowing smile. "I can relate to that. I spend most of my days here, undisturbed, which is perfect for my work. Though, I do enjoy traveling from time to time."

"What kind of work do you do here?" Selaina asked, glancing around at the natural embellishments within the tree hollow.

"I cultivate rare plants and experiment with their properties," Elowen explained, her eyes lighting up with passion. "Each one has unique essences that are quite powerful when properly harnessed."

Selaina was intrigued but confused. "Powerful for what?"

"For healing, for enchantments, sometimes just for the sheer beauty they can bestow," Elowen said, gesturing toward a small collection of luminescent flowers that emitted a soft glow, illuminating part of the room.

Selaina glanced around the dim room, her eyes narrowing thoughtfully. "You should put some windows here," she suggested, pointing toward the dark, enclosed walls. "Let some light in. I'm sure they would grow much better with some sunlight."

Elowen chuckled softly, shaking her head. "No, no, I much prefer the flame of candles to sunlight," she said, moving to adjust a candle on a nearby table, its flickering flame casting dancing shadows on the walls. "These plants don't need sunlight. They grow in the darkness of the swamp."

The liquid began to boil over the fire, a comforting, familiar sound that reminded Selaina of home. Her mother often brewed tea in the early evenings, a ritual Selaina had found mundane yet now realized she missed dearly. Elowen poured the steaming liquid into a small clay cup and set it down before Selaina.

The aroma was intoxicating. Selaina had never encountered a scent quite like it, rich and complex, beckoning with layers of unknown essences.

"One cup before you go," Elowen offered with a gentle insistence.

"Thank you," Selaina replied, lifting the cup to her lips.

The tea tasted peculiar, its flavor not as exquisite as its aroma suggested. Breathing in slowly, she savored another whiff. The scent was so delightful that she preferred inhaling it rather than drinking. After another tentative sip, she set the cup down on the table, her senses awash in relaxation.

Unable to resist, she hovered her nose over the rising steam. Closing her eyes, she drew in a deep breath, wishing she could capture this fragrance forever in her memory. The effect was so soothing that Selaina's awareness of her surroundings began to fade. She felt as though she were drifting upward into the sky, like a leaf falling to the ground in reverse.

"As I watched the flames last night, a vision came to me in the smoke," Elowen whispered, her voice barely audible over the crackling of the small fire. "A Lith, cloaked in shadows, stood at the edge of the forest, bathed in a light that shimmered like the essence of the Wishing Stone. I saw this figure approach my door, a seeker of truths long buried."

Selaina's mind soared, her thoughts as light and free as clouds drifting across a serene sky. Wrapped in this peaceful reverie, she didn't perceive the moment her balance wavered.

"And now you sit here, a Lith in my home, drawn here perhaps by fate. Could it be that you are the seeker my vision foretold, searching for the Wishing Stone?"

"What's a Wishing Stone?" Selaina asked, her voice thin as mist, fluttering with genuine curiosity and a hint of confusion.

Slowly, almost gracefully, she slipped from the tree stump seat. As she collapsed onto the soft, earthen floor, a deep, undisturbed sleep enveloped her. The world around her faded completely, her last fleeting thought carried by a whisper of wind, soaring her across boundless skies, far from the dark forebodings of the forest.

CHAPTER 11

As the new dawn shattered the dark veil of night, the sun burst forth, casting its vibrant light over the clearest sky Rykan had seen in weeks. Strands of sunshimmer wove through the air like prismatic ribbons reaching for the horizon. They had crossed from the realm of Nordravin back into the Kingdom of Elenior, home of Tathara and Rowanar.

Following a modest breakfast of small game Garrick had skillfully caught, Rykan sprang into action, helping to dismantle their temporary camp. They folded the tent with ease, tucking it away into one of Garrick's well-worn bags. Rykan slung one of the packed bags over his shoulder, feeling the familiar weight settle against him.

The path ahead snaked through a dramatic canyon, each twist revealing layers of brown, yellow, and red rock that rose starkly against the morning light, each layer telling a story of ancient geological battles. By midday, they navigated past the harsh embrace of the jagged rocks and precarious ledges, descending into a lush gorge dressed in moss and lichen. The ravine eventually yawned wide, unveiling a grand vista—a wild expanse laid bare before them.

After they stepped out from the confines of the rocky pass, verdant fields greeted them, undulating in shades of green under the wide sky. Forests awaited them on the horizon, promising mysteries and adventures, yet no sign of civilization was in sight. With the foothills receding behind them, the path they followed dissolved, leaving them to forge their own way toward whatever lay ahead, unguided and untamed.

As they traversed the open field, Rykan and Garrick encountered little more than scattered bushes and shrubs. A pack of wild dogs eyed them from a distance, maintaining a wary but unthreatening stance. Ahead, Rykan focused on a distinctive landmark—a row of begula trees that reminded him of the forests outside Tathara. Their stark white trunks contrasted sharply against the darker wood and vibrant green leaves of the surrounding acera trees, drawing them onward with their unusual beauty.

As the afternoon progressed, Rykan and Garrick followed a winding path that gradually merged with one of the main roads, a well-trodden route that delved deeper into a densely wooded area. Ancient trees made up the thick forest canopy above them, their branches interlocking to form a verdant veil that filtered shafts of sunlight into shimmering patches on the forest floor. The scent of pine and earth filled the cool fresh air, a stark contrast to the dusty trails they had traversed in previous days.

They walked in silence, the only sounds the crunch of leaves underfoot and the distant calls of forest birds. After several miles, the road began to ascend gently. With each step, Rykan felt a growing unease, a sense of anticipation accompanied with dread. He noticed the faint smell of smoke carried on the breeze, a sharp, acrid sign that something was amiss.

As they approached the next rise, signs of trouble grew more evident. Plumes of smoke rose into the sky, thick and black against the green backdrop. The once-faint scent of burning now overwhelmed the forest's earthy fragrances, stinging Rykan's nostrils and tightening his chest.

When they finally reached the gates of Rowanar, the scene before them was heart-wrenching. Most of the city lay in ruins, reduced to smoldering rubble and charred timbers. Rykan stopped dead in his tracks, his eyes scanning the devastation that had once been a bustling, vibrant city. The walls that had stood proud and welcoming now were but broken fragments, and the smell of ash and loss thickened the air.

Overwhelmed by shock and spurred by a desperate hope that his uncle's house might have survived, Rykan dashed forward.

"Rykan, wait!" Garrick called after him.

He ran through the gaping maw of what once were the gates, his feet carrying him instinctively toward the heart of the city, the market square that had once been filled with laughter and lively chatter. Now, silence and desolation awaited him.

Past scattered swords and shields resting near fallen corpses, Rykan darted down one of the side streets into the craftsmen's quarter where his uncle lived. The devastation before him was overwhelming. Once bustling with the sounds of hammers on anvils, saws against wood, and the general hum of creative energy, now the quarter lay in silent ruin. Workshops that had stood for generations were reduced to charred frames, their intricately carved signs hanging askew or lying amid ashes.

The streets, normally cluttered with stalls showcasing finely wrought goods and raw materials, were strewn with the remnants of their wares—splintered furniture, twisted metalwork, fragments of pottery, and half-finished projects abandoned in haste.

Everywhere he looked, Rykan saw the signs of sudden flight—tools dropped as if their owners might return any moment to pick them up, stools overturned, a child's doll lying beside a scorched loom. It was not just homes and livelihoods that had been destroyed. The quarter was a cradle of heritage and skill passed down through generations, now irrevocably disrupted.

The small square that once served as a gathering place for the artisans to sell their crafts and share news had been hit especially hard. The fountain at its center, once a proud symbol of the quarter's prosperity and craftsman-ship, was now a pile of rubble, its cheerful gurgle replaced by the occasional drip of water from a broken pipe.

Rykan stared ahead, his mind rebelling against what his eyes witnessed. The sound of quick footsteps approaching from behind barely registered until Garrick caught up to him.

"We should go. The Iron Flood could still be nearby," Garrick warned with tense urgency.

"Is this what you call saving the world!" Rykan exploded in anger, his voice echoing among the ruins.

Garrick remained silent, allowing Rykan a moment to wrestle with his emotions. When Rykan's breathing slowed, Garrick spoke gently, "Rykan, there's a chance some escaped before the worst hit. We might still find survivors in nearby towns that haven't been touched by the Iron Flood."

"Someone has to stop this," Rykan said, his fists tightening. "We need to gather as many as we can—towns, cities, kingdoms—and band together against them. Vatreus must answer for my father! For everything he has done! The Iron Flood, they must all be hunted down and punished for their crimes!"

Garrick placed his hand firmly on Rykan's back. "First, let's get you away from here. It may not be safe."

Leaving the smoldering remains of Rowanar behind, Garrick followed traces on the ground indicating that many had fled eastward. Soon, a vast lake unfolded before them, bordered by rolling hills and verdant meadows. As the acrid smell of smoke gave way to the sweet fragrances of wildflowers, Rykan felt a slight lift in his spirits. He gazed out at the serene landscape, pondering deeply. The world was such a beautiful place. Why must people mar it with conflicts over trivialities? If they didn't stop the Iron Flood's reckless path of destruction, there would be no lands to explore, no loved ones to cherish, and nothing worth living for.

Before they reached the new forest ahead, Garrick abruptly stopped and turned south. A figure approached, staggering under the weight of their journey. Sunlight glinted off their silver armor, catching Rykan's eye just as the stranger spotted them and began running in their direction.

Though Rykan sensed no danger, Garrick cautiously parted his coat, his hand drifting to the sheath at his side. The approaching stranger was clad in a soldier's armor, yet the armor was battle-worn—the plating on their left arm was missing, exposing a deep, red wound.

As the stranger neared, she removed her helmet, releasing a cascade of long golden hair onto her shoulders. Despite the scratches and cuts marring her features, there was a striking beauty about her, underscored by the determined set of her jaw. Her ivory skin stood in sharp contrast to the grime and blood. Her armor was more ornate than that of a typical soldier, adorned with intricate decorations that caught the light—each shoulder plate featured a fierce owl, a symbol that might denote her allegiance or heritage. In her left hand, she carried a shield, boldly emblazoned with the same owl motif.

"We are overrun!" she called out, her voice urgent even before she came within normal speaking distance. Panting, she continued, "Go! Round up any allies you can find. We must fight them back!"

Garrick approached her cautiously. "What allies?" he asked skeptically. "We are just travelers."

"Where are you heading?" the woman asked urgently. "If it's not far, we can rally reinforcements there and reclaim Guvallus."

"I'm looking for any place with a nice warm bed," Garrick retorted.

"If we do not defeat them," the woman countered, her expression hardened, "the only place you'll find to rest your head will be a tomb."

"Our chances of finding reinforcements grow thinner by the moment. We came from Rowanar, and there's nothing left there but ashes and soot. We would do well to gather what supplies we can and leave these lands," Garrick advised, his voice stern. "Prepare to live among the wilds. They are all that will be left free."

"I won't leave my people behind," the woman declared.

"Nor will I until Tathara is free," Rykan said.

"It appears you already have," Garrick said coldly. "Consider yourselves fortunate to have escaped. Go, live out your days in the free wilds."

"I've only left to gather allies," the woman replied, her voice quivering. "My people will suffer and perish in labor camps, enslaved by the Iron Flood, if I fail to liberate them."

"Few get the chance you've been given," Garrick countered sharply. "I suggest you seize it."

"She's right, we're not giving up," Rykan interjected, his jaw clenching as he spoke. "We can't just watch them destroy everything. My mother is still in Tathara. I can't abandon her. Someone has to stop Vatreus."

"Kid, haven't you seen enough?" Garrick shot back, frustration coloring his tone. "Both of you are underestimating them. Their ranks swell daily, and their elite warriors wield powers beyond our understanding. There's no defeating them."

"Then we'll fight until the end!" the woman declared fiercely. "In the long dream, find your truth. In the Everdream, find your peace. I'd rather die in battle than live under their tyranny."

"There was a time when I would have agreed with you," Garrick admitted, his voice softening with a hint of sorrow. "But eventually, you'll both come to see things as I have. I only hope you realize the truth before it's too late."

"There were signs that some fled Rowanar," Rykan chimed in as he tapped his finger against the side of his leg. "We are searching for them now."

"Why didn't you say so? Let's find them," said the woman, her face lifting.

"I didn't want to give you false hope," Garrick said. "I don't know how many made it out."

"May this be the tumbling stone that starts the avalanche," the woman said.

"That wound needs attention first," Garrick pointed out, nodding toward her arm.

"It's merely a scratch," the woman dismissed. "That can wait."

Garrick shook his head. "If we don't dress it now, it could get infected," he warned, and a wry smile played at his lips. "You wouldn't want to forever be known as the warrior who fell to 'a mere scratch,' would you?"

The woman sighed in resignation. "Fine, but make it quick."

Garrick dropped one of his bags and rummaged through it until he pulled out a small cloth sack. He gestured to Rykan. "Take some water," he instructed, pointing to a flask. "Clean the dirt around the wound."

Rykan poured water from the flask onto a piece of clean cloth. As the woman extended her arm, revealing the deep, jagged cut, Rykan hesitated upon seeing the severity of the injury. The flesh was split, moving grotesquely, as if each side had a life of its own. Trying not to stare directly at the gash, he gently dabbed around the edges with the damp cloth.

"My name is Elysia," the woman said, her voice steady despite the pain.

"I'm Rykan," he responded, his focus momentarily shifting back to her face. "And that's Garrick."

Rykan resumed cleaning, and Elysia winced when the cloth brushed too roughly on the raw wound. "Sorry," Rykan murmured, redoubling his efforts to be gentle.

Garrick then reached into the sack and withdrew a handful of a jelly-like substance. Carefully, he began to apply it over her wound. "We're going to have to close this up," he said apologetically but firmly.

"Maybe we should wait until we find a healer," Elysia suggested, pulling her arm back slightly.

"I don't think we should wait," Garrick insisted. "We need to close it now."

Elysia groaned, her eyes darting down to her arm. "You'd better be good at this!"

Garrick retrieved a linen cloth and a needle from his bag. "I've done this more times than most healers," he remarked confidently.

He worked the linen between his fingers, unraveling it until he had a single strand, which he then threaded through the needle. Carefully, he held Elysia's arm steady as he pierced her skin with the needle. She remained stoically silent, though her eyes occasionally shot him a stern look as he sutured the wound.

Once Garrick finished, Elysia marched off toward the rows of trees ahead, eager to get moving. The shade from the trees softened the harsh sunlight, making their journey through the underbrush more bearable. As they moved, two kulir birds flitted about under the tall trees, their gray-and-black striped feathers and distinctive white underbellies catching Rykan's eye — he had only seen such birds in sketches. Startled by Elysia's approach through the tall weeds, the birds quickly took flight, disappearing into the canopy.

A peculiar scent permeated the air, a potent mixture of earthy musk and wild growth that signaled the untamed heart of the forest. The sounds here were wild too, a cacophony of birdsong and insects clashing as if vying for dominance in an auditory battle. Everything about this place danced to its own rhythm, unrestrained by the orderly confines Rykan was accustomed to in the city.

The forest unfolded before him in a riotous display of nature's creativity. Crooked branches reached out like gnarled fingers, their tangled embrace forming a dense canopy overhead. It was a stark contrast to the neat lines and polished facades of Tathara. Here, life pulsed with raw vitality, each creature following its own unpredictable path. Insects hummed and darted in erratic patterns, while unseen animals rustled through the underbrush. Birds swooped and soared with reckless abandon, their flights embodying the boundless freedom of the wild.

The chaos of the forest both disoriented and mesmerized Rykan, who was accustomed to the structured routines of urban living. Amid the unpredictability, he found a strange beauty, an untamed energy that resonated within him, speaking to something primal that thrived on spontaneity and surprise.

After a while, Garrick glanced over at Elysia, his voice soft as he broke the quiet. "If you feel like talking about what happened in Guvallus … We may have a way to go yet."

Elysia kept her eyes on the path ahead, her sword slicing through the underbrush. After a moment, she responded, somewhat reluctantly, "Talk about the attack? There isn't much to say."

"How did you manage to escape?" Garrick asked gently. He seemed to be testing her willingness to open up.

"It wasn't anything heroic," Elysia admitted, her voice resigned "Mostly, it was just luck."

"Luck? You're more than a mere soldier," said Garrick. "You're one of the Noble Guard."

"If you're referring to my armor, it isn't mine," Elysia said. "I put it on when the Iron Flood attacked. We needed all the fighters we could get."

"How did you gain access to such armor?" Garrick asked.

Elysia paused, pressing her lips together before speaking. "My father is Lord Firion Guvallus."

"The Baron?" asked Garrick. "Rykan, brush those trousers off and straighten up, you're in the presence of nobility."

Rykan couldn't be sure if Garrick was serious or simply toying with him. Still, he stopped walking and offered a bow.

"My lady," he said.

"Please don't start that," Elysia said, brushing a loose strand of hair from her face in frustration. "I should have known better than to tell you that. I am a soldier. A defender of Guvallus, just like any other."

"Where is the Baron now?" Garrick asked, leaning toward her with concern.

"He and my mother were taken prisoner," Elysia replied, her voice faltering. She clenched her fists tightly at her sides. "I tried to defend them. I am trained to fight, but there …" She closed her eyes for a moment, pain darkening her features. "There were too many."

"You are brave, worthy of the armor you wear," Garrick reassured her, placing a gentle hand on her shoulder. "There was nothing more you could have done against the likes of the Iron Flood."

"I should have been better," Elysia murmured, shaking her head. "As a descendant of Ardalion Guvallus, I have fighting in my blood."

"Sorry, I'm not familiar with the history," Garrick admitted, his expression apologetic.

"Who was he?" asked Rykan, stepping closer, eager to hear the story.

"Ardalion Guvallus was one of the Zhal Evurah," Elysia began, her voice gaining strength as she spoke of her ancestor. "Thousands of years ago, he defeated the giants and returned peace to Galanor. He became king of these lands."

"The giants," Rykan mused, nodding slowly. "I've heard about them."

"But destinies, of course, are not inherited," said Elysia. She stooped to pick up a fallen branch, then snapped it in her hands to punctuate her words. "The rest of his bloodline, while strong, did not have the great destiny that he did. He was one of the last few Zhal Evurah. Now that Ethyllion has been destroyed, there can be no others."

"There are others who believe Zhal Evurah can be sent without the crystal of destiny," said Garrick.

"Not one has seen one in a thousand years," Elysia said. "Not since the crystal was shattered."

"How was the crystal destroyed?" Rykan inquired, looking at Elysia for the answer.

"Throughout history, the conflicts between the immortal realms Archeinor and Pandemora have raged. It is believed that chaos energy corrupted Ethyllion and it had to be destroyed. We could certainly use Zhal Evurah now," she said, "in these times."

"It's on us then," declared Rykan as he clenched his fist, "to defeat the Iron Flood."

"You don't know them the way I do," said Garrick, shaking his head. "Vatreus has power beyond anything this world has seen. He imbued his Dreadstorm Knights with unnatural strength."

"How do you know so much about them?" asked Elysia, narrowing her eyes as she scrutinized Garrick.

The birds clinging to the branches of a distant tree suddenly took flight, scattering in the air before regrouping as they soared, seeking another perch. Garrick's hand clamped down on Elysia's shoulder, halting her progress. She tried to shake his grip, but he pressed down on her, forcing her to the ground where he knelt. Rykan ducked with them behind a group of bushes as the low sound of thunder approached.

Through the tangle of leaves, Rykan watched men on ridgebacks rumble through a clear part of the forest ahead. Soldiers of Iron Flood, clad in black-plated armor, marched behind them, carving a wide path through the forest. His heart skipped a beat when a large garnarok stomped into view. Its long, powerful legs heaved as it strode through the brush, rigid black fur bristling, and snaggle-toothed fangs protruding from its mouth. It breathed vaporous steam in the cool air.

Atop the creature sat a man encased in decorative cloth and steel, his long black hair bouncing with the movements of the great beast. The man's eyes, burning with blue flame, held a gaze that felt like it could cut through the forest itself. A metal piece that descended from an ornamental headdress hid the left side of his face. Rykan felt a deep dread in his bones.

CHAPTER 12

SELAINA FELT COLDNESS against her cheek as her senses slowly returned and conscious thought flickered back to life. Her shoulder throbbed with a deep soreness. Her mind swirled, trying to piece together her whereabouts until, at last, it all came back into focus. With a jolt, she opened her eyes and found herself lying on the earthen floor of Elowen's house in the hollow of the old tree.

With no sign of Elowen around, Selaina sat up, feeling a dull ache in her head. How long had she slept? She realized her hands were bound with rope tied to a hook in the wooden tree wall. Selaina scanned her surroundings for anything she could use to escape.

Something bubbled in the kettle over the fire, a gray concoction that smelled as foul as it looked. The table held a candle, its flame extinguished. On the shelf beside the hearth, flowers glowed with a dim light. Her bow and quiver full of arrows rested on a chair leaning against the opposite wall, but the rope didn't allow her enough slack to reach them.

Selaina's heart pounded in her chest as her breaths grew rapid and shallow. She leaned against the table, and her fingers started to tingle. Her vision blurred momentarily, overtaken by a sudden, vivid vision. She saw Elowen placing one of the flowers in a ceramic pot on the table and then clumsily tipping it over. The pot shattered on the floor, soil sprinkling the floor as the ceramic pieces scattered. Some pieces slid under the table, while one lodged in the crevasse between the hearth and the wooden shelf.

Selaina glanced under the table but found only crumbs. She moved to the shelf and reached into the crevasse, her fingers hitting the sharp edges of a ceramic shard. After carefully prying it out, she tried to cut the ropes binding her hands, but they were too tightly wound. Eyeing the grooves between the planks of the table, she jammed the shard into one of them, pressing until it stuck. Rubbing the rope against the sharp edge, she weakened it until it separated.

Once she'd freed her hands, Selaina snatched up her bow and quiver, readying an arrow as she made her way outside. The swampy forest was dark and misty, but sunlight glimmered above the treetops. With her bow at the ready, she hurried through the thicket, ignoring the Nadrok that leaned around the trees. Occasional sounds of crackling wood diverted her attention, but everything remained still.

Selaina's response to the feeling of being watched began to change from fear to irritation as she felt the eyes of the Nadrok surrounding her. She made her way through in a haphazard manner, redirecting her path to avoid murky pools and sharp thorns. After she had been walking for a while, the forest opened up, allowing more sunlight to spread through the trees.

Ahead, a pathway carved through the stalks of grass and wound around a corner into the more welcoming forest beyond. Standing on the path, she began to feel safe. The ache in her head subsided as she stepped onto the road, but the soreness in her shoulder lingered. Pulling her cloak and tunic aside, she inspected the source of the discomfort but found nothing out of sorts. She must have slept in some awkward position while she was tied up. The thought of what Elowen might have planned made her uneasy, but she pushed it aside, focusing on the reassuring warmth of the sun filtering through the trees ahead.

With her feet firmly on the hard clay, she felt whole again, ready to travel onward and find her mother. After winding through the woodlands and over the meadowy hills, Selaina glanced back to where she had come from. With no sign of the dark, misty forests, she was glad to have the swamps of Ravendrith behind her. If this was any indication of what the wicked world was like, Selaina now understood why her mother had fled these lands so many years ago. Though it explained why her mother never wanted to talk about her earlier life, it made Selaina wonder more than ever what exactly had happened.

Placing the arrow back into her quiver and the bow over her shoulder, Selaina quickened her pace. Dark clouds that began on the horizon, rolled past as she continued on. A blanket of misty droplets tickled her skin, and she pushed forward away from the trail and into the shelter of dense undergrowth. The rhythmic patter of raindrops echoed softly around her, punctuated by the occasional distant rumble of thunder. Selaina pulled her cloak tighter, seeking refuge from the chill that seeped into her bones.

The forest seemed to come alive with the rain, each leaf and blade of grass glistening with moisture, the earth releasing a heady scent of dampness and life. Streams formed along the forest floor, snaking their way between moss-covered rocks and fallen branches, their gentle babbling providing a soothing counterpoint to the distant storm's fury.

Keeping the trail in sight, she followed its curves and contours from afar. The forest canopy thinned out ahead, causing her to move deeper into the forest to avoid the rain. One tree with a massive trunk stood out among the rest. Though not as thick as the one Elowen used as a home, it wasn't smaller by much. Its branches spread out wide, overtaking this region of the woods.

As Selaina ventured closer to the colossal tree, a sudden movement caught her eye, causing her to freeze in her tracks. Instinctively, she sought cover, pressing herself against the tangled undergrowth, praying the man seated beneath the tree remained oblivious to her presence.

"Is someone out there?" The voice of the man emanated from the tree ahead. Selaina fought to keep every part of herself still and silent. After a long pause, the voice sounded again. "Don't be frightened. Come and dry off, there is no sense staying in the rain."

Though his words carried a sense of warmth, Selaina remained wary, her instincts on high alert. She refused to be lured into complacency again, not after what she had experienced before. Braving the rain seemed preferable to risking another encounter like Elowen.

"If my presence disturbs you, I will move on," the man offered, rising to gather his belongings.

Dusting the leaves from his trousers, the man began walking away. Selaina's heart sank with the sudden weight of guilt.

"Wait!" she shouted, surprised at the volume of her own voice. Before she spoke again, she measured her sound to a more normal tone. "You don't have to leave."

The man stopped and turned around, watching as Selaina dodged bushes, shrubs, and trees on her way. Selaina crept underneath the wide canopy of the great tree, where hardly a droplet made it through to splash on her skin. She stood still, staring at the man. Their eyes met, and she felt a sudden connection. Images flashed before her.

In the first, she saw a pretty woman with dark hair and eyes as bright as the sun smiling with dark red lips. In the second, the same woman lay in bed, her lips now devoid of color, the light in her eyes diminished. In the third image, she saw a grave with the initials B.W. carved on a stone that rested on a mound of freshly dug earth. With these images, Selaina felt a deep sorrow. The same grief she felt for Jeth, only this was stronger. The woman in this vision had been everything to the man in front of her. She could tell he felt alone in this world now without her. He, like Selaina, was a victim of the wicked world.

Selaina was no longer afraid. She felt a kinship with the man. He was going through struggles similar to her own. It made her feel less alone, and she hoped she could bring that to him as well. Setting her bag, quiver, and bow on the dry grass at the base of the tree, Selaina lowered herself to the ground, leaning her back against the trunk.

The man returned to the trunk of the tree and sat down nearby while maintaining a respectful distance. He appeared older than Selaina but not by much. A crossbow with short arrows lay beside him. They sat in silence for a few moments, listening to the rhythm of rain tapping against the leaves above.

"My name is Darian," He finally broke the silence as he clasped and then unclasped his hands.

"Mine is Selaina," she replied.

"It isn't safe to travel alone," Darian observed with a bit of concern. "Especially for someone as young as you."

"I can take care of myself," Selaina asserted, compressing her voice to sound firm.

Darian rummaged through his bag, pulling out something that crunched loudly as he bit into it. "Want a piece of bread?" he offered, extending a hand toward her.

Selaina hadn't realized how hungry she was until he made the offer. There had been little time to hunt or fish since leaving the cabin. Before she could respond, Darian stood and reached out, offering the bread. She accepted it with a tentative smile. Though stale and hard, the bread tasted surprisingly good, though it could have been because of the emptiness of her stomach.

"I'm heading to Aldenglade," Darian mentioned casually. "I would welcome the company if you'd like to travel together."

Selaina finished chewing the bread before responding. "No thank you, I am traveling to Silvaren."

"I can go to Silvaren with you," Darian proposed. "It's not far out of the way to Aldenglade."

"What's in Aldenglade?" Selaina inquired with growing curiosity.

"Nothing much," Darian sighed. "Work. A new life, I guess. Away from the Iron Flood."

"The Iron Flood?" Selaina echoed, puzzled.

"You haven't heard?" Darian asked, surprised. "They're a rising power that's becoming a great concern for Galanor. Imperion Vatreus is consolidating control over everything in the Kingdom of Elenior. It won't be long before they march on Sybara."

"Why would they want to control everything?" Selaina asked. "Are they trying to save this wicked world?"

"No, they aren't saving anything. They only destroy. They embody everything wicked in this world," Darian said, looking distantly toward the treetops. "Some men get a taste of power and can't get enough. Most know when to stop, or they meet a swift end before gaining too much control. But then there's some like Imperion Vatreus—a master tactician with control over natural forces. He'll control the entire kingdom soon, and who knows how much more he'll try to take."

"Sounds like a terrible situation," Selaina remarked soberly.

"It is," Darian affirmed. "But Aldenglade is far enough from Elenior and Sybara, from the war. I thought it would be the safest place to start over, a new life. I only wish that ..." He paused, his expression clouded with emotion, and after a moment, he closed his eyes without continuing.

The wind howled through the trees, making Darian shudder. He closed his eyes, tensing his arms toward his chest. Once it quieted for a moment, he glanced at Selaina with an embarrassed smile.

"I don't like the sounds the wind makes," he said, rubbing his arms as if to ward off the chill. "I suppose it comes from old tales."

"What kinds of tales?" Selaina asked, sliding closer to make sure she could hear.

"My mother used to tell us about Windwraiths that ride on the air and steal the breath out of those who didn't go inside the house," Darian replied, his eyes cautiously scanning the treetops. "Whenever we heard the screeching howls the wind sometimes makes, we thought Windwraiths were near."

"Are we safe here?" Selaina asked, trying to make herself heard over the wind.

Darian let out an uneasy laugh. "It's probably just a made-up story, mothers trying to keep their children from going far from the house on cloudy days."

"Why would she lie to you?" Selaina asked, frowning as she peered out toward the dark reaches of the forest.

"I wouldn't call it a lie," Darian said, shaking his head. "When fearing their mothers wasn't enough, they would frighten the children in other ways to get them to obey. It was a well-known tale in my village. I still remember the first part."

He cleared his throat as he began to recite:
"When stormy winds begin to wail,
And shadows creep o'er hill and dale,
Beware the wraiths that ride the air,
With eyes aglow and ghostly glare."

Selaina shivered, her imagination conjuring eerie images of the Windwraiths. "But it must be true, or she wouldn't have told you that," she insisted, glancing around nervously.

"I've never seen anything like a Windwraith before," Darian replied, offering a reassuring smile, "or known anyone who has."

Listening intently to the wind and rain for a moment, Selaina realized how unnerving it could be. To take her mind away from thoughts of these Windwraiths, she tried to think of something else to talk about. She bit her lip, her brow wrinkled in thought, before finally breaking the silence.

"Tell me about the woman," Selaina began tentatively. "Did you have to leave without her?"

Darian halted his movements, his gaze sharpening on Selaina. "How do you know about her?"

"Visions," Selaina confessed. "When we connected, I saw a woman with dark hair lying on a white bed by a large window as you knelt beside her."

Darian brushed away tears, his voice thick with emotion. "You have a gift. Sight beyond seeing."

For the first time, Selaina pondered the uniqueness of her visions. Why did she possess an ability others did not?

Darian took a deep breath, and his voice held a wistful tone as he recounted, "My Bellaria. We had such dreams ... She fell in love with a particular spot in Rivenath, by the hills where the river cuts through the meadow. Wildflowers bloomed there each spring—it was our escape. She wanted us to build a home there. I was to be a master tailor, she a painter, surrounded by nature and the laughter of the children we planned to have. It was a beautiful dream, perfect in every way she imagined."

Selaina listened, the imagery starkly different from the dark tones of the world she had experienced outside her forest. Darian seemed lost in the past, his eyes distant. Returning to the world, he began rummaging through his bag, pulling out a small painted portrait.

He handed it to Selaina. "This is Bellaria."

"She's lovely," said Selaina, recognizing the woman from her vision.

"She could light up the world," said Darian as he took the painting and placed it back into his bag.

"What happened to her?" Selaina hesitantly asked.

Darian's eyes reflected deep pain when he glanced at Selaina. "She became ill from contamination, according to the healers. We had spent a few days in Rivenath not long before. It might have been the water from the crescent lake off the river." He paused, swallowing hard. "The healers tried, but they couldn't reverse it. The night before she passed, she knew ... she knew she was going to die. She made me promise to continue our dream, to build the house in Rivenath. But now, with the Iron Flood spreading, that's impossible."

His face twisted with grief. "Sometimes I wonder why I ever left. Why I didn't stay and face the Iron Flood, even if it meant the end. Without her, the dream feels … empty."

"No, there is always hope," Selaina said. "It is the order of the forest, of everything. The flowers wither only to bring new life. You must keep going to keep her dream alive."

Darian absorbed her words, his eyes reflecting a blend of sorrow and contemplation. Slowly, a faint smile broke through the clouds of his grief.

"That's exactly what she would say," he murmured, a note of wonder in his voice. "You're right," he acknowledged, his tone steadier, infused with an uncertain hope. "Sometimes, in the shadow of loss, I lose sight of that. But you're right, Selaina. Life is a cycle—there's room for new dreams, even now."

"It's not always easy to find hope," Selaina added softly, understanding the weight of his struggle, "but sometimes holding on to it is the hardest part."

As they spoke, the drip of water from the trees slowed and the light filtering through the branches brightened.

"I think the storm has passed," Darian noted, rising to his feet and gathering his belongings. "I'd better keep moving, find a place to camp before nightfall." He paused, looking at Selaina. "As I said before, I don't mind taking a route through Silvaren if you wish to join me."

Selaina collected her bow, quiver, and bag. "I'd be glad to."

CHAPTER 13

RYKAN'S EYES NARROWED, his focus sharpening on the darkening edge of the forest where the figure emerged, casting a formidable silhouette against the fading light. The man, flanked by a retinue of mounted soldiers, held a commanding presence, his long black mane flowing behind him like a battle standard in the wind. Each thunderous step the garnarok took sent a shiver racing down Rykan's spine, the ground trembling beneath its weight, as the man sat atop it like a looming storm.

"Is that …?" Rykan murmured, tension tightening in his gut, but he already knew the answer.

"Vatreus …" Garrick replied, his voice urgent yet low, laced with a barely contained alarm. "We need to go, now."

"Imperion Vatreus?" Elysia's hand instinctively went to the hilt of her blade, her stance coiling like a spring. "This is our opportunity."

Garrick seized her arm with a firm grip. "You can't be serious. We're outmatched. Facing Vatreus directly would be certain death."

"We have to try," Elysia insisted, her conviction unwavering. "We may never have this chance again. Galanor's fate hangs in the balance."

Rykan clenched his jaw, the memory of his father falling to Vatreus's sword flooding back. "Garrick's right. I've seen Vatreus in battle, surrounded by seven men, and he laid them low without breaking a sweat."

"They were not skilled enough, then," Elysia snapped with confidence in her tone. "I fear no man. All I need is one clean strike."

Rykan's voice softened, strained with deep-seated pain. "One of those men was my father," he confessed as a whisper laden with loss. "He was among the finest swordsmen I've known."

Elysia's expression softened immediately, her eyes widening with surprise and sorrow. "Sorry, I—" she began, but Garrick's somber voice cut her off.

"Do not throw your life away on a vain hope. Vatreus thrives on others believing they have the upper hand. There will be other opportunities, better ones," Garrick said, his hand firm on Elysia's shoulder, steering her back into the dark embrace of the forest.

An ominous, heavy feeling hung in the air, thick as fog, pressing down on them like a suffocating shroud. Rykan trailed close behind, each step heavy with dread. His heart thudded wildly against his ribs, a drumbeat of shadows that twisted around them.

Danger wasn't just approaching. It felt as if it were breathing down his neck, lurking in every flicker of movement caught in the corner of his eye. Rykan's breaths came quick and sharp, mirroring the frantic pace of his thoughts—plans, escapes, confrontations all tangled in his mind like a knotted rope.

A voice, sharp and commanding, shattered the stillness. "Halt! By order of Imperion Vatreus, lay down your arms!"

As the order rang out, a group of riders broke away from Vatreus's entourage, bearing down on the three of them with alarming speed. In the face of imminent peril, Elysia assumed a defensive stance, her sword poised for battle. But the Iron Flood soldiers quickly surrounded them, cutting off any hope of escape. Garrick, with a heavy sigh, conceded to the inevitable, relinquishing his weapons with a resigned gesture.

"If we can get past one of them, maybe we can run for it," Rykan hissed under his breath.

Garrick shot him a grave look. "There are battles to fight and there are battles to flee. This, Rykan, is neither."

Rykan's mind raced with the horrors he had witnessed in the mountains. "But they'll take us to the gate," he insisted.

"We'll have a better chance of fighting our way out of that than here," Garrick replied.

Without Garrick's help, Rykan had little choice but to give up his sword as well. One of the riders, a tall figure clad in black armor, reined in his ridgeback before them, eyeing their disarmed state. Finally, Elysia laid down her shield and sword.

"Smart choice," he sneered, his gaze lingering on Elysia's lowered sword. "What purpose do you have roaming out here?"

Garrick met the rider's gaze with a level stare. "We seek only passage, nothing more."

One of the soldiers scoffed. "Imperion Vatreus has banned all travel without explicit permission between the cities of Elenior."

The rider signaled to his men. "Keep them here. Vatreus will want to see them."

As the soldiers closed in, they wasted no time in scooping up the trio's discarded swords. The soldier's tone was brusque when he issued orders to his comrades. With a commanding gesture, he directed Rykan, Elysia, and Garrick forward, guiding them into the heart of the clearing.

"My lord! We have the assassins in custody," the soldier announced, his voice ringing out with a note of triumph as he presented the captured trio to his leader.

Vatreus, mounted atop a colossal beast, bore down upon them with an aura of undeniable power. Rykan clasped his arms around himself in a feeble attempt to quell the involuntary shivers coursing through his body as the Imperion's imposing figure loomed ever closer.

An eerie azure light set his eyes ablaze. Rykan remembered the unsettling glow that had emanated from him when he wreaked havoc outside Tathara and slayed his father.

"Assassins, you say?" Imperion Vatreus's laughter sounded ominously across the clearing, and he dismounted his garnarok with lethal grace.

His towering form loomed over Garrick, casting an oppressive shadow that seemed to darken the very air. With a casual flick of his wrist, he summoned an unseen power that drove Garrick to his knees, his head bowed in involuntary deference.

Rykan, witnessing Garrick's sudden and uncharacteristic submission, felt a cold shiver of fear. He stood frozen, his mind a tumult of shock and indecision—should he kneel or remain standing?

Vatreus approached Elysia, his gaze locked onto hers. "What have we here? A member of the Baron's guard from Guvallus," he observed. With a mere gesture toward her, Elysia too was forced to her knees, her proud stance crumbling under the tyrant's will. "Leave her in her armor, and keep her shield," Vatreus commanded his soldiers. "I want her looking the part. She may prove useful."

Turning his dreadful attention to Rykan, Vatreus extended his hand, and Rykan immediately felt an overwhelming force press down upon him, pinning him to the earth as if the weight of the world bore down upon his shoulders.

Struggling against the crushing pressure, Rykan's eyes locked onto the burning blue ember eyes within the shadow of the metal plate on Vatreus's face. Hatred flared within Rykan, numbing his fear because he saw nothing outside of his father's murderer. Vatreus's fierce glare met his gaze.

"You dare to look at me!" Vatreus thundered, his voice reverberating with terrifying authority.

As Vatreus held Rykan's glare, the tension peaked. Then, with a cold, dismissive wave, he turned and remounted his beast.

"Take them," he ordered crisply, and his soldiers moved in swiftly to seize Rykan, Elysia, and Garrick.

The soldiers bound their hands and feet tightly with coarse rope that chafed against Rykan's skin when they unceremoniously shoved the three of them into a cramped carriage. Already inside, two other captives slouched, similarly trussed. The two men sat with vacant stares, seemingly oblivious to Rykan and the others being thrust beside them. Even though the Iron Flood soldiers had failed to notice his boot knife again, this time Rykan couldn't reach it. The carriage jolted into motion, its interior dark and stifling, filled with the scent of damp wood and fear. For the remainder of the day, they were tossed about as the carriage wound through rugged terrain, every bump and rut sending sharp pains shooting through Rykan's constrained body.

The journey came to an abrupt halt, and the ridgeback pulling them whinnied and stamped, its restless movement audible in the quiet of the cool air. The driver dismounted with a grunt, leaving them still tied in the dimming light of dusk. Outside, the camp buzzed with activity. Voices murmured orders, occasionally rising in sharp commands. The rhythmic thud of axes splitting wood melded with the metallic clang of soldiers tending to their gear, creating a backdrop of warlike industry.

Rykan strained to listen, catching snippets of conversation and the occasional clatter of saddle and reins, the sounds painting a vivid picture of the camp's preparations for the night. The carriage door creaked open, flooding the confined space with the dim glow of lanterns. Rough hands grabbed Rykan, Garrick, Elysia, and the other captives, yanking them out of the carriage and onto the uneven ground below.

Forced to their feet, they stumbled forward, their bound hands making movement awkward and cumbersome. The soldiers, clad in armor that gleamed in the fading light, prodded them forward with the tips of swords, their faces hidden behind helmets, but their intentions clear.

Once in the open, the soldiers herded the captives toward the center of the camp, where they'd begun setting up tents and arranging supplies. Torches flickered on wooden posts, casting elongated shadows that moved eerily across the ground.

Without a word, the captives were put to work. The ropes were removed from their hands and the ones on their legs were loosened enough for them to walk more easily. Rykan found himself hauling bundles of firewood, his muscles straining against the weight, and he staggered under the load. Garrick and Elysia were tasked with unpacking crates of provisions, their hands fumbling with the unfamiliar instructions.

Rykan dropped the wood onto the pile and headed back to where soldiers were chopping trees for more. He noticed one of the guards looming over Garrick and Elysia, mocking them as they organized items from the crates.

"Move faster, or I'll give you a reason to hurry." The guard sneered, shoving Elysia.

She stumbled and landed awkwardly, yelping in pain as she gripped her wounded arm.

"Oh, nursing a little cut, are we?" the guard taunted. "Pick up the pace, or I'll make sure those sutures come out one by one."

"She won't be any use to you then," said Garrick as he continued working.

Rykan slowed to a stop, his mind racing with anger and irrational thoughts.

"If I wanted your opinion, I'd have asked for it," snapped the guard.

He then grabbed Elysia, forcing her down into the dirt and gripping her arm tightly as he clawed at her wound.

Rykan couldn't stand by any longer. Without thinking of the consequences, he ran toward the guard. But before he could intervene, Garrick lunged, striking the guard across the face and knocking him out cold.

Three soldiers rushed over. They caught Garrick and beat him with punches and kicks. Rykan grabbed one from behind, holding the soldier around the neck and pulling him off Garrick. Another soldier latched on to Rykan, tugging him away from the soldier and tossing him to the ground.

"Enough!" bellowed a man clad in black shoulder plates and a distinguished gray tunic. "Stop harassing the prisoners, you fools! We need them working, not incapacitated. If they refuse to work, bring them to me."

"Yes, sir," one of the soldiers replied as he gripped Rykan's arms, pulling him back on his feet.

The others let go of Garrick and Elysia, giving them room to stand on their own.

"And move him out of the way," the man commanded, gesturing to the soldier Garrick had knocked out.

Two soldiers hurried over, their boots crunching on the dirt as they grabbed the unconscious man. They hefted him up with a grunt and carried him off to the other end of the campsite.

Rykan dusted himself off and returned to gather more wood, understanding that compliance was his only option for now. If he had any chance at escaping and gathering a force large enough to retake Tathara, he needed to bide his time. His thoughts raced: he had to free his mother from their occupation, avenge his father's death, and put an end to Vatreus's conquest.

After the camp was constructed, a large fire crackled and the soldiers gathered in a line to receive the evening meal. Rykan, Garrick, Elysia, and the other two men were tied to trees at the perimeter of the camp, left to smell the tantalizing aroma of roasting meat. Rykan's mouth watered at the smell of the savory fare as hunger gnawed at his stomach.

Vatreus made no appearance during the murmured conversation of the soldiers while they ate. With them all preoccupied, Garrick tested the ropes that bound him, struggling to break them, but it was no use.

"So, Lady Elysia, what do we do now?" Garrick asked, his voice barely above a whisper as he glanced around to ensure the soldiers didn't overhear them.

"Don't call me that," Elysia snapped, tugging at her own restraints with a sharp jerk. "How should I know what we should do?"

Garrick shrugged, though the ropes limited the movement. "Nothing was coming to my mind. I thought maybe you would have an idea."

Elysia's eyes narrowed as she muttered, "Not many options. If we'd fought them earlier, we'd either be victorious or awake in the Everdream by now, instead of stuck here."

"I don't have much faith in the Everdream," Garrick whispered back. "We don't know that there is any waking up after this world. Maybe we should ask the escape artist over here. Rykan, any ideas?"

"If I could just reach my knife …" Rykan muttered, his fingers stretching for the blade in his boot.

"I can't reach mine either," Garrick replied, his eyes shifting to where their weapons lay nearby but out of reach. "We need you to come up with something more creative than that."

Rykan let out a breath of frustration. "Yeah, I'll be sure to keep you posted," he replied.

As Garrick quieted down, Rykan focused on the conversations of the soldiers while they ate. A man in a dark blue cloak walked between the soldiers where they sat, occasionally talking with them, laughing, or giving some of them a pat on the shoulder.

"At the first light of dawn, we shall make ready to advance," declared the cloaked figure as he drew near the soldiers surrounding Rykan. "Leave the steeds behind. This shall be a march on foot. We shall proceed in square formation. Dralomar will not present much resistance. A mere display of our might shall suffice."

"What of the Dovar?" inquired one of the soldiers.

"He is to be captured alive," asserted the cloaked figure, offering a reassuring clap on the soldier's back before continuing on his way. "We need everyone to see his surrender."

Rykan shot a quick glance at Garrick and Elysia, their faces taut with concentration, all of them straining to eavesdrop on the murmured conversation. If only these ropes would give, Rykan thought, pulling at his bindings with a burst of futile effort. The ropes bit into his wrists, stubborn and taunting. As the cloaked figure approached, a chill shot through him, and for a moment, he held his breath, eyes locked on what he expected to be a threat. But the figure only carried a basket. He was not the menace Rykan had braced for.

He exhaled, relief and suspicion churning inside while the man began to scatter small pieces of bread on the ground before them. No words exchanged, just the quiet shuffle followed by his departure. Bound to the tree, Rykan could do nothing but kneel and reach for the bread with his mouth. Rykan awkwardly bowed his head to peck at the bread like some caged bird. The bread was dry, barely enough to touch the edges of his hunger, but it was something—a faint flicker of hope in the grim shadow of their captivity.

As night crept upon the camp and the bustle settled into silence, Rykan slumped against the tree. He shuffled around, seeking some semblance of comfort in the hard, unforgiving grass. The sudden buzz of an insect by his ear jerked him alert again, but it was just the mundane reality of the outdoors. Beside him, Garrick had already surrendered to sleep, snoring with a regularity that seemed absurd under the circumstances. How can he sleep at a time like this? Rykan wondered, his thoughts a jumble as he tried to settle into a rest that seemed as elusive as their freedom.

৯৵

Rykan was shaken awake, and he tried to place where he was. The scuffling of many feet in the distance with the clinking of armor brought his memory back. The sun had not yet risen, but the early dawn light was enough to make out the carriage driver and two soldiers standing over him.

The soldiers cut the ropes and led Rykan, Garrick, Elysia, and the two quiet prisoners to the ridgeback-drawn carriage. After the prisoners were secured with shorter leashes, the ridgebacks started up, heading out of the camp area and into the woodlands.

Ahead, the rest of the soldiers marched in a mostly aligned formation, avoiding trees when they had to. The ridgeback pulling the carriage trotted along at a slow pace, maintaining a certain distance from the troops. By noon, they reached a wooden fence that surrounded a mountain with a small community built around it.

Amid the rugged backdrop of towering mountains, the town of Dralomar throbbed with industry. Workers, their faces streaked with dust and sweat, trundled small carts back and forth from the yawning mouth of the mountain, where the dark maw of the mine swallowed men whole and spat out precious ore. The clang of metal on stone reverberated through the air, merging with the distant rumble of machinery within the mine's depths.

Iron Flood soldiers marched with relentless purpose toward the town's perimeter fence. Their boots kicked up clouds of dust as they advanced, unswerving and ominous. The miners, undeterred by the growing threat, continued their laborious trek to a large stone building that squatted like a guardian at the mountain's base. This structure served as both a refinery and storage, its ancient stone walls echoing with the ceaseless din of processing ore.

Without pausing, the soldiers breached a gap in the rickety wooden fence, flooding into Dralomar. The townspeople clustered around the mountain's base as if clinging for protection against the encroaching wilderness. As the carriage came to a jarring stop, Rykan watched a hastily assembled group of town defenders gather in the central square, a hodgepodge of stone cottages and wooden shacks scattered about them. Their faces were set, grim with the mettle of those with everything to lose.

The town's bells pealed a harsh, urgent call to arms, cutting through the noise of industry and impending battle. Children hurried indoors as their elders grabbed whatever weapons were at hand. The defenders, seasoned miners and young townsfolk alike, formed a ragged line across the main thoroughfare.

Imperion Vatreus strode confidently to the front lines, his dark hair billowing in the crisp morning breeze. He stood defiantly before the city's defenders, his posture a silent challenge. Suddenly, the blare of a horn from the mountain pierced the air. Archers positioned on the rooftops below the mountain and stationed on the high plateaus notched their arrows. In a synchronized motion, they loosed a deadly salvo that soared through the sky with lethal intent.

The arrows whistled down toward the soldiers of the Iron Flood, some finding their marks with a clang against metal armor, others piercing through to fell some of Vatreus's men. However, most of the arrows halted mid-flight, caught by an invisible barrier. Vatreus, with a commanding outstretch of his arm, seized control of the arrows in midair. With a mere flick of his wrist, he turned them around and hurled them back at the archers. Screams echoed as many archers fell victim to their own projectiles, while the survivors hastily nocked another volley, only to see them manipulated once again by the Imperion's formidable power.

The defenders, undeterred by the aerial assault, charged forward with swords drawn, their battle cries filling the air. But as they neared Vatreus and one of his Dreadstorm Knights, an unseen force swept through their ranks. Men were hurled through the air like rag dolls, turned into unwilling missiles against their comrades. Amid this chaos, the Dreadstorm Knight advanced, his presence marked by the eerie glow of blue flames that wreathed his twin blades and was mirrored in his eyes. Like a specter of war, he moved through the defenders with supernatural speed, his blades leaving a luminescent trail of blue fire in their wake. Each swing was precise and deadly, cutting down the city's warriors with chilling efficiency. The battlefield before them was a blur of motion and devastation, punctuated by the grim ballet of Vatreus and the Dreadstorm Knight, who seemed untouchable, unstoppable.

"Looks like you have gained some understanding," muttered Garrick. "We should have remained in the wilds while we could."

Elysia was silent, just staring, her eyes locked on the battlefield's madness. Rykan watched her, saw that dazed look—she'd seen battles, sure, but nothing like this, he thought. Nothing like the raw, terrifying spectacle of Imperion Vatreus and his Dreadstorm Knight, blades dancing with blue fire, cutting through life as if it were nothing more than air.

To Rykan, it felt like the world had slipped off its axis. The usual chaos of war, the kind he thought he understood, had morphed into something far darker, more profound. War wasn't just clashing swords and battle cries anymore. It was this … this orchestration of destruction, precise and cold, directed by a man who seemed more force of nature than human.

Rykan's thoughts drifted to the stories he'd grown up hearing, tales spun around campfires and whispered by elders under starlit skies. Stories of conquerors like Vatreus, ambitious and ruthless, each one burning bright and fierce across the history of Galanor before their inevitable fall. They were all stopped, eventually—heroes emerged, shaped by destiny, the Zhal Evurah as Garrick and Elysia referred to them, the heroes who stood firm when the world teetered on the brink of collapse. Their names still resonated, carved into the very bones of the cities they had saved.

But now, what if what Elysia said was true? That Ethyllion, the crystal core of all destinies, lay shattered? A shadow of uncertainty crept over him. What hope could they cling to if the fabric of fate itself was undone? In a world unmoored from destiny's guide, what force could possibly rise to meet Vatreus's overwhelming onslaught?

Could other forces birth a new kind of hero, unscripted by fate, driven by sheer will and desperation? The thought both terrified and exhilarated him. Someone would have to step forward to challenge the Imperion and tip the scales back toward balance.

The bell sounded again, and an older man dressed in green and white robes strode toward the Imperion. The dual-wielding swordsman rushed toward the man, intent on cutting him down before he could reach Vatreus.

"Zarothos!" shouted Imperion Vatreus. "Stand down!"

He pulled the swordsman away from the old man with his unseen force. The swordsman turned to the Imperion, giving a bow of his head before moving past Vatreus and into the crowd of Iron Flood soldiers.

"Centuries have passed, and the mines of Dralomar have stood proud, supplying Elenior with noctharil," the man in the robes declared. "Though some brand us as rebels, our people, these brave souls, would defend this town with every fiber of their being, even against your reckless ambition. Spare what remains, allow us to live here in peace and Dralomar will yield to you."

"Dovar Rodorien, gather every soul, regardless of age or station, and bring them forth from their dwellings," commanded Imperion Vatreus, his voice slicing through the tense air like a cold, sharp blade. "Once you surrender to me, we will all have peace under my rule."

"Galanor could be a world reborn in beauty," Rodorien responded in what seemed like defiance with a bit of resignation. "If only the virtuous were the ones blessed with the might you wield."

Vatreus whirled around, his cloak billowing, eyes locking with Rodorien's in a silent clash of wills. "Our virtue is beyond question. Lands far and wide have welcomed us through their gates."

"They extend that courtesy out of necessity, not admiration," the Dovar countered sharply.

"Wrong, old man," Vatreus retorted, his tone both triumphant and cold. "I've forged a unity across Elenior, unmatched by any monarch before. There will be no more tariffs on your mines by the capital, no more control over the farmlands of Hildithor that choke off production."

Rodorien gestured despairingly at the fallen defenders scattered across the town square. "Is this the unity you speak of?" His voice thickened with grief.

Vatreus responded with cold precision, "You should have bowed to the inevitable when it loomed before you. I had hoped for a peaceful transition," he continued sharply. "Remember, it was your choice to resist."

As Vatreus stepped back, aligning with his commanders, Zarothos leaned forward, "My lord, perhaps we should reconsider the commitment of so many soldiers to Dralomar. If you aim to fight on two fronts in the coming days, our forces will be spread thin."

"We cannot afford to lose Dralomar," Vatreus asserted firmly. "The mines are crucial for supplying the battles to come."

From his vantage point, Rykan felt a chill settle over him as he absorbed the weight of Vatreus's words. It was the first time he had seen Vatreus portray a glimmer of doubt. As powerful as he was, he knew he was not invincible. Rykan vowed to find his weaknesses, revealing them for other nations to exploit. As the Imperion and Zarothos melded back into the ranks, disappearing into the sea of troops, Rykan was left with a sinking sensation that clung to his bones. As dark clouds began to cloak the sky, the shadows seemed to whisper of wars yet to come and of choices that might define the fate of their world.

CHAPTER 14

A FTER A RESTFUL night camping in the calm of the forest and traveling for part of the day, Selaina approached the entrance to Silvaren, her hair and clothes now dry, thanks to the late morning sun. She pulled her hood over her head, hiding her unkempt hair. The dirt road branched into two, encircling large wooden structures set among towering green trees that stood like sentinels.

As they stepped into the town, the bustling activity on the main road captured her full attention. People navigated the thoroughfare with purpose. Some walked alone, deep in thought, while others chatted animatedly in groups. The diversity of the town's populace was a new spectacle for Selaina.

According to Darian, Silvaren was renowned for its lumber and exquisite wood-crafting, and this was evident in the artistry of the wooden buildings and finely crafted goods on display. The craftsmanship added an air of pride and elegance to the town, blending harmoniously with the natural surroundings.

Selaina stood still for a moment, trying to absorb the structured chaos of urban life, a stark contrast to the solitude of the forest. When a rider on ridgeback cantered too closely by them, Darian quickly reached out, gently pulling her back to safety, snapping her focus back to the dangers around her.

Fascinated, Selaina watched the ridgebacks, creatures she had only heard of in stories but never seen. Each one moved with powerful grace, their riders in sync with the animals' rhythms. Regaining her composure, she adjusted the strap of her bag and followed Darian, her senses heightened. With each step, she observed the patterns of movement around her, the layout of the streets and the architectural styles that spoke of Silvaren's rich cultural heritage. It was a living mosaic of tradition and innovation, and Selaina, keen on new understanding and knowledge, felt a growing appreciation for the complex beauty of what a town could be.

"Let's have a look around," Darian said. "If your mother is here, we will find her."

They moved along the road until they reached the next building. A man walked up to two women standing outside the shop and opened the door, allowing them to go inside. Through the glass window, Selaina could see chairs, tables, chests, and all manner of wooden items. She hurried to the door and pulled it open.

"I don't think you'll find anything in there," Darian said.

Selaina brushed past Darian and stepped into the shop, pausing to inhale deeply. The air was a complex fragrance of sweet, resinous woods and the rich, earthy aroma of aged timber. Her eyes quickly found a beautifully crafted chair made of dark wood. The back was intricately carved with designs of interlocking circles, and the legs were adorned with vine-like lines and delicate floral etchings. She couldn't resist touching it, tracing the carvings with her fingertips.

Beside the chair, a table caught her eye. Its legs were a study in artistic whimsy, carved in varying widths, shapes, and patterns. Each piece seemed to belong perfectly in its place, a harmony that Selaina found deeply satisfying. She ran her fingers along the length of the table, marveling at the smooth and textured surfaces under her touch.

Darian, catching up to her, started to warn, "You probably shouldn't touch the—"

But the shopkeeper, who had approached unnoticed, interrupted him. "You have great taste," he said, admiring her interest. "That table was created by Brennan Brooks, the most famous artisan in Silvaren."

"It's beautiful," Selaina acknowledged, not hiding her admiration.

"Indeed," the shopkeeper agreed, beaming with pride. "And it's only twenty aurin."

Selaina recalled Darian telling her about aurin, the gold coins used to trade for goods in the towns across the realm. How would anyone get twenty of those to trade for a table?

"I'm afraid I don't have that," she admitted, with a bit of disappointment.

"Hmm, well, I can show you some other pieces," offered the shopkeeper. "How many coins did you plan to spend today?"

As much as she would love to bring some of these items back home to the cabin, she had to focus on what was important—finding her mother.

"Oh, I didn't come to buy anything," Selaina confessed, her gaze still wandering over the exquisite woodwork. "I was just admiring what you have in here."

The shopkeeper's demeanor shifted subtly, his smile tightening. "I should have known a Lith would be so cheap. Keep your filthy hands away from anything then, hmm?" he chided sharply. "I can't sell items with smudges all over them."

The remark stung, making Selaina's cheeks flush with embarrassment. She quickly inspected her hands, turning them over and frowning. They were clean. Why would he say that? Her grip tightened on the table as she fought to control a rising wave of confusion and anger.

"We'd better leave," Darian suggested quietly, rubbing his hands together, as if sensing some rising tension. "Don't need them calling the guards on us."

"I didn't do anything wrong," Selaina asserted, as she reluctantly released the table and moved toward the door.

Outside, Darian leaned against the wooden railing in front of the shop with a thoughtful expression. "Any idea where your mother might be?" he asked, watching her closely.

Selaina paused, her frustration from the encounter lingering while she considered his question. "I don't know what any of this is," she admitted. "I don't think I could ever understand the wicked world."

"It's not wicked," Darian said, his tone softening. He gestured toward a group of townsfolk bustling about their daily tasks—merchants arranging their stalls, mothers shepherding children, elderly folks chatting by the roadside. "Well … perhaps parts of it are. But most of these folks are just like you and me, selling their goods and wares to make a coin or two so they can buy food for their families."

"Then why would they take my mother?" Selaina asked, as they moved away from the crowded market square toward a quieter part of town.

Darian sighed. "Most of these people would never stoop to such actions," he remarked, his gaze sweeping the passersby. "But in every town, there are those few, driven by desperation or greed, who are willing to do wrong."

They continued down the road, and a small shop with colorful ceramic bowls and pottery displayed in the window drew Selaina's attention. She paused for a moment, her eyes wandering over the different shapes of vases, cups, and pots. Jeth had once told Selaina that her mother used to make ceramic items to sell before they left the wicked world. She could almost see her mother's hands shaping wet clay into beautiful, functional pieces, each one unique and crafted with care. Her mother had made many pieces over the years to use at the cabin.

Selaina left the ceramic shop behind, her eyes scanning the surroundings as they approached a building that cast a wide shadow over the street. The structure's darkened windows and the quiet around it contrasted sharply with the vibrant market they had left behind.

"Where would we find such individuals?" she inquired, her mind grappling with the possibility of confronting the darker aspects of human nature.

"It's hard to say," Darian admitted, his gaze drifting toward the darkened alleyways that branched off from the main road. "I suppose we would have to think of the places you and I would normally avoid. Those types tend to lurk in the shadows, avoiding the light of day. They move in silence, unseen, until they strike."

As they passed by the ominous building, Selaina felt a chill. The stark difference between the light-filled market and this somber place seemed to embody the very dichotomy of good and evil she was struggling to understand. She looked back at Darian, seeking some comfort in his steady presence.

Suddenly, a guard emerged from the doorway, grappling with a struggling man. Startled, Selaina instinctively took a step back as the guard forcefully ushered the man past her. The guard gave the man a rough shove, and he stumbled and tumbled into the dirt-laden street. When he rose to his feet, his eyes met Selaina's, defiance and resentment flickering at their core. Snatching his hat from the ground, he shot her a venomous glare before storming away.

In that brief moment, Selaina found herself inundated with fleeting glimpses of the man's recent thoughts. She witnessed him engaged in conversation with a woman seated at a table, a palpable sense of rejection washing over him as she turned him away. The scene shifted to another woman, pleading with him desperately, evoking feelings of betrayal and resentment. Selaina could almost taste the bitterness of his self-loathing, his inner turmoil palpable. It was clear that, beneath his facade of defiance, lay a deep-seated anguish, born of love gone awry.

"Maybe we should start here," Selaina suggested with a confidence she didn't expect from herself.

Darian hesitated, his gaze flickering toward the dimly lit interior. "That's the local tavern," he cautioned with evident concern. "Not the most suitable place for a young woman like yourself. Let me go in and ask around."

Selaina squared her shoulders, hardening her features. "I didn't leave my home and travel all this way to wait outside," she declared, pulling her hood over her head as she strode purposefully toward the entrance.

As she reached the doorway, the sounds and bustle of the tavern hit her all at once. A moment of hesitation gripped her, and she paused, looking over the crowd inside. The overwhelming noise, the chatter, the shifting figures—she wasn't used to this chaos. She stepped back slightly, glancing at Darian.

Darian stepped past her, his confidence giving her the boldness to follow. The tavern's atmosphere enveloped them—a stark contrast to the clean, ordered world Selaina preferred. The interior was dimly lit, the air heavy with the scent of ale and wood smoke. Candles flickered on scattered tables and sconces along the walls, casting dancing shadows that played across the rough-hewn surfaces.

The unfamiliar smells and sounds overwhelmed Selaina for a moment, and she instinctively pulled her hood tighter around her head, shielding herself from the bustle. Yet, she pushed her discomfort aside, focusing on her purpose here. She moved with deliberate grace through the tavern, her senses sharp as she searched for any signs of suspicious behavior or hints that could lead her closer to understanding her mother's disappearance.

In the center of the tavern stood the enormous stump of a tree, its surface glistening with a protective sheen. The massive tree's remains appeared to be shielded by some mysterious substance, giving it an almost magical aura. It seemed as though the entire tavern had been built around this ancient stump, honoring its presence and history.

Selaina followed Darian as he navigated through the throng to secure a stool by the bar. He settled next to a burly man, and Selaina sat beside him. Darian's posture relaxed when he addressed the tavern keeper.

"A cup of water, if it's not too much trouble," he requested.

The tavern keeper nodded, pulling a pitcher from behind the bar and filling a ceramic cup with water. He slid the cup across the bar to Darian. "Welcome to Silvaren."

"Anything for you, miss?" the tavern keeper asked as he started to turn around.

"I'll have water as well, thank you," Selaina replied.

"Haven't seen you two around here before," said the tavern keeper.

"Passing through on the way to Aldenglade," Darian responded, taking a sip.

"You have a long road ahead, my friend," the tavern keeper remarked with a chuckle. "I hope you have good company or at least a sturdy ridgeback."

"No ridgeback yet, unfortunately," Darian admitted, setting the cup down as he glanced at Selaina. "But I'm in very good company, indeed."

"Aldenglade, eh?" the burly man beside him chimed in. "What calls you there?"

"Work, hopefully," Darian replied. "Starting a new life."

"What are you running from?" the man prodded.

"Only the war," Darian said, his voice steady. "Trying to get as far away as possible before I settle down."

"I doubt the war will reach these parts," the tavern keeper interjected. "We're a lumber town. If you can do carpentry or woodworking, you will always have work here."

"I'm a tailor's apprentice, actually," Darian confessed. "I wouldn't know much about woodworking."

Selaina took another drink, her attention sharply focused on the exchange. Each word, each nuance, was a potential clue, yet none led closer to her mother. Her frustration mounted when the conversation drifted.

"Can't have too many tailors either," the tavern keeper added with a shrug.

Feeling some urgency, Selaina edged closer, her impatience surfacing. "If I may, have either of you seen a woman come through here?" She reached into her bag and found the small painted portrait of her mother, showing it to the tavern keeper.

"A Lith?" the tavern keeper asked. "Haven't seen any of them in a while."

"There's no shiners around here." The burly man scoffed. "We ran them off some years ago."

"Ran them off?" Darian echoed, his brow furrowing. "Why? I know there are some tensions, but they are exceptional artisans and crafters."

"Murderers is what they are." The man spat bitterly.

Selaina's heart sank as the conversation took a darker turn. Her mother's heritage now seemed like a dire impediment to her search. She clenched her fists, her breath quickening as she pulled her hood even tighter, making sure her white hair and ears remained hidden. The weight of every hostile word felt like it was pressing against her, and she struggled to hold her composure.

"Murderers?" Darian asked with a raised eyebrow. "I know some don't trust Liths, but few of them are violent."

The tavern keeper leaned closer, his voice lowering to a whisper. "He's talking about those folk who went missing around here years ago. Some were just children. Never did find them."

"It was those shiners who did it," the burly man said with a grunt. "Always wandering off outside the town, using those kids for some shiner rituals."

The tavern keeper nodded slowly, a shadow of doubt flickering across his face. "I won't outright say they had something to do with it," he admitted, "but their behavior was odd, unsettling even."

Selaina's pulse quickened. The hostility toward Liths was thick in the air, and she felt the oppressive weight of their disdain. She could feel the eyes of the tavern's patrons on her, some of them already casting suspicious glances.

Darian noticed it too. "We're not getting any help here," he said quietly, his voice low but firm. "It's best we move on. We don't need to stir up more trouble."

Selaina nodded, reluctant but understanding. As they turned to leave, the burly man muttered something about "troublemakers", and Selaina's stomach twisted.

They exited the tavern into the cool evening air, the door shutting behind them with a heavy thud.

"Do you think anyone else in here might have seen her?" she asked.

"I'm sorry, Selaina," Darian said as he urged her toward the door. "I didn't realize these people would be hostile to Liths. If I had known, I would have suggested we go somewhere else."

As they stepped into the sunlight outside, Selaina pondered aloud, "What were they talking about? How could they think someone like me had anything to do with their missing people?"

"To them it doesn't matter," Darian explained, his eyes meeting hers with a look of both sympathy and frustration.

"But I haven't done anything to anyone here," Selaina protested, her voice rising slightly with the confusion and hurt brewing inside.

"Just because you haven't wronged anyone doesn't mean prejudice won't cloud their judgment," Darian said, his voice somber. He looked around the town square, wary of any further confrontation. "People fear what they don't understand, and fear often leads to prejudice, like their unwarranted accusations."

Selaina's gaze lingered on the faces of the passersby, each indifferent or wary as they glanced her way. It saddened her that her mere presence could evoke such strong reactions based solely on her heritage—a heritage she herself was only beginning to understand. Feeling a sudden vulnerability at her distinctive white hair and the unique forked shape of her ears, Selaina reached up to pull her hood back over her head more closely. Under its shelter, she sought a semblance of anonymity, a brief respite from the judgments of the world.

"Why do they hate my kind so much?" Selaina asked, curious with a bit of sadness.

Darian sighed, running a hand through his hair. "It's complicated," he began, his gaze shifting to the horizon. "There's a deep-rooted mistrust for some. It probably got worse after Vatreus. It seems Liths are often the easiest to blame when things go wrong."

"Vatreus is a Lith?" Selaina's eyes widened in surprise. "No wonder they hate me." She hugged herself, feeling a chill that had nothing to do with the weather.

"I thought you knew," said Darian, placing a reassuring hand on her shoulder. "Every race of people has its bad seeds. Vatreus doesn't represent you or the rest of your people."

"Why don't people trust us then?" Selaina pressed, her brow wrinkled in confusion.

Darian sighed, as if she had broached a subject difficult to talk about. "It's a long story, but it goes back to the very beginning. The Liths are said to be the blessed ones of Archeinor."

Noticing Selaina's puzzled expression, he quickly added, "Forgive me, I keep forgetting that this is all new to you. Archeinor is revered as the pinnacle of order by those who believe in such things. I'm a bit of a skeptic myself. The legends describe it as a realm beyond our reach, a sanctuary of perfect order and balance. Supposedly, it's where every law and principle that governs our world was first conceived. Its Orithars, the lore says, shaped our world from the chaos that preceded it. But chaos never fully disappears. The balance between order and chaos is what sustains Galanor."

"And why would they only bless the Liths?" Selaina inquired.

"The historic accounts suggest that the Liths were fashioned in a nearly flawless image, a form that pleased the divine Orithars of Archeinor themselves," Darian explained. "Gifted with unparalleled logic and reason, they supposedly earned Archeinor's special favor. This favor has fueled resentment and envy among others. Regardless of one's belief in these stories, the achievements of the Liths are hard to dismiss. They built Ederanis, a city of splendor and intellect, showcasing their mastery over mathematics, engineering, and even the arcane arts."

"I must visit this city!" Selaina exclaimed with excitement. "If my kin have built such a place, I must see it—after I find my mother, of course."

Darian's expression turned somber. "I'm afraid you might not find the welcome you hope for. Ederanis was conquered by the Grulnogs years ago. Your people were driven out. I would love to see it myself, but that is no longer possible."

Selaina's excitement faded to confusion. "But how? If we were truly blessed, how could we fall?"

"It has caused many to question the Liths' supposed divine status," Darian admitted with a heavy sigh.

"And yet my people are still despised?" Selaina asked, her voice a soft echo of despair.

"Yes." Darian nodded regretfully. "Sometimes, history's favor is a double-edged sword. After they were driven from Ederanis," Darian continued, "the Liths scattered across various realms, seeking sanctuary. Despite their exile, they thrived, often amassing wealth that surpassed that of local families who had been established for generations. This success fueled existing resentments, perpetuating animosity toward them."

Selaina felt a surge of sadness, grappling with this new understanding of her heritage. The notion that the world might harbor such specific animosity toward her kin was disheartening.

As if noticing her troubled expression, Darian's voice softened. "Yet, it's important to remember, many admire and even revere the Lith people for their contributions and resilience."

Selaina managed a small smile, grateful for this acknowledgment of her people's strength. "But those who despise us," she murmured, her thoughts returning to her mother's disappearance, "could they be the ones who took my mother?"

"It's possible," Darian conceded. "But you told me you were isolated from the rest of the world, so it's puzzling. How would they even know of her?"

Selaina pictured her mother at her age, living in a town like this one. If she had faced the same prejudice for being a Lith, it was no surprise that she'd chosen to leave and carve out a life on her own, away from the rest of the world. Unlike Jeth, who had often joked around, her mother had a solemn demeanor, rarely smiling or laughing. She focused solely on her work, chatting only about practical things. Had her mother's burdens left her unable to enjoy the lighter moments of life?

A young man's approach interrupted her thoughts. Dressed nicely in a suit and hat, he appeared to be one of the merchants.

"Excuse me," he said politely, "were you in the tavern just now?" His eyes flickered with recognition. "Ah, yes, I've been looking for you."

Darian bristled slightly. "If you're here to send us away, we won't be staying long."

"No, not at all," the merchant hastened to assure them, his manner conciliatory. "I want to apologize for the behavior you encountered. Please don't think all of Silvaren shares those views. Some of us greatly value the Liths."

"Thank you," Darian replied with a hint of gratitude. "That's reassuring to hear."

The merchant hesitated before continuing. "May I ask about the woman you mentioned in the tavern?"

"My mother," Selaina replied. "She's missing, and I am trying to find her."

"That's dreadful," the merchant sympathized. "I only mention it because recently, an old man came through, also looking for a Lith woman. He seemed distressed that she wasn't in Silvaren. Curiously, he showed a sketching of her to anyone who would listen, and she looked remarkably like you."

Selaina's heart quickened, her thoughts flashing back to the strange man she had seen lurking in the forest just before Jeth was killed and her mother taken. Could it be the same man?

"Did he say where he was heading next?"

"He mentioned heading north, toward the river towns," the merchant said thoughtfully. "He seemed determined, even a bit desperate."

"Thank you," Selaina said, her hope strengthening. This could be a crucial lead, and every bit of information edged her closer to finding her mother.

CHAPTER 15

I N THE MURKY depths of a dimly lit chamber, a sinister figure, his form contorted and obscured by swirling shadows, rifled through the contents of an open sarcophagus. With deliberate, almost reverent movements, the creature retrieved a skeletal hand from within the ancient tomb.

With a chilling hiss that reverberated through the chamber, the figure drew the hand closer to his shrouded face, his glowing eyes flickering with an unsettling intensity as he scrutinized the bones. Each jagged edge and hollow socket seemed to pulse with a faint, otherworldly glow, as if imbued with the echoes of a long-forgotten power.

As the creature hovered over the skeletal remains, a malevolent aura emanated from his very being, casting a pall of dread over the chamber. With each passing moment, the air grew thick with the palpable sense of ancient magic intertwining with the shadows that danced hungrily around the figure's form.

Nearby, other creatures rummaged through the ancient tombs. One uncovered a tome bound in animal skin. As he opened it, the pages oozed with a sickly sheen. The air grew thick with the stench of rot as he flipped through its pages, his ember eyes gleaming with hunger for the knowledge it contained. Several others moved about the room, their pale forms shifting silently through the gloom, scanning for anything of value—bones, relics, anything imbued with power.

"Anguish resonates within these bones," the first entity hissed with a sinister rasp, his voice moving through the chamber like a 

lamentation of the damned. "The pain of the dead lingers here, waiting to be unleashed upon the living."

The other nodded in agreement, his gaze fixed on the tome before him. "And this tome … It is a grimoire of curses," he said in a hoarse whisper. "Someone once delved into the abyss of forbidden knowledge, seeking the power of dark secrets beyond mortal comprehension. It could be instrumental in unlocking the true depths of—"

Suddenly, a faint sound disturbed the air around them, rippling through the chamber. Both creatures paused their work.

"Did you hear that?" The one with the tome lowered it, his eyes darting nervously around the room.

The other glanced up from the bones. "Something stirs beyond the veil."

"Our master calls from the rift!" the second creature said as he placed the tome onto the floor. They hurried to the far side of the chamber where a massive stone door loomed, sealed by ancient mechanisms. One of the creatures reached for a rusty lever embedded in the wall, pulling it with a creaking groan.

Chains rattled and clanked in the darkness when the stone door began to tremble, inching open to reveal a passageway beyond. Sliding open with a resounding thud, the door revealed the eerie expanse of a cavern.

As they crossed the threshold into the cavern, the sound of chains dragging along the stone floor echoed behind them, sealing the entrance once more with a final, heavy clang. They hurried into the eerie expanse of the cavern, surrounded by towering pillars that loomed like silent sentinels in the gloom. As they emerged, their footsteps echoed through the stillness, disturbing the former tranquility of the cave.

One of the ghostly entities held a glowing red crystal, oddly curved like a horn. Pressing the crystal into the surface of a great stone, he drew the shape of a circle. Unnatural flame trailed the crystal's movements until he completed the circle, forming a dark void inside the stone within the burning fire. Coming together with their brethren around a weathered gray boulder, they formed a circle, their movements quick and purposeful. With a sense of urgency, they knelt before the stone, pressing their hands against its rough surface.

A hushed silence fell over the group as a crimson glow began to crack through the boulder, casting eerie shadows that danced across their faces. The air hummed with an electric energy, the earth itself awakening to a powerful presence.

One of the entities addressed the pulsating red light with reverence. "My lord, Nociferon, we have long awaited your call. What has stirred you from the shadows?"

A voice, eerie and unearthly, emanated from the fissure, his intonation akin to wisps of smoke curling from a flame. "A disturbance has echoed through the cosmos. Something previously unobtainable in Pandemora now lies within my reach. A fragment of pure order, once spilled into the mortal realm long ago, has returned."

"An artifact from Archeinor?" queried one of the entities, disbelief lacing his tone. "How is such a thing possible?"

"It assumes the form of a Stone," the voice said. "Its potency must not be wielded by the unworthy."

"What shall we do with it, my lord?" asked one of the creatures, anticipation evident in his voice. "Is this Stone a part of your grand design?"

"All will be revealed in time, my faithful," the voice assured. "For now, concentrate your endeavors on locating the Stone."

"We shall do as you command," said another creature. "The Stone will be ours."

"Go forth, my faithful. Let the whispers of chaos guide your steps, for the fate of Galanor hangs in the balance," the voice said.

Rykan jerked awake, his heart pounding as the vision of red flames encircling a void in the stone faded—a haunting echo of the dead tree in Nordravin. His breath came in ragged gasps, the weight of the dream pressing on his chest like a vice. Whatever he had touched in that old burnt tree had done something to him. Shaking off the lingering tendrils of the nightmare, he took in his surroundings under the weak, flickering light.

The place around him was akin to a forgotten barn, its once sturdy structure succumbing to decay. Musty odors of damp straw and rotting wood weighed down the air, speaking of years without proper care. He was shackled to beams that felt rough and splintered under his fingers, likely once serving as ties for beasts now long gone. Moonlight seeped through the wooden slats, casting ghostly shadows across the hard-packed dirt floor, well trodden by countless hooves and feet over the years. Nearby, Elysia's shield, emblazoned with the emblem of an owl, lay discarded among the debris, reflecting faint glimmers of light.

Muted voices pierced the stillness. A fellow prisoner, his facial hair neatly trimmed and skin tinted bronze, quietly strategized with Garrick.

"There are only two guards outside but taking them both is more than I can manage," he whispered. "If I get you out, can you handle one with your bare hands?"

"I could take both of them with my bare hands," said Garrick with an earnest tone. "But how do I know I can trust you? I don't even know you."

The prisoner flashed a sardonic grin. "Ah, well, in that case, let me formally introduce myself. I'm Kadin, of the distant and exceedingly mysterious lands of Korafal, and notorious for my trustworthiness, or so the stories claim," he quipped, his tone dripping with mock solemnity. "Does that put your valiant heart at ease?"

"Korafal," said Garrick. "I think I passed through there once."

"Wow, we practically grew up together then," Kadin joked, arching an eyebrow. "So, does this fleeting connection make us comrades or are you still on the fence?"

"I'm in. Elysia can fight too, so we should be more than enough," said Garrick.

Kadin nodded, but his expression was one of mock caution. "Sure, we could turn this into a parade with fanfare and all, but let's aim for stealth this time. I can't have everyone running free, turning this escape into a town festival."

"I'm not leaving her behind," Garrick said firmly. "The kid either."

"It would be unwise not to include the rest of us," said Rykan as he rose.

Kadin rolled his eyes. "Great, no pressure then," he retorted with a dry chuckle. "We have only a moment to strike and bolt for the mountains. Look around, Garrick—there's a whole casting call of replacements they can press into service. If we get caught, they'll kill us."

"What about your friend over there?" Garrick said, referring to a man sleeping in the corner. "You going to leave him too?"

"He's no friend of mine." Kadin shrugged. "If I could take out the guards myself, I'd have waved goodbye to this charming establishment hours ago."

Garrick chuckled under his breath. "How do you plan on getting out of these chains?"

With a sly grin, Kadin raised his hands into the light, holding loose shackles. "Oh, these old things?" he mused, giving his wrists a casual twirl. "I've been enjoying freedom for hours now. Just waiting on the right company to make an exit."

Garrick's eyes widened. "We can pull this off," he insisted. "But we don't leave anyone behind. They can stay put until the guards are taken care of."

"Garrick and I took out a whole group of bandits," said Rykan. "We can handle a few guards."

"Too risky," Kadin shot back.

Garrick shook his head firmly. "It's risky no matter how you slice it," he argued. "But if this falls apart, it won't be because we turned this into a free-for-all."

Kadin rubbed his temples, frustration etching his features. "And what makes you think they're even up for this kind of risk?"

Before Kadin could further his point, Elysia's voice cut through the tension. "I'm willing," she declared, her eyes snapping open, "and quite able."

Kadin sighed deeply, annoyance flickering across his face. "You talk too loud," he hissed at Elysia before turning back to Garrick. "I think I'll wait until they capture someone who can be a bit more discreet."

"You'll find no one more capable than us," said Rykan.

Elysia's tone hardened. "If we don't go through with this now, someone may talk." She glanced at Kadin. "Who knows? I might even receive some privileges for foiling a breakout." With a pointed stare, she held the man's gaze, daring him to defy her ultimatum.

Kadin grunted in frustration. "Fine," he muttered. "You want in? You take all the risk. You and Garrick handle the guards, and I'll make sure everyone stays quiet."

"And what do I do?" asked Rykan.

"Drag the bodies inside," said Kadin. "Make sure no one finds them until we're long gone."

"But I can—" Rykan started.

"Let's not argue right now." Garrick nodded to Elysia. "Let's make this quick and quiet," he said.

Elysia leaned away from the beam she was chained to. "You going to release us first or do we have to fight them from here?"

"Just make sure this doesn't turn into a circus," Kadin said as he slipped a small, slender blade from the sleeve of his tunic, deftly inserting it into the lock of Garrick's cuffs.

With precise, calculated movements, he manipulated the mechanism until a satisfying click sounded and the cuffs fell open. Garrick rubbed his wrists and exchanged a silent nod with Kadin.

Turning his attention to Rykan, Kadin's fingers worked with practiced skill. He twisted the blade at just the right angle, exerting subtle pressure until the metal yielded with a sharp snap. The cuffs released, and Rykan flexed his arms, the sudden freedom almost foreign after hours in bondage.

Rykan rolled his shoulders, easing the stiffness that had set in from the prolonged restraint. He rotated his wrists, trying to shake off the lingering numbness, his muscles protesting the movement after being immobilized for so long.

After releasing the other man from his chains, Kadin moved toward Elysia. He whispered in a low voice, his words brushing against Elysia's ear as he worked on her bindings, "We can't forget about you now, can we?" His hands moved deftly, but he deliberately worked slowly, the blade picking the lock on her cuffs. "Don't worry, my dear, you can thank me later."

The moment the chains loosened, Elysia's hands sprang free. In one fluid motion, she grasped Kadin by the neck, pushing him back with a force that belied her delicate form. As Kadin stumbled backward, gasping for breath, Elysia's lips curled into a sly smirk.

"I could let you struggle a bit longer," she teased with mock seriousness. She released her grip, stepping back and adding with a wink. "Consider us even now. No need to thank me."

Rubbing his neck, Kadin gave her a rueful grin. "Intriguing," he conceded. "I've always appreciated a woman with a strong grip.

Rolling her eyes, Elysia grabbed her shield off the floor, turning to see Garrick approaching.

His face barely contained any concern over Elysia choking Kadin. "You ready?" he asked, his gaze shifting between the two.

"As I'll ever be," Elysia replied, stretching her arms and flexing her fingers, preparing for what was to come. Garrick reached for the door handle.

Rykan grabbed Garrick by the shoulder. "Don't we need some kind of plan first?"

"Furthermore, do you even realize how much noise that door will make when you open it like that?" Kadin interjected, keeping his voice down." The guards will be on us before we can even step outside."

Garrick scowled at Rykan. "What's there to plan?" he asked. "I take one guard, she takes the other."

"I could help too," Rykan said. They were making him feel like a helpless child who had to be cared for.

Kadin exhaled sharply, a hint of irritation in his gaze as he searched the debris on the floor. "At the very least, decide who's going left or right," he insisted. "We can't afford sloppy mistakes."

Garrick raised an eyebrow at Elysia with a hint of challenge. "I'll take the left guard. You good with the right?"

Elysia nodded, her expression steely. "Watch and learn."

Kadin shook his head as he meticulously prepared a makeshift tool from a piece of rope. "It's truly a miracle you two have managed to survive this long," he quipped, slicing the piece of rope. He then inserted the rope between the door and its frame, cushioning the bolt. Slowly, he turned the lever with a thief's precision. "Stealth, my friends, is the art of survival."

Rykan, holding his breath, watched the bolt turn with painstaking slowness—it seemed to take an eternity but lasted only a few seconds. With a muffled click, the bolt slid back. Kadin raised a finger to his lips, signaling silence.

The tension was palpable. Even the stranger, silent until now, began to pace, his boots scuffing quietly against the stone floor. Garrick shot him a sharp look, motioning him to stillness with a stern hand.

"Remember, lift as you open to avoid any creaks," Kadin instructed in a low whisper, wrapping more rope around the door's hinges. "The devil is in the details."

Garrick's hand was steady on the handle as he eased the door open just enough for a sliver of cool air and dim light to slip through. Pressing his eye to the narrow opening, he scanned the scene.

"He's right," Garrick murmured, keeping his voice quiet. "Just two guards."

"Then let's move," Elysia whispered, inching closer.

"Hold on," Garrick hissed as he squinted through the opening. "Third one … just walked by."

Elysia bit her lip while she leaned against the rough wall. Beside her, Rykan felt his heart pound as they waited in the dim shadows.

"I'll take the third one," Rykan whispered.

Garrick waved him back as he kept watching. "He's stopped. Talking to the guards now."

From behind them, the sound of restless shuffling filled the small space.

"Will you keep it down?" Kadin's whisper stopped the stranger in his tracks.

"What are they saying? Can you hear?" Elysia's voice was barely audible.

"Just small talk," Garrick responded, keeping his eye glued to the gap. "The patroller's caught up in a chat about one of the guard's swords. Looks fancy."

"What kind of sword?" Elysia tried to get a better look, nudging Garrick slightly. "Shift over, let me see."

Garrick shot back quietly, "Is that really what we need to focus on right now?" But after a moment, he sighed and stepped aside, allowing her to peer through.

"What kind of metal is that?" Elysia murmured, squinting through the gap in the door. "It looks robust."

"How does one blade look stronger than another?" Garrick muttered, skeptically.

"Well, it's shiny," Elysia replied, still watching.

"Shiny doesn't necessarily mean better," Garrick pointed out. "A blade without nicks hasn't been through enough to prove its worth—"

Kadin turned to Rykan. "This is never going to work," he muttered.

"Hey, he's moving on," Elysia interrupted.

They watched for a moment, and Garrick nodded, pushed the door wider, and then slipped out into the shadows, Elysia right on his heels.

Outside, the sound of a brief scuffle was quickly followed by the heavy thud of bodies hitting the ground, signaling their swift handling of the guards. Kadin, who'd been keeping watch, darted out and began dragging one of the limp figures back inside.

Rykan grabbed the legs of the other guard sprawled just beyond the doorway. He grunted, pulling hard, but the guard's bulk resisted his initial efforts. Gritting his teeth, Rykan hauled again, managing to drag the body across the dirt and into the safety of the shadowed room.

Once outside, Kadin led the way, gesturing urgently for silence. They slipped through a group of trees, avoiding patches of moonlight as they made their way toward the rocky hills looming in the distance.

They had just cleared the tree line, venturing into an open field, when a shout halted them.

"Who's out there in the dark?" a voice called from behind.

Rykan's heart skipped a beat, his eyes darting between his companions and the approaching soldier. Elysia spun around, the stolen sword in her hand gleaming under the moon's gaze.

"Think you can sneak past me, huh?" the voice taunted, closer now. A lone soldier approached, his stance cocky. "Must not have much skill with that blade if you're sneaking around like a thief."

Elysia's grip on her sword tightened, her posture defensive yet poised. "Sometimes, silence is sharper than steel," she retorted.

As the soldier muttered more taunts, Rykan noticed Garrick appearing from the shadows, his sword lightly pressing against the soldier's back.

"Care to dance?" Garrick asked as he playfully tapped the flat of his blade against the soldier's spine, issuing a silent, deadly challenge.

With a graceful step backward, Garrick allowed the soldier space to turn and face him. Kadin, eyes wide, made frantic gestures for the others to escape, but only the other man with them took heed. Elysia clenched her teeth, clearly chafing at Garrick for interfering with her chance to prove the soldier wrong. Rykan, caught between the impulse to run and the pull of the unfolding duel, remained frozen, his breath caught in his throat.

The soldier sneered. "You might have stood a chance if you'd kept your advantage." His voice oozed with disdain as he faced Garrick squarely.

Garrick responded with a swift, clean stroke aimed directly at the soldier's heart. But the soldier parried with surprising agility, his own blade meeting Garrick's with a clang that resonated through the night air. Their swords locked in a fierce struggle, both of them trying to discern the other's next move.

As the soldier attempted to break the deadlock with a quick maneuver, Garrick adjusted his stance, ready for anything. The soldier aimed a quick thrust at Garrick's side, but Garrick avoided the blade, countering with a sharp, precise movement of his own.

As the soldier lunged forward again, Garrick's instincts seemed to kick in with lightning speed. With a swift pivot, he sidestepped the attack, his blade slicing through the air in a deadly arc. The soldier's eyes widened in alarm when he realized his mistake too late.

Garrick's sword found its mark, piercing the soldier's armor with a satisfying crunch. The soldier staggered back, a look of disbelief crossing his face as he clutched futilely at the wound. Blood seeped from the tear in his armor, staining the ground beneath him.

With a final, desperate gasp, the soldier sank to his knees, defeated. Garrick stood over him, his breathing heavy but controlled.

Elysia smirked and nudged Garrick playfully. "Looks like you fancy the shiny ones after all," she teased, nodding at the sword in Garrick's hand.

Garrick chuckled, wiping sweat from his brow. "I picked up the first one I saw. If you want it that bad, I'll trade with you," he offered, extending the sword toward her as he walked past.

Elysia accepted the sword, eyeing it critically. "You could have at least wiped it off first," she remarked with a playful roll of her eyes.

The fallen soldier's weapon drew Rykan's eyes. He quickly moved forward and picked it up, testing its weight in his hand. The sword felt solid and well balanced, it was better than the one he had taken from the bandits, possibly even better than the one he had used in Tathara.

"This will do nicely," Rykan muttered to himself, gripping the hilt tightly. He looked up at Garrick and Elysia, with a glint in his eye. "Let's keep moving."

CHAPTER 16

Selaina and Darian came out of the shady forest onto a vast grassy plain. The slender dirt path beneath them had overgrown in some areas, but they could follow it easily enough. A pesky itch on her right shoulder was annoying Selaina. It was so far underneath her sleeve that she couldn't properly scratch it. She tried her best to ignore it.

The plain stretched out before them, dotted with wildflowers that painted the landscape in bursts of color. Across the sky, greenish patterns of sunshimmer cascaded toward the horizon. Selaina had meant to thank Darian for his support, but the thought of bringing it up now embarrassed her for some reason. After rehearsing it in her mind for a while, she finally got up the nerve to say it.

"You're a good man, Darian," Selaina said, breaking the silence as they navigated around a large rock that jutted out of the path. "I appreciate you coming with me. Hopefully, we will find my mother soon and you can get on with your quest."

"It's nothing," Darian responded, his gaze wandering over the expansive view. "I'm in no real hurry. Like Bellaria used to say, 'Sometimes you have to divert your eyes from your destination long enough to appreciate the scenery along the way.'"

Selaina watched a butterfly flit from one flower to another, considering Darian's words. "My mother never said anything about there being good people in the wicked world," she reflected aloud. She plucked a small daisy from the ground, twirling it between her fingers.

"There are good people all over," Darian reassured her as they skirted a muddy patch on the path. "If you expect to see the bad in people, that is what you will find. I'm sorry to say, it sounds like your mother must have had some unfortunate experiences."

"She never talked much about the world outside of our forest," Selaina admitted. "She always got irritated when I asked about it."

"Whoever took her must be someone from her past," Darian concluded, pausing to look back at the forest they had left behind. "If you can remember anything she ever told you, it could be helpful."

"I'll try," said Selaina.

It had been weighing on her mind ever since she had heard an unknown traveler was searching for her mother. How did this man know her mother? Were his intentions for good or for ill? Was he connected with the stranger in the forest?

Ahead, a golden field of tall stalks of grass shone in the beams of sunlight as they parted the clouds. Out of the corner of her eye, Selaina caught a dark shape against the rows of wheat, but when she turned, there was nothing there. She could have sworn she had seen something, one of the Nadrok watching her.

As they drew closer, Selaina realized the stalks were nearly as tall as she was. She could barely see over them. She reached out to touch one that leaned toward the road. It had a soft leathery feel with a texture of many small creases running up and down the stalk. Wrapped inside the grass covering was a bundle of chaff.

As she slid her hand down the stalk, Selaina became aware of something poking the back of her hand. When she turned it to check, she found a large oblong insect walking across her skin. Selaina brought her hand toward her eyes to get a closer look at it. It had six legs and a triangular shaped head with three red dots on each side of its head for eyes. Of all the insects she had seen in the woods of her home, this was not one of them.

"What is this?" She reached out her hand toward Darian, who jumped when he first saw the bug.

"It looks like a loramantis," he said, eyeing the strange creature.

"Do they bite?" Selaina asked, as she cautiously watched the insect.

"I don't think so," Darian reassured her, watching as the loramantis navigated her fingers. "They're more interested in plants. This field is probably their feast."

"Back home, we had olivaras that wreaked havoc on our wheat," Selaina mused, watching the loramantis scuttle across her hand before it jumped back into the wheat. "Most things have a purpose, but I'll never understand why some creatures are so destructive."

Darian plucked a blade of wheat and rolled it between his fingers. "It's not about good or bad for them," he explained, his gaze following the flight of a bird overhead. "They're part of a bigger cycle. These loramantis feed the birds, who don't eat the wheat, but they get the nutrients they provide from these bugs."

"I guess that makes sense," Selaina conceded, her gaze shifting to follow his. "My friend Jeth would say things like that, about the cycle of life. With the way things have turned out, I can't always see it."

"Perhaps," Darian added softly, "it's about finding balance. Sometimes, what seems harmful at one moment could lead to necessary changes or growth. Life ... it finds a way to push through, to adapt and continue."

Selaina looked at him with a sense of admiration. "It's amazing you can see that, even after ..." she paused, searching for the right words, "even after your own loss."

Darian sighed, a faint smile flickering across his face as he gazed into the distance. "When you're caught in the midst of it, what you see is horrific," he confessed, his voice almost a whisper. "But from a distance, the resilience, the ebb and the flow of nature, the endless striving for balance—I suppose there's a certain beauty to it. It's strangely inspiring."

The trail curved around a small hill toward a crossroads ahead. As they neared the crossroads, a rumbling rose from the direction of the hill. Selaina paused, listening intently. She heard the sound of voices as well.

Darian motioned for Selaina to hide, and they both ducked low in the cover of the tall stalks of wheat. The clatter of people marching grew louder.

"Several people approaching," Darian whispered. "It could be the Iron Flood."

Staying as low as she could, Selaina cautiously peered through the tall grass as the group passed by. The wheat whispered around them, the world above undulating with the breeze. Darian's eyes were hard and alert, scanning the environment, while Selaina's hand trembled. She feared the uncertainty more than anything else.

A sudden voice, clear and commanding, cut through the tension like a blade. "Look there!" exclaimed a woman. "Someone hiding in the grass."

Selaina's breath hitched, her eyes meeting Darian's in a silent exchange of alarm. The reality of their discovery set in, and the rustle of the wheat seemed deafening as they waited for what would come next.

"An ambush, no doubt," declared a stern man's voice, now closer. "Form ranks! Draw swords!" The sound of metal sliding against leather filled the air.

After a moment's hesitation, Selaina pushed herself to her feet, parting the tall wheat with shaking hands. "I apologize. We mean no harm. I mean—I—I mean no harm," she stammered, her voice sounding small in the openness of the plain.

Darian rose beside her, casting a disapproving glance her way.

"Who are you?" demanded the same man who had called for swords. "And what are you doing out here?"

"You're a Lith," observed the woman who had first called out. She eyed Selaina curiously. "How intriguing to encounter you as we journey to Luanthor. Are you headed there as well?"

"I don't think so," Selaina replied, turning to Darian for reassurance. "I haven't heard of many places around here."

The woman's expression shifted to one of confusion. "Oh, I thought all Liths were well aware of your legacy."

"I'm only just beginning to learn," Selaina admitted, a flush of embarrassment coloring her cheeks. "What is this city you're traveling to?"

"It's not a city," the woman clarified, a smile touching her lips, as if she were explaining something to a child. "It's more of a tower, designed to study the heavens. The wandering stars Auronia, Verantis, and Zaryneth are aligning in the convergence. The last time this happened was one hundred and fifty-four years ago. It marks the return of the Wishing Stone. But more than that, thousands of years ago, it was said to give a glimpse of the hidden realm beyond the stars, a vision that signaled the birth of one who would become Zhal Evurah."

"If you believe in that sort of thing," Darian interjected. He sounded skeptical but kept his tone light, as if not wanting to escalate any remaining tension.

"Please, tell me more," Selaina urged. She was intrigued despite the awkwardness of the situation. "There's so much I don't know. What is Zhal Evurah?"

Murmurs rose from the group behind the woman, with a bit of quiet laughter and perhaps judgment, which made Selaina shrink back.

"She's been sheltered from much of the world," Darian explained quickly, his voice sounding protective.

"I understand," the woman responded sympathetically. "Many have lost interest in such matters. You're not alone in your lack of knowledge about the past."

"Before Ethyllion was shattered, it contained all the destinies of mortals," a man chimed in, his voice deep and resonant. "Since the beginning of Galanor, Archeinor had given every living thing a purpose. Though many drifted from the path they were given, some outright defied it, choosing their own instead. This would sometimes lead the world out of balance, leaning toward chaos. It had to be corrected."

"The Zhal Evurah were chosen for destinies of significant importance at a time in which they were most needed to restore the balance," said one of the women with reverence. "The essence of Zhal Evurah is to understand that strength is not in wielding power over others but in mastering it within oneself, much like a river that carves its path—not by force, but by persistence."

"We share so many commonalities," said another woman, "even if our beliefs vary."

"My apologies," said the first woman. "I should have mentioned that."

The second woman continued. "Like many here in the Kingdom of Sybara, some of us believe in the Rhythm of Being. The beating pattern of life through its many cycles, through life and death and all the realms of the unseen. Once you have completed the cycle, you return to life as a new being with greater knowledge and wisdom. What some call Zhal Evurah, we call the Resonant."

"We all consider the tower an important place, we are on a pilgrimage there," another man added, his voice filled with conviction. "In the same way that many in the old days would gather to rejoice that a new Zhal Evurah had been sent by Archeinor to correct the wrongs that would otherwise lead to chaos. Our people have carried that tradition even after the shattering of Ethyllion."

"The Resonant is the same person returning after passing through all the realms of the unseen," said the second woman. "We hold hope that there will be another, even without Ethyllion."

"Well, we haven't seen a Zhal Evurah since Ethyllion was destroyed," said the first woman.

"Society has largely moved further away from the divine paths of Archeinor that were lost," continued one of the women, a melancholic sound in her voice.

"Even some of the Liths no longer practice the old traditions," said an older woman, glancing at Selaina.

Selaina nodded, her gaze sweeping over the group of pilgrims as a breeze rustled through the tall grass around them.

"Yes, it is true," said the woman with a serene smile. "But we still cherish the old ways. In these troubled times, even without Ethyllion, we have hope."

"Hope that Zhal Evurah will find a way to return," said one of the men.

Another man, his hair silvered with age, gestured toward the horizon where the sunshimmer painted the sky in hues of orange and purple. "Luanthor is one of the few remaining structures controlled and maintained by the Liths," he explained, with a note of pride.

An old woman leaning on a walking stick looked up with bright eyes. "I am fortunate that I was able to live to see this convergence in my lifetime," she said, her lips trembling with emotion.

"You would be most welcome to join us on our journey," interjected another woman, stepping forward to offer Selaina a warm, inviting smile. "Luanthor would be a great place to learn where you came from."

Selaina paused, her foot hovering above the soft earth as she considered the offer. "There would be Liths there like me?" she asked, longingly.

"Yes, and I'm sure they would embrace you as one of their own," the woman replied encouragingly.

Emotions welled up achingly within Selaina. After her harsh treatment in Silvaren, the prospect of her own kind welcoming her, away from the disdain she had experienced, felt deeply comforting yet painfully distant.

Selaina took a deep breath. "As much as I would love to go, I must find my mother first," she said. "She's been taken captive."

"That is troubling to hear," the woman responded with genuine concern. "I hope that you are able to find her." Her eyes held Selaina's, offering silent support.

Selaina carefully removed a small painting from her bag and held it out to the woman. "I don't suppose you have seen her during your travels?"

The woman leaned closer, her companions gathering around her, their faces reflecting curiosity and sympathy as they looked at the painting of Selaina's mother.

"I'm sorry, but I have not," the woman said softly. "It has been a while since we last saw one of your kind. It seems the hatred toward them has only grown over the years, I'm sorry to say. I'm sure no one knows that better than you."

"We wish you well in finding your mother," a man in the group added, his voice gentle.

"Good wishes unto you as well," Selaina replied, managing a small smile as she tucked the painting back into her bag.

The pilgrims resumed their march, and Selaina watched them disappear into the distance, a pang of longing tugging at her heart. She waved to the last person in line, then turned to follow Darian.

"I wonder why my mother never told me about any of this," she mused aloud, her gaze sweeping over the rolling hills that bordered the trail. "The stories of our people … why keep them hidden?"

Darian looked over his shoulder, his eyes thoughtful. "Maybe she wanted to protect you or perhaps she hoped to shield you from the weight of history or from false hope."

"You think those pilgrims have false hope?" Selaina asked. "Why do they go to such lengths? What are they holding on to?"

Darian paused as he considered her words, his gaze lost on the horizon. "When people are going through hard times, they tend to cling to anything that will give them hope," he explained, kicking a small stone along the path. "Whether it makes any sense or not, they do it because they want to believe these signs in the stars mean that someone is going to come and save them."

"But if destinies were shattered," Selaina countered, stopping to pluck a wildflower from the roadside and examining its intricate petals, "how can anyone believe in them anymore?"

"They may not truly believe it will change anything," Darian replied as they passed a swarm of tiny insects only visible under a certain angle of sunlight. "But somewhere deep down, they hold on to hope. It may be all they have left to keep them going."

"Surely there's more to our lives than false hope," Selaina insisted, her gaze turning toward the distant mountains, their peaks shrouded in mist. "Why do we need someone with a great destiny to save us? Why can't we all work together to make things better?"

"Even in the legends, a Zhal Evurah was bestowed with immense power," Darian said. "Without such strength, we'd be helpless against—"

Selaina's breath caught in her throat when she detected a subtle movement amid the towering stalks of grass. Swiftly dropping her bag to the ground, she instinctively reached for her bow, fingers tightening around the familiar grip.

"What?" Darian asked, resting a hand on her shoulder.

"There's something out there," Selaina replied. She nocked an arrow and raised her bow, eyes trained on the shifting shadows.

"What is it?" Darian asked, his hand reaching for his crossbow.

"An animal of some kind," Selaina said, scanning the horizon. "I'm not sure."

The dark form vanished momentarily, but Selaina remained vigilant, her senses on high alert. The rustling of grass grew nearer, and she adjusted her aim, ready to confront whatever lurked in the surrounding foliage. Darian's hand eased away from Selaina's shoulder as the creature drew closer, its presence indicated by a deep growl resonating through the field.

"Keep still, Darian," Selaina commanded as she tracked the creature's movements by the faint sounds of its approach.

Selaina fought to steady her breathing, her palms slick with sweat as they clenched around the bow. The creature plowed through the dense stalks and then revealed itself to be a formidable four-legged beast, its sleek black fur bristling like jagged spikes. Its ears, pointed skyward like horns, twitched with alertness, while two menacing fangs jutted from its snarling maw. Muscular legs coiled with potential energy, hinting at its daunting speed—far surpassing their own.

Darian, glancing over his shoulder, retreated a few paces, his voice barely a whisper. "It's bigger than I thought," he murmured, his footsteps cautious on the soft earth.

"Keep still," Selaina urged him, her bow poised and ready. She awaited the perfect moment to unleash her arrow upon their foe.

But in a sudden and unexpected turn, Darian pivoted on his heel and fled. The creature burst forth from the field, hot on his heels. Selaina's heart raced as her target dwindled in the distance, but she didn't hesitate. Drawing back her bowstring, she loosed her arrow with precision, the shaft finding its mark with a satisfying thud. The creature let out a piercing shriek as it tumbled to the ground, but it quickly regained its footing, now fixing its gaze on Selaina with a primal intensity.

With lightning reflexes, Selaina notched another arrow, her muscles tensing as the creature charged toward her. She knew she had only one shot, one chance to halt its advance. Focusing her aim on the creature's center mass, she released the arrow, hoping against hope it would find its mark.

The animal yelped in pain, its movements slowing as it gingerly approached Selaina, the arrow protruding from its chest. With each labored breath, it inched closer, until finally it collapsed onto its side, breaths growing loud and raspy. The tall grass rustled softly while the beast's life ebbed away, a poignant scene of life and death in the wild.

Selaina stood nearby, her bow hanging loosely by her side, emotions churning within her. She couldn't shake the feeling of a strange connection with the dying beast. As memories of her past experiences flooded her mind, she couldn't help but recall the same sense of reverence she had felt when she had once shot an elk alongside Jeth. Yet, this was different—a creature that would have torn her apart in an instant lay dying before her. For a brief moment, Selaina was acutely aware of the fragile thread connecting all living beings, a connection only fully realized in the moments of their arrival and departure from this world.

When the beast took its final breath, Selaina couldn't suppress the twinge of guilt that washed over her. Despite the necessity of her actions, she couldn't shake the weight of responsibility for ending its life. She knelt down beside it, her fingers brushing against its coarse fur.

Darian approached Selaina with a hesitant stride. "I suppose I'm not the best company," he confessed, rubbing his hands together. "You clearly don't need me to protect you." His tone started out weak but gained strength, as if he were repressing wounded pride.

Selaina offered a reassuring smile, rising to her feet. "That's not entirely true," she said, making sure her tone sounded light but sincere. "You handle the crazy people like those in Silvaren and I'll keep the wild animals away."

A soft chuckle escaped Darian's lips, his features relaxing when he looked around the quiet field, the tension easing from his shoulders as he began to breathe at a normal pace again. "Deal," he agreed.

As they resumed their journey, the trail winding through fields of swaying grass and golden wheat, the distant silhouette of towering mountains beckoned them forward. With every step, they ventured deeper into the realm of the unknown, where the rugged peaks and untamed wilderness held the promise of both peril and discovery. And amid it all, Selaina clung to the hope that their path would lead them ever closer to finding her mother.

CHAPTER 17

Layers of fine linens enveloped Rykan in a silken bed, their gentle caress embracing his skin. Sunlight sifted through sheer curtains, casting a warm glow that danced across his eyelids as he hovered on the edge of sleep. In these fleeting moments of semiconsciousness, he envisioned his mother bustling in their old kitchen, the familiar clatter of pots and the rich scent of breakfast weaving through the air. He could almost hear her chiding him for lounging in bed while school duties waited. Yet, the luxury of the bed's embrace tempted him to linger in this sweet laziness a while longer.

A soft conversation drifted through the air, mixing with the scent of fresh linen and morning dew that seeped in through an open window. Someone must have come to visit, Rykan thought dimly, hoping their presence might afford him a few more moments of solitude while his mother attended to the guests.

"Are they dead?" One of the voices suddenly pierced the tranquility.

"No, they're not dead," replied another voice, distinctly masculine with a certain degree of amusement.

The sound of footsteps and the swishing of cloth approached.

"How can you tell?" the first voice asked with a tone of relief.

"The big one over here is snoring." The man chuckled softly, his voice drawing nearer.

Rykan could sense the shift in the air as the man paused by the side of his bed, likely observing him with a keen eye.

The swishing of robes drew closer, setting Rykan's nerves on edge. The murmured words, initially dismissed, now echoed ominously in his mind. What were these visitors discussing? The more he pondered, the less sense it made. A sudden realization jolted him upright—he wasn't in his comfortable bed but rather in a makeshift camp on the plateau of a hill. Rykan's brief escape into the past was interrupted as the pieces began to fall into place. Anxiety prickled at the back of his neck when he realized there were strangers among them in the here and now.

An elderly man in flowing robes navigated around the prone forms of Rykan's companions, with a young woman trailing behind him. Their presence seemed almost spectral in the morning light filtering through the towering trees around the campsite.

"Who are you?" Rykan demanded, his voice intentionally loud, hoping the urgency would rouse his friends.

The two figures halted abruptly, turning to face him with expressions of surprise. As they did, Elysia's eyes fluttered open. Instinctively, she reached for the shiny sword lying beside her, clutching it tightly while she scrambled to her feet.

"Garrick!" she called out. But only his snoring responded.

The elderly man raised his hands, his face creasing into a calm, if cautious, smile. "We mean no harm," he assured, his voice steady yet gentle.

The young woman beside him nodded, leaning on a wooden staff with one hand. She was of the Anvir race, exuding an ethereal quality that seemed almost native to the dense forest. Small, branching antlers adorned her temples, poking through holes in the hood over her head. Each antler was intertwined with strands of beads and shimmering jewels that caught the morning light, casting a soft glow around her face. Her long, tapered ears rose like delicate crescents, holding the trim of the hood behind them and accentuating her distinctive features. Her skin, a pale bluish gray, stood in stark contrast against the rich, dark waves of her hair, which fell around her shoulders like a midnight cascade.

The old man stood still, his robe catching a slight breeze, casting a shadow that flickered over the dew-covered grass. "You didn't choose your camp very wisely," he noted, his voice sharply stirring the morning stillness. "We spotted you from the road."

Kadin, brushing leaves and dirt from his clothes, pushed himself to his feet with a sardonic smirk. "We're not exactly trying to win any honors for our camp here," he retorted. "But thanks for the observation. Very astute of you."

The woman beside the old man chuckled softly, amusement flickering in her eyes. "You were sound asleep when we arrived," she pointed out. "Had we been less friendly, you might have woken up in a far less comfortable situation."

Elysia raised an eyebrow, scanning their attire with a skeptical look. "I don't see any weapons on you," she observed with a touch of challenge.

The woman's smile broadened. "We're mavins," she explained gently, as if revealing a well-kept secret. "We have no need of such things."

"You bear the marks of shackles," the old man observed, his gaze settling pointedly on their wrists. "An unusual choice for accessories, wouldn't you say?"

Kadin glanced down at his wrists, then flashed a rueful grin as he crossed his arms. "Not at all," he quipped. "It's the latest fashion in the dungeons these days—highly exclusive, you know."

"We were held captive by Imperion Vatreus himself," Elysia explained. She brushed a lock of hair back from her face. "We fled during the night. It's been quite an exhausting ordeal."

"The Imperion is nearby?" the woman asked, her eyebrows knitting together in concern as she glanced toward the dense trees surrounding them, like she half-expected Vatreus's forces to emerge. "I'm impressed that you were able to escape."

"He was holding us in Dralomar," Elysia continued, her gaze drifting to the old dirt road that wound its way through the forest. "A mining town about an—"

"I know of Dralomar," the old man interrupted, his expression turning grave while he stroked his beard thoughtfully. "I hadn't realized the Iron Flood had reached so far."

The woman spoke to the old man solemnly, her voice cutting through the quiet. "Their power grows. If we can't find this Lith soon, time will be our greatest enemy."

The statement hung in the air, mingling with the rustling leaves around them.

Garrick leaned forward. "You're searching for a Lith?" he asked.

The woman nodded solemnly. "Have you encountered any on your travels?"

Garrick shook his head as Kadin stroked his chin thoughtfully. "There's a Lithian district in Rosenlend, and I've seen a few in Iravedra."

The old man settled onto the grass nearby, easing his weary bones. "Rosenlend, you say? I don't think she would have ventured that far south."

"Myrradin," the young woman addressed the old man with a respectful tone, but there was a hint of impatience in her voice, "we've searched everywhere you suggested. Isn't it time we consider alternatives?"

Myrradin reached into the folds of his robe and pulled out a small triangular object that swirled with dim light. His fingers caressed the surface, as if to draw strength from its contents.

"We must proceed cautiously, Ysadora," he said quietly, mindful of prying ears. "We need to gather more information on the Iron Flood's movements before we venture into unknown territory. There is one more place I wish to check before we move on to other regions."

Ysadora shifted her weight, leaning heavily on her wooden staff. Her eyes darted toward the thickening shadows that crept around them, a sense of urgency radiating from her posture.

"Caution may no longer serve us," she murmured, her gaze moving to the skies overhead where an arc of sunshimmer could be seen nearly from one horizon to the other.

As Myrradin twirled the magical object between his fingers, its hues shifting subtly, Rykan couldn't contain his curiosity any longer. "What exactly are you talking about?"

"Saving the world," Ysadora answered solemnly, her gaze sweeping across the sprawling fields around them. "Our steps are not merely our own. Each choice carries the weight of countless lives."

Myrradin's expression was somber as he looked out over the grassy landscape. "It's becoming more of a dream than a hope, I'm afraid."

From his spot under the shade of a large tree, Kadin interjected with a skeptical tone, "Saving the world from what, exactly?"

Garrick, who had been mostly listening up to this point, joined the conversation with a firm voice. "From Imperion Vatreus and the Iron Flood."

"And you two plan to defeat the Iron Flood with what? Magic?" Elysia, who was polishing the reflective metal on her shield with her sleeve, added with a touch of sarcasm.

Myrradin, holding the magical object up toward the sunlight, letting its colors refract into small rainbows, responded enigmatically, "There are ways to fight that don't involve swords and arrows."

"Ah, this should be good," Kadin remarked as he leaned back against the tree trunk. "Indulge us, won't you? I've always had a fondness for lunacy and madness."

Elysia shot Kadin a look of mock annoyance. "Ignore him," she said, her tone half-serious. "We're a bit skeptical, as you can imagine."

"What if I were to tell you that I possess knowledge of the Wishing Stone?" Myrradin continued, as he carefully placed the magic object back into his robes. "I know how to use it and the very spot that it appears during the convergence."

"The Wishing Stone?" Rykan's eyes widened, his earlier weariness washed away by a surge of interest. "You're going to use it to wish away the Iron Flood?"

Ysadora adjusted her cloak as she corrected him with a hint of exasperation. "That's not exactly how it works, but essentially … yes."

"If you know where it is," Garrick interjected, squinting under the bright sun, his arms crossed skeptically, "why don't you have it already?"

"It's not something that can be found and taken," Myrradin replied. "We must bring the woman to the Stone."

"You can only use the Stone to return to a space and time where your energy lingers," Ysadora explained with a tone of superiority, tracing a circle in the dirt with her staff. "It must be an event you were present for. It's basic temporal knowledge, really."

"What event are you going to change?" Rykan asked.

"Some years ago, a pact was made," said Myrradin, "a pact that gave Vatreus his power."

"The only person we have been able to identify who was present at that moment is the Lith woman we are looking for," Ysadora added, her tone dripping with certainty. "Her presence at the event is crucial to altering the course of history. Without her, none of this will work."

"You're holding on to the chance that there's some magic Stone that can change something that has already happened?" Garrick asked.

"I don't have to believe," Myrradin declared, his eyes growing intense. "My studies have uncovered volumes of historical records detailing the manifestation of the Stone. Every instance is marked by the extraordinary—wars diverted, disasters forewarned, and the emergence of innovations before their time."

"For those who have wielded the Stone," Kadin mused, looking thoughtfully at the group, "why would they ever surrender such formidable power? Shouldn't someone in history have transformed Galanor into a paradise?"

"Don't fall prey to the illusion that the Stone guarantees bliss," Myrradin cautioned, folding his hands solemnly. "Once an event is altered, its effects will ripple across time, altering destinies in ways unforeseen. Lives that should have been spared may be lost, and fates that should have been sealed may be rewritten. It's a force meant to be invoked only in the direst of circumstances, for to tamper with it is to assume the weight of reshaping history itself."

Ysadora used her cloak to shield herself from a gust of wind. "It can only be used once. Each time it is invoked, it fades away, propelling forward in time. We won't see it again in our lifetime."

Elysia stepped forward, her eyes alight. "I would do anything to see Guvallus restored to its former splendor," she declared earnestly, "to reclaim my parents' rightful standing. Please, tell me how I can aid your cause. I stand by you, ready to act."

Thoughts merged with memories beating through Rykan's mind. If this was true, he could return home and find his mother.

"I as well," Rykan chimed in. "If there is any chance to destroy the Iron Flood, we have to take it."

Garrick, rubbing a grass stain off his tunic, shook his head. "Our best chance against Vatreus is to hide," he muttered, "find some place to live out the rest of our lives in peace."

Ysadora fixed her intense gaze on him as if seeing into his mind. "Is it fear that compels you to hide," she questioned sharply, "or is it shame?"

Garrick's jaw tightened, and he glanced away to stare at the sprawling landscape.

Kadin strolled over to a tree, leaning against its rough bark as he surveyed the group. "As much as I'd love to put an end to the Iron Flood," he began, rubbing his chin thoughtfully, "I don't see much profit in this journey."

Elysia's eyes narrowed slightly at Kadin's comment. "Well, that makes it simpler. Because you're not invited."

Kadin stood upright, a glint of mischief in his eyes. "Even after seeing my talents firsthand? You would still be in chains if it weren't for me. The real question is, do I want to go?" He pulled an aurin coin from his pocket, holding it up for all to see. "If it lands on the Archeinor side, I go with you. If it lands on Pandemora, I leave and go on my own."

"Where did you get a coin?" Elysia asked, her tone a mix of curiosity and suspicion.

"From one of the guards you and Garrick took down," Kadin said as he tossed the coin into the air. It spun and glittered in the fading light before landing near Elysia.

"Pandemora!" she said, crossing her arms. "I guess this is goodbye then."

Kadin picked up the coin, a smirk playing on his lips. "Actually, I think I will go on this excursion."

"But you said—" Elysia started. "What was the point of tossing the coin then?"

"When it landed on Pandemora, I was disappointed," said Kadin with a shrug. "That told me I wanted to go after all."

Elysia shook her head in dismay, a sigh escaping her lips as she turned away.

Rykan stepped closer to Garrick. "Garrick, we need you," he said. "You're one of the best swordsmen I've ever seen. This is your chance to make things right, to fight for something better." Rykan knew how much Garrick regretted his time with the Iron Flood, and this felt like an opportunity for him to find redemption. "For all of us."

Garrick shifted uncomfortably, his eyes narrowing as he scanned the faces of Myrradin and Ysadora. "I don't want to see you get false hope," he replied gruffly, skepticism written all over his face. "I don't believe the Stone exists, but if this can somehow lead to others willing to fight the Iron

Flood, I'm prepared to take the chance." Turning toward the mavins, he added, "And if you two are playing some kind of trick, I will hunt you to the ends of the world." His hand touched the hilt of his sword.

Myrradin, who had been quietly scanning a small map, looked up, meeting Garrick's intense gaze. "None of you were part of our original plan," he admitted, calmly. "But if the Iron Flood's presence has expanded, your added strength might just be what we need to get past them on our way to Virelda."

"Virelda?" Kadin asked. "Have we crossed into the Kingdom of Sybara?"

Ysadora, leaning on her staff, surveyed the sky as if calculating the time. "Yes, you have," she confirmed. "And we need to get moving," she pressed. "If we don't find the Lith in Virelda, I don't know where else we will end up looking next."

"If you need someone found," Kadin boasted, brushing off his clothes, as if to ready himself for a challenge, "I am your man. With my contacts and resources, I could track down even the most elusive of individuals."

Elysia crossed her arms, eyeing Kadin with a raised eyebrow. "Who have you ever needed to track down?" she asked. "I find it hard to believe you've ever helped anyone in need."

Kadin shrugged nonchalantly, scratching the back of his neck as he responded. "Well, there have been instances where people have been more than willing to pay a hefty sum to locate someone indebted to them," he admitted, avoiding direct eye contact.

"I should have expected as much," Elysia retorted dryly. "Are we certain we want this scoundrel tagging along with us?"

Myrradin glanced up from the map, his wise eyes studying Kadin for a moment. "If he truly does have such experience, he may yet prove his worth," he said. "I would give him the chance." He folded the map and tucked it into his robe, signaling it was time to move on.

As Myrradin and Ysadora prepared to resume their journey, they walked toward a white ridgeback tethered to a nearby tree. The ridgeback, unsaddled but laden with packs full of supplies, stood patiently as Ysadora approached. She gently took the reins, murmuring a few soothing words to the animal, and began leading it back toward the road. The clink of the supplies and the soft crunch of leaves underfoot punctuated the quiet as they made their way. Myrradin followed closely behind, adjusting his robe and glancing back to ensure everyone was ready to move on.

Rykan straightened out his tunic but paused as a thought struck him. "What happened to that other man? The one who also escaped with us?"

Kadin, busy tying the laces on his shirt, glanced up and shrugged. "He ran off during the night," he said with a hint of amusement in his voice. "Seems he wasn't too fond of our company."

Garrick, who was methodically checking the sharpness of his blade, gave a short, humorless laugh. "Smart man," he muttered under his breath as he slid the blade back into its sheath.

Elysia gathered her sword and shield. "I'm keeping my eye on you," she said to Kadin.

Kadin watched her go by. "Ah, but where's the fun in being so blatant?" he called back teasingly. "Subtlety, my dear, adds a bit of mystery to the game."

Rykan couldn't suppress a chuckle, his imagination painting a picture of Elysia's probable scowl. It was clear Kadin was exactly the kind of character his mother had warned him about, yet his presence brought an undeniable intrigue to their group.

His gaze shifted to Garrick. With a nod and a faint smile, he strapped on his sword, signaling for Rykan to lead the way. A sense of relief washed over him. With Garrick's participation confirmed, Rykan felt more confident about the path ahead, grateful for the familiar strength by his side.

CHAPTER 18

Selaina cautiously made her way across the creaking wooden bridge, her gaze fixed on the swift-flowing water below. The pungent scent of fish permeated the air, emanating from the buckets beside several men lounging with their legs dangling over the edge of the bridge. Some of them used weathered wooden poles, while others hauled in nets heavy with their catch.

The river snaked around the eastern edge of the city, giving it both an abundant source of water and a natural defense against enemies. Small watercraft lined the riverbanks, and fishermen prepared their vessels for their next excursion. Ridgebacks stood at the outer walls, tied to iron stakes in the ground. As her eyes wandered over the people who seemed to be taking care of the animals, a man wearing a scowl on his face noticed her. He gave her a stern nod as he looked back at her. Selaina diverted her attention to the city ahead.

After entering the city, they navigated through rows of tables that crowded what would have otherwise been a broad path. Merchants hawked furs and leathers, their calls mingling with the sounds of bartering. As Selaina moved deeper into the market, a merchant's sharp call cut through the bustle.

"My lady!" he shouted, drawing her attention.

Her pace slowed, her heart tightening when she met the eager eyes of the man behind the table. The merchant beckoned her over with an outstretched hand, and Selaina's pulse quickened, a knot of apprehension tightening in her stomach.

"My lady, step right over here!" he pleaded. "Exquisite jewels and trinkets await to adorn your beauty." His insistent voice, brimming with eagerness, only heightened her unease.

Rooted to the spot, Selaina felt overwhelmed by his barrage of praise. Her fingers twitched nervously at her sides, her mind racing to identify an escape from the unsettling attention. The necklace he brandished gleamed tantalizingly in the sunlight, but to her, it felt like a heavy chain tethering her to this unfamiliar world of commerce and flattery.

"This necklace was made for you," the merchant insisted, softening his voice to a persuasive whisper. "It would complement your lovely hair perfectly."

Selaina inched closer to Darian, seeking his comfort. He responded by draping an arm around her shoulders, his presence a reassuring weight.

Another vendor's voice cut through the air. "Fine leather goods here! Belts, pouches, and gloves, perfect for traveling!"

"Not good enough for a shiner girl?" A woman sneered as Selaina and Darian passed her stall.

"That's what I've been saying," a man across from her added disdainfully. "They think they're better than the rest of us."

Selaina pulled her hood up over her head, covering her ears and most of her hair. The market felt like a maze, each turn presenting a new barrage of voices. She tried to block out the cacophony, yearning for the tranquility of her forest home. Despite her discomfort, she couldn't help but notice others enjoying the marketplace. Children laughed and played, while adults perused the stalls.

As they walked, delicious aromas of savory meats and freshly baked bread filled the air, stirring the hunger she had ignored until now.

"Will you be well here for a moment?" Darian asked, squeezing her shoulder gently.

"Where are you going?" she inquired, anxiety edging her voice.

"Just over there." Darian pointed to a nearby stall. "I'll be right back."

Selaina watched him move through the crowd, heading to one of the tables. Between the people passing by, she could see him reaching into his pocket and handing some coins to the woman on the other side of the table. When he returned, he held out one of the pieces of meat in his hand, offering it to Selaina.

"What is this?" she asked as she took the meat wrapped in a piece of parchment.

"Roasted sunbird leg," Darian said, smiling. "You must be hungry."

The sunbird leg was golden brown and quite warm, even through the wrapping. Her mouth watered from the smoky aroma mingled with scents from the herbs and spices it contained. She tentatively took a bite. Her taste buds awakened to a burst of flavor she had never experienced before. The tender meat was succulent and juicy, infused with a smoky essence. Each bite revealed a subtle blend of herbs and spices that enhanced the richness of the meat.

They ate as they walked, but Selaina couldn't help but pause on occasion to savor this newfound pleasure. Before she knew it, nothing was left but the bone.

"Looks like you were even hungrier than I was," said Darian as he continued eating.

"Thank you," she said, expressing her gratitude with a smile. "That was the most delicious meat I have ever tasted." She never wanted this flavor to leave her mouth. If only it could endure forever.

"Why don't you have the rest of mine?" he said, offering her the leg.

"No, absolutely not," Selaina insisted. "You need to eat as well."

As they passed through the final stretch of bustling merchant tables, Selaina's awe deepened with each step. The merchant area gave way to an expansive open square, its grandeur unfolding before her. Majestic structures crafted from intricately carved stone encircled the space, their architectural elegance dwarfing anything she had seen before.

In the center of it all was an oval-shaped pool of shimmering water, flanked by four imposing statues. The stone figures, with swords held aloft in commanding poses, guarded the tranquil pool with unwavering vigilance.

Nearby, the vibrant chords of a lute caught her attention, a stark contrast to the simple tunes of Jeth's whistling that had once filled her forest home. The musician, a man with nimble fingers and a deep concentration, drew spirited melodies from his instrument, weaving notes that danced through the air like playful sprites.

Intrigued, Selaina felt herself drawn toward the melody. She navigated through the crowd, moving closer to observe the musician's skilled hands. His fingers shifted with fluid grace, coaxing out a melody that pulsed with the life of the city itself. Around him, a small crowd had begun to gather, their bodies swaying and feet tapping in rhythm with the music.

As she watched, the rhythm of the music enthralled her, creating an island of serenity amid the chaos. For a moment, the cacophony of the market—the clamor of bartering, the random movements of the crowd—faded into a mere backdrop against the music's embrace. Selaina found herself standing at the intersection of two worlds: on one side, the chaotic flow of the merchant tables with their jumbled sounds and haphazard activity, and on the other, the ordered harmony of the dancers, their movements synchronized to the tranquil melodies that cut through the disarray.

The dancers twirled and leaped with infectious joy, their laughter ringing out amid the lively rhythm of the music. It was a new, delightful discovery in a world that was still so unfamiliar and overwhelming. Selaina turned around, her eyes searching for Darian through the crowd. He waved back at her when they made eye contact, smiling.

Amid the dancers, a sense of tranquility enveloped Selaina. The music and movement momentarily lifted the weight of her burdens. She recalled the moment she had touched the blue energy emanating from the cracked rock in the forest, feeling an overwhelming connection to all things—as if her body were merely a vessel confining her spirit.

She closed her eyes as she began to lose herself in the rhythm, when a sudden jostle from behind snapped her back to reality.

A young man, moving hastily through the crowd, bumped into her, causing her hood to slide back and reveal her distinctive white hair and forked ears. He stopped abruptly, his eyes widening as he took in her appearance.

"Sorry, I didn't see you there," he stammered, his gaze lingering on her. "Are you … a Lith?" His voice held a certain curiosity, different from the disdain she was now used to when people said 'Lith' or 'shiner.'

Selaina quickly adjusted her hood, her moment of tranquility shattered by the intrusion. "Yes," she answered cautiously, her guard up as she assessed the stranger. "Why do you ask?"

"This place reminds me of my hometown," the traveler remarked as if he hadn't heard the question. "It's been weeks since I've heard music like this."

As her eyes connected with his, she saw a vision, jumbled with countless images of thoughts. Though difficult to distinguish, she saw a great city, a man and a woman lecturing, fighting, and burning cities. A man killed by the long sword of a masked man with long dark hair. Selaina's brow furrowed in confusion. The young man studied her expectantly, prompting her to respond.

Sensing no escape, she relented. "Are you not from here?"

"I'm from Tathara," the stranger explained. "I was able to escape the Iron Flood before they took over."

Selaina instinctively stepped back, the clamor of the crowd pressing in around her and creating a cacophony that muddled her thoughts. She scanned the sea of faces for Darian, but he had been swallowed by the swarm of strangers. A surge of confusion and unease washed over Selaina, her heart pounding as the young man approached, breaking her focus. She needed to find a swift exit and focus on her primary mission—finding her mother.

"I imagine you're concerned about the Iron Flood reaching this place," the young man said, his voice softening as he edged closer, trying to reengage her attention. "Forgive me for mentioning it."

"It's not that," Selaina replied, her voice laced with a hint of impatience as she took another cautious step away.

She certainly did not have time for distractions. She needed to start asking around about her mother, maybe she would even run into the mysterious old man rumored to be searching for her.

"Understood. Before you go, there's something I must ask," the stranger persisted, his earnest tone slicing through the ambient noise.

"I've been away too long," Selaina said briskly, her anxiety mounting as she turned to weave through the crowd, hoping to lose him in the shuffle.

But the young man was undeterred, trailing after her with determined steps. "I understand that being a Lith doesn't mean you all know each other …"

Selaina's eyes narrowed, her patience fraying at the edges. "I really need to find my mother," she said, her tone clipped, betraying her growing frustration.

The stranger's expression softened, his voice carrying an urgency that halted her in her tracks. "Please, just hear me out for a moment …"

"I'm sorry, she's missing," Selaina interjected sharply. "It's rather urgent that I find her."

"Have you heard of a woman named—" the young man started.

But Selaina cut him off, desperate to end the interaction. "I'm not acquainted with anyone here," she said quickly, eager to move on.

"—Thessalia Saerwolf," the stranger finished, his words catching her off guard.

Selaina's heart skipped a beat, her breath catching in her throat. Thessalia Saerwolf. The name echoed in her mind like a haunting refrain, sending a chill down her spine.

"How do you know that name?" she demanded, her voice thick with suspicion.

"There's a man, a mavin, here that is looking for her," the stranger explained, his eyes earnest. "I take it you know her."

Selaina stepped closer, her expression hardening. "What does he want with her? Who are you?"

"My name is Rykan," he replied, taking a cautious step back from her growing distress. "The Iron Flood will take control of all of Galanor unless we do something. We need her help."

"Someone has taken her," said Selaina. "Do you have any idea who might have done it?"

"Follow me, let me introduce you to him," said Rykan, a promise of answers in his voice.

"Only if my friend can join us," Selaina responded, her tone cautious yet hopeful.

Rykan nodded earnestly. "Of course."

Selaina quickly navigated through the bustling crowd, her eyes sweeping over the sea of heads until she spotted Darian. He stood near a group of street performers, a smile on his face while he watched their antics.

"Darian!" Selaina called out with excitement. "Will you come with me? I may have found someone who knows about my mother!"

"That was fast," Darian remarked with a raised eyebrow. "Weren't you just—"

"There's no time to explain," Selaina said, grabbing his hand with an urgency that surprised even her. "Please, just come!"

Darian allowed himself to be pulled along, seemingly surprised by the sudden shift in her demeanor. As they made their way along the crowded street, dodging vendors and shoppers alike, Selaina led Darian to where Rykan tapped his fingers against his arm as he waited.

CHAPTER 19

s Rykan burst into the bright interior of the tavern, he was immediately enveloped by the flickering glow of an open hearth, its warm, dancing light casting lively shadows across the room. Every corner was alive with plants, their vibrant greenery creating a lush, inviting sanctuary. Vines snaked up the stone walls, and potted plants swayed gently from the ceiling, caught in the currents of moving air. The smooth stone floor grounded the space, enhancing its earthy, welcoming feel.

He quickly turned to check on the Lith girl and her companion, catching a fleeting look of apprehension on her face when she stepped into the bustling, crowded room. The rich aromas of roasted meats and herbs mingled in the air, a sensory feast that almost overwhelmed him. The large stone hearth blazed brightly, its heat drawing patrons close as they chatted and drank.

A few of the patrons scowled at the girl as she passed by, so Rykan leaned closer to her and offered a reassuring smile.

"Don't worry," he said, his voice steady against the layered atmosphere. "These people are friendly." He wasn't entirely sure if that was true, but it felt right to say, and sometimes, confidence was enough to make things true.

Rykan moved between the stone tables, his boots making a soft echo against the floor. The chatter of patrons and the clinking of mugs created a lively backdrop while he searched for Myrradin and Ysadora. He zigzagged through the room with little concern for subtlety, his movements quick and fluid. After walking the length of the tavern, he headed along the tables on the other side, glancing back occasionally with a confident smile. At last, his eyes found the familiar faces of old Myrradin and young Ysadora as they sat chatting between sips of their drinks.

"Already conceding defeat?" Myrradin asked, twirling his magic object between his weathered fingers. His lengthy silver locks cascaded down to meet his equally impressive beard, and the wrinkles etched around his eyes and deeply furrowed lines on his forehead hinted at a lifetime spent accumulating both knowledge and wisdom. "Surely, you couldn't have interrogated every soul in the town square within the span of a single hour."

Rykan cleared his throat, his eyes shifting between Ysadora and Myrradin as the latter drummed his fist on the stone table. He found a spark of enjoyment in being the center of attention, even for a moment.

"I found someone you should speak with," he began, his voice rising above the hum of tavern noises. He paused, realizing in his haste that he had never asked for the girl's name, and turned to her with an apologetic look. He gestured for her to introduce herself.

"Selaina," she said simply, stepping forward, her eyes meeting Ysadora's.

Ysadora scrutinized Selaina, her gaze intense. "She bears a striking resemblance to Thessalia," she commented, her tone analytical. "But this isn't her. Thessalia would be older than the portrait suggests."

"Thessalia is my mother," Selaina responded quickly, her voice tinged with urgency. "How do you know her?"

Both Ysadora and Myrradin froze, their expressions shifting from calm detachment to stunned disbelief. They exchanged a glance, the weight of Selaina's words sinking in.

"We didn't know she had a daughter," Ysadora admitted, her voice softer now, almost apologetic.

Rykan leaned forward, unable to suppress a grin. "You see? I told you I'd find something," he said.

"We must speak with Thessalia. The fate of Galanor depends on it," Myrradin interjected as his right eye twitched slightly.

"I was hoping you might have some idea where she is," Selaina continued, her gaze flickering between the two. "I have been looking everywhere for her."

"You don't know where she is?" Myrradin asked with a sharp tone, the shadows in his brow darkening. The tavern's ambient noise seemed to recede as the gravity of their conversation deepened. "Where did you last see her?"

Rykan gestured toward a pair of empty chairs at the table, which was cluttered with maps and papers. Darian took a seat, while Selaina chose to remain standing.

"She was taken by two men," Selaina disclosed, her voice cracking slightly as she recalled the harrowing memory. "It happened while I was outside our cabin. They … they even killed Jeth."

Myrradin slammed his fist onto the table, causing the candle to flicker wildly. "I knew it! They got to her first!" he exclaimed in frustration. "Our plans are all but ruined now."

"With all of us working together, we will find her," Rykan said confidently, stepping in to offer a solution.

His voice was firm, intending to steer the group away from despair and toward action. Inside, he felt a glimmer of impatience. Why did people always think it was hopeless? There was always a way, even if it meant making it up as you go.

Selaina turned to Ysadora. "How did you know her?" she asked.

Ysadora opened her mouth to speak, her eyes softening as she regarded Selaina. But before she could voice her thoughts, Myrradin interjected.

"We've never met her before," he explained. "All we know is what Ysadora has determined from her portrait."

Selaina's brow furrowed. "What portrait?" she asked, a hint of confusion in her eyes.

Shuffling her hand underneath her robes, Ysadora produced a small, worn sketch. It depicted a young Lith woman in a simple dress, standing beside an ornate chair surrounded by flowers. Her posture was almost unnaturally straight, as though she was leaning back too far.

"I can read energy from objects," said Ysadora softly but with a certain intensity. "Energy marked by strong emotions. When this portrait was created, Thessalia had recently endured a traumatic experience. The energy is clear—she was consumed by thoughts of a great power. A power she both feared and hoped for."

As Ysadora spoke, Rykan noticed Selaina's hand trembling, her eyes fixed on the woman in the sketch. Rykan watched her, empathetic, understanding too well the turmoil of missing a mother. Though he knew where his own mother was, she remained just as unreachable.

The crackling hearth cast a warm glow over the room, its light reflecting off the stone walls and the verdant plants that adorned the tavern, creating an earthy tranquility at odds with the tension of their conversation.

The glow of light played in Selaina's silken hair like whispers of magic. Rykan found his gaze irresistibly drawn back to her, pulled by an unseen force. What was it that made her so captivating? It was more than the symmetrical perfection of her features, more than her smooth, flawless skin. It was elusive, difficult to define. Perhaps it was the spark of life in her eyes, the gentle flush of her cheeks, or the subtle allure of her smile. Gazing at her felt like uncovering the mysteries of the universe, each moment revealing something profoundly beautiful.

Rykan felt a tinge of guilt for being distracted by her appearance while she was going through so much. He tried to keep his focus on her words.

"The timing adds up," Ysadora continued, her eyes on Selaina. "Thessalia was present when Vatreus was bestowed with immense power."

"Vatreus?" Darian interjected sharply. "The Imperion of the Iron Flood?"

"My mother could not have been there," Selaina protested with a bit of emotion in her tone. "Why would she have been with him?"

"He was little more than a child at the time," Myrradin interjected. "She could not have known what he was to become."

"There is no doubt she was there," Ysadora insisted. "I have seen it. The vision was unmistakable." She folded her arms, as if the matter was beyond debate.

"What did you see?" Selaina demanded. "Tell me."

Ysadora exchanged a glance with Myrradin, who gave a subtle nod. The old mavin's eyes were heavy with unspoken knowledge.

"From the emotional energy on the sketch," Ysadora began, her voice lowering as she spoke, "I saw two men, a boy, and a woman standing before an enormous gate in the side of a mountain. The woman was indeed Thessalia Saerwolf."

Rykan nearly choked on his breath, past horrors flashing before his eyes—the image of a terrifying hand emerging from the gate, its grip tightening around the girl. Her screams echoed in his memory, mingled with that unsettling chant he'd heard: *Bleeding veins, pulsing life. Skin to peel, bones to slice.* The memory made him tense, but he shook it off.

"She's the only one we have been able to identify who was present at this event," said Myrradin. "Other than Vatreus himself."

"So what? Even if she was there, how does that help anything?" Selaina asked, her frustration mounting.

"Because only someone who was present can undo it," Myrradin explained, meeting her eyes with a stern intensity.

"If it already happened, how can anyone undo it?" Selaina's voice rose in disbelief.

"The power of the Wishing Stone," interjected Ysadora. She leaned closer to Selaina. "Since Ethyllion was destroyed, the destinies and fates of Galanor are no longer immutable. The purposes of the world can be broken, the balance of nature can be destroyed, and the world can be dominated. But it also means that it can be undone."

Selaina's eyes widened. "Undone? You mean we can change everything that already happened?"

Ysadora nodded with a knowing look. "Exactly. The Wishing Stone holds the power to alter the temporal order of reality itself."

"I've heard of the Wishing Stone," said Selaina as she rubbed her shoulder, her tone reflective. "There was a strange woman in Ravendrith looking for it."

"Yes, there are all manner of beings aware of its arrival." Myrradin nodded slowly. "But very few who know where to find it. We must keep it that way. If it found its way into the wrong hands, we could be even worse off than we are now."

Selaina sat in the chair next to Darian, rummaging through her bag. She extracted a painting of her mother, more detailed and richer in color compared to the sketch.

"Can you read anything from this?" she asked, holding it out toward Ysadora.

Ysadora took the small, framed painting gently, holding it in both hands. She closed her eyes, concentrating deeply.

After a moment, she spoke, "She was happy, but like in the sketch, there was a disturbance in her mind. She felt new hope and relief but also the stain of death and the burden of guilt. This was painted around the same time that the sketch was done."

"We have Selaina right here," Rykan said, turning to Ysadora. "Can you read anything from her?"

"My ability only works on objects, not on people," Ysadora replied, lifting her eyebrows as she extended her hand toward Selaina, silently asking for permission. "But I can try."

Selaina nodded and lifted her hand to Ysadora. "Go ahead."

Ysadora gently cradled Selaina's hand in hers and closed her eyes. After a moment, she shook her head, her expression one of frustration. "Too much information with people, too many memories and thoughts, always changing," she murmured. "I can never make sense of it."

"A glass of ale please," a man shouted as he stomped up to their table. The rickety wooden chairs creaked under his weight as he propped his foot up. "Ah, I see you were able to convince someone else to have a drink with you at least."

"We've gathered more info than you have, Kadin," Ysadora said. "What have your sources discovered so far?"

"Nothing yet, are you sure this shiner woman even exists?" Kadin asked as he slid his chair further.

"Please, don't use that word," Darian interjected with a firm voice as he clasped his hands together.

"What? Shiner?" Kadin raised an eyebrow, puzzled. "I wasn't aware that was offensive."

"Well, now you know," Darian replied curtly, his eyes narrowing.

Rykan felt a knot tighten in his chest. He'd never heard the word used that way before, but he was glad to have learned. The idea of using it unthinkingly made his stomach churn. He made a mental note to watch for it and call it out if he ever heard it again.

"Anyway, I am out of leads for the moment," Kadin continued, shrugging. "We can only hope the others fare better." He leaned over Ysadora's shoulder as she studied the painting. "What kind of flowers are those?"

Ysadora glanced up from the painting, annoyed by the interruption. "In the painting? I don't know. Lunoras, I think. What of it?"

"Yes, shiners seem to be quite fond of those, for some reason," Kadin started.

Rykan glared at Kadin as Darian cleared his throat loudly, as if warning him.

"Liths," Kadin corrected himself hastily. "Liths if you prefer."

"What about my mother?" Selaina cut in. "What can we do about finding her?"

"Getting your mother back would be an impossible task," Myrradin declared. "Our only option is to identify the two men who were present at the event and track them down."

Selaina abruptly stood from her creaking wooden chair, frustration evident in her tense posture. "Do what you will. I'm going to find my mother," she asserted firmly, reaching out to Ysadora, who handed the painting back to her with a sympathetic nod.

Darian rose swiftly and followed her, casting a worried glance back at the group.

Rykan felt a hollow ache inside as he watched them leave. He had believed they were close to a breakthrough, and now it seemed to be slipping away. He refused to let the opportunity fade.

Pushing himself out of his chair, he said, "I'll be right back," and hastened toward the tavern's doorway.

"Selaina!" he called out into the bustling street, his voice barely cutting through the music and commotion of the market.

She paused and turned, allowing Rykan to catch up.

"I'm sorry things didn't work out," he admitted, his words coming slowly as he struggled to find the right ones. "But I'm not giving up, and neither should you."

"What do you mean?" she asked, curiosity and a hint of skepticism in her voice.

"We're so close to finding answers," Rykan said with an earnest tone. "If you leave now, we might lose our only chance to set things right. You're looking for your mother—I promise we'll help you. But we need to do this together."

Selaina searched his eyes, as if looking for sincerity. "You hardly know me," she said softly, her voice laced with doubt. "Why would you risk so much for a stranger?"

"Because I've lost people too," Rykan replied, his voice steady. "And I won't stand by and let someone else go through that alone. Stay with us, and we'll find her. I swear it."

Selaina sighed, a bit of resignation in her expression. "I appreciate that, but it doesn't seem like your friends are as willing to continue the search. I don't have time to convince anyone. I will go alone, if I must. I do hope that you find what you're looking for, Rykan, and that everything works out."

"Thank you," he managed, his voice quieter now, as he watched her give him a final, lingering look before she and Darian disappeared around the corner toward the town square. With a heavy heart, he made his way back to the tavern.

"There he is," Kadin quipped as Rykan sat down. "You were so taken with that Lith girl, we wondered if you'd come back."

Rykan's cheeks flushed with irritation and embarrassment. "What are you talking about?" he retorted, trying to mask his discomfort.

"You were staring at her the whole time," Ysadora teased, her voice mingling with the boisterous laughter and clinking of tankards from nearby tables.

"I was not," Rykan countered defensively. "I was listening."

"You must be an extraordinary listener," said Kadin. "But let me ask you this. Do you usually focus so intensely on the same person even while another is speaking?"

Myrradin and Ysadora chuckled at the exchange.

"Well, she's certainly easier to look at than the rest of you," Rykan said as he eyed the three of them. "Except you, Ysadora, I didn't mean that about you."

Ysadora responded with a reassuring smile. "Love can make one say the darndest things."

Rykan rolled his eyes, his cheeks tinged with red as he glanced away toward the flames coming from the huge hearth. "I'm not in love with her."

"Perhaps you could give her some lunora flowers," Kadin suggested jokingly.

"Why do Liths favor lunora flowers?" Ysadora asked. "Is there something significant about them?"

"They're white with black-tipped petals," Myrradin explained. "In nature, they only bloom in the spring, though some skilled gardeners can cultivate them year-round."

"Do you think their presence in the painting has meaning?" Rykan asked, glancing at the sketch.

Ysadora's brow furrowed as she examined the flowers more closely. "They bloom in spring … a time of renewal."

"Some cultures see them as symbols of vitality and potential," Myrradin added thoughtfully. "Perhaps they were meant to reflect that in the painting."

"Maybe they're something given to people when they're ill?" Rykan suggested, trying to piece together the clues.

"But why would she commission a portrait if she was unwell?" Kadin countered, frowning.

"It must have been a significant moment in her life," Ysadora murmured, deep in thought. "Marriage, perhaps?"

"If it were her wedding, I doubt she'd be depicted alone," Myrradin reasoned, scanning the image.

Kadin's expression shifted as a thought dawned on him. "What if she was pregnant?"

Ysadora's eyes widened. "Motherhood!" she exclaimed, her voice cutting through the room's chatter. "Rykan, hand me that sketch!"

Rykan quickly passed the thick paper to Ysadora. She scrutinized the image, focusing intently. Her eyes suddenly widened further. "Look at her hands—they're resting over her belly. Kadin's right. Thessalia was pregnant when this was drawn." She looked up, realization hitting her. "Which means—"

Myrradin stood abruptly, drawing curious glances from nearby patrons. "Rykan! Find that girl and bring her back here, immediately!"

CHAPTER 20

As the sun dipped toward the horizon, casting long shadows across the ancient cobblestones of the town square, Selaina found herself surrounded by the city walls, which rose like old guardians over its inhabitants. The fading warmth of the day and the cool promise of evening tinged the air. Around her, some of the crowd began drifting away from the bustling shops and vibrant market near the entrance, their voices melding into a harmonious din of daily life winding down.

Surveying the rounded archways that led to the outer streets, Selaina felt dwarfed by the enormity of her quest. The world was much bigger than she had ever imagined. How could she ever hope to find her mother in all this expanse? If what Myrradin said was true, that the Iron Flood held her mother, how would she ever free her?

"Not to break your spirit, Selaina, but I'm not sure what is left to do." Darian rubbed his hands together slowly. "But tell me where we can go next, and I'll take you."

Her eyes darted back toward the archway leading to the tavern they had recently left, the wooden sign creaking gently as a breeze teased its edges. She wished she had an answer for him.

"You are welcome to come with me to Aldenglade," Darian offered, his gaze following a group of children chasing each other around a nearby statue, their laughter lifting the evening air. "Perhaps you can find a new life there, just as I hope to."

Selaina shifted her attention back to him, the fading light

casting his face into silhouette. "You should continue on your journey. I wish I could repay your kindness, but I can't give up on this," she acknowledged, trying to keep her voice steady despite the conflict within. "Something weighs on my heart, giving me pause. I can't shake the feeling. I will find someone out there who knows more."

"Of course," said Darian, nodding toward a small inn with glowing windows that promised warmth and rest. "We should find accommodations for the night regardless."

The sound of rapidly approaching footsteps quickly drew her attention. She turned to find Rykan weaving through the people who still lingered in the square.

"Selaina!" he shouted breathlessly as he caught up to her, drawing a few curious glances from the townspeople. The excitement on his face left her wondering what had changed. Could he have decided to join her? They barely knew each other. The thought seemed unlikely, yet anticipation stirred within her.

"Please come back to the tavern!" Rykan huffed, nearly out of breath when he caught up to Selaina. "We found something crucial!"

Selaina turned, skepticism clear in her expression. "Found what exactly?"

"I don't know all the details," Rykan admitted, wiping the sweat from his forehead. "But it's something that could help us use the Wishing Stone."

Selaina crossed her arms, her eyes narrowing. "Unless it involves finding my mother, I'm not interested."

Rykan's eyes widened with urgency. "If you help us, we could set everything right, and you wouldn't have to find her."

Darian, standing beside Selaina, stepped forward. "Why do you need her help? We don't plan on wasting any more time on this."

"Please," Rykan implored, his voice almost desperate. "Just listen to what Myrradin has to say. They found something new in the sketch of your mother."

Darian rubbed his temples. "It's been a long day. We're both hungry and tired. If we see you again in the morning, perhaps Myrradin can explain then."

Rykan's face fell, but he quickly rallied. "If you just come talk to him,

I'm sure Myrradin would make it worth your time. He'd probably offer you dinner on his coin."

Darian held up a hand to still Rykan. "Excuse us for a moment," he said.

Rykan stood by, shifting nervously as Darian and Selaina stepped aside near the shadow of a nearby building.

"I hate to say no, but this is getting tiresome," Selaina murmured, keeping her voice low.

Darian nodded, his expression softening. "I know. I wanted you to have a chance to decide without feeling pressured. If you don't want to go, I'll tell him."

Selaina placed a hand on Darian's arm, her eyes warm with gratitude. "I appreciate you, Darian. Always watching out for me. But I'll go, if only so you don't have to spend more aurin to feed me."

"Don't worry about that," Darian said, shaking his head. "You saved my life. No amount of aurin can repay that."

Selaina sighed, glancing toward the tavern. "Still, any coin saved would help. Let's go eat and they can talk all they want."

Darian smiled faintly, giving her a reassuring nod. "Let's do it then."

They walked back to Rykan, who looked relieved when they told him their decision.

"Thank you," he said earnestly, leading them back toward the tavern. "I promise, this will be worth your time."

As Selaina, Darian, and Rykan stepped back into the tavern, the evening revelry was beginning to reach its peak. The warmth of the crowded room hit Selaina like a wave, mingling with the cacophony of laughter, chatter, and the clinking of glasses. The scent of ale and the rich, earthy aroma of roasting meat thickened the air.

Navigating through the throng, they made their way past the open hearth, where patrons clamored for the roaster's attention. The lively murmur of conversations filled the space, punctuated by the occasional burst of hearty laughter. In an animated corner, a group of revelers sang with boisterous abandon, their voices weaving through the din of the tavern's other sounds.

Selaina spotted Myrradin, his demeanor noticeably lighter as he finished his ale with a satisfied gulp. Seeing Selaina, Rykan, and Darian, he waved them over with a broad smile.

"Ah, there she is," he called out, his voice cutting through the background noise. "Join us! Can we offer you a drink or perhaps some bread and cheese?" His eyes twinkled invitingly, making it clear that the evening was far from over.

The first time she had seen Myrradin, a fleeting vision of old men in robes gathered in a circle came from his recent thoughts. In another, she saw him sitting on a crystal chair. Attendants carefully trimmed his silver hair and beard while he deliberated with advisers.

"I was told there would be a meal." Selaina pulled out a chair and sat down at the table. "I hope you had more in mind than bread and cheese."

Myrradin glanced at Rykan for a moment before returning his focus to Selaina. "What about some roast sunbird or maybe some pork?" His eyes brightened with what seemed like genuine hospitality.

Without a moment's pause, Selaina responded, "Roast sunbird!" Her mouth watered as she remembered the sunbird leg from the market. She noticed Darian reclaiming the chair he had previously occupied. "For Darian too, please."

"Tell the maid, would you, Rykan?" Myrradin instructed, his eyes shifting to the bustling activity near the hearth.

Rykan nodded and turned toward the hearth. Just as he started off, Kadin rose from his seat.

"I think I will partake as well," he announced. "Make sure it's from the top shelf of the kitchen, Rykan. I'm in the mood to taste what royalty eats—not that the usual swill wouldn't do."

"If you want to eat, it will be on your own coin," Myrradin quickly added with a playful sternness as he turned back to Selaina. "Now, my dear, there's a new matter that has come to our attention." He began twirling a triangular trinket in his hand, an object that captured the bright glow from the hearth. "How old are you now?"

Selaina thought for a moment. She didn't dwell on her age often. When she was a little girl, her mother would remind her of her birthday, but as she grew older, that had all but stopped. The last time she remembered her mother mentioning it, she had been twelve years old. Silently counting the seasons that had passed since then, she came up with a number.

"Seventeen," she replied. "I must be seventeen now."

Myrradin exchanged a knowing glance with Ysadora, his grin widening. "That seems to fit with everything we know," he affirmed. "It seems your mother was pregnant with you at the time she witnessed the transfer of power."

"What does that tell us?" Selaina wondered. "Does it offer some clue to her whereabouts?"

"It tells us that you were there too," Myrradin revealed dramatically, "which means you can use the Wishing Stone to undo Vatreus's power, to reverse the Iron Flood and all the havoc they've wreaked."

Just then, Rykan returned, carefully placing a plate of steaming roast sunbird in front of her—much more than the leg she'd had earlier. The tantalizing aroma reached her nose, and she couldn't wait any longer.

"Are you certain?" she asked, skeptically, picking up a piece of sunbird. "Wouldn't I have to remember this to be able to use it?"

Myrradin shook his head solemnly. "It's a lot to take in, but we believe it's the truth. Your energy was there, and that is all that is required."

Selaina watched the candle flame on the table as she took a small bite. It flickered under the draft from the old, wooden tavern doors, casting wavering shadows across the room.

"Say you'll do it," Rykan said as he rapidly tapped his fingers on the table. "You have to."

"She doesn't have to do anything," said Darian, tearing a piece of bread and dipping it into some gravy.

Selaina set down her fork. "And what would happen if I used the stone?" Selaina asked as she raised her eyes to meet Myrradin's gaze.

"Your mother would never be taken, for there would be no Iron Flood," Myrradin declared with a certainty that filled the room. "You would go on living the same life you had before."

As Selaina considered the possibility of altering her past, a painful throb of hope and duty pulsed through her heart. Maybe Jeth would never be killed. But along with that hope, doubt crept in.

"Wouldn't that change the order of fate itself?" she asked, her voice trembling with uncertainty. She had only recently learned about the realm of order, and this felt like it violated everything she understood. "If what has happened was meant to be, wouldn't reversing it go against the will of Archeinor?" Her gaze shifted to Darian, searching his eyes for reassurance.

Darian, silent until now, met her gaze with a grave expression and nodded slightly, confirming her concerns. "It's a valid fear. Tampering with the order of events could have unforeseen consequences."

Myrradin sighed, his tone soft but resolute. "Destiny was disrupted when Ethyllion fell, not by what we do now. We're merely guiding fate back to its true course."

"And how do we know their intent?" Selaina asked, her brow furrowing in confusion.

"Do you think Vatreus was Archeinor's intent?" Myrradin challenged. "Do you think your mother being taken was their intent? Did the order of the universe depend on any of those?"

"My father was murdered by Vatreus," Rykan interjected, his voice quaking with anger. "And my city is now controlled by the Iron Flood."

Selaina could see the pain in their eyes. They had been through the same or worse tragedies than she. "My heart aches for all of us, for every tragedy we have endured," she said with a heavy tone. "But at least we have something to rebuild, to carry on with the memory of those no longer with us". "I hesitate because I must be certain that pulling at the threads of time will not unravel the very fabric of our existence."

She glanced around the table, reading the array of expressions. Darian wore a grave and pensive look, his eyes shadowed with concern, while Kadin appeared skeptical, his brow furrowed as if he doubted her motivations. Intrigue filled Myrradin's aged face, but a surprising spark of hope lit his eyes, and thoughtful curiosity marked Rykan's youthful features, as if the idea fascinated him. Ysadora raised her eyebrows, but her expression remained unreadable.

"This wouldn't be the first time the Wishing Stone has been used," said Myrradin. "It was left for us by Archeinor. Since we lost Ethyllion, they have provided the Wishing Stone, to give us the ability to undo what has been wronged. To continue order without the stone of destiny."

"What is your decision?" Ysadora asked Selaina, cutting through the tension.

Taking a deep breath, Selaina squared her shoulders, feeling the burden of history, of the future, and of everyone at the table pressing down on her. "I need time to think," she began, her voice steady. "I feel the weight of what you ask. But if there's even a chance that the consequences could be greater than the reward, I have to be sure I am doing the right thing."

"I have researched ancient texts, studied all that is known of Archeinor and the ordering of chaos into Galanor," Myrradin said in little more than a whisper. "I have put more thought into this than you possibly could. I would not advocate this if I were not certain". "Meet us here at sunrise tomorrow morning. We will await your decision."

Myrradin excused himself and left the table, slowly making his way up a stairway at the back of the tavern.

Selaina watched him go, then turned back to the table, her mind swirling with thoughts and uncertainties. She picked at her food, her appetite nearly gone, but she knew she needed the strength for whatever lay ahead.

Ysadora stood from her chair. "There are dormitories for anyone short on coin," she said helpfully, gesturing toward the front door of the tavern to the street.

"How did you two get so wealthy as to afford a room at the inn?" Kadin asked, leaning back and scrutinizing Ysadora.

"We help people," Ysadora replied simply.

Kadin raised an eyebrow, the corner of his mouth twitching. "There's gold in that, is there?" he mused. "I suppose next you'll tell us that alms fill coffers as well as hearts."

☙

The building across the street was a humble, two-story structure made from aged timber and rough-hewn stone. Its design was simple, and it had peeling paint and weathered shutters, giving it an aged appearance. As patrons pushed open the creaky door, a warm, albeit dimly lit, common room greeted them. The scent of burning wood from the fireplace mingled with the faint aroma of ale drifting over from the tavern.

The innkeeper, an elderly woman with a kind but tired face, managed a small counter to the right, offering basic necessities to the lodgers. As Selaina looked around, Darian took care of the payment: a single aurin coin. A few rickety tables and chairs sparsely furnished the common room, with travelers sitting, eating simple meals, and sharing stories from the road around them.

After ascending a narrow, creaking staircase, Selaina reached the heart of the lodging—a large, open dormitory that stretched out beneath a low ceiling. The chamber was a single, expansive room filled with rows of simple wooden beds, each bearing a thin straw mattress and a threadbare woolen blanket. The beds were arranged in crooked lines, with narrow walkways between them, allowing just enough space for guests to shuffle through.

A few flickering oil lamps mounted on the walls dimly lit the room, casting long shadows across the floor. The walls themselves were bare, save for a few hooks where guests could hang their belongings. The atmosphere was quiet and subdued, with the occasional cough or murmur breaking the silence.

Each bed, with its crumpled sheets and lumpy pillows, offended Selaina's love for neatness and symmetry. She moved with hesitance, her eyes scanning for the least disheveled option. Finally settling on a relatively tidy bed near the far end, she carefully placed her bow, quiver, and bag beside it, ensuring each item aligned perfectly with the bed's edge. Not far from her, Darian also chose a spot, lowering his belongings with less concern for precision, a few rows down.

She lay awake on her back as she stared up at the ceiling. The back of her shoulder began to ache with a sharp soreness. Sitting up to inspect it, Selaina felt a large welt in the same spot that had been itching the last few days. At least now it only hurt from contact. She welcomed that over the irritating itch.

Glancing over at Darian, she saw him staring at a small portrait, the painting of his wife, who had passed away. Adjusting her position on her bed, Selaina tried to ignore the quiet conversations around her of distant lands, lost loves, and dreams of the future. She thought back to her secret place in the forest. Selaina remembered the connection she had felt to other souls through the pocket of blue energy on the hill.

Slowly, her eyelids grew heavy, and she drifted into an uneasy sleep.

ഏഏ

Selaina awoke to a soft touch on her hair. Everything was calm and quiet, surreal like a dream. Gentle hands combed through her hair as her thoughts drifted. Her mother had not stroked her hair like this since she was a girl. Selaina realized now how much she missed those moments of affection.

As her thoughts swirled, a deep concern began to well up through the serenity. Her mother was missing. Had she somehow found her? Selaina's eyes fluttered open, her vision blurred and unfocused at first. She blinked rapidly, trying to clear her sight, and slowly the room came into view. A figure sat on the edge of the bed, shrouded in the dim light from the oil lamps that cast eerie shadows across the room. The figure's presence unsettled Selaina, a cold dread settling in her stomach.

She squinted, trying to make out the figure's features, and her heart lurched when the face became clear. It was Elowen. Her eyes gleamed with a strange, almost predatory intensity. The corners of her mouth curled into a chilling smile, the flickering light creating a sinister dance of shadows on her face. Selaina's breath caught in her throat as the realization hit her like a physical blow.

Selaina's immediate reaction was to get up, to shove Elowen away and put as much distance between them as possible. But her body betrayed her—she couldn't move a muscle. Panic surged through her veins, her heart pounding like a war drum. Elowen's fingers continued to run through her hair with an unsettling tenderness, each stroke sending a shiver down Selaina's spine. The feeling of helplessness overwhelmed Selaina, and her mind raced, desperately searching for a way out of this nightmare.

"Sleep well, child of silver snow," Elowen whispered, her voice sending chills down Selaina's back.

With every ounce of effort she could muster, Selaina struggled to break free from the invisible grip that held her to the bed. Her muscles strained, but it was as if iron chains bound her.

Elowen's lips curled into a sinister smile. "You left too soon, my dear," she purred, her voice dripping with malice. "I wasn't quite done with you yet."

Selaina tried to call out. If she could wake someone up, they could get Elowen away from her.

Elowen leaned in closer, her breath warm against Selaina's ear. "Where is the Wishing Stone?" she whispered in a menacing tone.

Struggling with all her might, Selaina heard a ripping sound, like fabric fraying as if she were beginning to break through the spell that bound her.

"Tell me," Elowen demanded in a sinister hiss.

With the sound of a deep sigh, the power holding Selaina in place released, and her scream echoed through the darkened room. The murmur of people chatting in the corner returned to her awareness. Selaina sat up in bed, frantically scanning for any sign of Elowen. Darian rushed over to her.

"What happened?" he asked, eyes wide with concern.

"She was here!" Selaina said, rubbing the deep soreness in her shoulder and noticing the other lodgers now sitting up in their beds, their faces lit by nearby lamps.

"Who?" Darian asked, glancing around at the curious onlookers.

"The woman who imprisoned me," Selaina whispered urgently. "She was sitting right here on my bed."

"I didn't see anyone," Darian said gently. "It was just a dream, a nightmare."

Selaina's eyes darted to the unfamiliar faces surrounding her. She was drenched in a cold sweat, her breaths coming in heavy, ragged gasps. Darian sat beside her, his presence comforting her as she began to breathe more calmly.

"I'm sorry I woke you," Selaina said quietly.

"I had barely closed my eyes," Darian said softly, his eyes searching hers. "Are you well enough to get back to sleep?"

Selaina nodded, though she wasn't sure if she believed it herself.

"I'll be right over there if you need me," Darian said, giving her a reassuring pat on the shoulder before returning to his bed.

As she lay back down, questions tumbled through Selaina's mind like an unstoppable current. Was it just a dream, or had Elowen really been here? How had she found her? What did she want with the Wishing Stone? Selaina felt a gnawing sense of unease—the strange connection she had felt during the encounter was too real, too vivid to simply dismiss. Her mother's warning had always been clear: the outside world, the "wicked world," was dangerous.

She shuddered, the memory of Elowen's predatory smile still fresh. Could it have been more than a nightmare? Was Elowen watching her even now? The thought kept Selaina's eyes wide open, and she was afraid of what might come if she closed them again.

Exhausted, Selaina's mind drifted back to Jeth's teachings. He had spoken of a time when the world wasn't so wicked, when people came together in harmony to provide for one another. She remembered the moments on her secret hill in the forest, sensing glimmers of light amid the darkness. Darian, and perhaps even Rykan, had shown her the spirit of compassion still lived on in some. But her encounters with others, those who wished to harm her, reminded her of the world her mother had tried to protect her from.

Could the Wishing Stone change all of that? What if its power could undo the wickedness that now seemed to dominate the world? Selaina's pulse quickened at the thought. Was it worth risking everything for the chance to mend what had been broken? If she had the power to reshape the world, wouldn't standing idly by be as grave a mistake as misusing the Stone?

These questions weighed heavily on her, keeping sleep at bay. Her mother's warnings echoed in her mind, but the choice before Selaina was now hers alone to make.

CHAPTER 21

I N THE DIM light of a forsaken chamber, the trembling, gnarled hand of a shadowy being clutched a strange orb. Its surface was a turmoil of swirling colors, like a captive tempest sealed within an arcane lattice. Placing the orb against a cold, unyielding stone, the being watched the runes of the metal casing flare to life, casting a sickly glow upon the twisted features of the dark creature.

The orb pulsed violently, a heartbeat of pandemonium. With a sound like the breaking of the world's spine, a rift tore through the face of the monolith, a gaping maw of swirling darkness.

A voice, laden with the depth of ages, resounded through the rift. "Who dares breach the veil?" it asked.

"It is we, Lord Nociferon, your devoted servants, the Sullen," said the creature, its voice trembling as it cradled the glowing orb in unsteady hands. "We seek your guidance to locate any traces of the Stone."

The voice boomed with displeasure. "In the realm of mortals, nothing remains hidden from those who possess the will to seek it out. Redouble your efforts. The fate of our dominion hangs in the balance."

"We have scoured the scrolls of ancient mages, sifted through the ashes of the fallen, yet the Stone eludes us. The whispers of magic lead us in circles," said one of the other creatures, standing just outside the red glow of the rift.

A low, rumbling chuckle, like thunder rolling over barren landscapes, filled the air. "It seems the world clings desperately to its

secrets, its little shard of Archeinor. But fear not, for every lock has its key, every riddle its answer. The time has come for greater intervention."

"We stand ready, my lord. Command us, and the world shall quake at your will," said the creature with the orb.

The voice spread through the rift like a plague. "I offer a few of my ravagons. Seek any who dabble in the rigid magics of Archeinor. The Conclave, in all their so-called wisdom, may hold the key to our conundrum. Drive them from their sanctuaries, into the open, where the veil between realms thins."

"By your will," said one of the creatures.

A dark chuckle echoed through the chamber. "I will shepherd them to the very threshold of your domain. It is there you will corner them, there you will tear from their minds the knowledge we seek—the location of the Wishing Stone."

Several orbs emanated from the portal. As they touched stone, they melted, transforming into beasts of living flame, pulsing with a life of their own, blending hues of red, orange, and black. Their eyes burned with malevolent light, and their jagged, molten teeth gleamed within their gaping maws. As the dark figures commanded them, the burning ravagons dashed through the cave, heading out into the unsuspecting world.

Rykan jolted upright, his breath ragged, skin clammy with a sheen of cold sweat. The haunting images from his dreams clung to his mind like smoke, fading slowly but leaving an uneasy residue. What was the meaning of these nightmares? The other beds, with their tousled blankets and drowsy murmurs, indicated he wasn't the only one yanked early from the realm of dreams. Garrick was already up, stretching his tall frame, casting long, wavering shadows in the gloomy half-light. As Rykan hurriedly dressed, his thoughts entangled in the remnants of his unsettling dream, he barely noticed the dormitory emptying around him. By the time he shook off his reverie, he found himself alone. His companions had already left.

The street outside greeted him with the fresh bite of morning, the sky a pale wash of colors not yet bold enough to claim the day. He spotted Elysia and Garrick emerging from a small shop across the road. Rykan entered the tavern to find Kadin already seated with Myrradin and Ysadora at a table. With fewer patrons, the tavern was much quieter than it had been the night before. Garrick pulled out a chair for Elysia before sitting down himself. Kadin, ever restless, picked at his fingernail with the tip of his dagger. Rykan tried to calm his nerves by breathing slowly and methodically.

"Has she been here yet?" he asked, fearing he had missed what might be his last chance to see Selaina.

"No," said Ysadora, her voice edged with impatience. "We're still waiting."

With a resigned sigh, Myrradin pushed a plate of sausages toward them. "You may as well eat something."

Without further hesitation, Rykan grabbed one of the sausages and bit into it. A peppery blend of spices greeted him as he gulped it down. The savory aroma filled the air as the others began to partake. Just then, the tavern door creaked open, drawing Rykan's attention.

Selaina and Darian walked inside. She saw them seated at the table and made her way over. There was a determination in her eyes that he hadn't noticed yesterday. Her movements portrayed a quiet grace. She strode with purpose, unaware of those around her.

"Good morning," Ysadora greeted them, gesturing toward the remaining sausages. "Please, have some."

Elysia greeted her with a warm smile. "Good awakening."

Darian remained standing as Selaina sat down beside Ysadora.

"As you've probably guessed, this is Selaina," Ysadora said to Elysia and Garrick, tapping Selaina on the back.

Selaina winced, the touch aggravating the welt on her shoulder.

"A blessing to meet you, Selaina," said Elysia, extending a hand. "I'm Elysia."

"Lady Elysia," Garrick said, bowing his head with a grin.

She gave him a light slap on the arm. "It's just Elysia."

Garrick nodded respectfully at Selaina, while Rykan leaned forward, resting his arms on the table. "Good morning, Selaina."

She glanced at him, and for a moment, their eyes met, making his heart race.

Myrradin wasted no time. "Have you made your decision?" His one visible eye, peeking through his unkempt hair, fixed intently on her.

"I will come with you," Selaina declared. "But I want to learn everything you know about the Wishing Stone."

Myrradin sat up straight, brushing the hair from his eyes. "Excellent," he said.

Rykan was overjoyed that Selaina would be coming with them. He couldn't help but applaud. Ysadora soon joined him, and the others exchanged knowing glances as if they'd already known her answer.

"I will protect you on the journey," Rykan declared with conviction. "All the way to the Stone."

"Yes, consider his body your shield against both the sword and the arrow," Kadin interjected with a grin.

Rykan nodded, feeling an uncertain pride. He was certain that Kadin was making fun of him, but he chose to let it slide. His focus was on Selaina and the promise he had made.

"Will I need protection?" Selaina asked, her brow furrowed.

He found himself captivated whenever he heard her voice.

"No more than on any other journey," Myrradin reassured her. "But you are now central to our quest. We must guard you at all times."

"If you would have me, I would like to come as well," said Darian.

Selaina raised an eyebrow. "Darian, are you sure?"

"I wouldn't feel right about leaving you alone with strangers," Darian said, steadying his voice. "Though ending the Iron Flood won't bring back my Bellaria, I believe she would want me to help in any way I can. There's a part of me that clings to the hope that, in helping you, I might find a way to start over, to bring something back that was lost. The dreams of her presence guide me, and maybe, in the end, we'll find a way to set things right—for all of us."

Rykan felt for Darian. Though he didn't know the full story, he recognized the pain in the man's eyes—he knew the agony of losing a loved one all too well. The vision of his father being cut down by Vatreus was still fresh, a wound that hadn't yet begun to heal. Rykan couldn't help but wonder why he hadn't dreamed of his father or sensed him near, as Darian claimed to with Bellaria. Maybe it would come in time, or perhaps, he feared, the connection was lost forever.

"Only Selaina will be aware of going back to that moment when she uses the stone," said Myrradin. "The rest of us will awaken to a new world without the Iron Flood, as if nothing had ever happened."

"That would be perfect," said Rykan, his eyes lighting up with hope.

Selaina leaned against Darian from her chair, her expression softening. "Thank you, Darian. It means a lot to have you with me."

Rykan's gaze lingered on them for a moment too long, a sharp feeling twisting in his chest. He quickly looked away, pretending to adjust the strap of his satchel. He wished he were closer to Selaina, that she might turn to him more often, but he didn't doubt her trust in Darian. Darian had been kind to her, protective even, and Rykan couldn't deny that she seemed to lean on him for support. The thought stuck with him, though, as Rykan longed for the same bond with her.

As they gathered outside the gates, Rykan kept close to Selaina, walking just behind her, trying to catch her eye now and then. Her white hair sparkled in the morning light, with small strands waving wild and free in the gentle breeze. She looked so at peace, standing with Darian. A knot of frustration tightened in Rykan's stomach, though he fought to hide it. He felt protective of her—more than protective—but it was hard to admit, even to himself, that his feelings went beyond just their shared mission.

Being near her made him feel alive, and yet, seeing her so close to Darian sent a bitter undercurrent through that joy. He stayed silent, keeping his distance, wondering if she noticed him at all.

They came alongside Myrradin and Ysadora, who was leading their ridgeback, carrying bags filled with supplies.

Myrradin moved off the path onto the grass and came to a halt. "From this point on, we live off the land. We will stay off the roads. We will avoid towns and villages."

Kadin smirked. "Ah, nothing like roughing it in the wild with good company. Let's hope the wildlife is friendlier than our Iron Flood hosts."

Though he enjoyed the freedom of the wilderness, Rykan was relieved by Garrick's presence. He may not fare as well otherwise.

Kadin tossed his bag on top of the others secured to Ysadora's ridgeback.

"What are you doing?" Ysadora snapped. "Carry your own bag. Frey is at her limit. She doesn't need to carry anything else."

Kadin gave Ysadora a cheeky grin as he lifted his bag back down. "Fine,

fine. I'll carry it. Wouldn't want Frey to think she's doing all the heavy lifting around here."

Ysadora led the ridgeback by the reins as they trekked over the rolling grasslands past rows of hills bathed in the light of the sun. Rykan watched the cascade of grass, rippling like waves in a green sea, as the wind swept over them. Single trees stood tall, watching over the land. In some areas, strange rock formations sat above them on the hills, looking down like silent sentinels.

They moved at a steady pace, their footsteps crunching softly against the earth. The scent of wildflowers and fresh grass filled the air, mingling with the distant chirping of birds. After they passed a glade of blue wildflowers, Rykan noticed something out in the fields in the near distance. Eager to see what it was, he broke away from the group, running toward the object.

"Rykan ..." Myrradin muttered in exasperation as he dashed away.

In the grassy meadow, Rykan found an object made of carved stone. A crudely carved circle of rock, a monument of some kind, sat on a flat base. He ran his fingers over the weathered surface, trying to decipher its purpose.

When he returned to the group, Myrradin's expression was stern. "We must not stray from each other," he said. "There is no way of knowing who might be lurking about. You could lead someone back to the rest of us. If we are fortunate, we will make it to the Wishing Stone without issue."

"Where is it we are going?" Garrick asked, squinting at the horizon. "Where is this Wishing Stone?"

"I dare not utter its location aloud," Myrradin replied, his eyes scanning the surroundings warily. "I will tell you all when the time is right."

Kadin chuckled, shaking his head. "Mysterious as always, Myrradin. You really know how to keep us on our toes."

"You would be wise to understand how cunning some can be when it comes to the chance to obtain power," warned Myrradin. "Mavins have been expelled from the Conclave for trying to gain secrets such as the Wishing Stone's location."

"You mean Gwenna?" Ysadora interjected. "She's not that strong, is she? I don't think she's anything to worry about."

"I would advise you not to underestimate her. She is no doubt searching for the Stone as we speak," said Myrradin, a shadow crossing his face. "If she ever got her hands on it, who knows what dreadful thing she would use it for."

"What is the Conclave?" Rykan asked.

"They govern those of us with magical potential," Ysadora explained, as if reciting from a book. "And they safeguard powerful secrets."

"Like the Wishing Stone?" Selaina pressed.

"Yes." Ysadora nodded, a slight smirk on her lips. "Myrradin is one of the few members of the Conclave who is Sanctified. It's a rare honor, reserved for those who have demonstrated exceptional mastery and wisdom. One day, I expect to be one of them."

Rykan mulled this information over. Powerful secrets? How many secrets were out there?

"You don't know where we are going either?" Garrick asked, looking at Ysadora.

"I do not," Ysadora admitted, though she didn't seem bothered by it. "But I'll find out when you do. The journey is part of the learning process."

"And you trust us all with that knowledge?" Kadin asked, raising an eyebrow.

"Once the wish is made, any knowledge you have gained will be wiped away," said Myrradin. "The Stone will vanish once it is used," he added, his voice grave, "and won't reappear in your lifetime."

Elysia, who had been quietly observing, spoke up. "We won't remember anything at all from this?"

Myrradin looked thoughtful. "There is a chance you may see fragments of it in dreams," he said slowly. "Otherwise, you will not be aware that anything happened. Selaina would be the only one who remembers both timelines. Even then, her mind would gradually adjust, reconciling memories to align with what makes the most sense for the new timeline."

Darian frowned, glancing at Selaina as he rubbed his hands together. "Not sure how to feel about that. How far back will that go?"

"From the point where Vatreus acquired his power," Ysadora replied promptly, her tone sounding a bit condescending. "Anything affected by that is subject to change. It's quite simple, really. His gaining power was a pivotal event, creating ripples through time and altering countless lives. Reversing that means every single one of those ripples might be undone. It's basic temporal theory."

Rykan felt a bit of disappointment wash over him. He had longed to see Vatreus brought to his knees, to feel the satisfying resistance as his sword plunged through armor, piercing his dark heart beneath. Using the Wishing Stone would never give him that satisfaction. But if this was the only way to end Vatreus's reign, to have a chance to see his father and mother again, to see a free Tathara standing proud once more, he would accept it.

"So, everything I do, at least, from this point on, will be undone?" Kadin asked, a sly grin spreading across his face. "Now that's a wild thought."

Elysia shot him a sharp look, her eyes narrowing. "I could use Kadin as a practice dummy without remorse."

Kadin smirked, feigning surprise. "So, you're saying you'd normally feel remorse? I'm touched. But let's not get too emotional—we can't afford to show weakness in the wilderness."

Their shadows shrank and then grew again as they trudged down a hill through a stand of trees. A group of small round furry creatures scurried through the grass away from their path. Ahead was a well-traveled road crossing their path between the hill they were on and another. Myrradin motioned for them to stop as he gingerly made his way down, keeping behind the trees to stay hidden.

Rykan hoped Selaina wouldn't notice how tense he was. He stole another glance at her. Even standing here in the wilderness, her posture and the way she carried herself were elegant. He had to stay strong for her.

As Rykan waited, a sense of dread crept over him like a shadow in the dusk. The rhythmic clatter of approaching ridgebacks grew louder, echoing in his ears with a foreboding rhythm. Myrradin's unexpected gesture of surprise only heightened Rykan's unease.

With wide eyes, Rykan watched as the branches of the trees near Myrradin seemed to come alive, swaying and reaching out as if guided by some unseen force. A cold sweat broke out on Rykan's brow as he struggled to comprehend the unnatural spectacle unfolding before him.

The sight of the black-armored riders of the Iron Flood sent a chill coursing through Rykan's veins. He could feel the weight of their presence like a heavy cloak, suffocating and oppressive. They couldn't afford to be discovered. Not now. As the foot soldiers marched by in disciplined formation, Rykan's heart pounded in his chest, each beat growing louder in his ears.

Throughout it all, Myrradin remained eerily still, hidden amid the foliage as if part of the forest itself. Rykan dared not make a sound, his breath catching in his throat as he prayed for their safety.

Once dust clouds were all that could be seen, Garrick made his way downhill. After their encounter with Vatreus, Rykan worried he would be seen if he moved. Elysia joined Garrick as they made their way onto the road. They both paused for a moment, Elysia squinting toward the distant soldiers before they crossed over into the dense foliage on the other side.

"Who do you think they are off to conquer now?" Elysia wondered quietly.

"Those were outriders," Garrick responded, glancing back to ensure they weren't being followed. "They would only be sent to chart defenses and report back to the vanguard."

"Outriders? There were enough to take a small village," Elysia remarked, her forehead creasing.

Garrick shook his head as he looked toward the dust clouds. "The Iron Flood never invades without at least one Dreadstorm Knight."

Elysia pondered his words for a moment, then nodded and pushed ahead, the leaves crunching under her boots.

As Selaina strode past Rykan, stepping down the incline to the road, he realized he couldn't afford to show any signs of fear. He had to prove he could protect her. Eager to keep up, he jumped ahead, nearly stumbling in the process. A sharp pain shot through his ankle, forcing him to take the descent more cautiously.

He winced as he shifted his weight, the discomfort lingering but manageable. It wasn't the first time he had twisted his ankle, and he knew from experience it would likely ease with a bit of walking. Rykan silently hoped Selaina hadn't noticed his momentary stumble.

The sunshimmer blazed with fiery oranges, pinks, and reds as the sun crept behind the distant horizon, casting long shadows across the rolling grasslands. The air cooled quickly, and the first stars began to twinkle in the deepening twilight.

With a wave of her hand, Ysadora ignited the crystal atop her staff. It shined bright in the darkness, casting a soft, warm glow that illuminated their path.

"What is that?" Selaina asked.

"If you mean the crystal," Ysadora replied, "it's called a sunkeeper. It absorbs the light of the sun during the day so we can use it at night. Ingenious, really. We have to use it sparingly, as it may draw unwanted attention, although I think we are quite safe here."

"I've never seen anything like it," Selaina said, marveling at the crystal's soft, radiant light.

"That doesn't surprise me," Ysadora replied. "It's all in how you cut the crystal. It requires very precise magical imbuing as well. Myrradin taught me, of course, but it's not something just anyone can master. It takes a special kind of understanding."

As they continued walking, Myrradin found a campsite on top of one of the hills, nestled beneath a cluster of trees. The spot offered a panoramic view of the landscape, with the last light of day painting the sky in a riot of colors.

"Here will do," Myrradin announced, setting down his pack. "We'll be sheltered by the trees and have a good vantage point."

Elysia and Ysadora immediately began gathering wood and dried grass to build a fire. Selaina watched them for a moment, then joined in, collecting twigs and branches from the forest floor.

Garrick walked over to Darian, eyeing the crossbow slung over his shoulder. "Unless you're an expert with that crossbow, you mind if I borrow it?"

"I'm far from an expert," Darian said as he removed it from his back and handed it to Garrick.

Selaina took her bow from her shoulder. "I can hunt too."

"I don't doubt that you can," said Garrick, as Darian handed him his quiver. "But only one of us needs to go. Why don't you rest until I get back?"

"Rest?" Selaina asked with a hint of defiance. "I want to contribute."

"You are everything to this journey, our reason for being here," said Garrick as he made his way down the hill into the twilight. "How much more do you need to contribute?"

Selaina watched him go, her expression telling of her frustration. Rykan sympathized. She wanted a chance to prove herself, just as he did. Deciding to keep himself busy, Rykan joined Elysia and Ysadora as they gathered wood for the fire. He bent to pick up a few substantial logs, feeling the rough bark against his palms. He tested the weight of each before adding it to the pile they were assembling near Myrradin.

Soon, they had a fire going. Ysadora held Myrradin's arm, giving him support as he lowered himself to the ground to sit near the fire. Elysia and Selaina settled close by him. Myrradin took a drink from a flask and passed it to Ysadora, who took a quick gulp before handing it to Elysia.

Elysia eyed her suspiciously.

Ysadora remarked, "It's only water," she assured with a knowing smile. "If you want anything more potent, you'll have to ask Myrradin."

Rykan made his way over to stand near the fire, adding more wood and stoking the flames to ensure they burned brightly. Once the fire was roaring, Rykan moved around the perimeter of their campsite, his eyes scanning the shadows between the trees.

He eased closer to Selaina, leaning one way and then the other. Wanting to sit next to her but without letting everyone know it, he meandered around until he found a place to sit. Making sure it wasn't too close to her, he slowly lowered himself onto the grass, scooting a bit further away for good measure.

He wished he had the courage to sit beside her openly, but the fear of making things awkward held him back.

"The enemy extends its reach ever broader," Myrradin intoned, staring into the fire. "Our path demands not just courage, but the utmost prudence."

Rykan couldn't shake the feeling of dread that had settled over him since seeing the Iron Flood soldiers. "What do you think they're up to?" Rykan asked, breaking the contemplative silence. "Those soldiers marching on the road."

"To conquer more land, no doubt," said Elysia.

"But why?" Selaina asked, frowning. "Why spend all this time and effort to take control of more and more land?"

Myrradin sighed, his gaze distant. "Power, greed, fear. These are the forces that drive men to such lengths. The Iron Flood seeks dominion, to shape the world in their image, regardless of the cost."

Rykan felt a chill run down his spine at Myrradin's words. The idea of a world shaped by Vatreus terrified him. He drew the sword he had taken from the fallen Iron Flood guard. Inspecting the hilt, Rykan was surprised at how simple its design was. Though it was well made, it didn't have the fancy carvings of many others he had seen had.

Kadin, flashing his characteristic grin, added, "Or perhaps he sees himself as the great healer of the realm's ills, though it seems his method involves more of the leech than the balm."

"He's deranged," said Elysia sharply. "His intentions aren't rooted in any desire to heal."

"Well," Kadin drawled, leaning back with exaggerated contemplation, "considering that our realms squabble over a blade of grass like it's sacred ground, one might ponder if he's not so misguided in believing the world tilts on the edge of reason."

"So, this bloodshed is supposed to bring unity?" Elysia countered, unamused. "What good is unity under tyranny?"

"You almost sound like you're rooting for him," Rykan remarked, eyeing Kadin with a hint of suspicion.

"Far from it," Kadin replied with a dismissive wave. "I'm only turning the question over, as posed. Besides, fewer distinctions between realms mean fewer opportunities for profit, and where's the fun in that?"

"Every conqueror harbors their own justifications," Myrradin reflected, still watching the dancing flames. "They are but dreamers, toeing the edge of ideals, not yet brought to kneel by the stern hand of reality."

Rykan thought about Myrradin's words for a moment, imagining a boy with grand ideas of making the world a better place, ridding it of its ills, only to become its worst enemy. A rustle in the grass nearby caused Rykan's reflexes to jump.

"Who's hungry?" said Garrick as he emerged from the shadows, carrying four of the furry round creatures they had seen earlier.

Selaina stood, brushing off her hands. "I'll help prepare them."

Garrick handed two of the dead critters to Selaina, keeping the other two. She took a knife from her bag and set one of the animals on a nearby log. Rykan watched with awe and dismay as Selaina expertly butchered and skinned the animals, preparing them for the meal to come.

Under Myrradin's instruction, Rykan untied the sacks from the ridgeback, retrieving a box filled with cooking utensils, pots, skillets, and stirring spoons, among other items. He set them out methodically, creating a makeshift kitchen in the wilderness. From another box, he took out bottles of various spices and herbs, their aromatic scents promising a flavorful feast.

Once the fire was ready, Myrradin handed Rykan a metal grate from a bag on the ridgeback's saddle. He worked with it until he figured out how to unfold its legs and stand it over the flames, creating a perfect platform for cooking. Garrick took some of the spices and covered the meat with them.

"Where did you get all this stuff?" he asked.

"He collects it," Ysadora replied with a faint smirk. "You'd be surprised at some of the gifts he's managed to procure."

The prepared meat was placed on the grate, the sizzling sound and savory aroma quickly filling the air as the fire danced beneath. When the meat was done, Ysadora passed out Myrradin's plates. The food tasted far better than expected for some small animals prepared in the wild.

"I have to hand it to you, Myrradin," said Kadin as he chewed the meat. "You know how to travel. Why go to a tavern when you bring the tastes of the finest taverns with you?"

After finishing the meal, Rykan helped Ysadora unload the remaining equipment from Frey. They spread it out on the ground, revealing a large, intricately designed tent. Carefully, they began assembling it, driving sturdy stakes into the ground and raising the central pole. Rykan held one corner to keep it straightened out as they secured the lines and adjusted the fabric to ensure it was taut and stable.

The tent gradually took shape, its walls standing tall and firm against the wind. Once it was complete, its spacious interior promising a comfortable refuge from the wilderness, Ysadora and Rykan carried in two thick bedrolls, along with fluffy pillows and high-quality quilts, arranging them neatly inside.

Kadin raised an eyebrow, watching the process unfold. "What is this, a portable palace?" he asked, incredulous. "This is what Frey's been lugging around? No wonder we have to carry our own bags. She's been hauling the royal suite!"

CHAPTER 22

As THE SHADOWS deepened across the land, so did Selaina's sense of isolation. Hearing Garrick, Elysia, and Kadin's stories about their travels and adventures only distanced her further. Selaina listened, feeling as though her own experiences of the quiet of her forest home paled into insignificance. Their world seemed vast, vibrant, and thrilling, while hers was confined to the familiarity of trees and hidden paths. Feeling more like an outsider with each story, she quietly moved away from the warmth of the fire. Her thoughts meandered like the brook in the forest she called home. She wondered where in this enormous world her mother could be right now. Was she safe? Selaina hoped she was on the right course to finding the Wishing Stone and that it truly could undo the mistakes of the past and the other hardships her mother had endured.

Out of the corner of her eye, Selaina noticed Ysadora sitting a distance away from the group, her pale bluish skin almost glowing under the soft lamplight. The mavin was absorbed in a book, the small hornlike antlers on her head catching shadows and light in turn. Selaina wondered if Ysadora felt as much like an outsider in this group as she did.

Selaina approached quietly, mindful not to startle Ysadora. As she focused on her book, the strands of jewels intricately woven between her horns shimmered with each turn of the page. Ysadora raised her head when she noticed her watching, her black hair framing her face elegantly.

"Is something wrong?" she asked, marking her place with her finger.

"What are you reading?" Selaina asked as she stepped closer.

Ysadora seemed a little perturbed, her eyes moving back to the book as she turned another page. "It's a book of magic."

"There are books about magic?" Selaina asked with a spark of interest.

"There are books about everything," Ysadora said, keeping her eyes on the pages. She adjusted her position as if inviting Selaina to sit beside her.

"I never learned to read," Selaina admitted, sitting down carefully on the rocky ground. "My friend, Jeth, taught me a little, but my mother didn't think it was important, with all the other duties of the forest."

Ysadora looked up again, incredulous. "Not important? You didn't have any books at all?"

"Only one that Jeth had," said Selaina. "I have it with me, maybe you could tell me what it says."

"Perhaps another time," said Ysadora, softly. Her interest in the conversation seemed to be waning as she tapped her book's cover with a slender finger adorned with a silver ring. "I have to study."

"Anyone who can read that book can learn to do magic?" Selaina asked.

"Not anyone," said Ysadora. "You need an aptitude for magic first, which few possess. Then it takes a lot of study and practice."

"Is that how you became a mavin?" Selaina asked.

Ysadora closed the book with a soft thud, her eyes bright, as if she had waited a long time for someone to ask this question. "I showed an aptitude when I was at the orphanage. Myrradin found me and became my mentor. He showed me what it takes to be a great mavin, how to practice, how to study. You have to demonstrate your skill to the Conclave to advance."

"That's how you learned how to discern things from objects?" Selaina asked, leaning closer to get a glimpse of the leather-bound cover of the book.

"I could always do that," Ysadora said with a look of pride. "That's how they knew I had the aptitude, but I have learned to hone it."

"I have visions like that at times," Selaina shared, a hesitant confession. "I saw my mother get taken when I touched the place where she held on to the table."

"You? You think you have an aptitude?" asked Ysadora as her eyebrow raised, a hint of professional interest crossing her face. "Are you certain it's not just your own memory?"

"It's definitely not my memory," Selaina insisted. "Sometimes I see people's thoughts in their eyes, but a few times, I have seen something more. It doesn't happen much though."

"Everything that has happened or will happen has already existed," Ysadora mused, her voice taking on a lecturing tone as she grew excited by the topic. "Before this world, before everything, there was a single thought containing all possibilities. When it was unraveled, the ordering of time was created. It is the only way we can experience the Azsh Rozaht."

"The what?" Selaina asked, struggling with the unfamiliar term.

"The Azsh Rozaht is the all-encompassing thought," said Ysadora. She seemed to relish having someone interested enough to share her knowledge with. "Without the framework of time, we could not exist to experience it. All events were once a single moment, so they still have a connection. Everything we interact with leaves traces of energy, like a memory. When our emotions are strong, the energy left behind is powerful enough to sense."

"So I'm sensing energy?" Selaina asked, trying to grasp the concept.

"Correct," Ysadora affirmed, nodding. "Since it has only happened a few times, it may need to be particularly strong for you to sense it."

"What about seeing people's thoughts?" Selaina asked.

"I don't know," Ysadora admitted, her confidence fading. "Perhaps you are simply speculating what others are thinking."

"But they are true," argued Selaina.

"What am I thinking now then?" Ysadora challenged, a playful smirk on her face.

Selaina brushed a lock of hair behind her ear. "It doesn't work like that," she said. "It only happens when I first see someone. I get a quick image of their most recent thoughts. When I first saw you, I saw a place on a hill with a view of the surrounding countryside. It was filled with books. I saw Myrradin scolding you, and there was a woman who wore some type of hat I've never seen. She handed you a blanket."

Ysadora's eye became distant, as if she were embroiled in deep thought. "That doesn't prove anything," she said as her eyes regained their focus.

For a moment, Selaina wasn't sure what to say next. She could walk away, but that seemed even more awkward. "What kind of magic can Myrradin do?" Selaina asked, changing the subject.

Ysadora rubbed her nose, clearing her throat before she spoke. "Myrradin is a master of the Interflux, the energies between. He can create a binding force around objects or living things called the Aedavaris. It's quite impressive." Her eyes beamed with a certain pride. "I, on the other hand, am learning Ardrial, sensing creative energies to harness and direct. I can do a lot more than read objects. I can use the ordered energy inside smaller organic compounds to create a reaction."

"What does that mean?" Selaina asked, her eyebrows coming together.

"It means that I can shape some rock and stone," explained Ysadora, using her hands to illustrate. "I can direct plants and vines against our enemies."

"Really?" Selaina asked with some measure of disbelief. "Can you show me?"

"It's forbidden to use magic without a purpose," said Ysadora, glancing toward Myrradin as she lowered her voice. "Myrradin would not be happy if he noticed. Perhaps there will be a use for it before this journey is over."

"Of course, I didn't mean to ask you to do something you aren't supposed to," Selaina said quickly, her cheeks warming slightly.

"It's fine," said Ysadora, reassuring her with a gentle smile before opening her book. "But I'd better get back to my studies."

৵৽

As dawn broke over the horizon, casting a soft, golden light on the awakening world, Selaina was already in motion. She meticulously packed her bag with the essentials for the day's journey, slung her bow over her shoulder, and secured her quiver filled with arrows. With a sense of urgency, she hastened her steps, her boots lightly crunching over the dew-laden grass.

The cool morning air brushed against her face as she navigated through the early stirrings of the forest, the chorus of birdsong accompanying her solitary trek. Selaina's keen eyes scanned the path ahead. For a moment, she saw something silhouetted against the light, a single Nadrok standing just outside of her vision, but once she turned to look at it, the thing was gone. Some of the others had already gotten a head start, making their way down the hill to fill their canisters with water from a pond.

Up ahead, Darian's figure emerged from the morning mist, a lone silhouette against the brightening sky. As Selaina closed the distance between them, Darian turned, alerted by the soft cadence of her approach. Their eyes met, and for a fleeting moment, the corners of Darian's lips curled into a semblance of a smile—one that didn't quite reach his eyes, hinting at something amiss.

"You weren't going to wait for me?" Selaina quipped, a playful lilt in her voice.

"Just needed to stretch my legs," Darian replied, his voice slightly more formal than necessary. He rolled his shoulders in a manner that seemed overly deliberate, as if he was consciously trying to appear at ease. "I had a hard time sleeping in the grass. What's your secret?"

"It's comfortable out here. I love it," she said, her eyes gleaming. "You'll get used to it soon enough."

Darian nodded slowly, almost reluctantly. He shifted his weight from one foot to the other, his movements slightly jerky. "Maybe," he said, his voice lacking its usual warmth.

"I hope you don't regret coming on this journey," Selaina said, trying to gauge his mood.

Darian shook his head, his movements stiff. "Not at all," he said. "Like you said, I'm sure I'll get used to it."

A rustle in the grass made them pivot where they stood. Rykan, Elysia, Myrradin, and Garrick strode toward them, their figures taking shape through the morning mist.

"Ah, there she is. This one knows how to live off the land," said Garrick, pointing to Selaina. "If you're as good with that bow as you are at skinning those tuffels, we won't need a stone to defeat the Iron Flood."

Selaina couldn't suppress the grin on her face. "Thank you, I've had years of practice."

"Really? Is that common for your people, to live off the land?" Rykan asked.

"I don't know what's common for my people," she replied, a touch of sadness in her tone. "I lived in the forest all my life. I was taught to help my mother and my friend, Jeth. For as long as I can remember, I've helped them maintain the house, take care of the animals, and prepare food."

Ysadora secured the bags carried by the ridgeback and untied it from one of the trees. Selaina gathered her bag and bow, readying for a new day's journey.

Kadin, leaning against a nearby tree with a smirk, added, "Too much work for my taste. Honestly, I would've bolted as soon as I could toddle. Give me the bustling cities any day—where the clever thrive and you can always find someone eager to do the heavy lifting for the right price."

"I'm not fond of cities," Selaina said, undeterred by Kadin's remark. "They are crowded and chaotic, a maze of brick and stone with no soul. The forest where I lived was beautiful, full of life and spirit. Every creature has its purpose, every routine a rhythm. Where decay is found, new growth follows."

"You would like my city," Rykan said with a hopeful smile. "We have big celebrations where almost everyone comes together to dance, sing, and share stories. It's a place where new friendships are made, and even some Liths live there, like you." His expression darkened, and his smile faded. "At least, it was like that before Vatreus came."

"That does sound inviting," said Selaina. "But I still prefer the forest. You should see it someday. There's a place where the sun filters through the trees in golden rays near the end of the day. You can sit by the brook, listening to the water as it flows over smooth stones, all in the cool, peaceful shade."

She paused, as she contemplated further. "There's something profound about being alone in the woods, with just your thoughts and the sounds of nature. It's like being connected to something greater than yourself, something beyond reasoning. It's a feeling of deep peace and purpose, as if the whole world is in harmony and you're a part of that divine balance."

"Sounds like something a Lith would say." Kadin pushed off the tree, joining the group as Myrradin and Ysadora started off. "They would see a sunrise and call it a sign of their divinity."

"Maybe you should spend more time in the forest," Selaina said softly. "You might find more than you expect."

"If you ever find a tree that grows gold coins, I'll take you up on that," said Kadin with a wink.

"You must have been raised by nobles, with the way you obsess over gold," Ysadora remarked, a hint of sarcasm in her voice.

"Quite the opposite," Kadin retorted, his tone growing serious. "When you're left alone in the world with a niece and nephew to care for, gold is all you think about. If you have to beg, cheat, lie, or steal—all that matters is having enough coins to feed them."

"I'm sorry, Kadin. I didn't know. It must have been hard for you," Selaina said. "But lying and stealing are the tools of a wicked world. If you had been in the forest, it would have provided everything you needed. Nature takes care of its own."

"Yes, if only the forest bowed to my every whim like it does for the Liths," Kadin retorted with a bitter edge. "You don't know what the world is really like. You do whatever it takes to survive. Everyone is born into different circumstances, and not everyone's surroundings are as kind and forgiving as your forest. Don't presume you would never lie and steal when the situation demanded it."

Selaina continued walking, biting back the impulse to declare she would never stoop to such actions. Memories surfaced of the times she had crossed the brook against her mother's wishes and lied to cover her tracks. The truth was more complicated than she cared to admit.

As if reading her thoughts, Elysia's voice was warm with sincerity. "The world is more complicated than any of us realize. I spent most of my life with my family in Guvallus, knowing nothing of the world beyond until I traveled to other cities. People's experiences shape them in ways we can't always see. When you see where and how they live, you begin to under-stand why they think and act the way they do. That is the journey you are just beginning."

Elysia cast a sidelong glance at Kadin and added with a sigh, "Aside from that, you might find it best to tune Kadin out. Honestly, I sometimes question why we even allowed him to tag along." There was a hint of jest in her voice, but Selaina couldn't tell for sure.

Kadin, unfazed, retorted with a smirk, "Such ingratitude. Without me, you'd be relegated to scrubbing floors on your hands and knees in Dralomar."

"It wasn't out of the kindness in your heart," Elysia countered, her tone edged with skepticism. "You needed us."

Kadin's response was swift, "Ah, but mutual need, now that's the foundation of a truly reliable friendship, wouldn't you agree? No one is wholly virtuous. If purity is your requirement, then trust is impossible."

"There are a lot of good people," said Rykan. "Look at Selaina. She stopped looking for her mother to come help right the world. She is selfless."

Selaina's cheeks warmed with embarrassment. She wished Rykan had not said that, especially knowing that Kadin would have something to say about it.

Kadin flipped his coin in the air, catching it on its way down. "Selfless, you say? Let's not forget, her involvement is tied to the hope of reuniting with her mother. That aligns more with mutual benefit, which, frankly, sits better with me. It's the reliance on mutual need that I find trustworthy. Tell me, when have your actions been solely altruistic, without any gain for yourself?"

"I'm here to help save the world from Vatreus," Rykan retorted. "Isn't that what we're all here for?"

"And what does 'the world' mean to you?" Kadin prodded, his tone teasing yet pointed.

"My city, Tathara," Rykan admitted. "My family, my friends."

"There you have it," Kadin said with a knowing look. "You're driven by your ties to them. It's natural, but let's not dress it up."

"And what about you, Kadin? What drives you?" Rykan challenged.

Kadin shrugged nonchalantly. "Each to their own, Rykan. You fight for your Tathara. I look out for my own interests. We're all heroes in our own tales, after all."

"We should reach Harunel River by the end of the day," interrupted Myrradin. "From there, it will only be a few more days if everything goes as planned."

"The sooner the better," said Garrick as he stared ahead.

They arrived at a patch of barren land, the rocky outcroppings jutting out of the hard, cracked earth. Though trees covered the horizon ahead, the ground beneath their feet seemed lifeless and desolate, a stark contrast to the lush hills and forests they had trekked through before.

"Do you hear something?" Rykan asked, his eyes scanning the horizon.

Garrick paused, tilting his head to listen. "Nothing unusual."

"Nothing," Elysia echoed. "What does it sound like?"

"Screeching, screaming," Rykan replied, uncertainty in his voice. "I'm not sure."

Selaina felt a chill despite the heat. Her instincts prickled with a sense of impending danger, making her grip her bow tighter.

Myrradin came to a halt, his eyes narrowing as he focused. "He's right. There's something coming."

Suddenly, a high-pitched squeal roared toward them. A fiery creature burst into view, snaring Myrradin as a trail of red zoomed by. Garrick and Elysia drew their swords, prompting Selaina to ready her bow. As the creature dragged Myrradin across the plain, he managed to conjure a white energy shield around himself. The nearly invisible barrier flared up, repelling the creature with a violent force. Myrradin was thrown backward, tumbling over the dusty ground as Selaina and Ysadora rushed to check on him.

The sight of the creature filled Selaina with awe and dread. It was nearly the size of a ridgeback, composed entirely of red, orange, and black flames. Massive white-hot horns curved menacingly from its head, and it stood on limbs that ended in blazing claws.

How do you fight something made of fire? Selaina's mind raced for a solution.

Myrradin quickly transferred the shield from himself to the beast, trapping it within the magic barrier. Ysadora helped Myrradin to his feet as a second creature, equally fierce, dashed toward him. With a swift movement, Myrradin shifted the shield to ensnare the second creature, but in doing so, he released the first one.

Ysadora pointed her staff, causing rock to rise from the ground and encase the flaming beast. Garrick and Elysia moved in to protect Myrradin as the first beast broke free of Ysadora's rock impediment. It attacked Myrradin, and Garrick slashed at it with his sword, but the burning flames forced his hand away before the blade could fully penetrate its molten form.

Selaina's heart pounded in her chest. What chance did they have against creatures like these?

Elysia raised her metal shield, protecting herself and Myrradin from its fiery assaults. The flaming beast crashed into the shield, heat pouring off it. Myrradin cast his magic barrier from the other creature to Elysia's sword, engulfing it in white energy. Elysia bashed against the beast with her shield, then somersaulted forward, slicing through the creature with her enchanted weapon. The flaming beast crackled as it withered and exploded into a black cloud of smoke.

Selaina released an arrow at the remaining creature. It struck the burning beast but quickly ignited from the flames. Her frustration grew.

Garrick circled, trying to draw its attention, while the flaming creature stalked Myrradin and Elysia. Elysia swung at the beast, but it dodged her blows, seemingly waiting for the right moment to strike.

Garrick kicked dirt at the creature, causing its flames to sizzle and flicker. It turned, eyeing Garrick menacingly. Backing up on its haunches, it charged at Garrick, just as Elysia cut through it with her shielded sword. The fire beast flamed out, leaving nothing but ash on the ground.

Myrradin brushed himself off, his breathing heavy. "Ravagons," he said. "Abominable creations of Pandemora. The veil between realms has weakened."

Rykan's eyes widened in recognition. "I've seen creatures like this," he said. "In a dream. Summoned by dark beings in search of the Conclave."

Myrradin's face tightened with surprise. "When did this dream occur?"

"The night before we set out," said Rykan.

"We must not tarry," Myrradin said, his voice urgent. "Someone knows we are here."

Garrick sheathed his sword, glancing around warily. "Agreed. Let's move before more of them appear."

Ysadora nodded, her grip firm on her staff. "Stay close. We don't know what else might be lurking," she added, her eyes scanning the shadows.

Selaina attempted to retrieve her arrow, finding mostly ashes in the sand. Her mind raced with the realization of the danger they'd faced. She looked at Myrradin, who gave her a reassuring nod, and they continued their journey across the barren land, the oppressive heat bearing down on them as they moved forward, more guarded than before while they looked for the next threat.

As the day aged, the once-clear sky began to brood, shrouded by an advancing army of dark clouds that swallowed the sun whole. The air grew tense, as forceful gusts of wind coerced the towering trees into a reverent bow. Across the vast plains, a herd of deer galloped in a synchronized sprint. Above, flocks of birds, silhouetted against the darkening sky, streamed past in hurried formations. A storm was coming.

The wind whipped fiercely, transforming Selaina's hair into a billowing white blur that fluttered wildly across her eyes. Myrradin steered their group away from the vulnerability of the open plains, guiding them toward the relative shelter of the groups of clustered trees. As they moved, a peculiar scent came in on the air—moist and earthy, rich with the promise of rain.

Elysia clutched her cloak tighter around her shoulders, her eyes scanning the darkening sky. "Are you certain we should keep going?" she asked, her voice fighting against the volume of the wind. "They say that Windwraiths ride on storms like these."

Kadin's eyes darted nervously. "They will steal your breath," he said, his hand tapping nervously against the dagger on his belt. "Drain the life right out of you. Why did we have to stray so far from villages or towns?"

"Those are just folktales, I think," said Darian, though uncertainty betrayed his words.

"I've seen artwork of them," said Kadin. "Dark, shadowy figures with long, trailing tendrils."

Ysadora gripped her staff and moved closer to Myrradin. "Everyone knows that Windwraiths don't exist," she declared, her confident tone drifting toward doubt. "Do they, Myrradin?"

"More than Windwraiths, we should be concerned about the fury of nature itself," shouted Myrradin over the wind as it howled through the hollows of the trees. "These trees won't be shelter enough."

As Selaina registered the chill of raindrops on her skin, she pulled her hood over her head, seeking a semblance of shelter. The first few drops quickly burgeoned into a steady downpour, urging her and her companions to hasten their steps. The gentle pitter-patter on the leaves overhead and the whisper of rain against the grass exploded into a relentless deluge that enveloped them. The rain's intensity blossomed, rendering the tree canopy above ineffectual. The refuge failed to hold back the onslaught, leaving them exposed to the elements as the rain surged around them, transforming the landscape into a blur of water and wind.

Myrradin spread his left hand, conjuring his nearly invisible barrier, which radiated with white energy. He used the barrier to shield them from the elements as the sky flashed with light, followed by the crack of thunder.

"Away from the trees!" shouted Myrradin. The group sprinted with the wind at their backs out into the open plains. Selaina's boots sank into the soft mud, forcing her to slow her steps to avoid slipping.

No stranger to the capricious moods of the forest's weather, Selaina found herself astounded by the sheer ferocity of the rain now engulfing them. The downpour transformed the grasslands, turning tufts of grass into burgeoning pools as rivulets of water raced toward the dips in the terrain, creating ephemeral ponds that shimmered in the dim light. Amid this watery chaos, small oily brallops seized the moment, emerging from their hidden dens beneath the grass with an enthusiasm reserved for such deluges. They hopped around the expanding puddles, their croaks a vibrant chorus against the drumming rain, reveling in the sudden abundance as they danced under the tempest's veil.

The hairs on the back of Selaina's neck stood on end, feeling hard and prickly. A burst of lightning tore through the sky, followed by a deafening crack. Balls of flame erupted as it struck a distant tree, igniting it instantly. Rykan froze, his eyes wide, awestruck by the power of nature. Something about this storm felt different.

Ysadora tried to rein in the ridgeback, but it broke free of her grip, bolting into the gray mist. "Frey!" she cried. Ysadora started after her, but the ridgeback was too fast to catch up with.

"We have the bare essentials, I suppose," Myrradin called out, his voice barely audible over the growing storm. He sighed, casting a wistful glance at the vanishing ridgeback. "Though I'm not sure how well I will get along without my silk pillows and incense."

"Who knew your portable palace would be the first casualty of this journey?" Kadin jabbed. "Guess you'll have to rough it like the rest of us commoners."

Ysadora, still looking into the mist where the ridgeback had disappeared, shook her head. "It's not just about the supplies. I'll miss Frey. She's been a loyal friend."

"I'm sorry, Ysadora," said Selaina, trying to offer a comforting smile. "I hope that Frey will find her way back to you one day."

Ysadora's eyes softened as she turned to Selaina, the sorrow in her face evident despite her attempt to remain composed.

Garrick glanced around at the encroaching mist. "Maybe we should follow the ridgeback," he suggested. "She probably knows the best way out of the storm."

Myrradin, wiping rain from his face, looked in the direction Frey had gone and shook his head. "If she weren't going in the opposite direction of our course, I would," he replied firmly.

Selaina shivered as another lightning bolt struck nearby, the thunder rumbling through her chest. "I don't think I've ever seen a storm this bad," she said, barely able to hear her own voice over the howling wind.

Another lightning bolt struck nearby.

"This way! This way! We must get to the bridge!" Myrradin shouted over the stampeding rain, while he motioned for everyone to follow.

"We need shelter!" Elysia shouted, her voice cutting through the chaos. "Forget all the secrecy! Where is the nearest village?"

The group instinctively huddled closer, forming a tight-knit cluster behind Myrradin. Myrradin cast his Aedavaris ability in front of him, using it to block the brunt of the wind and rain. The barrier provided some relief, allowing them to press forward with a bit more confidence, despite the storm's fury.

"Perhaps you're right. Fallodan is near," said Myrradin. "If we can make it across the river, we can stay on the road to Fallodan."

"We need to move fast," said Garrick urgently. "This storm isn't letting up."

They hurried ahead, sloshing through the wet grass. Surveying the ground ahead, Selaina picked out the steadiest terrain, running in haphazard patterns but maintaining their general direction. With one miscalculated step, her foot sank deep into the mud, her momentum carrying her foot free of its boot. She tried to shift her body to account for the change in balance, but it was too great. She found herself landing face down in the muddy grass.

Her hands slid around slick surfaces as she struggled to pull herself up. Someone grabbed her under her arms and lifted her back to her feet. Turning around, she realized it was Kadin, who continued to hold her up until she found her footing. Rykan hurried to her side, brushing the thick mud from her missing boot.

The others came over to her as the rain continued beating down on them. She didn't want to slow them all down.

"Go on ahead," she told them. "I'll catch up to you."

"Without you, this is hopeless," said Ysadora, shaking her head defiantly. "We're not leaving."

"We stick together," added Darian firmly. "That's the only way we'll get through this."

Rykan held her boot low where she could step into it as she leaned on Kadin for support. It took a moment to get her wet foot in the proper alignment with the soaked, muddy boot, but she managed as Rykan pushed from the other end.

The storm unleashed its fury with unyielding intensity as the day wore on, the rain descended like a barrage of arrows, each drop striking the earth with force. Lightning rent the sky, its jagged fingers illuminating the tumultuous scene in brief, stark flashes. Darkness smudged the once-distinct line where sky met land. Roiling clouds seemed to merge with the horizon, cloaking the landscape in a veil of shadow and mist. Visibility dwindled to mere shadows in the gloom, the world reduced to the immediate and the elemental, with each flash of lightning providing fleeting glimpses of the storm's wild dominion.

Towering trees came into view as they neared the edges of the river, its current moving swiftly. Myrradin led them northeast along the stone-covered banks, until the stone arc of the bridge emerged from the gloom. Selaina and the others picked up speed as the prospect of finding shelter became real. Pushing against the wind, they made it up the incline to the road that led to the bridge.

The concrete and stone were broken in the middle, and the rising waters of the river flowed up to the underside of the bridge.

"We're too late," said Myrradin, his voice heavy with frustration. "The bridge is washed out."

Elysia, her face pale with worry, glanced at the surging river. "We shouldn't have come to the river," she said.

"What do we do now?" Darian asked, his eyes scanning the chaos around them as he wrung his hands.

"Make for higher ground," Myrradin commanded, pointing toward the hills that loomed in the distance. He continued along the banks of the rising waters, a sense of immediacy in every step. "We can cross at Petra Vianor."

Selaina tightened the hood of her cloak so it covered her face, shielding her from the wind and pelting rain. She followed closely behind Myrradin and Ysadora, each step a struggle against the storm's relentless assault.

"There had better be shelter there," Elysia muttered as she hesitantly marched after them.

"Keep moving!" shouted Garrick, his voice barely carrying over the howling wind. He urged the group forward, squinting against the driving rain. "We'll make it!"

Kadin glanced at Selaina. "Try not to lose another boot," he said with a grin, earning a faint, grateful smile from her.

As they moved ahead, the ground beneath them began to incline above the river and the grasslands gave way to a rockier landscape. Climbing the hill with the wind pressing against them slowed them down quite a bit. The rain felt like tiny needles hitting Selaina's body.

The hazy remnants of the sun, obscured by black clouds, neared the bottom of the sky as they came to the side of a cliff with steps carved into the rock. The steps appeared to be naturally formed into the rock, but as she ascended them, Selaina found it hard to deny that someone had to have made them. Reaching the top of the cliff, Ysadora and Rykan helped Myrradin up, with Selaina right behind him. The bridge here was high enough above the water that it had not been affected by the storm, but the water was quickly rising.

Myrradin stepped onto the bridge. "Let Selaina cross first," he said. "She is crucial to our quest."

The wind blew the rain sideways into them, making Selaina fear that it would push her or someone else off the bridge. The river surged below them, dropping into a cascading fall not far past the bridge. Trying to keep her focus on the floor of the bridge and not the river, Selaina took a deep breath.

She moved onto the bridge tentatively, as her boots were still slick and muddy. Fortunately, the stone making up the bridge was coarse and irregular, giving her more confidence in her footing. As she made it halfway across, a sudden gust of wind tried to shove her off the edge. Holding steady, she maintained her balance and slowly crept across.

Her heart pounded as she made it to the other side. Allowing her pulse to slow, she waited for Myrradin, who trailed right behind her. She watched anxiously as he moved past, followed by Ysadora, Elysia, Kadin, and Garrick. Rykan appeared nervous as he let Darian go ahead of him. Selaina stood at the edge of the river, making sure everyone made it safely across.

As Rykan crossed the bridge's arch, the stone began to give way under the rising currents. With a sudden lurch, Rykan was thrown into the water, his hands desperately clinging to what remained of the collapsed bridge. Selaina's heart skipped a beat as she saw him struggling.

"Rykan!" Selaina shouted, her voice drowned out by the roaring river.

Elysia and Garrick bolted toward the bridge, but Kadin's urgent voice cut through the chaos.

"Don't!" Kadin shouted. "Too much weight could cause it to crumble!"

Selaina stood helplessly at the edge of the river. At any moment, Rykan would be swept downstream. She couldn't bear to see him struggling only a few feet away, while she did nothing. She was perhaps the lightest person among them. Selaina sprinted across the broken stone.

"Selaina, wait!" Myrradin cried out.

But she dropped to her knees as low as she could, reaching down with all her strength to find Rykan's hand. The cold water splashed up, soaking her sleeves. It was much colder than the rain, but she ignored it.

"Hold on, Rykan!" she cried, her fingers stretching to grasp his.

Rykan's grip on the remaining stone began to slip, his knuckles turning white. "Selaina!" he shouted, with panic in his voice.

Selaina lunged forward, her hand clasping around Rykan's wrist. She braced herself against the edge, using every ounce of strength to pull him up. She managed to tug him just enough to where he could support himself with his other hand. She could feel the current tugging at him violently, but she held firm, her muscles straining.

"Almost there," she whispered, more to herself than to Rykan, as her voice trembled with exertion.

Slowly, Rykan pulled himself onto the stone while Selaina gave him the leverage he needed to climb onto the splintered surface next to her.

With a final surge of strength, Rykan hoisted himself up and over the edge, collapsing onto the broken bridge beside her. He lay there for a moment, gasping for breath.

"Thank you," Rykan managed to say, his voice hoarse and shaky.

As they hurried toward the bank of the river, Myrradin and Darian reached out to Selaina, pulling her away from the crumbling remains of the stone bridge.

"Are you well?" Darian asked, as she bent over with her hands on her knees.

"Selaina!" Ysadora yelled, her voice cutting through the rain. "You can't risk yourself like that! The whole point of you crossing first was to protect you!"

"You must understand that, no matter what happens to the rest of us on this journey," Myrradin said, "as long as you are able to use the stone, we will all be safe in the new time path."

Selaina began to catch her breath as Myrradin's words echoed in her mind. She had not thought of it that way. Their lives depended on her in a way she had not realized.

The road from the bridge cut through the uneven, rocky mounds as rainwater poured through cracks and crevasses in the stone around them. Lightning continued to fill the murky skies, occasionally touching the ground and causing a loud boom to echo across the area.

As the trail curved through a wooded area ahead, Myrradin moved off the path, heading further up the incline. Keeping clear of the runoff, they took a haphazard path as they made their way through the rain. Selaina wondered if Myrradin even knew where he was leading them anymore. The wind changed direction, pushing hard against them, causing Myrradin to adjust and lead them on a new path.

"Are we still on course?" Selaina asked after a while.

"If you're asking if we're lost, I'd say not exactly," Myrradin replied, squinting through the downpour. "But if you're wondering if I know exactly where we are, that would also be a no."

"So, we're lost," said Elysia with frustration as she hugged her cloak tighter against the storm.

Darian's voice pierced the thick veil of mist, drawing attention to a peculiar shadow amid the trees, against the cliff wall. "What's that there?" he asked, pointing toward the anomaly in the gray expanse.

Garrick squinted, his gaze following Darian's finger. "Looks like a cave entrance," he said, the outline of the dark void becoming more distinct as they neared.

Without hesitation, Myrradin veered toward the mysterious opening, his usual caution dampened by the urgency of their situation. Selaina trailed closely behind him, her body trembling not just from the biting cold and her drenched clothes, but from the anxiety that gnawed at her.

As they approached the cliff face, the initial impression of a natural cave dissolved. The entrance before them was framed by intricately carved columns, unmistakably manmade, more befitting of a temple's grandeur than a mere shelter. Flanking the opening, two peculiar trees with twisted roots stood tall, their gnarled branches casting eerie shadows on the stone.

Myrradin paused, momentarily caught in awe. He studied the ancient symbols etched into the stone with a keen eye, while Ysadora joined him, their curiosity piqued yet tempered by caution. The carvings told stories of old, their meanings partially obscured by the passage of time, but the craftsmanship was undeniably exquisite, hinting at a long-forgotten civilization.

Elysia, driven by a more practical concern for immediate shelter, brushed past the pondering duo and stepped into the embrace of the temple's entryway. Her decisiveness spurred the others into action, and they quickly followed, seeking refuge from the relentless storm outside.

Inside, the sound of the rain softened, replaced by the eerie silence of the temple's interior. They huddled together, seeking comfort in shared warmth as the darkness enveloped them, a stark contrast to the chaos of the storm they had fled.

Myrradin huddled inside with the rest of them, but his gaze remained fixed on the entranceway. He absently stirred the dirt on the temple floor with the tip of his staff, drawing aimless lines as if his mind was wandering far from their current shelter. Selaina wondered what weighed so heavily on him, until at last he spoke.

"It's odd we should be so far off course and find this place," he said.

Ysadora glanced at him, nodding in agreement. "You think it's more than coincidence?"

"It's almost as if …" Myrradin began, his words trailing off into a quiet murmur, his staff continuing to etch shallow patterns in the dirt.

"As if what?" Ysadora asked.

"Nothing," he muttered, shaking his head. "The rambling thoughts of an old man."

"Like the storm led us here," Selaina said softly, her eyes on the swirls of dirt beneath Myrradin's staff.

Ysadora glanced at him again, a tension in her gaze. "Then we were meant to find this place."

Selaina shivered, pulling her cloak tighter around herself. "I don't know if that's comforting or terrifying."

A subtle, low rumble, akin to distant thunder, reverberated through the stone underfoot. With her senses dulled by exhaustion and the numbing cold, Selaina paid little heed until a startling realization dawned on her. The sliver of gray light from the entrance, their only visual tether to the outside world, began to narrow alarmingly.

Rykan's voice broke through the mounting panic. "The door is closing!"

In a frantic scramble, their silhouetted figures dashed toward the shrinking light, their efforts futile as the entrance sealed with a resounding boom that echoed ominously through the temple's depths. Plunged into absolute darkness, the reality of their situation settled heavily upon Selaina—they were trapped, with no choice but to wait out the storm and confront whatever lay within the temple's ancient walls.

CHAPTER 23

IN THE SUFFOCATING darkness, Rykan could only hear the sound of their ragged breathing, each exhale a desperate whisper against the oppressive silence of the sealed temple. The air felt thick, almost alive, pressing down on them with a palpable weight. Rykan's hands groped blindly in the void, seeking anything familiar or stable. His fingers brushed against the cool, uneven surface of the stone walls, their ancient carvings worn smooth by centuries yet still whispering secrets of a forgotten past.

A surge of frustration overwhelmed him. The darkness clawed at his sanity, each moment stretching into an eternity of confinement. Rykan's breaths grew sharp and erratic, his heart pounding fiercely, as if trying to escape the prison of his chest. He kicked at the ground, sending small stones skittering across the floor.

"Get this thing open!" Rykan spat, his voice cracking through the eerie quiet.

He beat his fist against the wall, the dull thud of flesh resonating against the stone. Pain shot up his arm, but it was a welcome distraction from the dread that threatened to consume him.

"Rykan, relax," Selaina urged, her voice a calm contrast to his agitation. "Take a deep breath."

He leaned his forehead against the cool stone, trying to gather his scattered thoughts, his breath coming in short, heavy gasps.

Suddenly, a soft glow pierced the darkness. Ysadora's sunkeeper crystal illuminated Myrradin's weathered face, casting his deep wrinkles into stark relief. The interplay of light and shadow accentuated his features, making them appear like ancient scars etched by time. Its light was dimmer than before, unable to gather sunlight during the storm.

Reaching the light near the wall, he traced it along the doorway. Garrick grabbed at the edges, the light reflecting off the droplets of water in his beard. His fingers found the edges of the stone door. Positioning for leverage, he pushed all his weight against the stone door, but it would not budge. Rykan ran over to help Garrick. The others soon joined, trying to place themselves in a manner that would allow each of them to lend their strength. Even with all of them pushing, they could not move it in the least.

"Here," Kadin called out. "I found it."

"Found what?" Elysia asked.

"Giant stone doors don't close by themselves," Kadin replied with a knowing grin. "Ysadora, shine your light this way," he directed.

Obliging, Ysadora moved her light along the wall, illuminating the area where Kadin stood by a massive chain attached to the door. It ran through a pulley system toward the ceiling.

"Simple enough," Kadin observed dryly. "We only need to follow the chain to the fulcrum that's holding the door shut."

Ysadora followed the chain with the light above them, while Rykan crept behind her, not wanting to be left in the dark.

"If doors don't move by themselves," Selaina said, with concern growing in her tone, "does that mean someone in here closed it?"

Stopping abruptly, Myrradin banged his foot into something on the floor. It appeared to be a big chunk of rock with smaller pieces lying near it. Grumbling something under his breath, Myrradin lowered his head, watching the floor instead of the ceiling as he moved. Debris littered the ground. Rykan kicked several objects out of the way, noticing an old thick book lying in their path.

The cloth cover of the book was torn at the corners, covered with symbols Rykan didn't understand. He reached down to pick it up.

"Leave it," Myrradin commanded sharply.

Rykan glanced back at him. "What is it?

"A book of curses," said Myrradin. "Chaos is forbidden magic. Difficult to control. You are as likely to inflict terrible things on yourself as you are anyone else."

Rykan hesitated, staring at the book for a moment longer before reluctantly stepping over it, the warning echoing in his mind. Ysadora continued on until she reached a junction with three passageways. Rykan moved ahead of the group, kicking and shoving objects out of Ysadora's path as she raised her staff toward the ceiling. She revealed that the ceiling was lower in the hallway straight ahead, where the chain disappeared into a hole in the stone. Moving into the hallway, Ysadora quietly stepped forward. The hall became increasingly narrower the further they went. It curved slightly to the left, then back toward the right.

They came to a row of steps. While Myrradin and Ysadora hesitated, Rykan moved ahead and descended the stairs that went down into a space that widened into a larger room. Some of the stones in the walls seemed to glow with their own light, revealing the rectangular shape of the chamber.

Intricately carved into the walls were figures of people set in between columns that displayed great artistry and craftsmanship. Detailed arches were formed out of the rock above each section. A few of the statues had toppled over, with broken pieces scattered about on the floor. Each statue that remained standing held a faint blue light illuminating it, casting strange shadows that rose above them to the ceiling.

As Rykan crept onward, Ysadora's light caught a rectangular box along the left side wall. The top of the box was shaped like a squared-off roof with complex designs cut into it. After she took a few more steps, Ysadora's light reached another box, this one missing its top. She and Myrradin peered inside, jumping back once she moved the sunkeeper over it.

Before Rykan could get a look, they moved ahead, taking the light away from the object's interior. Rykan surveyed what he could still see, an eerie feeling growing inside him.

"There's something familiar about this place," said Rykan. "Like I've been here before. But that's impossible."

He wandered around the room, staying close to Ysadora's light. Pieces of rock and debris lined the floors, prompting him to sweep them aside with his feet. Eyeing a big round stone that lay on the floor near a lump of cloth, Rykan stepped toward it, gasping as he recognized what it was. The skull was mostly intact, its body wrapped in cloth robes.

Myrradin glanced back at him, noticing what he had found. He then turned to the rest of the group. "It appears we have discovered some ancient catacombs." He paused, allowing the words to sink in. "Let us tread upon these sacred grounds with respect and caution."

"I think it's too late for that," Ysadora said, her eyes fixed on one of the open sarcophagi. "These tombs have already been disturbed."

"Grave robbers," Garrick said. "One of the lowest forms of life."

Kadin stepped through the debris. "Well, you can't deny their rationale," he said. "It's not as though the dead are going to miss anything they take." His foot crunched on the bones of a skeletal hand on the floor. "I'm beginning to miss the storm already," he said, twisting his face in disgust.

Myrradin bent forward, picking up a gold ring set with smoky gray gemstones. "If they were grave robbers, why would they leave this behind?" he asked, handing it to Ysadora. "What can you see?"

She examined it, turning it between her index finger and thumb. "It once held powerful magic. Its bearer was old when he died, wearing a long robe with three golden triangles imprinted on the chest."

"A mavin of the old days, before the Conclave," said Myrradin. "How did the ring lose its power?"

"Hard to see," Ysadora murmured, her brow furrowing in concentration. "There is darkness obscuring my vision, shadows tearing at the light. I have never encountered this before."

"I would venture to guess that all of these trinkets are or once were enchanted," Myrradin said. "This is a vault of mavins, sorcerers, and disciples of order. Magrin Necrovar. Its location is known only to a few and has never been documented."

"It couldn't be Magrin Necrovar," Ysadora replied, handing the ring back to Myrradin. "It would have been sealed where no one without specific knowledge could enter. Even we would have no way of opening it."

"I fear something sinister is at work here," said Myrradin squinting at the golden ring.

Rykan leaned against the walls, his feet aching from standing and walking all day. Ignoring the pain, Rykan moved ahead, not wanting to show any signs of weakness. Rounding a bend, he stopped when he saw the faint light of flame, a torch mounted on the wall of the long hallway. As he looked back, he noticed Ysadora appeared unsettled, and suddenly it dawned on Rykan that this could only mean someone had been here recently.

Once the rest of the group had caught up, they all stood still, gazing at the torch and listening to the silence. For a moment, Rykan thought he heard faint whispering coming from somewhere in the darkness ahead. He glanced at Selaina, and her eyes darted back to him as if she heard it too. He wondered if her pointed ears gave her better hearing. Ysadora's may too.

Kadin scrutinized the walls. "I don't think the chains lead down here," he said. "They must be somewhere above us."

Myrradin turned around, waving his hands at them to go back. The terror in Myrradin's eyes stirred something in Rykan. As he followed the others back through the hall where they had come from, he was on the edge of panic. Patting his chest to the rhythm of his heart, he tried to steady himself. Selaina wore a look of concern but retained her calm demeanor. Her slow, deliberate movements kept Rykan from bolting ahead and pushing aside anyone in front of him.

Selaina followed closely as Rykan made his way back through the burial chamber to the junction of four halls. Rykan and Selaina moved aside, allowing Ysadora past so she could bring her light to the front. Garrick and Elysia followed when Kadin took the passage to their right instead of going straight ahead. Rykan's feet splashed through puddles of water in the hallway. Perhaps they could find out where the rain was coming in.

As the hallway ended, they found themselves in another chamber, the walls lined with the flat ends of coffins that had been pushed into carved-out spaces. At the end of the room was a big statue of a man in robes, his hands clasped together in front of him. The air was silent and damp. Drops of water echoed through the pathway ahead. Several coffins had been pulled out of their places in the walls and opened, the corpses that were once inside missing. A pile of books lay in one corner, their disheveled appear-ance indicating they had been thrown there rather than placed. A thick gnarled stick stood against a wall, the top of it divided into two short pieces as if it were once a limb that branched off into two parts. Fitting perfectly between the two parts was a violet stone. Many other metal trinkets were scattered across the floor.

Rykan's attention was drawn across the room, and he noticed Kadin crouching to collect small daggers from the floor. With quick movements, Kadin tucked them into his belt. He then spotted a set of large, finely crafted daggers along the wall and moved to gather them as well, securing them at his side.

His focus shifted to a wooden sheath nearby. Rykan picked it up, feeling its weight, and noticed the gold hilt of a sword sticking out from the end. He drew it out, revealing a silver blade with strange symbols etched into its flat surface. The symbols were filled with a pale blue crystalline substance.

"It would be unwise to desecrate this place of rest," said Myrradin.

Rykan gripped the sword, spinning the hilt in his hand. "It was desecrated before we found it."

"All the more reason to put it back with the dead it belonged to," Myrradin said.

"How do I even know who it belongs to?" he asked.

Rykan dropped the sword when a horrible screech sounded through the chamber. A dark figure materialized out of the shadows. Myrradin raised an open palm to the creature as it charged them. The dark creature stopped in its tracks, unable to escape the Aedavaris as Myrradin kept his hand aimed at it.

Though the attacker had a head, arms, and legs, its form was inhuman. Most of it was solid, but parts appeared held together with a sort of spectral aura that faintly reflected on the wet floor. Wearing ragged robes with a hood that concealed its face in shadow, the being began to coil and writhe. Its left arm was stretched and elongated with a large, clawed hand that was disproportionate to the size of its body.

"What is this creature?" Elysia asked with apprehension, her eyes wide with unease as she gripped her shield tighter. "A Windwraith?"

Myrradin stepped closer, his eyes narrowing as he studied the apparition. "No," he said, his voice measured. "Nothing like a Windwraith, though it appears powerful."

Somewhere in the haunted depths of nearly repressed memories, Rykan looked at the creature with recognition. "This thing," he said, "I have seen its likeness before … in a dream."

"A dream?" Ysadora asked as she eyed Rykan curiously. "You saw this moment in a dream?"

"Not exactly this moment," said Rykan, his eyes never leaving the creature. "None of us were there. But I saw creatures in a place like this."

"How many were there?" asked Ysadora, her grip tightening on her staff.

"Many. More than I could count," Rykan said, swallowing hard. "Moving through the shadows as if they were a part of them."

Ysadora's eyes narrowed as she processed this information. "If your dream holds any truth, we must be cautious. Dreams are often windows to deeper truths and hidden dangers."

"Is that what you read in your books, Ysadora?" Kadin quipped, though his tone held more seriousness than usual.

"Yes, Kadin," Ysadora replied sharply. "And it's something you should heed if you want to stay alive."

The creature writhed inside the shield, the group instinctively drawing away from it and raising their weapons in defense.

"Don't worry," Myrradin said. "Nothing can break out of the Aedavaris until I let go."

Rykan joined the others, readying his sword as he stared at the creature. They surrounded the creature while it continued to slash and claw at the shielding, its movements growing more frantic.

"Be ready," said Myrradin.

Garrick stabbed at the creature, but Myrradin's field around it repelled his sword.

"Not yet," Myrradin said, straining to maintain the barrier.

Wringing his hands from the impact, Garrick gathered himself. "I thought you said you were ready."

When Myrradin released the spell, the fiend swung at him with its oversized claw. With a flash of light, Elysia's shining blade cut through the creature's arm, but instead of falling, the severed claw writhed and reformed in midair, attempting to reattach itself.

The creature swatted its remaining hand at them, and Garrick swung at the creature's head, slicing into its neck. The hood collapsed, as whatever was underneath dissolved into ash and dust, but the body began to pulse and shimmer, as if trying to pull itself back together.

"Stay back!" Myrradin warned, his voice tense. "It's not done yet!"

The creature's body reformed, its spectral aura flaring brighter. It swung its newly regenerated claw at Myrradin again, but Kadin threw his daggers, pinning the creature's arms to the stone wall behind it.

Garrick stepped forward, his face set in determination. "We need to strike together."

As one, Elysia, Rykan, and Garrick attacked the creature, their blades flashing in the dim light. Each strike seemed to weaken it further, but it took several combined efforts before the creature's aura flickered and dimmed.

With a final, desperate lunge, Elysia's sword pierced the creature's heart. The spectral aura around it imploded with a flash of dark energy, and the creature dissolved into black and purple dust, its remnants falling onto the discarded corpses lining parts of the floor.

Breathing heavily, Myrradin steadied himself. "That was only one. If there are more, we must be prepared. They are not easily vanquished."

With a sigh of relief, Rykan tightened the sheath of the sword to his side. The chamber and hall ahead seemed more familiar from this angle. "I've seen this place before. I think I know the way out of here!"

He dashed ahead into the hallway, unconcerned that he didn't hear the others following. If they didn't believe him, he would show them. Fortunately for him, some torches remained lit in this section too, and he came across another junction. Rykan took the hallway to the right. A second junction with four paths lay before him. The floor and walls here were uneven, smoothed out in long streaks. Between each smoothed pathway were sharp ridges.

As he approached an archway, the one he recalled from his dream, Rykan heard moans coming from inside. Fear gripped him, but he was too close to turn back. The archway should lead to an altar where chains attached to a fulcrum lever that controlled the doors to the outside. The sounds of footsteps behind him made him feel at ease. They would see he was useful. He would get everyone out of these catacombs.

A screech rang out, sounding as if it was close behind him. Rykan turned to see another creature charging at him. He swung his blade wildly at the creature, forcing it to pause before swiping its claws at him. The creature's form shimmered and distorted, making it difficult to predict its movements. Before it could strike him, the sound of metal rang out, and the creature toppled over. Most of its body turned to smoke and dust that stained the floor, revealing Garrick standing with his sword at the ready behind it.

Before Garrick could react, another creature attacked him from behind, clawing into his back with a force that knocked him to the ground. As Rykan prepared to defend him, Selaina fired an arrow into the creature's back, violet dust spilling from the wound. It turned, charging at her with alarming speed. Rykan tried helplessly to reach it with his blade, but it was too fast. Elysia stepped in front of Selaina, slicing into the creature with two swift cuts. Blue smoke poured from its wounds as it collapsed to the floor, but even then, it writhed and clawed at them. Darian fired his crossbow, hitting it with two bolts, and it finally disintegrated.

Before Rykan could take a deep breath, three more creatures poured from the archway, their screeches echoing ominously. Myrradin held one still with his Aedavaris, and Ysadora raised rocks from the ground, sharp spikes shooting up and impaling the creature, pinning it in place. The third fell to another shot from Selaina, the arrow going straight into its head. However, instead of collapsing immediately, the creature thrashed violently, flinging the arrow out and lunging forward. Garrick managed to thrust his sword into the fiend by propping himself against the wall. The dark being collapsed, succumbing to the damage.

The creature held by Ysadora quickly broke free of the stone prison, its eyes glowing with malevolent intent. But before it could charge, Rykan managed to run his sword through its chest. Its claws grabbed at his blade, as the blue dust gushed out of its wound, and it continued to fight, forcing Rykan to twist the blade multiple times before it collapsed into a pile of dry soot.

"If you are ready," said Myrradin, his voice strained from maintaining the spell, "I will release this one."

Elysia and Rykan stood on either side of the creature with their swords, while Selaina trained her bow on it. "Ready," said Elysia. Before either of them could swing their blade, a dagger hit the creature at the moment Myrradin released it from his shielding spell. As the creature tumbled over, Rykan glanced behind Elysia to find Kadin pumping his fist.

"That was a thing of beauty! The timing!" Kadin shouted, narrowing his eyes as Elysia and Rykan stared at him.

"You could have hit us with that," said Elysia.

"I couldn't let you have all the fun," said Kadin with a smirk. "And thus far, you haven't been polite enough to get out of the way."

Garrick moaned as he rolled himself onto his knees. Rykan and Elysia ran to him while he tried to stand but grunted in pain.

"I'm fine," he said through gritted teeth. "Just help me up." He roared again when they lifted him to his feet. Blood stained the back of his tunic, and his face was pale, but strength still burned in his eyes.

"I can help," said Ysadora, stepping forward with her staff. "This won't be pleasant, but it can keep the wound from getting infected."

"Whatever you need to do," Garrick replied, his voice strained but resolute.

Elysia gently lifted his tunic, exposing three slashes on his back, one of which was especially deep. She winced at the sight of the wounds, their edges ragged and bleeding. Ysadora held her staff near Garrick's back. The staff began to glow blue, and a flame appeared from Garrick's wounds. He yelled as the flames quickly extinguished, leaving the wounds blackened with a few tiny orange embers that slowly faded out. The bleeding had stopped.

"One of those wounds is deep," said Myrradin, his brow furrowed with concern. "We need someone to suture it. Anyone?"

They all exchanged glances, but no one responded.

Garrick sighed. "If I could reach it, I would do it myself."

"I will try if there is no one else," said Elysia. "Since you did it for me. But I don't know what I'm doing."

"Does anyone have anything small to pierce the skin?" Myrradin asked, his eyes scanning the group.

"I have my sewing needles," said Darian, stepping forward and rubbing his hands together.

"You're a tailor?" Myrradin asked, his expression brightening. "Perfect. Just imagine you're sewing leather together."

Darian's eyes widened, but he nodded, accepting the task. "Is there anything to set him on?"

"There should be an altar in the next room," said Rykan, pointing toward the archway.

They carefully guided Garrick into the next chamber, where a stone altar stood in the center. The faint glow of Ysadora's staff dimly lit the room, casting eerie shadows on the walls. On the altar lay an old man, bound and unclothed, his writhing movements the only thing telling he was alive.

Garrick grunted in pain as he lowered himself onto a broken pillar, his breath coming in short gasps. Darian approached Garrick, threading one of his sewing needles with a steady hand. He glanced at Myrradin for reassurance, who gave him a nod of encouragement. Elysia and Selaina stood close by, ready to assist if needed.

Rykan turned his gaze toward the man on the altar. Despite the urgency of their situation, he offered the old man a reassuring look, silently hoping that he would hold on. The man's labored breathing was faint, but Rykan's expression conveyed his quiet support.

"This will hurt," Darian warned, his voice soft but firm.

Garrick merely nodded, bracing himself.

Darian began to suture the deep wound, and Garrick clenched his jaw, suppressing groans of pain. Elysia held his hand as the needle moved methodically through the torn flesh, each stitch drawing the wound closer together. The others watched in tense silence, the dim light of the staff reflecting in their eyes.

As Garrick tried to suppress the voice of his pain, Rykan turned away, distracting himself by glancing once more toward the altar. He watched as Myrradin threw a blanket over the old man to cover him, then knelt beside the altar where the man lay. The man's eyes widened with surprise when Myrradin approached. Coughing as he tried to speak, the man's chest convulsed with a raspy, deep hack that made Rykan rub his own chest in sympathy.

"Myrradin?" asked the old man, his voice weak and strained. "Is that really you?"

"Indeed, Telarion. It is I," Myrradin replied, his tone softening with recognition. "What are you doing in this dreadful place?"

"Beware." Telarion coughed again, his body shaking. "The Sullen. They have taken up residence here, siphoning remnants of magic to keep what remains of their mortal bodies from dying."

"The Sullen," Myrradin repeated, his expression darkening. "This is worse than I feared."

"I was caught by ravagons. They carried me off into the wild before burning out into ash and dust. But something led me here," Telarion continued, his voice faltering. "I thought it was my own clairvoyance guiding me to Magrin Necrovar. I've always wanted to discover what history and knowledge this place contained. Now I know, it was a trap."

He began coughing violently, and Myrradin quickly took a flask from his robe. He opened it but frowned at the empty container.

"Ysadora," Myrradin called, his tone urgent. "Hold this for me." He handed her the flask and wrung rainwater from the sleeve of his robe into it. After collecting a few drops, he gave it to Telarion to drink.

"They tried to extract secrets from me, Myrradin," Telarion said, his voice barely above a whisper. "Though I told them nothing, I fear they were able to glean something from my mind."

"Nonsense," Myrradin said firmly. "You are too strong to be broken by the likes of the Sullen."

"I hope you are right, old friend," Telarion murmured.

"What did they ask you?" Myrradin inquired. "What was it they wanted to know?"

"The location of the Wishing Stone," Telarion replied, his eyes glazing over with exhaustion.

Myrradin's eyes widened in alarm. "Surely you guarded your mind against them."

"I can't be certain of anything," Telarion said, his voice trembling. "All my strength has been taken."

Myrradin leaned in closer, speaking quietly. "You know how the winds carry secrets, Telarion. Even a whisper can be heard if you listen carefully." He placed his hands gently but firmly on Telarion's shoulders.

"Myrradin …" Telarion said, his voice growing weaker as he tugged at Myrradin's robe. "You don't have to …"

"Stay with us, Telarion!" Myrradin said, his voice urgent, tinged with desperation. "How many of them are here?" He leaned in even closer, his eyes searching Telarion's for any sign of life, but the old man's gaze was vacant, the color draining from his face like water from a broken vessel. His head lolled to the side, lifeless. Myrradin grabbed his face, shaking it gently. "How do we get out of here, Telarion?"

The silence was deafening, the oppressive atmosphere of the catacombs closing in on them. Myrradin's grip tightened on his friend's shoulder, his expression a blend of grief and resolve.

"What happened to him?" Ysadora's voice was soft, her face a mask of sorrow as she knelt beside Myrradin.

"I'm afraid he succumbed to his wounds," Myrradin replied, his tone heavy. "They must have been keeping him alive with dark magic." He released Telarion's shoulder, his fingers lingering for a moment as if reluctant to let go.

Ysadora's eyes moved between Myrradin and the still form of Telarion. "What should we do with him now?" she asked quietly. She placed a gentle hand on Telarion's forehead, closing her eyes for a brief moment, as if offering a silent prayer.

"We must find our way out," Myrradin said, his voice steely. "And quickly. The Sullen will not be far behind."

"Almost done," Darian said after what seemed like an eternity. He tied off the last stitch and stepped back, wiping sweat from his brow.

CHAPTER 24

Selaina watched Darian carefully finish sewing up the wound on Garrick's back. The flickering torchlight cast long shadows across the ancient stone walls, giving the catacombs an eerie atmosphere. Despite the oppressive surroundings, Darian's focus remained steady, and the stitches were precise.

"I don't think I could have done it better myself," said Garrick, wincing as he ran his fingers over the part of the stitching he could reach.

"We're grateful you are with us, Darian," said Elysia warmly. "I don't know that I could have managed."

Darian grinned with a glimmer of pride, the torchlight catching in his eyes. Selaina felt a sense of relief that he was there. His presence had eased her mind since she'd joined these strangers. She wondered if he felt out of place among them, lacking the fighting skills they possessed. But now, seeing him in his element, he seemed more at ease, his demeanor more confident.

Turning her attention to Myrradin and the others, Selaina stepped toward the altar. Myrradin gently placed his hand over the dead man's eyes, closing them where he lay motionless.

"Telarion will be the first mavin dead in Magrin Necrovar in over five hundred years," Myrradin said, flashing a quick, sad smile at Ysadora.

Ysadora returned the smile with a sorrowful nod. "I hope he finds rest," she replied softly. "And that the Sullen don't desecrate his body."

"Perhaps we killed them all or frightened them off," Myrradin mused, though doubt lingered in his tone.

"Do you think they know where the Wishing Stone is?" Ysadora asked, her brow furrowed with concern.

"Difficult to say," Myrradin responded. "Even if they do, I doubt they would be able to find their way to the Stone. But we must proceed as though they know everything."

"We need to get out of these catacombs and back on course," Ysadora said, her eyes scanning the shadowy corners. She took a step forward, her staff illuminating the path ahead. "The sooner we leave this place, the better."

"The fulcrum should be over there in the corner." Rykan pointed, his voice echoing off the stone walls.

As they moved along the wall's edge, they spotted two thick chains descending from a pulley in one corner of the room. Myrradin tugged at one of the chains, but it didn't budge.

"No, no, no," said Kadin, striding past Myrradin with a grin. "That's not how it works. You have to swing the lever."

He pulled the lever of the fulcrum, and one of the chains began rapidly moving into a slot in the floor. The sound of stone grinding against metal echoed through the halls.

"See?" Kadin winked at Ysadora. "Like magic."

"It's open," said Garrick, his voice urgent. "Let's move. Back to the door!"

"That sound didn't come from behind us," Darian said, frowning. "It came from ahead."

"He's right," Selaina added, her heart pounding. "It couldn't have been the door we entered."

"Now there's another door?" Garrick asked with frustration. "Look, sounds can be deceiving. Especially in a space like this."

"Actually, there must be another door. In my dream, they moved further ahead from here," Rykan said, glancing into the darkness.

"We need to press forward," Myrradin urged. "Find the door that we opened. There may be another way out of here."

"That's our plan?" Kadin asked, raising an eyebrow. "Relying on this kid's dream?"

"Dreams are significant," Elysia interjected. "If Rykan dreamed of this place, we should take heed."

Everyone stood around, waiting for someone to take the lead. Selaina decided to act, striding purposefully toward the hallway. Myrradin, Ysadora, and Rykan were the first to follow, their footsteps echoing in the confined space. As Ysadora's sunkeeper cast a soft glow from behind her, Selaina noticed a wide passage ahead where a large metal door was separated into two. Perhaps this was the door they had opened. She stepped inside, greeted by the musty scent of ancient, undisturbed nature wafting from within.

The hallway soon narrowed, the walls closing in until there was only enough room for one person to pass at a time. Selaina moved forward cautiously, her senses heightened, aware of the weight of the darkness pressing around them. The confined space made her uneasy, and she couldn't help but notice the cobwebs clinging to the corners and the occasional scurrying of unseen critters, sending shivers down her spine.

The passage tilted downward unexpectedly. Her foot caught on a step she hadn't noticed, sending her stumbling. With heightened caution, she focused intently on the path ahead, navigating the rock-carved stairs that descended deeper into the earth. To her right, the solid comfort of the wall receded, replaced by an expansive darkness as the staircase spiraled further into the shadows. The uneven steps grated on her nerves, making her long for the familiar pathways of the forest she knew so well.

A whisper of a breeze brushed against her, teasing strands of hair across her face. The air grew heavier with the scent of moisture and the unmistakable earthiness of wet stone, becoming more potent with each step downward. Reaching the base of the stairs, Selaina stepped onto a rugged expanse of natural stone, its surface marred by irregular pits and scattered debris.

Torches mounted along the walls illuminated the cavernous chamber as they moved forward. The steady roar of a waterfall, just out of the edges of the light, filled the air with noise. Three unusual rock formations stood ahead, each etched with strange symbols. They pressed on, and Selaina noticed a faint red light on the ground next to a large pillar.

Moving away from the others, Selaina circled the pillar, her eyes searching for the source of the strange glow. The cavern's damp air carried a chill that seeped into her bones. Footsteps approached while she stared at the pulsing red lines etched into the stone. Rykan hurried over just as she discovered a dark hole in the side of the pillar. Outlined with pulsing red streaks, the dark cavity hummed with strange energy.

"I've seen this before!" Rykan exclaimed, reaching out to touch the stone.

"Step away!" Myrradin's voice thundered with an urgency that sent a jolt through Selaina.

Both she and Rykan recoiled from the enigmatic pillar. The harshness in Myrradin's tone was uncharacteristic, sparking fear and curiosity within Selaina.

She found it impossible to tear her gaze from the portal's dark heart. What was once a void now teemed with a mesmerizing dance of colors. Swirls of red mist, like the outer bands of a storm, twisted and turned, intertwining with crystallized hues of violet that shimmered with an otherworldly light. Yellows and oranges flowed like molten suns, their luminescence ebbing and flowing, while arcs of raw electricity leaped across the chasm, illuminating fragments of unknown matter caught in their frenetic ballet.

"You never know what might be on the other side of a portal," Myrradin cautioned, his voice softening as he approached. His eyes, wise and wary, fixated on the swirling vortex, betraying a deep concern for what lay beyond.

Selaina felt a shiver run down her spine at Myrradin's words. It reminded her of the blue energy breaking through the cracks in the rock on the hill in her secret forest. That place was mystical and serene. Yet, this portal was its stark antithesis. Here, the energy didn't merely seep through the environment, it roiled and churned with volatility. The air around it seemed wild and untamed, as if it possessed its own consciousness, keenly aware of their presence.

"I remember it from my dream," Rykan confessed, a tremor in his voice. "There was a voice on the other side, calling out …"

Selaina, sensing the significance of Rykan's revelation, exchanged a loaded glance with Myrradin. The air around them hummed with an unspoken understanding that what lay before them was not merely a phenomenon of magic but a gateway to untold secrets, possibly answers to questions they had yet to ask.

Myrradin stepped closer to the portal. "If voices reach out from its depths, we must tread carefully," he murmured, more to himself than to them. "The entities of outer realms are rarely bound by our notions of friend or foe."

His voice held concern. "The Sullen have no doubt been communing with dangerous forces," he stated, his gaze lingering on the remnants of the portal with a discerning eye.

Positioning himself squarely in front of the enigmatic pillar, he extended his hands, palms outward, as if to embrace the unseen energies swirling around them.

Selaina watched with bated breath as Myrradin closed his eyes and drew in a deep breath, entering a state of deep concentration. The air around them stilled, charged with anticipation. Moments later, a faint glow emanated from his hands, gradually intensifying into a brilliant blue energy that danced like flames along the edges of his fingers.

With a graceful motion, Myrradin directed the azure flames toward the pillar. The blue energy cascaded over the dark center of the portal, its light washing over the swirling mists and chaotic colors. The energy worked its magic, sealing the breach.

As the blue flames subsided, the stone surface of the pillar began to knit itself back together. The cracks and rifts mended as the colors and storms within the portal receded, swallowed by the closing gateway, until with a final pulse of energy, the portal vanished. The humming sound quieted, and the stone was now as it once was, unmarred and whole, with no trace of the dark passage that had been there moments before. Myrradin lowered his hands, his breathing steady but showing signs of the effort expended.

"Where do we go from here?" Myrradin asked Rykan, his voice echoing in the chamber. "This cavern is wide open."

Rykan shook his head. "At this point, I don't know. I don't remember seeing a way out in the dream."

The faint scuttle of unseen creatures echoed through the cavern, swiftly followed by an unsettling chorus of low moans. Myrradin gestured for Selaina and Rykan to quicken their pace toward the safety of their companions. They hastened along a narrow waterway that snaked through the cave's brittle foundation, the eerie sounds intensifying behind them. Abruptly, a cadre of Sullen flitted by, their presence menacing yet oddly non-aggressive.

"Strike them down!" Garrick's command pierced the tense air. "They're maneuvering to surround us."

As Selaina readied her bow, Rykan countered, "Wait! Perhaps we should let them! If they're angling to cut us off from the exit, they'll unwittingly guide us to our escape."

The idea of allowing the Sullen to gain an advantage by surrounding them within the cavern's shadows did not rest easy with Selaina. Rykan's bold suggestion clashed sharply with her instincts for caution and meticulously planned actions. In the brief time she had known him, she had come to expect the unexpected. Yet this reckless strategy seemed particularly jarring. It deepened her reservations about him, casting a new layer of doubt over his unpredictable nature.

"Madness. This is what you call a strategy?" Disbelief tinged Ysadora's voice, and her gaze flitted between Rykan and the shadowy figures moving stealthily around them.

Myrradin's eyes narrowed, scrutinizing the shadows with caution. "Rykan, your proposition teeters between brilliance and recklessness," he admitted, but there was a reluctant admiration in his voice. "Wandering these caverns without direction is a fool's errand."

"Are we seriously considering the whims of a whelp?" Kadin asked.

Garrick, his back to the group, kept a vigilant watch. "Now's the time you choose to be bold, lad?" he muttered under his breath.

Suddenly, a surge of Sullen emerged, heading toward their flank.

Darian's voice cut through the tension, urgent and clear. "We must act now!"

With a swift motion, Selaina drew her bow, the string taut as she aimed at the advancing Sullen. The atmosphere crackled with tension, every heartbeat echoing in the cavernous space. Myrradin's hands glowed faintly with residual energy as he prepared another spell, while Ysadora tightened her grip on her staff.

"Get ready," Garrick growled, positioning himself defensively. "We fight our way out, or we follow Rykan's lead. Either way, we move together."

With a decisive nod, Myrradin barked, "Forward!" He led a swift charge toward the Sullen that had just passed, a move that positioned them squarely between two factions of the enemy.

The air was thick with tension as they advanced. The cave's dim light cast eerie shadows on the stone walls, making the Sullen's movements appear more sinister. Garrick's frustration was obvious as they regrouped, the Sullen encircling them with chilling precision.

"Rykan, your gambit has backfired," he accused, his eyes darting nervously around the tightening circle. "We're cornered, with no way out and no plan to speak of."

Selaina's keen eyes scanned their ominous adversaries, noting a trio among them that were larger and more imposing, their eyes ablaze with an intense flame. The larger Sullen moved with a deliberate, menacing grace, their forms flickering with dark energy.

"Actually, he's onto something," Selaina said, pointing toward the looming figures to their left. "Those three look stronger. They're blocking that path."

"I concur," Myrradin affirmed, his gaze sharpening as he assessed their foes. "If we can break through those three, we might find the way out."

The larger Sullen shifted, their glowing eyes locked onto the group. The cave echoed with their low, guttural growls, and the air grew colder, the presence of the dark entities chilling them to the bone.

"Go quickly," Myrradin said, his voice steady despite the chaos. He extended his hands, a faint glow of blue energy beginning to form around his fingertips.

The group charged toward the largest of the Sullen. Garrick and Elysia advanced with swords at the ready, their movements nearly synchronized. Rykan, with his sword drawn, flanked their assault. From a distance, Selaina's focused aim preceded the swift release of an arrow, which found its mark in the chest of one of the Sullen, causing an ethereal blue essence to seep from the wound and stain its tattered garments.

The Sullen, reeling from the precision strike, retaliated with a ferocity that matched its towering stature. Its elongated, skeletal claws swiped at Garrick, who nimbly evaded, the air whistling with each missed swing. The creature's focus on Garrick left it vulnerable, and Elysia capitalized on the moment, her blade slicing through the air to sever its arm. But instead of falling, the arm twisted, regrowing with dark energy, and the Sullen howled in fury.

Meanwhile, Kadin hurled one of his long daggers with lethal accuracy, embedding it deep into another Sullen's glowing blue eye. The creature staggered but did not fall. Kadin, with a flick of his wrist, sent his second dagger spinning toward a different target, striking its throat. The Sullen gurgled but continued to advance, its body fueled by dark magic.

Darian fired his crossbow at an approaching Sullen. His shot was less precise, the bolt grazing the creature's shoulder. The Sullen barely reacted, its attention fixed on the more immediate threats. Darian reloaded clumsily as he fumbled with the mechanism.

As the skirmish intensified, Myrradin's magic conjured a barrier of shimmering energy around one of the Sullen, isolating it from the fray. Ysadora stood vigilant beside him, ready to support.

The remaining Sullen began to converge, their numbers a dark tide threatening to engulf them all. Yet, they kept their focus on the three largest Sullen, hoping to open the way ahead.

Ysadora pointed her staff, raising barriers of stones from the floor just in time and ensnaring one of the advancing Sullen before it could attack Rykan. As it struggled against the magical constraints, Rykan attacked with a swift turn and a practiced swing. He cut deep into the essence of the creature, releasing a cascade of blue, life-giving magic. It dissolved, its form crumbling into little more than dust on the cavern floor.

Maintaining her focus, Ysadora used her powers, enveloping another Sullen in a binding of stone. This allowed Garrick the moment he needed, as the creature reached for his sword with elongated, claw-like fingers. With an agile sidestep and a powerful thrust, Garrick drove his sword through its chest, turning its threatening advance into a crumbling defeat.

The battle's tide was turning.

"Move quickly!" Myrradin commanded, his voice cutting through the chaos of the skirmish. "Let none stand in our way!" His directive was clear, urging them to capitalize on the opening they had fought hard to create.

Selaina and the others sprinted toward temporary safety as more Sullen closed in. With precise aim, Selaina loosed another arrow, striking one of the encroaching creatures in the shoulder. The impact was less lethal than she'd hoped—her arrows seemed less effective than her companions' swords. But she recognized the need to keep moving. Having difficulty notching another arrow while running, she swiftly stowed her bow and accelerated, her boots pounding the cavern floor as she raced to catch up with the group.

Kadin demonstrated remarkable skill with his daggers, his movements fluid and precise, even in the heat of battle. With a swift motion, he hurled a smaller dagger from his belt, striking a Sullen in the chest. In the same breath, he spun to parry another attacker with one of his long daggers, its blade flashing as it deflected the blow. His belt held several more smaller daggers, ready to be thrown at a moment's notice, while his long daggers excelled in the brutal, close-quarters combat he seemed to relish.

The creatures thudded to the ground, clearing a path for Selaina to dart through. As she wove her way between the fallen and the flanking Sullen, a gnarled hand suddenly grasped her arm, halting her escape. Struggling fiercely, Selaina kicked and clawed at her captor, but to no avail. The Sullen tightened its grip, its other grotesque, malformed hand encircling her throat. Selaina's heart raced when she realized the perilous strength of its grasp, knowing a single squeeze could be lethal.

With a surprising burst of agility, Darian sprang into action, his figure a blur as he lunged at the Sullen menacing Selaina. He swept his crossbow across the creature's hooded visage, momentarily stunning it and allowing Selaina to escape its grasp. Rykan hurried toward the Sullen while Selaina tried to ready her bow for a shot.

The Sullen swung its claws at Selaina, but Darian was quicker. After grabbing a dagger from his belt, he drove the blade into the creature with relentless precision. His arm moved in a furious rhythm, each strike finding its mark. Rykan raised his sword to strike, but paused, realizing it was no longer necessary.

Darian's strikes were punctuated by the spatter of eerie blue magic, which sizzled and then turned to dust upon Darian's hand and the steel of his dagger. The Sullen staggered, its form disintegrating into a cloud of dust that mingled with the shadows of the cave, leaving no trace of its presence. Selaina stared at him, wondering where that instinct came from. She supposed all the surrounding danger they were faced with had changed him. It was surely changing her as well.

With the immediate threat subdued, they hastened their escape, navigating toward a murmuring waterway that snaked through the rocks. The sound of cascading water grew louder as they approached a series of natural waterfalls, the clear water tumbling down terraced rock formations into a stream below. Rykan, seizing the initiative, leaped onto a prominent boulder adjacent to the waterfalls and ascended the rock tiers, which resembled a rough staircase sculpted by nature itself.

The others quickly followed suit, with Garrick lending support to Myrradin, helping the elder mavin navigate the uneven terrain. As Selaina reached the summit of the rock wall, fresh, cool night air greeted her. It brushed against her face, reviving her senses after the stifling confines of the cave. Gazing into the water coursing over the threshold, she noticed her reflection in the rippling surface. The three wandering stars approaching their convergence nearly touched her face as they sparkled in the watery mirror.

Positioned now on the elevated ground just beyond the doorway, they prepared to make their stand. The strategic vantage offered them a clear view of the cavern below. Standing shoulder to shoulder with the others, she felt strong enough to take on whatever may come. Selaina readied her bow, her eyes sharp and focused on the shadows of the cave, awaiting the incoming assault of the Sullen.

CHAPTER 25

Rykan's chest heaved as he stared down into the cavern, adrenaline still surging through his veins after their narrow escape. Silvery light sparkled on the ripples and splashes of the water that ran into the cliff wall. The moon emerged from behind the clouds, casting a ghostly pallor over the land and illuminating their surroundings with an eerie glow.

Tapping his fingers restlessly on the hilt of his sword, Rykan watched, every muscle tense, waiting for the first sign of the Sullen emerging from the shadows. The cool night air did little to calm his racing heart. He wiped the sweat from his forehead, his eyes darting to every shift of movement. Beside him, Garrick slid his blade behind him, absentmindedly rubbing the dull side against the wound on his back.

"Stop that!" Elysia said with exasperation. "You're going to break the stitches."

"Scratch it, would you?" he asked, a pained yet sheepish grin on his face.

"If you'll leave it alone," she replied, shaking her head.

She slowly reached her hand through the tears in his tunic, rubbing her fingers gently around the sutured wound. Garrick arched his back as she scratched, taking a deep breath.

"That's it, like that. Maybe a little harder."

"Are they being cautious?" Ysadora asked, tensely. "I don't hear them at all."

"This opening would serve as a choke point, a place where their 

numbers will count for little," Myrradin said, his eyes narrowing while he surveyed the cave entrance. "Bear in mind, these are not mere brutes. The Sullen were once magi, possessing both intelligence and cunning."

"Maybe they were only protecting their territory," Selaina suggested, her brow furrowed in thought. "Now that we're gone, they have no need to follow."

"No," said Myrradin. "They need us. They know there's a chance Ysadora and I may know the location of the Wishing Stone."

Ysadora channeled her power, focusing it on her staff as she pointed it at the opening of the cave. Rock and stone protruded from the threshold, forming pillars that resembled teeth covering the cavernous maw.

"That should hold them for a while."

"Unless they're heading around to the entrance to meet us with their full force," Kadin remarked.

"We shouldn't stay around to find out," Darian said, his eyes darting nervously as he rubbed his hands together.

"Doesn't that hurt?" Elysia asked as she scratched Garrick's back more vigorously.

"Stings a bit," he replied, "but in a good way."

Myrradin turned, walking away from the group. "We need to find a place to camp for the night, somewhere hidden but that we can defend if need be."

Rykan's thoughts swirled as he pondered the mystery of the Sullen. If they were once magi, how did they become what they were now?

"The Sullen?" he asked within earshot of Myrradin. "What happened to them?"

For a moment, only the rhythmic swishing of feet through tall grass and the occasional chirp of nocturnal creatures answered him. Rykan wondered if his question had gone unnoticed or if it had stirred memories Myrradin preferred to leave undisturbed. The moon cast a pale glow over their path, the silver light reflecting off the dewdrops that clung to the blades of grass.

"They were once a great order of magi," Myrradin finally said with a hint of reverence. "Like myself, they studied everything we have available about the aspects of Archeinor."

Rykan noticed Selaina had moved closer, her curiosity kindled by their conversation. The group continued to navigate the marshy terrain, the soft squelching of mud underfoot a reminder of the unstable ground they traversed.

"Like most orders, they had a creed, a unified vision," Myrradin mused, almost to himself, as he led them away from the marsh. "But personal ambitions always weave through such grand plans. It reminds me of my youth. I too was once driven by a vision, a belief that my profound aptitude for magic was destined to reshape our world."

He paused, his gaze lingering on the distant horizon, as if envisioning the world he'd intended to create. The night was still, the air crisp with a hint of the approaching dawn.

"I was to be a beacon of change, a paragon. Not just another mage feeding the hungry or tending the sick but a true architect of a new era. After all, isn't the mark of a great man to envision and forge a future others only dare dream of?"

Myrradin glanced at his companions, his expression one of earnest self-reflection mixed with pride.

"I envisioned a world reordered by magic, where its application was interwoven with the very fabric of society. Not merely to aid in mundane tasks but to fundamentally transform how we interact with the world, how we govern, how we live. The potential for magic to be a catalyst for global change is immense, and I—well, I've always seen myself at the forefront of that transformation."

"But what of the Sullen, Myrradin?" Rykan interjected cautiously, confused by the conversation veering far from his initial question.

"The Sullen?" Myrradin mumbled to himself, snapping back to the present. "Oh, yes, yes. Where was I?"

"You hadn't even started yet," Selaina said teasingly.

"Long ago, before the Conclave, there were many smaller orders of magi scattered across Galanor," Myrradin began again, delving into the history of the Sullen.

Rykan tried to keep his focus, though he couldn't help catching Selaina's eye, sharing a fleeting smile of amusement at the elder's tendency for long-winded tales. The brief connection with her warmed him more than the evening air.

Rykan's gaze lingered on Selaina a moment longer, captivated by the soft glimmer of moonlight in her eyes. She smiled back, but this time, Rykan noticed a faint unease in her expression. Realizing his attention might be making her uncomfortable, he quickly averted his eyes, heat rising in his cheeks as he turned back to Myrradin's ongoing narrative.

"It has been said that they discovered a great well of magic in the pockets of the earth, potentially left over from Archeinor during the molding of the world," Myrradin continued.

As they walked, their shadows stretched long and eerie against the ground, cast by the moon's light.

"They attempted to use it to bind this pure Archeinor essence to themselves, but it was too raw, too potent, to bind. They tried to alleviate this by joining together in a binding ritual, synthesizing the essence between them all to allow them to use it."

Myrradin's voice grew more somber as he continued.

"Something caused the energy to become volatile, rupturing the land around it and twisting their physical forms into grotesque shapes, leaving them as fragments of what they once were."

The group moved steadily, the distant hoot of an owl punctuating the night. Myrradin's words hung heavily in the air.

"Now they must feed on essence to survive. They have been known to comb the battlefields where mavins and sorcerers fought and died, draining any residual magic that remains."

Rykan's brow furrowed. "I guess the catacombs are the perfect place to make their home," he said, his voice reflecting a mix of understanding and unease.

"Indeed," Myrradin replied, his tone carrying the weight of unfortunate truth.

"In the forest where I grew up," said Selaina, "there was a blue light that could be seen through cracks in stone. Could that be one of these wells of magic?"

"It certainly could be," said Myrradin. "I'm sure there are smaller pockets in the world that have yet to be discovered."

"Why have I never heard of the Sullen before?" Rykan asked with curiosity as well as concern.

"They are mostly unseen, keeping out of the way of most folk. They have not been known to attack," Myrradin explained. "They have been seen in certain places where the veil between the mortal world and that of Archeinor and Pandemora are thinnest, places only those who dabble in magic would have interest in."

Rykan's thoughts returned to his dream. "Who were they speaking to in my dream?" he asked. "Through the portal."

Myrradin stopped abruptly, turning to face Rykan, his expression serious. "Be careful of the words you utter into the night," he cautioned, his voice low and ominous. "Do not repeat the names you may hear in dreams. It may take only vocalizing a name to summon the influence of entities that would do great harm to the world."

Rykan's skin turned cold, a shiver running down his spine as Myrradin resumed his path around the lake. He wondered if he had said something wrong. Glancing at Selaina, he searched her expression for her thoughts, but she didn't look back this time. Her focus remained on their path ahead.

As they neared the other side of the lake, they came upon a small hill, or what seemed more like a very large boulder with moss and trees growing on top. The hill loomed in the moonlight, casting long shadows that danced with the swaying trees. Myrradin headed toward it, climbing up the slope with the ease of someone familiar with such terrain.

"We should make our camp here," he announced, his voice cutting through the quiet night.

The group set to work, their movements efficient and purposeful. Rykan helped gather firewood, the scent of damp earth and fresh moss filling the cool night air while they prepared for the evening. The soft crackle of the fire soon mingled with the symphony of the night—crickets chirping, leaves rustling in the gentle breeze—providing a sense of warmth and security pushing back against the mysteries lurking in the darkness.

Rykan settled by the fire, his thoughts lingering on Myrradin's words and the Sullen's tragic fate. The night was still, the stars twinkling overhead like scattered diamonds, reminding him of the vastness of their journey and the mysteries yet to unfold. The fire crackled softly, casting flickering shadows on the surrounding trees and rocks, creating an almost ethereal atmosphere.

He glanced at Selaina once more, her face bathed in the warm, gentle glow of the firelight. Her features appeared serene and contemplative, adding a sense of calm to the otherwise tense evening. Not wanting her to catch his gaze on her, he quickly turned away, his heart quickening as he hoped she hadn't noticed his lingering look. The cool night air brushed against his skin, and he took a deep breath, trying to steady his racing thoughts.

Rykan surveyed the land behind them, making sure there were no Sullen in sight. His eyes caught something out of place against the reflections of moonlight on the lake. A silhouette stood silently, watching them. Its slanted stance defied the natural balance any human could achieve without falling over. Panic surged through him, and he quickly drew his sword. Behind him, Garrick unsheathed his weapon as well, and Elysia followed suit, her eyes scanning the shadowy figure.

He continued to stare into the night until he noticed another form shifting almost imperceptibly in the gloom, its movements slow and unnatural. The air seemed to grow heavier with each passing moment, the night pressing in around them like a living thing.

"Don't be alarmed," Ysadora said calmly. "They are the Nadrok, the neverborn, the watchers from the deep. Their nature is strange, but they will not harm us."

"What do they want?" Rykan asked, his grip tightening on the hilt of his sword.

"They want nothing," Myrradin replied. "Consider yourselves fortunate to have seen them. Few ever do."

"I've seen them before," Selaina added, keeping her voice quiet. "They did nothing that would harm me."

"What do they watch?" Rykan asked tensely, his eyes never leaving the eerie figure.

"No one knows for certain," Myrradin said, his tone thoughtful. "It is speculated that they exist in past, present, and future all at the same time. Their presence here could signify that something significant happened long ago or will at some point in the future. Though I have never heard of them being seen in this area before."

Rykan shifted uneasily. "Maybe we should keep moving."

"I'm with the kid," Garrick muttered, his eyes narrowing at the silent watcher. "I prefer not being watched while I sleep."

"I am weary, I'm sure we all are," Myrradin interjected, "from the storm, from fighting. We have a lot of travel ahead of us tomorrow. This is the best place we will find."

As they settled into the camp on the hill, Darian passed around a small jar of nuts and berries he had gathered along the journey. Rykan took it first, measuring what he guessed was enough to split between the eight of them into his hand and putting back the rest. It wasn't much, but it was something to put in his belly until they could find something else.

Sitting quietly around the campfire, no one seemed comfortable enough to sleep with the dark creatures nearby. Rykan watched as Selaina got up to retrieve something from her bag. She returned to the fire and sat next to Ysadora.

"Here's the book I was telling you about. Could you tell me what these words say?" Selaina asked, hopeful as she offered the book to Ysadora.

After only a short moment, Ysadora rubbed her temples, as though trying to ward off an intense headache. "I'm sorry, Selaina," she said, her voice strained. "I can't hold this any longer. This book … it's saturated with suffering, sickness, death, pain, guilt—it's overwhelming."

She quickly closed the cover and handed the book back to Selaina, who looked disappointed but understanding. Rykan opened his mouth to speak, but before he could, Elysia's voice cut through the tension.

"Bring it over here," she called from across the fire, a warm smile on her face. "I'll read it."

Selaina hesitated, concern in her eyes as she glanced back at Ysadora. "Are you well?"

"Yes," Ysadora replied, exhaling deeply. "I'm fine now."

Relieved, Selaina's eyes brightened as she stood and crossed the small camp to where Elysia and Garrick lounged. Handing over the book, she watched as Elysia gently caressed the leather cover.

"This is a beautiful book," Elysia remarked, her fingers tracing the embossed patterns. "Where did you get it?"

"It belonged to my friend, Jeth," said Selaina with a touch of sadness. "After he was killed, I kept it to remember him."

"I'm sorry," Elysia responded softly as she opened the book. "The short dream whispers, the long dream teaches, the Everdream embraces. I pray he is dreaming well."

"My mother spoke of the Netherwood, a spirit world in the forest," Selaina said, her eyes fixed on the dancing flames. "She believed that's where the living go when their spirits leave this world."

Elysia nodded thoughtfully. "The Netherwood and the Everdream may be the same place, just known by different names in different cultures."

"I hope he's happy," Selaina murmured softly, more to herself than to anyone around her, "wherever he is."

Elysia's eyes moved over the pages of the book as she read aloud. "In the dawn of days when the world was young…" she began, "the celestials gathered to shape Galanor, the world where the wild, unbridled chaos of the cosmos merged in perfect harmony with the steadfast structures of order."

She paused, looking up briefly at Selaina.

"One by one, the celestials presented their visions of how the world should be shaped. There were dreams of seeds that would grow into great expanses of green, forests so vast and ancient that they remembered the planting of the first seed." Her hands traced the words as she spoke them.

Rykan began to recognize the story, moving closer to listen to Elysia.

"Others spoke of oceans that would stretch beyond the horizon," Elysia continued, her voice rising and falling in a rhythmic pattern. "Their waves would one day tell stories of ancient civilizations swallowed by time and of creatures that dwelled in the abyss guarding secrets as old as the world itself."

She turned another page, her eyes scanning the text before she relayed the next part.

"Another brought ideas of vast dunes, sculpted by the winds of time, under a canopy of stars. The sands would whisper secrets to the moon, each grain of sand a keeper of stories untold. The deserts would be places of beauty and mystery where silence spoke louder than the rain."

Elysia's voice adopted a reverent tone.

"Unable to come to an agreement, they chose to unite all their visions, spreading out from the center of the world. The celestials worked together, forming a great mountain that rose to the heavens. Kylinshan stood as the heart of the world."

"I know this story," Rykan chimed in. "Kylinshan is where the Sky Serpents are."

"I've heard about the Sky Serpents," said Selaina.

"The summit of Kylinshan is where the Zhal Evurah must go to be judged," Ysadora added. "If the Sky Serpents give their blessing, they bestow some of their power on the Zhal Evurah so they can return balance to Galanor."

"There are pilgrimages still made to Kylinshan," Elysia noted. "Most for the history and beauty of the mountain, but others actually believe they are Zhal Evurah climbing to the summit in hopes of receiving the Sky Serpents' blessing. Now that Ethyllion is gone, they all return disappointed."

"What makes them believe they are Zhal Evurah if it is no longer possible?" Selaina pondered aloud.

Elysia shrugged. "They are eager to see themselves as more than they are, I think, chasing grandiose delusions."

After a while, their growing weariness made most of them forget about the Nadrok, and they each began to seek out a place where they could lay their heads. Rykan discovered that the driest spots on the ground were those away from the trees, the rest still damp from the storm. It seemed contradictory, but he supposed the trees weren't much help in shelter from that kind of rain. The open places would have dried faster in the sun if the storm had subsided before nightfall. Though he hadn't expected to get much sleep here, he was out as soon as he laid his head down.

❧

In the stillness of the night, Rykan stirred from his sleep, his throat parched and his mind momentarily lost in the remnants of a fading dream. The moon had long set, leaving only a ghostly light that lined the clouds overhead in silver. Adjusting to the darkness, he noticed someone standing alone near the edge of the hill.

It was Selaina.

Feeling a compelling urge to join her, Rykan quietly made his way over, intentionally scuffing his boots against the grass to alert her to his presence.

"Why aren't you sleeping?" he asked gently, hoping to draw her out of her thoughts.

"I was," she responded, her voice soft and distant. "But I woke up and couldn't fall back asleep."

"You know, lying down might help," he suggested half-jokingly, trying to bring a smile to her face.

She didn't laugh. "I was listening to the night birds," she explained, turning slightly to face him. "They remind me of home. There's a lot on my mind … I was hoping the sounds would calm it."

"Is it working?" Rykan inquired, stepping closer to her side.

"A little," she admitted, her eyes drifting back to the dark horizon.

Rykan found himself opening up more than he had intended. "A few weeks ago, I would never have imagined I'd be this far from home."

"Neither would I," Selaina agreed, finally turning to face him fully. "I always wanted to see what there was out beyond the forest. I never thought it would be like this. That seems so long ago now, everything seemed so much simpler then."

"If you were back there now and nothing had changed, what would you be doing?" Rykan asked.

"We would have finished dinner by now," she said, her eyes reflecting the starlight. "I would have cleaned the table. Mother and Jeth would have retired to their rooms. I'd be tucked into my bed." Selaina's hands absently picked at a loose thread on her sleeve. "Sometimes, at night, I'd keep my lamp burning, just a small light to push back the darkness. But even with the lamp, the world outside my window felt like a different place—one I wasn't part of. I used to wonder what happened out there in the dark. What was it like, the wicked world beyond the forest? And I wondered if there were others like me, lying in bed, feeling lost, yet unable to find each other."

Rykan grinned. "Finding the people in this group, what do you think of the world now?"

"It's amazing and terrifying," said Selaina. "There is so much I don't understand, but it isn't all wicked the way my mother described. What about you, what was living in the city like?"

"There are too many rules," Rykan said with a dismissive wave. "Most of them don't even make sense half the time. I get why they exist, sure, but the whole 'get up, get dressed, be here at this time' routine? It's like the world's constantly telling you where you need to be. I love Tathara, but it feels like we never get enough time to actually live. Festivals and celebrations—they're the best part, when everyone comes together to just be. But even then, we have to leave early because there's always some pointless task waiting for us the next day. It's exhausting, always getting ready for the next boring thing."

"Festivals sound wonderful," said Selaina, her face lighting up. "I've never been to anything like that. But you shouldn't despise the work you have to do every day. I had chores to do every day, things that needed to be done so that we had food, shelter, and clothing. I can't imagine not having something to work for, just to walk about aimlessly with no direction. Responsibilities give you purpose."

"Now that you're free, do you feel you don't have purpose?" Rykan asked, his voice lowering slightly.

"I'm not free," said Selaina. "I am bound to this quest. I committed to using the Wishing Stone and helping to set the world right again."

"We aren't keeping you here," Rykan said. "I definitely don't want you to leave, but you have the freedom to leave if you wanted to."

"I suppose I always have," said Selaina. "I could have left my mother and Jeth long ago and gone out on my own, but something held me there. Maybe it was my responsibilities or maybe it was out of love. This is the same way. If it weren't for this responsibility, I don't think I would walk across the land, through storms and dark catacombs."

"The whole world is depending on you," he said softly, aware of the weight of their quest. "And no one even knows it."

"It's not just on me," she corrected gently. "I couldn't do this alone."

"None of us could," Rykan concurred, remembering the eerie depths of the catacombs. "Down there, it felt like we were a team. I didn't think we'd make it out, but we supported each other. Like a family."

"It does feel like we've grown closer," Selaina said, a faint smile playing at her lips. "I don't feel as isolated in the group as I did at first."

Encouraged by her words, Rykan instinctively reached out, his hand brushing against hers in the darkness. He intended it as a comforting gesture, a physical affirmation of their bond. However, she stiffened, her hand pulling away.

"What are you doing?" she asked, her tone laced with surprise and a hint of caution.

"Nothing," Rykan stammered, suddenly self-conscious. "I just thought—we were getting closer."

"I thought you meant mentally, like trusting each other," she explained, taking a step back to put a gentle but definite space between them. Her voice remained soft, yet resolute. "We don't need to be touching, do we? It only makes me feel more closed in."

Rykan nodded, a flush of embarrassment warming his cheeks. "Right, of course," he said quickly, respecting her space. He hadn't considered that she might not see his gesture the same way he did, especially given her secluded upbringing. "I'm sorry," he added. "I didn't mean to make you uncomfortable."

She nodded, her smile returning, though still a bit hesitant. "No harm done. I just need some time to … understand all this."

They stood together in silence, Rykan contemplating the vast night and the journey ahead. He realized then just how much distance remained, not only from the Stone, but between him and Selaina and their understanding of each other.

CHAPTER 26

I N THE EARLY light of the sun, Selaina walked behind Myrradin and Ysadora as they discussed how to get back on course. The dawn's gentle rays cast long shadows across the landscape, painting everything in a soft, golden hue. A cascade of sunshimmer curved through the sky, scattering prismatic sparks that danced across the morning air. They crouched low in the weeds as they neared a small trail. Selaina held her breath in anticipation. The earthy scent of damp soil mingled with the crispness of the new day, heightening her awareness. Myrradin, watching and listening, paused for a moment until deciding it was safe. After crossing the path, they hurried toward a group of trees ahead, hoping to stay out of sight of any potential travelers.

Selaina tried to keep a certain distance from Rykan, even though he stayed near her. Walking close to Ysadora, she used her as a shield to keep Rykan's gaze from fixing on her. The embarrassment of the previous night was still fresh in her thoughts. She wasn't even sure what she was embarrassed about exactly, only that she couldn't look him in the eye right now.

The feeling of being so far from home and everything unfamiliar weighed heavily on her. How had she ever allowed herself to think she could be anything more than an outsider? She didn't know the customs of these people. Was it normal to touch their hands together when feeling a level of trust between each other? It seemed like something more. She felt something more, but it was strange. Whatever it was, she wasn't ready for it. And now she had broken any trust that Rykan shared with her. How could she face him again? She couldn't say anything to undo it.

After a morning of relentless travel, Myrradin finally paused for a much-needed rest, settling onto a large white stone that jutted from the earth like a weary throne. Selaina sat down next to him. The stone was cool and smooth, offering a brief respite from the rigors of their journey. Her thoughts were adrift in memories of home when a sudden tap on her shoulder jarred her back to reality. She turned to find Garrick beside her, his expression earnest.

"Come with me," Garrick said, a spark of adventure in his eyes. "Let's see if there's anything to hunt."

A smile spread across Selaina's face, not out of eagerness to hunt, but because she felt a sense of belonging—being chosen, being needed. She nodded, and together they steered away from the resting group, heading toward the denser part of the woods.

Behind them, Myrradin's voice carried a note of concern. "Do you really think it wise to take her away from the larger group?"

"She's the only other hunter we have," Garrick replied without looking back, his voice carrying a definitive edge, as if no further justification was needed. "And I know you won't leave if she's with me."

Kadin rubbed his stomach exaggeratedly. "Seriously, try to bring back something big. I'm so hungry I could eat an entire forest right now."

"We could all use a good meal," Ysadora chimed in, her tone earnest and slightly insistent. "Some real sustenance would do wonders." She looked around, daring anyone to disagree.

"Don't take too long," Myrradin called after them, his voice fading as they delved deeper into the woods. "We still have a long way to go."

Garrick seemed to dismiss Myrradin's caution, his focus set on the hunt as he led Selaina into the thicket. The trees here were not particularly tall, but the undergrowth was dense, a tangle of bushes and ferns that clutched at their clothes and obscured their feet. Despite the challenging terrain, Garrick moved with a hunter's grace, each step deliberate and quiet.

As they pushed deeper, the forest seemed to close in around them, the light dimming under the thick canopy, the air cool and heavy with the scent of earth and leaf mold. Selaina followed Garrick's lead, her senses sharpening, listening for the rustle of game or the snap of a twig underfoot.

"I'll let you decide where to go. Where should we seek our prey?" Garrick asked.

"I thought you had some idea," Selaina responded, slightly taken aback.

"You said you knew how to hunt," Garrick pressed. "Where would you go?"

She realized now that he was testing her knowledge. "We always went near the brook back home," Selaina explained. "Animals would come to the pooled water to drink—it was a perfect spot."

"Smart." Garrick nodded. "So, think about it—where would you find water here?"

"How could I possibly know that?" Selaina's frustration showed. "I don't know this land."

"But you know nature," Garrick encouraged. "You have the answers, you just need to connect the dots."

Selaina hesitated, feeling out of her depth. "I … I don't know what you mean."

Garrick pointed toward a nearby hill. "Would you find water flowing up there?"

"Obviously not," Selaina replied, a touch of irritation in her voice. It clicked then—water flowed downhill. "It would collect in the lower areas … like a basin."

"Now we're getting somewhere," Garrick said with a small smile. "So, where from here?"

Selaina took a moment to observe their surroundings, her gaze settling on a gentle slope. "The land dips over there, toward that thicket."

"Lead the way," Garrick encouraged, stepping aside to let her take the lead. His challenge had sparked a flame of determination in her.

Selaina advanced toward the sloping land, using the trees as support to navigate the descent. At the bottom, she found herself on flat ground carpeted with moss and scattered leaves, a stark contrast to the uphill terrain. Standing in the quiet of the forest, she paused, trying to envision the passage of wildlife through this area.

Ahead, the forest framed a natural corridor where two trees arched gracefully away from each other, creating a picturesque setting. Selaina could almost see elk there, majestic and alert, lifting their heads at the slightest sound before returning to graze on the branches within their reach.

However, the reality of the landscape disappointed her hopes. There were no low-hanging branches here for elk to feast on. While the animals might pass through this area in their travels, they wouldn't linger to feed. Her eyes scanned the vicinity, searching for a better location, when a cluster of shorter trees caught her attention to the left. That seemed like an ideal spot for elk to browse.

Approaching the cluster, Selaina noticed a small footprint in the dirt beneath one of the trees—an encouraging sign. She followed the direction of the print, weaving between the trees with heightened awareness, her eyes peeled for more signs that could lead her to their quarry. Each step was measured and silent, her senses tuned to the subtle whispers of the forest in hopes of catching any further evidence of the elk that had once passed this way.

As Selaina ventured further, she encountered another cluster of trees tightly packed and forming a natural barrier, their leaves a lush, vibrant green. The ground underfoot grew softer, a gentle slope leading her deeper into the woods. With deliberate movements, she pushed aside the dense brush, revealing a hidden gem—a clearing with a small, secluded pond at its center.

The pond, seemingly unconnected to any stream or brook, appeared to be a natural basin where rainwater had collected, perhaps swollen from recent storms. It was a serene spot, with waterfowl dotting the surface, some paddling gently while others bathed or foraged along the muddy edges. The abundance of insects or amphibians that thrived in such undisturbed wetlands likely drew the birds to this place.

Selaina felt a sense of peace wash over her. She watched the birds, their simple existence a contrast to the chaos and conflict she had experienced the last few days.

"Something about finding these secluded spots brings that primal core to the surface," said Garrick in a voice that was softer than usual. "It's in moments like this you feel a part of the world. Not the civilizations we build for ourselves but the natural world. Though we are physically built like prey, our minds make us predators. Our inventiveness and skill at building and using tools and weapons."

Selaina nodded thoughtfully, her eyes following the ripples on the pond. "I think I know what you mean. When I take aim at a living target, I feel powerful, dangerous. I like that feeling, though I don't like hurting animals."

Garrick looked at her as if he understood. "You know that you are deadly, but you also have the control to restrain it, to only use it when necessary," he said. "That's the responsibility required of anyone with power. That is Vatreus's weakness. For all the power he has, he has lost control."

Selaina's jaw tightened. "That is why we must take it from him," she said.

"It's all we can do to stop him," said Garrick. "Now, move ahead and find a target."

As Selaina slipped quietly behind a fallen log, her movement startled a group of birds into flight, but not all were perturbed. She noticed several pheasants wandering near the grassy banks, pecking at the ground in search of food. The clearing offered a wide-open view of the sky above, framed by the encircling trees—a stark contrast to the dense forest surrounding it.

The tranquility of the place struck Selaina, making it feel almost otherworldly. It was hard to believe such a peaceful, secluded spot existed in the midst of the wilderness, much like a secret garden. She was part of the natural environment, a predator stalking its prey. With her heart quietly thrumming in her chest, she steadied her breathing and prepared for the hunt, her eyes fixed on the unsuspecting pheasants.

Garrick moved stealthily beside Selaina, his presence reassuring rather than imposing. When he gently placed his hand on her shoulder, it felt like a silent commendation of her skills, a gesture that surprisingly didn't unsettle her. It was guiding and supportive. Selaina reflected momentarily on why this touch felt different from Rykan's—perhaps it was because someone touching her hands felt more personal, more intimate, than touching her shoulder.

Focused on the task at hand, Selaina pulled an arrow from her quiver, nocked it, and pulled back the string of her bow, her eyes narrowing on her target. Just then, she felt Garrick's breath near her ear, his voice barely above a whisper.

"You're not accounting for the wind," he advised calmly. "There's enough wind that, at this distance, it's going to throw your arrow off."

Though it felt counterintuitive, Selaina trusted Garrick's judgment. With a slight adjustment to her aim, she targeted a spot just to the left of the pheasant. Her muscles tensed as she steadied her breathing and released the arrow. It sailed through the air and struck the pheasant on its side with a thud. Almost simultaneously, the other pheasant, startled by the commotion, flapped its wings frantically, attempting to take flight. But before it could ascend, another arrow, swift and precise from Garrick's bow, brought it down.

When they returned to the others, each carrying their kill, they were greeted with applause. Those who remained had already started a fire in preparation. With their lack of time, Garrick showed Selaina how to skin the birds rather than spending time plucking them. After gutting the birds and cleaning them with some water from Myrradin's flask, they had them ready to cook. Garrick decided to split both birds down the back to flatten them out and reduce the cooking time.

As the birds cooked over the stones placed in the fire, Selaina made a small cut to check that the meat was no longer pink near the bone. Once it was ready, she could hardly wait for the meat to cool before taking a bite. The meat was a bit tough, but it had a hearty flavor, even though they lacked anything to season it with.

Selaina observed her companions eating, talking, and sharing laughter around the fire, and a soft smile touched her lips. The group had endured a fierce storm, navigated the perilous depths of the catacombs, and faced the Sullen in harrowing encounters to reach this moment of respite. Seeing them relish simple joys, with the meal she had helped provide, filled her with a warm sense of accomplishment.

The laughter and camaraderie that rippled through the group lit a spark of belonging within her. For so long, she had felt like an appendage to the group—valuable only for her connection to the Wishing Stone. Now, as she watched them, their guards lowered in the glow of the campfire, she felt her role within the group shifting. She was no longer just a means to an end but an integral member of their makeshift family.

Selaina's earlier embarrassment over Rykan's touch had faded into the background, replaced by a newfound concern. She noticed him sitting quietly on the grass between Darian and Elysia, unusually subdued. This was a marked change from the Rykan she had come to know, and she couldn't help but wonder if he felt like an outsider—the way she once had—merely along for the ride.

Her heart sank at the thought that her reaction to his touch might be haunting him. It had been meant as a way to establish personal boundaries, not to alienate him from the group. The discomfort she felt stemmed partly from the unexpected intimacy—a concept foreign to her, as she had never witnessed such affectionate exchanges between her mother and Jeth. At the time, Rykan had seemed more concerned about her feelings than his own, which only added to her guilt.

But there was more to her hesitation than just unfamiliarity with closeness. Selaina knew that, once they used the Stone to change time, everything would be different—perhaps irrevocably so. They would likely never meet again, never share these moments, these bonds they were slowly forming. The thought of growing too attached, only to have it all undone, filled her with a sense of impending loss. How could she let herself get close to anyone when their very existence in her life might be erased?

Friendships, she realized, were far more complex than she had anticipated. If only she could share her past experiences and her fears about the future with Rykan, perhaps he would understand that her reaction wasn't a personal rejection. It was a defense mechanism, a way to protect herself from the inevitable pain of losing him—or never having known him at all.

After the meal had settled, they carefully extinguished the fire, covering it with dirt and shifting the rocks to erase any trace of their campfire. As they resumed their journey, trekking deeper through the woods, subtle changes in the environment began to hint at the landscape ahead. While the forest remained dense, the vibrancy of the leaves started to wane. The green hues of the foliage subtly shifted toward yellow, hinting at a drier climate ahead.

The air gradually lost its moist chill, growing slightly warmer and drier with each step. The soil underfoot, previously rich and loamy, began to show patches of harder, more compact earth. A dull yellow color tinged sparse areas of grass that bordered the path, the vegetation struggling under less frequent rains.

As darkness fell, they made camp on a ridge overlooking a vast valley below. Above it loomed a group of mountains in the distance, nearly blending into the dusk sky. After feasting on Garrick's recent kill, they sat around the fire telling stories of their exploits, many of them sounding a bit too far-fetched to be completely true. Rykan remained subdued, as he had all day.

"Who is she?" Ysadora asked as she stood next to Darian, who held the small frame of Bellaria's portrait.

"Bellaria," said Darian, his voice carrying a fond sadness. "My wife."

"She's a lovely woman," Ysadora remarked as she looked at the portrait. "Where is she while you are on this journey?"

Darian nodded, his eyes not leaving the painted image. "She passed a few months ago."

"Oh, I'm sorry," said Ysadora as her expression softened.

"When we had this painting done, I didn't fully realize just how precious it would be," said Darian. He adjusted the frame slightly, as if ensuring the firelight caught her features just right. "This gives me the chance to look at her face each night before I close my eyes, praying to meet up with her in a dream."

Selaina's heart ached for Darian, but he seemed to like showing his wife's portrait to people. Perhaps sharing his grief with others helped to relieve some of the pain.

Garrick sat shirtless as Elysia leaned close to him. He polished the blade of his sword with a cloth, while she rubbed something over the wound on his back. They seemed to be listening to Kadin ramble on with another story. It amazed her how a group such as this could end up getting along so well. She realized she had come to feel something for each of them. As much as she missed her life in the forest with Jeth and her mother, she would miss these people nearly as much.

The campfire had dwindled to embers, casting a gentle glow that barely touched the edges of the darkness. Myrradin excused himself, his silhouette merging with the shadows as he sought a quiet place to rest. One by one, Garrick, Elysia, and the others followed, their conversations tapering off into the night.

Selaina watched Rykan for a moment, his quietness pulling at her. When he stood and walked away from the dying fire, presumably to find solitude, she seized the moment. This might be her only chance to bridge the distance that had crept between them.

She found him at the cliff's edge, a solitary figure against the vast, moonlit valley. He sat with his hands propping him up from behind. His gaze was lost to the horizon where the night sky met the rugged earth. The gentle rustle of leaves under her feet announced her approach, and he turned, his face etched with surprise.

"Do you mind if I sit with you?" she asked gently, not wanting to spoil the serenity of the night.

"No, you're welcome to," Rykan replied, his voice warm but weary, as he cleared a spot beside him.

Selaina settled next to him, mimicking his relaxed pose. They both stared out into the valley.

"It's a lovely view," she remarked, her words floating between them.

"Yes, it is," Rykan agreed, his eyes reflecting the tranquil scene. "You can see the water down there in the valley."

Following his gaze, Selaina noticed the gentle shimmer of a brook winding through the valley. "You're right," she confirmed, "there's a brook. It's beautiful."

"The world almost seems like a beautiful place from here." Rykan sighed, a hint of melancholy threading through his tone. "You would never know there's any fighting or war going on."

"The world is always a beautiful place." Selaina nodded, feeling the weight of his words. "Sometimes our actions make us forget that."

Rykan looked out over the moonlit landscape, his voice carrying a hint of wishful thinking. "Maybe if they saw it the way we are right now, it would inspire us all to do good," he mused.

Selaina sighed, her gaze drifting to the distant shimmer of the brook that caught the moonlight like threads of silver. "I don't know if I have ever truly done anything especially good," she admitted, as the uncertain breeze changed direction, blowing her white hair across her cheeks.

"Of course you have," Rykan countered with warmth, turning to face her fully. The soft glow of the moon illuminated his features, casting light on his earnest expression. "Look at what you're doing now, traveling across the world to help everyone."

"I haven't done anything yet," Selaina protested softly. "But I hope to."

"You have a kind heart," he insisted gently. "You care about others. That counts for a lot."

Selaina shook her head as she looked down at the grass beneath them, dewy from the night air. "I do care, but I don't know if I can actually help anyone."

"Most people are difficult to help. You never know what they really want or need," Rykan reflected thoughtfully.

Selaina watched him, noting the lines on his brow and the distant look in his eyes. She hadn't thought of him as being someone contemplative, who looked out at the world and wondered.

Rykan glanced at her, breaking the quiet. "I guess the others are asleep. What's keeping you up?"

Selaina hesitated for a moment. "I wanted to make sure you were well," she replied honestly. "You haven't been talking with everyone much lately."

Rykan's eyes opened in surprise, his gaze meeting hers. "You noticed?" As his features relaxed, he spoke again. "I suppose that proves what I was saying—you're kind enough to care about how others might be feeling."

"Not all the time," Selaina confessed, her eyes meeting his. "There's a lot I could have done differently."

"Me too," he agreed, his voice softening. "Everyone has regrets. We just have to keep doing better, try to keep them to a minimum."

"Yeah." She nodded, her gaze lingering on him with a bit of concern and curiosity. "So, have you been well lately?"

"Yes, I've been fine," he answered a bit too quickly, his eyes briefly flickering away toward the valley below.

"There must be something bothering you," she pressed gently. "You haven't been yourself."

"I just didn't feel like talking, I guess," he said.

"I suppose you were right," she said. "Most people *are* difficult to help."

Rykan exhaled sharply, stifling a laugh, which in turn made her smile. Selaina let the silence hang for a moment before she leaned back, spreading her hands out behind her. Accidentally, her hand brushed against his, and he quickly withdrew.

"Sorry," he muttered.

"No, all is well," she reassured him, smiling slightly from embarrassment. "It was my fault."

He repositioned himself, sitting straight and crossing his legs. Above them, the crescent moon began to dip behind the mountain range.

"What's been bothering you?" Selaina asked again, her voice soft but insistent.

"Nothing that important." He shrugged, and his voice betrayed a bit of hesitance. "It's stupid, really."

"If there's something on your mind, it's not stupid," she said earnestly, her eyes searching his. "I used to talk to my friend Jeth about things that I couldn't talk to my mother about. It always helps to have someone who will listen."

Rykan's voice trailed off, laden with uncertainty. "It's just … I don't know, the other day when you and Garrick went hunting and brought back food, I realized something. Everyone has a role in the group, except me," he confessed, his tone edged with frustration. "No one really needs me to be here."

"How could you say that?" Selaina countered firmly, turning to face him directly. "You fought bravely in the catacombs, and you were the one who came up with that plan to find our way out. I would have never thought of that."

"It didn't work out like I thought," Rykan admitted. "If it weren't for your keen observations, we still wouldn't have found the exit."

"That's because we make a great team," Selaina said, her tone light, trying to lift his spirits with a warm grin.

Rykan responded with a hesitant smile and looked down, his attention caught by a small leaf, which he began to twirl between his fingers. The night deepened around them, and the stars began to twinkle more brightly as the moon dipped behind the distant mountains, casting long shadows across the landscape.

The stars were magical, no matter how many times she saw them.

"Maybe it's like the stars," Selaina said. "They don't need to force their way into the sky, they simply exist where they are meant to be, shining light down on us." She noticed Rykan glancing at her, but she kept her eyes on the sky. "Maybe we don't need to try so hard to prove our worth. Maybe it's more about finding where we fit in the universe."

Rykan turned away, joining her in gazing up at the sky. They sat silently for a few moments. Selaina wondered if he was pondering her words.

"See those three bright stars close together?" Rykan pointed. "They say that's the sign of the Wishing Stone returning."

Selaina followed his gesture. The three stars of the convergence. They were all close, but two of them were closer together than the third.

"The convergence," she said. "They stand out, even against all the other stars."

"Auronia, Verantis, and Zaryneth," Rykan named them. "They were three celestials who watched over the world."

Selaina's eyes widened as she remembered. "The Sky Serpents are stars?"

"They aren't the same as the others," Rykan said. "They wander across the sky independently. It seems odd that the celestials are supposed to be perfect, but even they can disobey. I always wonder what tragedy made them do it. They weren't supposed to intervene in matters of the mortal world."

"I don't see what's so wrong with that," Selaina said. "If I could stop a tragedy, I would do it too."

"They interfered with the divine plan," Rykan explained.

"But why does a divine plan include tragedy?" Selaina asked. The idea frustrated her.

Rykan sighed, a thoughtful glare in his eye. "You can't have triumph without tragedy. At least, that's what my mother told me. She said it was a story told to explain hardships to people going through them. To help them see a broader view of their life and to continue on through the hardships, because even the celestials and the Sky Serpents have a purpose and are part of a greater design. To remind them that triumphs are waiting on the other side."

Selaina looked at Rykan, her eyes searching his face. "Jeth said their punishment was that they became physical but without hands, so they couldn't shape the world anymore."

"Their purpose was changed, as physical beings in the mortal world," he said. "To herald the coming of those with great destiny."

"That doesn't sound so bad," Selaina mused.

Rykan chuckled. "I don't know. Maybe to a celestial, becoming a physical being is the worst punishment there is."

Selaina wasn't sure if she found that idea funny or frightening. She gazed skyward again, her voice filled with wonder. "There are so many stars out there. Do you think they are all celestials?"

"Maybe," Rykan replied, his gaze following hers. "The rest of them must be more obedient than those three. They all stay in the same position relative to each other."

"How many stars do you think there are up there?" Selaina asked.

"More than I can count," Rykan murmured. "It always makes me feel tiny knowing there's so much more out there beyond this world."

"It does," Selaina agreed, her eyes also tracing the stars. "But it also makes all our troubles seem smaller, more manageable."

He nodded. "You see the good in everything."

Selaina felt a shift within her—a softening, a readiness to embrace the moment more fully than before. She remembered their earlier encounter and how she had recoiled from his touch. But now, with the vastness of the universe above them and the uncertainty of the future weighing on her, something had changed. The thought that this moment, this connection, might be erased if they used the Stone was strangely freeing. It stripped away her usual caution, her constant overthinking, leaving her with only the present—only this moment and the desire to live it fully.

Without a word, Selaina slowly reached out her hand toward Rykan's. Her movement was tentative at first, but as her fingers gently brushed against his, she didn't pull away this time. Instead, she let her hand rest near his, giving him the chance to pull away if he chose.

Rykan looked at her hand, then at her, a question in his eyes. He turned his palm up, inviting her to link her fingers with his. Selaina responded by slipping her hand into his, their fingers intertwining.

For once, she wasn't concerned with the consequences or what the future might hold. In this fleeting, fragile moment, she allowed herself to simply be—to feel without restraint, without the burden of what might come next. And in that, she found a freedom she hadn't known she needed.

They both looked at their joined hands for a moment, acknowledging this new, unspoken agreement of mutual support. Communicating through glances and playful expressions, they sat silently under the stars. Selaina's eyes moved back to the three wandering stars of the convergence, two of them so close now they seemed to be connected.

CHAPTER 27

THE FOLIAGE THINNED as Rykan and the others emerged from the woodlands the next day, revealing an uneven, rocky landscape, covered mostly in red clay. Sparse vegetation dotted the terrain, with bushes and small trees interspersed among patches of yellow grass. Without the shelter of shady trees, the sun blazed down, its rays relentless and unforgiving.

"We've passed into the region of Nordravin," Myrradin announced. "You would do well to cover yourselves as much as you can. The sun can be unforgiving."

Heeding his advice, Rykan pulled his hood up over his head, glancing at Selaina as she did the same. A strange feeling washed over him as he returned to a land he thought he had left behind.

"Nordravin?" Garrick asked, his brow furrowing. "What's in Nordravin? I lived here in the mountains for the past several months."

"If that is where Myrradin says we must go," Ysadora replied as she adjusted her cloak, her tone leaving no room for disagreement, "then that is exactly where we shall go."

Garrick's frustration erupted. "Enough with all the mystery," he demanded. "I think it's time you told us where we're heading." He slowed to a stop, crossing his arms and challenging Myrradin with his stance.

"It is too early yet," said Myrradin, keeping his gaze on the horizon. "You will know soon enough."

"I'm with Garrick," Kadin interjected with more than a hint of irritation in his voice. "We've been through enough on this quest

of yours. Battled with fire beasts, slogged through the worst storm I've ever heard of, and fought our way through catacombs of dead sorcerers. We deserve to know where our destination is." He threw up his hands in exasperation.

Myrradin's eyes darkened. "That is precisely why I haven't told you," he said, firmly. "I fear there are already sinister forces on our trail. If they were to discover the location now, they wouldn't need any of us alive." He scanned the rest of the group with a grave expression.

Rykan shifted uncomfortably. "Couldn't you just write it down or something?" he asked, hoping to mediate the discussion.

"I will not allow the secret anywhere outside of my head!" Myrradin shouted with an uncommon intensity.

Rykan felt his eyes widen, not expecting the outburst. He exchanged glances with the others, finding the same surprise on their faces.

Garrick sighed, rubbing the back of his neck. "What if something happens to you, Myrradin?" he asked, concerned. "What if you're killed in battle or on the journey? Then what?"

Myrradin's expression softened for a moment before hardening again. "Then we must make sure that doesn't happen."

"Lead the way then," Garrick said, his voice reluctant but resigned.

They approached the rim of a vast canyon, where imposing rock walls segmented the enormous chasm stretching out below them. Myrradin led the group along the cliff's edge, navigating between these natural barriers to find a well-trodden path that bridged the expanse. As they stepped onto the pathway, wide enough for four to walk abreast, the sheer drop on either side sent a shiver of apprehension through Rykan.

Casting a wary glance at Selaina, he noticed the unease mirrored in her eyes. She moved with exaggerated care, each step deliberate and measured, as though she were balancing on a high wire. Garrick and Kadin brushed past, their confident strides causing Selaina to stiffen momentarily until they were clear.

Sensing her discomfort, Rykan gently brushed his hand against Selaina's arm, a silent offer of support. She slipped her hand into his. Her fingers were small, yet her grip conveyed a surprising strength. As they walked together hand in hand, she appeared to be grateful and relieved, stepping across the rocks with more confidence. Rykan felt more stable too, now seeing the canyon's beauty for the first time.

The canyon walls themselves were a mosaic of geological history, with vibrant stripes of sediment layering down their faces. Below, a verdant canopy of trees hinted at a more humid, life-rich zone at the canyon's base, contrasting starkly with the arid breezes that swept the upper paths. Despite the pathway being polished smooth by countless previous travelers, it was not without its challenges. Large stones disrupted the surface, and the path occasionally sloped steeply, requiring careful navigation and occasional climbs. Ahead of them, Myrradin was having no trouble at all, despite his earlier complaints of sore joints and tired bones.

The pathway gradually expanded into a spacious plateau adorned with bushy trees, their leaves a vibrant display of orange and yellow hues. Selaina's grip loosened, a sign of her growing ease as the ground beneath their feet became more stable. Her lips curved into a smile at the sight of two lizards darting playfully among the crevices of the rocks, their swift movements a lively contrast to the serene landscape.

As they neared the mountain, a sense of unease washed over Rykan. The towering peak ahead seemed oddly familiar, a vague memory tugging at him—a feeling that something about this place was intimately connected to him. The silhouette of the mountain against the sky echoed a scene from a dream. An unsettling thought crept into his mind: the thing behind the gate was somewhere in these mountains. The air grew cooler and thinner as they ascended, the scent of pine and damp earth mixing with the crisp mountain breeze, but Rykan couldn't shake the feeling that something waited for them ahead.

"What mountains are these?" Rykan asked, the discomfort coming through in his voice.

"These are the Velsarath Peaks," Myrradin replied, his tone lowering to a whisper, as if the very name carried weight. "Many a soul has vanished amid their winding paths. It is said that an ancient terror dwells within, lurking in the shadows, forever bound to the crags and gorges."

A chill ran down Rykan's spine. The towering peaks cast long, foreboding shadows over the group, and the distant cry of an unseen creature added to the eerie atmosphere.

"I've seen such a terror," Garrick said, his voice grave. "A monstrous entity, ensnared behind an iron gate wrought into the mountainside."

The image of the flaming blue claw pulling the girl underneath the warped corner of the enormous gate flashed through Rykan's mind, sending a shiver through him.

Myrradin immediately came to a stop and turned around. "You've seen it?"

The whole group came to a halt as Myrradin stepped closer to Garrick. Each breath felt weighted, as if the very air around them carried the whispers of unseen threats. Shadows grew longer and seemed to twist unnaturally, casting an eerie pall over the landscape. Every rustle of leaves and distant, indistinct noise heightened their apprehension, amplifying the sense that something ominous lurked just beyond the edge of perception.

"Describe it to me," Myrradin said, his tone almost demanding.

Garrick's face darkened with the memory. "All I saw was a hand," he said. "A claw formed of blue energy, fire, but it contained something solid too."

"Was there anything else?" Myrradin asked, his eyes intense. "Anything at all?"

Garrick shook his head, a haunted look in his eyes. "I've tried to forget that day ever since."

"Did it make a sound?" Myrradin pressed. "Maybe a powerful resonance?"

Shuddering, Rykan recounted the words that were burned into his soul. "Bleeding veins, pulsing life. Skin to peel, bones to slice. Those were its words after it dragged a girl beneath the gate."

"You witnessed this too," Myrradin affirmed with a grim expression. "If only we knew what these words truly mean."

The group stood in a tense circle, a sense of dread thick in the air. The distant rumble of thunder reverberated through the mountains, each growl of the storm amplifying the sense of imminent danger. Though the sun still hung in the sky, its light wavered, casting long shadows that shifted unnaturally.

"What are we even talking about here?" Kadin asked. "Don't tell me our grand quest for the Wishing Stone now includes a tour of this horror show.

The catacombs were quite enough. If we're expected to face anything else like that, you'd better believe I'll be demanding substantial compensation."

Myrradin started along the pathway on the canyon wall. "Do not fear. We won't be going into the mountains."

The path began to narrow, leaving the plateau behind. Selaina squeezed Rykan's hand, her grip firm as they navigated the treacherous ledge.

"But what is the creature behind the gate?" she asked quietly.

Ysadora glanced questioningly at Myrradin as they continued along the ledge. The canyon wall loomed on one side, while a sheer drop stretched out on the other, making every step a test of balance and nerve. Myrradin slowed his pace, turning back to Selaina.

"We don't know for certain what it is," he said, pausing to gauge her reaction. "It is said that the presence in the mountains is an Orithar, an immortal being from Archeinor."

"That can't be right," Rykan interjected with disbelief. "Why would the Iron Flood be bringing people to a divine being, and why would it be eating them?"

"I highly doubt it was eating anyone," said Myrradin, attempting to reassure him.

"I heard the crunching of bone," said Rykan. "The sickening sound of …" The sounds crept back into his mind. Closing his eyes, he tried to shut them out and wipe them from his memory. The thought that the girl's was a fate that should have been his unsettled him endlessly.

"There was a mischievous one from Archeinor," said Kadin, breaking the tension. "At least in the stories I was told. He wanted to free mortals from our preordained fates, driven by the realm of order, and give us a chance to make our own way."

Elysia, who had been walking beside Myrradin, paused to adjust the strap of her pack before glancing at Selaina and Rykan.

"That's not how it goes," Elysia said, breaking the momentary silence. She glanced at the jagged peaks surrounding them, as if drawing strength from their steadfast presence. "In the constant battles between Pandemora and Archeinor, Ethyllion eventually became corrupted by chaos. With the stone accumulating too much chaotic energy and no longer functioning,

Azragal destroyed it to prevent a catastrophe that would endanger the fabric of reality."

Myrradin turned to face her, his eyes narrowing thoughtfully as he pondered her words. "Interesting perspective," he said, his voice barely rising above the sound of their footsteps crunching on the gravel path. "It seems the truth is as fragmented as the world that seeks to explain it."

As they walked, the group fell into a contemplative silence. The path ahead narrowed even further, forcing them to walk single file. Myrradin led the way, his staff tapping rhythmically against the ground. The jagged cliffs beside them seemed to close in, and the sky above turned a deeper shade of blue.

Myrradin tugged at the thick hairs on his chin. "No wonder the world is in the shape it is," he muttered, his voice carrying a hint of frustration. "After a thousand years, does no one even know the truth anymore? You seem to view Archeinor as purely good and Pandemora as evil. But they are not forces of good or evil. They are the energies of the beginning, of order and of chaos. Azragal viewed the world as a failure, something that needed to be fixed."

Elysia glanced toward him, her brow furrowed in thought. "I only tell the myth as I have learned it," she said softly. "The stories that have been passed down among my people for generations. It's not history, but a truth in the telling of a story."

"It is more than a story," Ysadora said, her voice unyielding. "Azragal destroyed Ethyllion to end destiny, to control us as he saw fit. He shattered that connection and entered the mortal realm."

Darian, tapping his foot against a large boulder, asked, "Control us? To what end?"

"To bring the world into complete and perfect order," explained Myrradin. "From birth, our behavior would be regulated, serving only the needs of Azragal and the colonies of all humanity. We would act on predetermined instinct rather than free will. Predetermined by him alone."

"Fortunately for us, he failed," Ysadora added, her gaze sweeping over the horizon. "The last Zhal Evurah, along with other Orithars from Archeinor, were able to seal him in a prison."

"Within the mountain," Rykan said as he looked up at the imposing peaks.

"And now he has given his power to Vatreus," Selaina added with concern.

"To wipe the world clean and bring it under control. Perfect order," Darian concluded.

"I don't believe that," Elysia said, shaking her head. "The power of Archeinor would never be used to subjugate us like that."

"That is the way of order," Ysadora said, her eyes meeting Elysia's. "It is why we must respect the balance. The world must be both."

"But you wield the power of Archeinor," said Darian. "Do you use it to bend the will of others?"

"We don't have that kind of power," Myrradin replied, his right eye twitching. "No one does. We can use it for protection or knowledge."

"No one has power like that except Vatreus," Ysadora said, her expression darkening. "He was given the purest form of power, directly from an Orithar of Archeinor."

"So we must undo it," Selaina said. "With the Wishing Stone."

"The power he wields is … fascinating," Myrradin mused. "Dangerous, of course, but it makes you wonder how much good could be done with it, if used properly."

"As you remind me all the time, life was never meant to be easy," Ysadora interjected. "That kind of power has no place in this world."

"I only wish I knew what my mother was doing there," Selaina said. "Why she was with Vatreus?"

"Liths tend to seek each other out," Myrradin replied gently. "In a world that both loves and hates them, they often find strength in numbers. But once you stop this from happening, it won't matter anymore."

Finally understanding the breadth of their mission, Rykan's frustration simmered just beneath the surface, a growing storm of indignation and grief. No one seemed to acknowledge the gravity of his city's plight or that he had narrowly escaped such a fate.

"None of this explains why they used the people of my city as fodder for that monster behind the gate," he said, his voice quivering with emotion. "I was almost among them."

Myrradin waved a dismissive hand. "Do not let your fear cloud your purpose, Rykan," he advised in a lofty tone. "Focus on the greater mission.

And remember, should the worst have befallen you, the power of my—our—wish would have undoubtedly restored you."

If there had never been an Iron Flood, so many things would be right again. His father would be home, never having needed to go to war. His mother would've continued living in peace. He would not have had to leave home until he was truly ready to find his way in the world.

Then there was Selaina. Would it mean he would never meet her? Rykan could not imagine never seeing her face again, her warm reassuring smile, her graceful movements. Being in her presence was almost worth all the calamity of the world. He would have to hope the fates would be kind to him. Perhaps they would reward him for helping to restore their vision of the world.

They moved from the canyon to a landscape of sandy soil at the foot of the nearest mountain. Patches of short yellow grass and trees with orange leaves were scattered in their path as they strode ahead. After a time, the dispersed trees became forests providing plenty of shade from the bright sun. Passing the first mountain displayed the full extent of the Velsarath Peaks. Many mountains, one behind the other, were layered into the distance.

"This area is patrolled by the Iron Flood," warned Garrick. "We shouldn't pass through here too close to the mountains."

"That is why we are traveling through this area," said Myrradin. "Further from the mountains is flat land and open space. You can see for miles."

In the shadows of the thicker part of the forest, they came to a trail worn into the grass between the trees. Rykan recognized it immediately as part of the road the caravan had traveled on to take them to the iron gate.

He could almost feel himself being jostled around the cart with the others. Echoes of the girl with scruffy blond hair speaking to him reverberated in his mind. Her scream as she was dragged under the gate still haunted his memories.

"This is it," he said. "The road that took us into the mountains."

He wasn't certain he could find the gate now. They had taken so many twists and turns through the ravines that he doubted he could remember the way. He was grateful for that, knowing neither his curiosity nor anyone else's could make him return.

As if seeing the discomforted looks on the others' faces, Myrradin added to his statement. "The presence is deep in the middle of the mountains. We are still quite far away."

As they crossed the road, Rykan saw something out of the corner of his eye move among the trees, but as he turned to look, there was nothing there. The feeling of being watched clung to him while they made their way across the path into the cover of the trees. Again, he noticed something there and turned, this time seeing a shadowy figure dart behind one of the trees. He glanced at Selaina. Her wary eyes told him she had seen them too, the Nadrok. Though they were only watchers who never interfered with mortals, their presence unnerved Rykan.

The leaves rustled nearby, and Rykan tapped the hilt of his sword, trying to ignore the sound and refusing to give into the fear imposed by the Nadrok. It grew louder, as if many ran through the forest without care for suppressing their footsteps.

A shout broke the tense silence, reverberating through the air. "You are trespassing in the territory of the Iron Flood." The familiar voice had a strange, metallic quality. "Surrender your weapons, and we will spare your lives."

Rykan and his companions instinctively looked to Myrradin for guidance. The old mavin's eyes narrowed, a firm resolve setting in.

"Surrender is not an option," he declared quietly. "Prepare to defend yourselves."

Garrick and Elysia unsheathed their swords with a swift, decisive motion, the metal gleaming under the scant light. Ysadora positioned herself, gripping her staff with both hands, ready to channel her magic. Rykan released Selaina's hand and stepped protectively in front of her, drawing his blade with a steady hand. His heart pounded in his chest as he scanned the terrain.

From the gloom, six swordsmen in black armor materialized, moving with a purposeful and intimidating gait. The leader brandished a sword that blazed with a mystical blue flame, his eyes pulsing with the fiery intensity of the Dreadstorm, a clear mark of Vatreus's dark empowerment. Rykan recognized the Dreadstorm Knight as Velkar, the one who had smacked him in the face when he passed by the ridgeback carts on the way into the mountains. Among them, Rykan spotted one soldier slightly out of step with the rest, a potential weak link.

His palms grew slick with sweat as the ominous echo of armored boots approached. Behind him, the taut whisper of Selaina's bowstring drew tight. Rykan's instincts screamed against the idea of waiting passively for their assault. Doubts swirled in his mind about his ability to withstand a direct attack. His best strategy now was to disrupt their advance. Taking a deep, steadying breath to quell the rising tide of adrenaline, Rykan fixed his eyes on the isolated soldier. With a determined exhale, he propelled himself forward, targeting the gap in their formation.

CHAPTER 28

Panic surged through Selaina as Rykan charged headlong at the Iron Flood soldiers.

"Rykan, wait!" she shouted, her voice slicing through the clamor, but he was already beyond hearing.

She directed her focus to the soldier ahead of him, her fingers trembling slightly as she aimed. The arrow whistled through the air, striking the soldier Rykan was about to engage. A metallic clang echoed as the arrow glanced off the black armor, ineffective. As the group entered the clash, Darian hesitated.

"Why is it always swords and magic? Why not a good parley once in a while?" muttered Kadin.

Despite his words, he readied two of his daggers, his eyes scanning for the best target.

Rykan's blade struck next, slashing across the soldier's armor with a harsh screech that did little more than score the surface. He ducked beneath a sweeping blow, finding a gap beneath the soldier's arm to drive his sword in with all his might and sending the soldier crashing to the ground. As Rykan grappled with the soldier, Selaina quickly nocked another arrow, her heart pounding as the enemy soldiers closed in with increasing speed. She watched Rykan struggle to pierce the soldier's armor. The desperation in his efforts filled her with dread but heightened her resolve.

Moving swiftly, Selaina dashed toward Rykan, stepping decisively on the downed soldier's hand to pin it. She fired her next

arrow point-blank into the T-shaped visor of his helmet. The soldier's grip slackened, his sword clattering to the ground as his body went limp.

The Dreadstorm Knight advanced on Garrick, who braced himself for the attack. Myrradin closed his eyes as he muttered silently, his hands glowing with mystical energy while he cast an enchantment that cloaked Garrick's sword in a radiant white aura just as the blue flames met the blade in a shower of sparks. Beside him, Ysadora focused, her hands drawing patterns in the air to control the roots beneath the ground that sprang up to form barriers, which funneled enemies into less advantageous positions and showcased her unique control over the forces of natural order.

Kadin's crossbow twanged as he fired, the bolt thudding into an enemy's chest plate with a denting impact. Beside him, Elysia was a whirlwind of motion. She bashed one soldier with her shield while parrying another's blade.

"Bet you ten aurin I take down more than you!" Kadin shouted over to Rykan, managing a quick grin.

With a fierce upward thrust, Elysia dislodged another soldier's faceplate, then delivered a crushing blow to his head, sending him sprawling to the ground.

Selaina drew another breath, steadying her trembling hands as she scanned for her next target. She released her arrow into the chaos, and it found its mark in the back of a soldier threatening Elysia. He staggered, and Elysia shoved her shield hard into his chest, sending him tumbling down.

As the battle raged, Ysadora's staff surged with a brilliant blue aura, her focus unwavering. With a slam of her staff into the earth, roots and vines erupted from the ground, snaking rapidly around the feet of two soldiers attempting to outmaneuver Myrradin. The thick undergrowth that bound them tightly muffled their surprised yelps. As the Knight's relentless attack forced Garrick back, Darian saw an opening. Despite his trembling hands, he aimed and fired. With precision, his bolt plunged into the Knight's leg, creating an opening for Garrick to exploit.

Concentrating on the Dreadstorm Knight, Selaina loosed another arrow into the thick of the battle. Her arrow glanced off the armor of the Knight, as he turned and pointed at her. "Take down the archer!" he ordered. She reached for another arrow when two enemy soldiers broke through the melee, their blades gleaming menacingly as they aimed for her. In a flash, Myrradin redirected his Aedavaris from Garrick's sword to Selaina. A dome of shimmering white energy encapsulated her just in time, causing the attackers' swords to clatter against the barrier with a streak of white light.

The swift act of protection came with a price. With the shield removed, the Dreadstorm's flaming sword sliced through Garrick's blade as if it were mere straw, cutting it clean in half with a terrifying sizzle and a shower of sparks. Selaina's heart sank as she realized her safety had cost Garrick dearly. Ysadora reacted swiftly, her staff shining as she summoned an array of protective vines to shield Garrick from further blows.

More soldiers poured in through the trees, alert to the sounds of battle. Noticing the immediate danger to Selaina, Rykan and Darian leaped into action with renewed fury. Darian, with a roar of battle rage, closed in on one of the soldiers, firing his crossbow into the visor of his helmet. Meanwhile, Rykan engaged another soldier, his sword finding a chink in the enemy's armor and driving in deep with a crunch of metal. Kadin positioned himself strategically behind a rock. Just as a soldier nearly overran Selaina, Kadin leaped out, throwing a dagger that struck the soldier squarely in the back. "Gotcha," he muttered, more to himself than anyone else, before ducking back into his makeshift cover.

Selaina returned her attention to the Dreadstorm Knight as his flaming blade carved fiery arcs through the air, Garrick narrowly evaded each deadly swing. However, the azure warrior, seizing an opportunity, delivered a powerful kick to Garrick's chest. The force of the blow sent Garrick tumbling back, his body crashing into the underbrush beneath a gnarled tree.

Selaina launched another arrow as the Dreadstorm Knight stepped toward Garrick. The arrow hit hard against the knight's helmet, tilting it sideways.

"Someone kill the archer!" the Dreadstorm Knight said as he adjusted his helmet.

Selaina nocked another arrow while Elysia sprinted to his Garrick's aid, just as the Knight prepared for a final, fatal strike. Her shield burst into radiant light as Myrradin redirected his Aedavaris toward her.

Before Selaina could fire her shot, Ysadora summoned roots and vines to snare the Dreadstorm Knight's legs. The Knight tore through the natural restraints with brute force, but the delay allowed Elysia to position herself between him and the vulnerable Garrick. A rustling sound in the bushes behind her drew Selaina's attention. A soldier with a blade drawn was attempting to sneak up on her. He charged, and Selaina pivoted swiftly, bringing her bow around and launching an arrow directly into the soldier's chest. The force and angle of the shot allowed the arrow to penetrate his armor, dropping him instantly.

Returning her focus to Garrick, Selaina watched as the Dreadstorm Knight's flaming sword clashed against Elysia's radiating shield, sending a shower of sparks into the air, each spark dancing like a firefly in the dark. She aimed her bow, but there was no shot she could take without risking Elysia being hit. Frustration gripped her as she held her breath, her fingers trembling on the bowstring, waiting for an opening.

Leveraging the tree for support, Garrick pushed himself to his feet, the glint of a fallen soldier's sword catching his eye. He grasped the weapon, testing its unfamiliar weight with a quick swing.

Selaina darted through the chaos, her breath coming in short bursts. She spotted a narrow opening between two soldiers, Rykan and Darian fending them off. Without hesitation, she rushed toward them, but before she could join her companions, two soldiers who had been advancing on Myrradin and Ysadora shifted their focus to her.

Her heart pounded as she evaded the first strike, feinting right and then dodging left. A second blade came for her head, and she barely ducked under it in time. As she tried to rise, a soldier's hand clamped down on her cloak, yanking her off balance. With a violent tug, he swung her toward his comrade, who was already thrusting his blade forward.

Selaina's body twisted in midair, and her boot caught the ground just in time to stop her momentum. The sword grazed past her, missing her by inches. Her heart raced as she scrambled for an arrow, but her fingers fumbled with the bowstring. Before she could steady her aim, the soldier was suddenly ensnared by thick, curling vines—Ysadora's magic at work— binding him to the earth.

Dodging the other soldier's attack, Rykan caught up to her, slashing into the soldier's armor and knocking him to the ground. Before the soldier could get back up, Kadin leaped on him, stabbing a dagger into his chest. Selaina continued on as Rykan followed, looking for a clear shot at the Knight.

Elysia skillfully managed to parry the relentless barrage of strikes from the Dreadstorm Knight's sword. Seizing a brief lull when the Knight over-extended, Elysia counterattacked, her blade piercing the thinnest spot in the middle of his armor. The fiery vanguard staggered from the blow.

Garrick, now armed, flanked the Dreadstorm Knight. With a powerful swing, he drove his borrowed sword into the knight's back. As he pulled the blade free, its tip was stained red with blood. His strike had reached flesh. The Knight faltered, pain evident even beneath the mask of his helmet.

The air was thick with the smell of scorched earth and iron, the sounds of battle echoing through the trees, as Selaina and her companions continued to fight the oncoming soldiers. In the corner of her eye, Selaina noticed Kadin fighting off three swordsmen surrounding Ysadora and Myrradin. She nocked another arrow, aimed, and fired, piercing the back of one of their helmets.

Dividing her attention between the Dreadstorm Knight and the remaining two soldiers attacking Ysadora, Selaina grabbed another arrow. Garrick aimed a fierce strike as Elysia assaulted with her shield. Selaina again could find no open shot. The flaming champion, using his sword to parry Elysia's blow, lost his balance momentarily when he retaliated with a forceful kick that Garrick was ready for. Taking advantage of the Knight's momentary instability, Elysia slashed with her sword, knocking him off his feet. Ysadora's vines, conjured from the earth, ensnared the Knight, pulling him downward to assist Elysia's attack.

Just as Garrick raised his sword for a decisive blow, the Dreadstorm Knight surged back to his feet with unexpected agility, seizing Elysia's shield and thwarting her next strike. With this surprising move, the Knight found a momentary opening and plunged his flaming sword into Elysia's abdomen. A piercing scream escaped her as blue flames spread from the wound, casting eerie light on their grim faces. Selaina was stunned as she felt all the air go out of her.

Ysadora reacted swiftly, her magical energies extinguishing the unnatural fire while Elysia clutched the searing blade, holding it with a death grip. Struggling fiercely, the Dreadstorm Knight attempted to withdraw his weapon, but Elysia's tenacity matched his strength. Garrick took this opportunity to strike, hammering a powerful blow into the Knight's helmet, creating a huge dent that warped its shape. Before Garrick could deliver another strike, the Knight wrenched his sword free from Elysia's grasp, the blade slick with blood, ready to counterattack.

Selaina ran toward Elysia, but something grabbed hold of her ankle, making her fall into the soft dirt. One of the wounded swordsmen held her on the ground, but Selaina kicked herself free, taking an arrow from her quiver to impale the soldier's arm. Myrradin, recognizing Elysia was down, shifted his protective magic to Garrick, enveloping his sword in the Aedavaris just as their blades met with a clashing spark. Selaina, bow raised and arrow nocked, searched frantically for an open shot, but the fighters were too intertwined, moving too swiftly for a clear aim.

Glancing toward the sounds behind her, she saw Rykan engaged fiercely with another soldier, blades clashing with metallic fury, while Ysadora supported him with her vines, attempting to restrain the soldier's movements. The Dreadstorm Knight, recovering from the earlier disarray, launched a series of rapid, vicious strikes at Garrick. Each swing pushed Garrick further back, his sword barely catching the fiery blows. Dodging a particularly lethal strike, Garrick rolled away, using the brief respite to catch his breath and reassess.

As he regained his footing, Garrick pressed forward, driving the Dreadstorm Knight into a defensive posture with a sudden flurry of aggressive strikes. Each clash of their swords illuminated the battleground with flashes of silver and blue.

Selaina made her way closer, her heart pounding as she knelt beside Elysia. She quickly tore a piece of fabric from her sleeve, pressing it firmly against the wound, her hands guided by the survival lessons Jeth had taught her.

"My long dream has ended. I will awaken in the Everdream, where all our journeys will converge." Elysia's voice was low, barely breaking through the clamor.

"No, we need you here!" Selaina's voice trembled with urgency as she applied more pressure, feeling the warm blood seeping through the cloth. "If anything happens, we'll use the Stone to bring you back!"

Elysia winced, her hand weakly grasping Selaina's wrist, grounding her. "Sometimes, the true power lies not in altering fate," she murmured, her eyes locking onto Selaina's, "but in embracing it."

Elysia's words hung in the air, a quiet truth amid the chaos. The clash of steel resonated as Garrick and the Dreadstorm Knight engaged in a fierce duel. The Knight's flaming blue blade met Garrick's sword, enveloped in a protective aura. With a skilled maneuver, the Knight forced Garrick's blade upward, exposing him momentarily. Garrick, however, sidestepped the Dreadstorm Knight's lethal thrust, closing the distance between them. Locked in close quarters, they struggled, too entangled to use their swords effectively.

Seizing the moment, Garrick used the pommel of his sword, smashing it down into the slit of the Knight's helmet with a crushing force. The Knight reeled back, dazed by the sudden impact. Garrick pressed his advantage, pounding the Knight's helmet with the side of his blade, each hit ringing out like a bell.

Regaining his composure, the Dreadstorm Knight lashed out with renewed vigor, his blows swift and relentless, forcing Garrick to retreat under the barrage. As Garrick struggled to maintain his footing, the Knight dropped low, kicking Garrick's legs out from under him.

Garrick lay sprawled on the ground as the Dreadstorm Knight loomed over him, the menacing glow of his flaming sword casting doomed shadows. The Knight stepped down on his right arm, leaning down as if taunting him. Selaina scrambled for an arrow, but it was too late for a clean shot now. With mere moments to act, Garrick tossed his sword from his fingertips, grabbing it with his left hand and thrusting it into the vulnerable space beneath the Knight's faceplate, slicing into his neck. The Knight's body jerked from the sudden assault, his knees buckling as the fierce blue light in his eyes dimmed to nothing. While he clutched at his wound, the Dreadstorm Knight's flaming sword clattered to the stones covering the ground before he collapsed forward into the sand, lifeless. The blue flame covering the sword burned out, the burned metal left behind crumbling into ashes.

"I can't stop the bleeding!" Selaina cried out, desperation edging her voice as she pressed down harder on Elysia's wound.

Myrradin and Ysadora, alerted by her shouts, hurried over, their faces fraught with concern.

Rykan, Darian, and Kadin, having dispatched the last of the soldiers, turned to see the grim scene unfold around Elysia. Their faces registered shock and disbelief, the weight of the battle's cost suddenly hitting them. Rykan's sword dropped, his focus shifting entirely to his fallen comrade. Selaina's hands trembled as she frantically searched the faces around her for any sign of hope. She sought a gaze that held a promise of salvation, a silent vow that they could yet mend the unspoken breach between life and death that Elysia teetered upon.

Garrick rushed over, grabbing hold of Elysia's hand. With some difficulty through his exhausted breaths, he spoke to her. "Stay with me!"

Selaina, her eyes wide with panic, looked up at Ysadora. "Can't you do something?"

Ysadora shook her head, her expression grim.

"But you kept the flames from burning her!" Selaina shouted, desperation cracking her voice.

"The flames came from magic," Ysadora said as she knelt beside Elysia, her voice tinged with sorrow. "This, however, we cannot fix."

Garrick wiped his eyes, his concern morphing into hopelessness. Seeing his despair nearly made Selaina crumble into the dirt, her own tears threatening to spill over.

"You fought well, Elysia," Garrick said to her, his voice breaking.

Elysia, with a faint grin, mustered her strength. "My proper name," she whispered. "Say it again."

Garrick spoke slowly, pronouncing every syllable with perfect enunciation. "Lady Elysia," he said, forcing a quivering smile across his pained face. "You fought well."

Elysia's eyes moved over everyone standing nearby. Her gaze turned skyward as her breathing slowed until it came to a sudden stop.

Selaina exhaled, as if she had been holding her breath the entire time. She rubbed her eyes, trying to hold back the deluge that would soak her skin.

"I pray you are dreaming well," she whispered softly.

Myrradin, standing a few paces away, glanced at the horizon. "We had better get moving," he said. "Gather anything we need. We don't have much further to go."

Darian, his voice thick with anger and grief, glared at Myrradin. "Do you not have a shred of decency? We just lost Elysia!"

"All the more reason to make it to the Wishing Stone," Myrradin said firmly. "If everything goes as planned, this too will be undone. Elysia will be alive."

Garrick nodded, swallowing his grief. "If what you say about the Stone is true, our need is even greater now. We must do this for Elysia. For all of us."

Rykan brushed the sand off his clothes and placed his sword into its sheath, then added, "So let's do it."

Garrick picked Elysia up, cradling her gently as he carried her to the base of one of the taller trees in the forest. He positioned her on her back with her shield over her chest, he laid her right hand on the shield, and in her left, he placed her sword. Selaina tried to imagine her spirit waking up after the long dream of life into the Everdream. She envisioned Elysia walking through a beautiful garden surrounded by woodlands, flowers of all colors everywhere. Wondrous creatures gathered around her as she made her way through.

Ysadora stepped forward, her expression grim but focused. She placed her hands on the ground, exhaling slowly. The earth trembled faintly as jagged rocks began to rise from the soil, forming pillars that framed Elysia's resting place. Though the edges were rough and crude, the stone provided a semblance of shelter, creating a simple, protective tomb.

"It's not much," Ysadora murmured, brushing dirt from her hands as she stood. "But it'll keep her safe from the elements."

Garrick ran his fingers over one of the jagged stones, nodding slowly. "She would have liked this," he said. "It's... fitting."

CHAPTER 29

RYKAN'S HEART RACED, pounding in his chest even an hour after the battle had ceased. The world around him felt surreal, detached, as if he were observing it from afar. For the second time, he had watched the life of someone he cared about drain away before his eyes. The powerlessness gnawed at him. His inability to change the outcome haunted him. Every moment replayed in his mind—a torturous loop—feeding the nagging thought that, somehow, he might have done something, anything, to save Elysia.

As their journey led them through a barren landscape, the group stumbled upon an unexpected oasis—a deep pool of water nestled among the sand. Driven by thirst and a desperate need for distraction, Rykan hastened to the water's edge, dipping his flask eagerly into the cool liquid. Before he could pass it to Selaina, Ysadora intervened with a cautious hand.

"You're really going to drink that? I'll purify it first," she insisted, her staff glowing faintly as she murmured a spell.

Moments later, the water in the flask stilled, its surface now sparkling subtly under the sun. Selaina took a grateful sip and returned the flask to Rykan, who drank deeply, hoping the water might wash away the haunting images that clung to his mind.

While the others refilled their canisters, Garrick pressed on, his pace undeterred by the brief respite. Catching up, Ysadora offered him her flask, and he drank deeply, offering a brief nod of thanks. Beyond them, the terrain stretched, flat and unyielding, dotted only with sparse trees and unusual, dome-shaped, ridged plants that broke the monotony of the desert expanse.

The further they went, the more Rykan worried they would end up stranded in an area where food was scarce. If the others shared the same concern, they didn't vocalize it. Garrick, Selaina, and the rest all appeared focused on the task ahead of them. Darian scratched the dried blood from his knife as he walked, while Kadin picked at his head, brushing sand out of his hair.

The wind made patterns in the sand, sweeping designs around the stones that dotted the landscape. Rykan stared at the elongated shadows as they seemed to move with the wind. Selaina rubbed her shoulder while they marched on through the sunbaked sand.

"Are you sure nothing hurt you during the battle?" Rykan asked, his eyes showing concern.

Selaina glanced at him, shaking her head. "Nothing like that," she said. "Just some soreness I've had for a little while."

Rykan gently brushed her hair aside and reached out to touch her shoulder. "If you'll allow me, it may be something I can fix." He pressed with a bit more pressure, his fingers kneading deeper into the muscle.

Selaina recoiled sharply. "Don't touch it!" she exclaimed, her voice tense. Then, much softer, she added, "Please, it's too sensitive right now, but I appreciate you trying to help."

Rykan stepped back, his hand falling to his side. "I guess we've all had our fair share of bumps and bruises on this journey," he said, trying to lighten the mood. "It will be good to rest and heal when this is over."

"According to Myrradin, we won't need to heal," Selaina said thoughtfully. "We'll go back to being as we were before this all started. For you, I guess it will be the point before the Iron Flood invaded your city."

Rykan's brow creased as he considered her words. "That's hard to imagine," he said. "So many things will change."

"Probably things we would never expect," Selaina added, her tone carrying a mix of hope and uncertainty.

Rykan looked at her with resolve. "Whatever happens," he said, "I swear that I won't forget you."

Selaina gave him a sad smile. "I don't know that you can control that," she said gently. "The Wishing Stone is stronger than …"

"Love?" Rykan interjected. "I don't believe anything is more powerful than love."

"Memory," she finished. "The memory won't exist after the Stone is used."

Selaina smiled sadly, her gaze softening. "Focus on the positive. The Wishing Stone is a blessing. Haven't you always wanted to do something that actually made a difference? We will bring a new Galanor, and you will find all the love you've ever hoped for. Our friendship will always exist in this pocket of time because we needed each other here."

Rykan sighed, his shoulders sagging. "Why is every blessing shadowed by a curse?"

Garrick, walking ahead, called back, "Shouldn't we change course?"

"No, keep to this same direction, and we will be there soon," Myrradin replied.

"But if we keep going straight, we'll end up in—Oh, that's where we are going, isn't it?" asked Garrick. "I should have known that's where a Wishing Stone would be."

"Where?" Rykan asked, confusion creasing his brow. "What are you talking about?"

Myrradin burst out. "Don't say it out …"

"He's taking us to Wekenwild," Garrick answered grimly.

"… loud," Myrradin finished with a sigh. "We don't know what ears might be listening."

"The place no one ever comes back from?" Dread tinged Rykan's voice.

"We're miles away from anyone out here," Garrick replied to Myrradin.

"I've heard of this place," Kadin chimed in. "I've known people who have searched for it. It's said there are artifacts of great power within its boundaries. I don't know if they ever found it or not. They were never heard from again."

"That's why he didn't tell us. If I knew we were going to Wekenwild, I would never have come," Garrick said firmly. "If that's the only way to get the Wishing Stone, then we have come all this way for nothing."

"Is it cursed?" Darian asked, his eyes wide as he clasped his hands in front of him.

"More like enchanted," Myrradin said calmly. "Do not fear. I can easily find the way to the Stone. It's getting out of Wekenwild that's the tricky part."

"That's why we cannot go," Garrick insisted.

"Once Selaina uses the Stone, we will all find ourselves back where we were before the Iron Flood affected us. We won't need to navigate our way out of Wekenwild," Myrradin reassured him.

"Ah, that's true," Kadin said, nodding. "It seems you've thought of everything, I must say."

"As long as nothing goes wrong while we're in there," Darian said, his voice tinged with worry.

"What could possibly go wrong?" Kadin grinned.

The sun dropped low near the distant horizon, bathing the sand and the mountains in an orange glow. The flat land made the world a vast expanse with an eerie, lonely silence. The only noise, other than the crunching beneath their boots, was a flock of large birds squawking to each other as they flew past.

"Where will you end up once the wish is made?" Ysadora turned to Kadin, her eyes searching his face. "Where would you be if there were no Iron Flood?"

"I would be home," Kadin said wistfully. "Counting the aurin I made during my journey. Handing out the gifts I bought for my young sisters and nephew. Grateful that they would be able to grow up in a world without the tyranny of a madman. Instead of getting myself captured by the Iron Flood."

"Is that aurin made legitimately?" Garrick chuckled.

"It depends on how you define legitimate," Kadin replied with a wink. "Personally, I would say yes. Others would not."

"At least, if he has stolen anything from us," Darian added, "we'll get it back when the Stone is used."

Rykan grinned as Garrick laughed. The others seemed less amused.

"My fear is that, once the Iron Flood is gone, what kind of suffering and evil will rise to take its place?" Selaina asked.

The others glanced at each other quietly.

After a moment, Myrradin spoke. "There hasn't been a kind of oppressive force like the Iron Flood in hundreds, thousands, of years, maybe ever. Any suffering that will come after the change will pale in comparison."

As they walked onward, they came to a row of trees with red leaves. The sun had dipped below the horizon, and the first star of the evening ignited. An elliptical radiance of dark gold remained where the sun had been. The barks of dorum, a small doglike scavenger, echoed in the distance. Somehow, they made the world seem quieter.

Under the trees, the shadows that remained took on a ghostly quality in the twilight. Rykan felt uneasy as the darkness spread. From behind one of the trees, he saw movement. Drawing in a deep breath, he tried to ignore the tricks that nightfall played.

Something to his right moved against the rhythm of the woods. Though he resisted the mockery of his senses, the others turned in its direction. Before long, they came out of the small forest, into a clearing that led to a salt flat.

Remnants of the last rain puddled in pockets of the wide-open landscape. The barking had gone silent now. Another shadow taunted him just outside his vision. His eyes darted toward it, finding a dark figure silhouetted against the twilit sky. It stood there motionless, watching. It was one of the Nadrok.

They continued over the flats, avoiding the small pools of water, and Rykan became aware of more shadows standing around them. Barely visible against the coming darkness, they seemed to multiply. Selaina rubbed her shoulder and turned her head right and left, keeping an eye on the Nadrok.

Rykan slowed, his pulse beating in his ears. Even if they were only watchers, he felt more threatened by them than anything he had ever encountered. The others seemed to be ignoring them.

One of them advanced in the blink of an eye, standing near while it watched them pass by. Selaina moved left, stepping on Rykan's foot when another Nadrok on their right moved in close. More shadows appeared, walking, advancing with strange, staggering movements.

Myrradin stopped as the shadows surrounded them. The Nadrok closed in. They seemed to all be staring at Selaina. She grabbed her shoulder tight, grunting in pain. One of the shadows froze in place, while the others staggered toward it. One by one, they each seemed to merge into the frozen

Nadrok, each making a different shape with their body position before losing all movement. It was as if they'd vanished, leaving a black stain on the sand and air. Rykan felt as if he were trapped in a dream, struggling to trust what his eyes revealed. They all stood transfixed, staring at the void left behind.

Something stirred from within the shadow's remnant. A hand reached out through the void. Rykan gasped as his breath was stolen away for a moment. A moment later, a figure stepped through the gateway, the figure of a woman with long dark hair. Dressed in old robes, she appeared disoriented.

Rykan turned to Selaina, realizing she was no longer standing beside him. Panic surged through him as his eyes darted back to the robed woman, who now held Selaina captive. The woman had her arm wrapped tightly around Selaina's neck, pulling her close as she stroked her fingers through her hair.

"So, the Wishing Stone resides in Wekenwild," the woman murmured, pulling Selaina closer until their faces were nearly touching. Her voice oozed with a sinister satisfaction. "Child of silver snow, I knew you would be the one to lead me here."

"It's Elowen!" Selaina gasped, struggling desperately to break free. "She wants the Stone!"

The woman's laugh was low and menacing. "I am known by many names, dear heart," she whispered, her eyes glinting with dark amusement. "But rest assured, Myrradin and I need no introduction."

Myrradin stepped forward, his eyes narrowing with recognition. "You are dabbling with dark magic, Gwenna," he said, his voice steady but tipped with concern. "Manipulating forces beyond our understanding is forbidden for a reason. You should know better than most that dabbling with things beyond your control will eventually consume you."

Gwenna's lips curled into a mocking smile. "Not everything needs to be controlled, Myrradin. I embrace the unpredictable and ever-shifting pulse of nature. I am allied with it, wielding power that surpasses your feeble attempts at order."

Selaina's struggles were evident, but Gwenna's grip tightened, keeping her immobilized.

"We are on a very important mission," said Myrradin gravely. "The fate of Galanor depends on it."

Gwenna laughed softly, a chilling sound that echoed in the stillness. "Why do you need them, Myrradin? If you've come to make a wish, why not come alone?"

"The Iron Flood is making travel difficult these days," Myrradin replied, attempting to sound casual, but his eyes betrayed his anxiety.

"Don't lie to me, Myrradin," Gwenna said sharply. "You know I will deduce your plan soon enough."

Selaina thrashed in Gwenna's hold, trying to break free, but Gwenna's grasp only tightened further. Rykan's hand clenched around the hilt of his sword, ready to strike if an opportunity arose.

"I have nothing to hide," Myrradin insisted. "Our purpose is noble. What do you hope to change with the Stone?"

"I have no desire to make any wishes," Gwenna said with a disdainful flick of her wrist. "The stone is not just a relic, it's the essence of Archeinor itself, pure crystallized power. The power to shape the abstract of Pandemora into something far greater." Gwenna tightened her grip on Selaina, her eyes glinting with newfound intent. "Who would have imagined that any fragments of Ethyllion still existed in this world?"

"Fragments of Ethyllion?" Ysadora turned to Myrradin, her eyes wide with surprise.

"Take us to the Stone, Myrradin," Gwenna demanded, her voice dripping with ambition. "We can all share in its power."

"Power is not why we are here," Myrradin replied firmly, his gaze unwavering.

Ysadora pounded her staff into the sand, sending strands of stone coiling around Gwenna's feet and climbing up her leg. Gwenna let go of Selaina, fire in her hands flaring up and shattering the stone bindings with a violent burst of heat. With a brief opportunity to escape, Selaina stumbled away, racing toward her group. Rykan and the others quickly closed ranks around her.

Gwenna, undeterred, brought her hands together, fingers weaving through the air as she conjured a formidable wall of black and red flame— an unnatural fire that spread out in multiple directions, splitting the night with its ferocious heat. Myrradin stepped forward to protect the group. He extended his arms, a bright aura emanating from his hands, forming a barrier that repelled the fiery onslaught. The air shimmered around them as the flames licked hungrily at Myrradin's shield.

Behind the shield, Rykan could feel the oppressive heat, his clothes sticking uncomfortably to his skin. Gwenna's face twisted with frustration as her attack faltered. She gasped for breath, her chest heaving from the effort of sustaining such powerful magic.

Rykan gripped the hilt of his sword, his muscles tensing as he weighed his options. Should he take advantage of Gwenna's momentary weakness?

As he unsheathed his sword, Myrradin's sharp command halted him. "Stay right here!"

Gwenna rallied, her hands moving through the air in complex patterns ending in a sharp thrust toward them. The sand at her feet erupted into molten obelisks, glowing bright orange-red and snaking toward them like sentient beings. They slithered in erratic patterns, some targeting the group directly while others circled around, attempting to flank them.

Myrradin clenched his jaw, the lines on his face deepening as he focused intensely. He extended his hands, channeling his magical energy. The air around him shimmered with the force of his spell as he targeted one of the flaming serpents. His robes fluttered as the energy surged through him, and with a forceful sweep of his arms, he managed to extinguish one. The fiery creature hissed violently as it turned into a stream of smoke, dissipating into the cool air. Beads of sweat formed on Myrradin's brow, his breathing heavy.

The group began to spread out slightly, dodging the unpredictable bursts of molten fire. Garrick drew his sword, and Rykan followed suit, both ready to defend their friends. Selaina grabbed her bow and took aim, her eyes narrowing as she tried to predict the movements of the fiery snakes.

One serpent zipped dangerously close, splitting the group as they dodged.

"Close the formation," Myrradin shouted over the chaos. "She wants us to scatter!"

CHAPTER 30

SELAINA FIRED AN arrow at one of the flaming serpents, but it speared harmlessly into the sand, missing its target. Garrick stood his ground, waiting for it to come near, his blade slicing through it, leaving two severed parts, smoldering and inert.

Ignoring the failed attempts to track the snakes, Selaina shifted her focus to Elowen, who she now knew as Gwenna, launching an arrow straight at her. The arrow, true in its flight, ignited midair, turning to ash before it could reach its mark.

"Pick your patch of sand and defend it," Garrick barked, parrying another serpent that sped toward him. "If you focus solely on the moving flames, they will outwit you."

Gwenna gathered her strength. Her hands came together once more, pulling from the depths of her power. Selaina, realizing the imminent danger, sprinted toward Myrradin, pulling Rykan by the arm. As walls of flame surged over the sand toward them, Myrradin raised his shield once more, enveloping them in a protective glow. Kadin and Darian squeezed in tight, trying to get further away from the flames.

The remaining fire serpents swarmed in, their movements more frantic as the flames around them thrashed wildly. With no room to retreat, the group braced for the worst.

Images flashed through Selaina's mind: the gloom of Ravendrith where Gwenna lived, the dark and moldy interior in the hollow of the tree. She recalled the vision from Gwenna's mind when

Selaina had first met her eyes. She had seen Gwenna in the bright daylight, desperately running toward the forest. She had seen her rubbing salve on her burned arms. She recalled her comment about preferring flame to …

"Sunlight!" Selaina gasped. "She hates the sunlight!"

Garrick, busy fending off another serpent, grunted in response. "Unless we can hold out until morning, I don't think that's going to help much."

"No, there's another way," Ysadora interjected.

She ignited the sunkeeper crystal on her staff. It shined brightly even through the darkness. Instead of allowing it to ambiently glow, Ysadora focused it, sending a concentrated beam of pure sunlight at Gwenna. The witch shrieked, shielding her eyes from the blinding light, her connection to the chaotic fire magic visibly weakening.

Ysadora advanced toward Gwenna with the beam of sunlight keeping the sorceress at bay. Gwenna tried to veil her skin as her hands and arms began to burn. Desperate to escape the piercing light, she threw weakened balls of flame at Ysadora, which the mavin dodged with ease. Rykan cut down one of the last flame serpents, as Gwenna, blinded and disoriented, stumbled toward the void gate. Garrick and Rykan charged ahead, their blades ready to cut her down. Gwenna glanced back once, a look of pure venom in her eyes, before disappearing through the portal.

With a sigh of relief, Selaina wrapped her arms around Rykan, feeling his heart pounding against hers. The chaotic heat of the battle gave way to a cooling breeze, the last of the fiery serpents reduced to mere glowing embers at their feet. The world around them seemed to pause, the aftermath of their skirmish fading into a moment of shared solace.

"Where is it?" Myrradin asked, breaking her attention from Rykan's warm embrace.

Myrradin's urgent tone cut through the air, disrupting the moment.

"Where is it!" he demanded, his gaze piercing into Selaina.

Startled, she stepped back from Rykan, confused. "What are you talking about?"

"You led her right to us!" Myrradin accused, his voice rising with intensity. "There's a curse upon you, some sort of mark!"

Selaina's hand moved instinctively to her shoulder, feeling the affliction beneath her clothing. Myrradin reached out abruptly, pulling at her collar to inspect.

"Hold on!" Selaina protested sharply, pulling away to loosen the lacing at her neckline herself. She gingerly pulled down the fabric, revealing the creeping black growth that had now spread ominously down her arm.

The group's eyes widened in alarm.

Darian stepped closer, wringing his hands, his face pale. "When did that appear?"

"It must have happened in the swamp, while I was asleep," Selaina explained, her voice uneasy.

"If we don't remove this curse immediately," Myrradin declared, "Gwenna will undoubtedly return, and she won't be caught off guard next time."

"You should have informed us about the curse," Ysadora chided, her tone carrying a hint of exasperation.

"I didn't realize it was a curse," Selaina replied defensively. "I thought it was something that would heal on its own."

"It's basic knowledge to anyone versed in ancient magic," Ysadora continued, crossing her arms.

"Keep the fabric away from it," Myrradin instructed, his expression stern. "This might sting a bit."

Selaina inhaled deeply as Myrradin focused on the cursed skin. She felt pressure, as though something were being drawn out of her body. Her skin grew warm, the heat intensifying until it felt like it was burning. Selaina gritted her teeth, trying to keep the pain contained. Suddenly, a blue flame burst from her skin, and her eyes began to water. Smoke drifted from the flame, carrying the stench of rotting death.

A scream escaped her lips as she unconsciously allowed her mouth to open. Ysadora used her staff to extinguish the flame, but the pain did not leave. Still burning, her shoulder was now bright red where the mark had been burned away. Ysadora poured water over her raw skin, lessening the intensity. She tied a piece of smooth cloth over the skin to rest underneath her clothing so the material of her tunic wouldn't irritate it.

"Let us hurry," said Myrradin breathlessly. "We are not far from Wekenwild."

Myrradin led them on, with a hastening to his steps Selaina had not seen from him before. The scattered, red-leafed trees passed in a blur as they hurried through the night, guided only by the pale glow of the moonlight. Leaving the barren salt flats behind, they entered a more fertile land teeming with wild grasses, ferns, and dense clusters of trees.

As they ventured deeper into the thick forest, strange chimes echoed ahead, creating an eerie symphony that sent shivers down Selaina's spine. The trees and underbrush grew increasingly dense, as if the forest itself were trying to bar their passage. A low rumble resonated through the air, a vibration that Selaina could feel deep in her chest, though the ground beneath their feet remained stable. The incessant chirping of insects layered over each other, creating an ominous, unnatural harmony that set her nerves on edge.

At last, the forest opened up, unfolding into a landscape where the concepts of moonlight and night seemed to lose all relevance. They found themselves on the threshold of a new domain, a forest unlike any Selaina had ever witnessed. The ground before them was black, not from the absence of light, but as a natural hue. The trees and foliage were similarly dark, punctuated by blue glowing orbs of varying sizes that created intricate patterns around every trunk and branch. The leaves, tinted in deep shades of blue and violet, radiated a light that mysteriously failed to reflect off the bark, casting an otherworldly aura around them.

In the distance, the trees stood in unnerving perfection, each one a clone of the one before in the pattern of its branches, shape, and height. The ferns unfurled in magnificent spirals, each one mirroring the next with only subtle variances that challenged the limits of perception. These organic spirals countered the rigid conformity of the trees, forming a mesmerizing display of geometric patterns throughout the forest. Beneath their feet, the black grass was alive with glowing moss and wildflowers, sketching complex circles, lines, and shapes that contrasted with the myriad other patterns in the forest.

"If you weren't already certain, this is Wekenwild," Myrradin said, his voice a hushed reverence. "You must stay with me or risk being lost forever."

As Selaina glanced back, trying to trace their path, the uniformity of their surroundings toyed with her senses. Had they been unwittingly following the subtle curve dictated by the ferns and fauna? Or were the trees themselves guiding their route, aligning with mysterious patterns? Her sense of direction had already faltered, overwhelmed in this bewildering place.

"What is this?" Ysadora asked with disbelief. "How could this be part of nature?"

"Exactly right," Myrradin replied with a solemn tone. "It is order, but not natural order."

"What do you mean by that?" Selaina asked.

"Natural order is balance," Myrradin explained. "The balance between order and chaos. Wekenwild is pure, rigid order. This is the closest you will find to Archeinor in the mortal world."

"It's not what I expected," Ysadora admitted. "It has a certain beauty that is almost horrific."

"A very apt description," Myrradin said, nodding.

"It looks more like chaos than order to me," Garrick commented, his eyes scanning the strange surroundings.

"The patterns are so complex that it's easy to lose sight of them," Myrradin said. "Your eyes will deceive you while your mind plays tricks on you here."

Selaina's foot kicked into a stone, nearly tripping her. She looked down to find not a stone, but a creature crawling along the ground in the same patterns as the plants, feeding on the grass as it moved. There were rows of them moving slowly across the turf in perfect alignment. They had shells on their backs like beetles but were larger than any beetle she had seen.

"How is this place out of alignment with everything else?" Ysadora asked, her voice strangely echoing over and over throughout the forest.

They all paused to look around, wondering what had caused the sudden echo.

After a moment, Myrradin focused on answering her. "Wekenwild is a remnant of the ancient world, a place where …" He paused as the echo happened again.

Selaina noticed a group of birds standing together on a branch of one of the trees, each one opening its beak along with the echoes. They were mimicking their voices, but in such a way that it sounded like an echo.

With the sounds moving across the forest, Selaina imagined there were more of these birds all around them.

"I think the echo is coming from these birds," she said as the birds repeated her words one at a time. "They're copying our voices."

"This place gives me the creeps," said Kadin as he glanced up at the trees around them.

"As I was saying," Myrradin began again, trying to ignore the echoing birds. "From my studies, this is where the mortal world connected to Archeinor through Ethyllion. When Ethyllion was destroyed, a part of Archeinor spilled into the mortal world, allowing Azragal to enter and enchanting this forest."

"Then Gwenna was right," Ysadora said, with awe and concern. "The Wishing Stone was once part of Ethyllion."

Myrradin muttered, his eyes scanning the symmetrical patterns around them. "No one knows for certain," he said. "But that is not why we are here. No matter if it is part of Ethyllion or not, we must use it to ensure that Vatreus is never granted his power." He paused, the blue orbs on the trees reflecting in his eyes.

Kadin, trailing behind with a nonchalant air, asked, "What is Vatreus's crusade anyway?"

Myrradin turned to face him, his expression stern. "The power he received has made him a madman," he said. "Whatever good he may have envisioned doing is now nothing more than justification for conquest. He's addicted to it." He continued walking, the blue glow from the trees casting long shadows.

Garrick, walking beside Selaina, clenched his fists. "He must be stopped, no matter what his cause is," he said. "The cruelty and suffering he has wrought have only made things worse for Galanor. More importantly, we have to restore Elysia. She should not have had to waste her life fighting for this." He kicked a stone out of his path.

"Yes, we have to restore the natural order," Selaina said. "For all of us." She glanced at Rykan, who walked silently on the other side of her, their earlier conversation still lingering in her mind.

Something moved along the radiant blue lines beneath her feet. Taking a closer look, she realized there were insects marching through the grass, tracing along the lined patterns. They all had some kind of glowing powder stuck to their tiny, fuzzy hairs. Maybe these insects carried pollen from other plants, crossing them with the flora in this part of the forest.

Was it the insects moving in these complex patterns that made the illuminated plants grow that way or were the insects simply following the pattern already made by the plants? Perhaps it was both. What exactly was it that instructed the creatures and plants to behave this way? A question she supposed could be asked not just in Wekenwild, but the world at large.

As they moved deeper into the enchanted forest, something rustled through the bushes. The echoing birds mimicked the sound, making it repeat over and over all around them. Suddenly, a man jumped out of the trees and grabbed hold of Rykan.

The man had long hair with a long beard, his clothes torn and tattered. "Tell me how to get out of here!" the man pleaded.

Selaina's heart raced as she saw Rykan struggling to push the old man away. The two grappled briefly before the man thrust a stone tablet into Rykan's hands. The etchings on the tablet shifted constantly, as if alive. Myrradin and the others quickly surrounded them, ready to intervene if the man posed a threat.

"I found it here, in the forest," the man said, his voice trembling. "If you lead me out, I'll give it to you."

"What is it?" Rykan asked as he stared at the changing patterns and text.

"It's a codex of infinite symmetry, a command of order in physical form," said Myrradin. "Do not take it. Make no attempt to read it. It is not for the mortal world."

"For those who can decipher it," the man said, his eyes wide with madness, "it contains the secrets of the universe."

"You'd spend the rest of your life trying to understand it," Myrradin warned. "And the little you did understand would only lead you to ruin. Just look at what happened to Vatreus."

Selaina felt a chill run through her as Rykan pushed the tablet back toward the man.

"I don't want it," he said firmly.

"You can't decline such an offer," the man hissed, his desperation growing. "I spent years of my life searching for this and many more trying to find my way out of this place."

"Maybe you should let it go," said Rykan. "Maybe the forest won't let you leave with it in your hands."

"You are a fool!" the man roared, his voice thick with contempt. "You are nothing, less than a speck in the cosmos! Your absence would leave the universe wholly unchanged!"

His hands clawed at Rykan in a desperate grapple until Rykan managed to shove him away. Regaining his stance, Rykan unsheathed his sword and aimed it at the man's chest.

"Do it," the man goaded. "End my torment. I have uncovered secrets too vast for any mind to bear. Everything you know and love, it all started with a singular thought, an all-encompassing thought. All possibilities without time or structure! Too many possibilities to comprehend. Why was this particular function chosen? Read it and make sense of it! Tell me!" he screamed. "Or drive your sword through my heart and free me from these relentless thoughts."

Selaina held her breath as Rykan hesitated. After a tense moment, he sheathed his sword and backed away, leaving the man shivering in the grass. Selaina watched the man, pity welling up inside her, but she knew there was nothing they could do for him.

As they continued onward, Selaina felt a growing unease. Myrradin walked along the strands of light. Circles and intersecting lines led to more circles and intersecting lines, making shapes and symbols on the ground. In certain moments, her mind refused to make sense of it all, making it appear as an insane mass of blue orbs, purple illuminations, white lights, and dark plant life.

They reached a clearing among the trees, a perfect oval cut out of the forest. The moonlight poured through the opening, casting an ethereal glow on the scene. As Selaina stepped into the clearing, she noticed the intricate patterns of blue light scattered across the ground. Her eyes widened when some of the lights lifted and floated in the air, forming a delicate grid pattern.

Curious, she moved closer and realized they were tiny insects, their wings a blur in the dim light. Luminescent like fireflies, they flickered gently, their light forming a shimmering veil. The air was alive with their soft glow, creating an otherworldly sight that felt both enchanting and unsettling. As she stood there, captivated by the luminous display, the insects began to settle down, landing gracefully on the surface to form yet another complex pattern.

Moving beyond the clearing, they ventured deeper into the forest, where cliff walls rose imposingly among the trees, curving over in spirals that defied gravity. Grass and trees sprouted sideways and even upside down from these formations, blurring the line between earth and sky. This alien labyrinth of vegetation and rock warped the very space around them.

As they navigated this surreal landscape, Selaina steadied herself against a tree that grew horizontally from the cliff. She ran her fingers over its bark, feeling the tiny grooves that spiraled into elaborate patterns. Faint strands of light glimmered within these textures, casting a subtle glow that added a mystical quality to the forest's already otherworldly beauty.

Amid all the cliffs, trees, plants, and intricate lines of patterns and shapes, one spot stood out. It was a focal point where everything seemed to converge. A rock formation, glowing with an ethereal violet light, protruded from the earth like a colossal stalagmite. Blue strands of luminescence swirled through it, pulsing rhythmically as if breathing in sync with the forest itself.

"The Wishing Stone," Myrradin said, his voice filled with awe and reverence.

Selaina's heart quickened as she stepped closer, her eyes wide with wonder at the convergence of nature's artistry and the magic that hummed through the air.

CHAPTER 31

BEFORE THEM LAY a massive crystal, its facets shimmering with an inner light that seemed to breathe life into the surrounding scene. Each pulse sent ethereal glows cascading across the dew-drenched foliage, painting the forest floor with dancing lights like the surface of a tranquil, starlit pond. The crystal hummed with a melodically delicate yet powerful vibration, a symphony of whispers weaving through the very air, resonating with the forest.

Rykan stared, his breath catching in his throat as his eyes widened with awe and disbelief. He had clung to the hope of this moment, a beacon drawing him onward through a maze of doubts and dangers, yet the reality of its presence overwhelmed him more than he could have imagined. The Stone was not just a legend. It surely must be the most powerful object in all of Galanor, a tangible force of nature he could see, hear, and almost touch with his soul. As the whispers of the crystal filled the air, they seemed to call to him, pulling at the edges of his consciousness and inviting him to step closer.

The air around the crystal thrummed with energy, palpable and electrifying. Looking around, Rykan saw his companions' faces, each reflecting his own wonder and trepidation. There was a unity in their shared astonishment, a silent acknowledgment that they had achieved what they'd set out to do. The Iron Flood's grip on the world was fading, dissolving into the past.

He felt an inexplicable strength as the Stone's radiant energy bathed him in a warm glow that seemed to seep beneath his skin, invigorating his very soul. They all stood in a cautious circle around it, maintaining a respectful distance. The Stone's power was inviting yet daunting—an allure wrapped in an aura of danger. It commanded their respect through its sheer presence, radiating a formidable essence that instilled a palpable fear in their hearts. Yet they were drawn to it, compelled by the promise of what it could offer.

"It's beautiful," Ysadora whispered, stepping closer to the Stone. "I can only imagine what Ethyllion must have been like." Her eyes reflected the Stone's light, giving her an almost otherworldly appearance as she gazed at it, clearly entranced by the light it emanated.

"I can't believe it's real," said Darian, his voice trembling with awe. He clenched and unclenched his fists, trying to steady his nerves.

Kadin took a step toward the Stone, his curiosity evident. "This truly is not of this world," he said, his voice filled with wonder. "Worthy of everything I have ever heard about Archeinor." He moved closer, his hand reaching out.

"Stay back!" Myrradin warned, sharply. "We can't risk it being used by anyone but Selaina."

Kadin stopped abruptly, his fingers a few feet from the Stone's surface. He backed away, his face covered with disappointment. Garrick stared in disbelief, his eyes fixed on the Stone, as if in a trance. Selaina slowly circled it, her white locks shimmering in its violet-blue light. Her face was full of questions, doubt, and wonder.

Darian's hands nervously shook, his awe manifesting itself as fear. "It's actually real."

"Selaina, are you ready?" Myrradin asked, gently but earnestly.

With steps of uncertainty, Selaina moved toward the Stone. "What exactly do I do?"

"Reach out to it," Myrradin instructed, his eyes locked on hers. "Not only with your body, but with your mind. Your first memory of your mother. Picture it, make it come alive, connect with her energy. And then flow with it, let it take you to a time before you were born. When you were still in your mother's womb."

Rykan's heart pounded. He knew he should keep quiet and let her focus, but he couldn't let her go like this. "Wait, Selaina," he called out with an edge of desperation. "Before you change everything."

Myrradin frowned, glancing at the sky. "Quickly then, we haven't much time."

"It will only take a moment," Rykan said, stepping forward and placing his hand on Selaina's shoulder.

Her cheeks turned pink as she glanced at the others watching before looking at the ground. Rykan wished this could be a private moment, but he wasn't about to let that interfere.

He gently wove his hand underneath her white hair, cupping her face with his palm. "I will do everything in my power to remember you." He slid his hand down her cheek and under her chin. "And when I do, I will find you."

His thumb gently touched the corner of her mouth, tugging on her soft bottom lip. Leaning closer, he searched her eyes for a sign that she wanted him near.

"If fate truly guides our steps, this will be the ultimate test," Selaina said, her eyes widening with nervous anticipation.

Her breath hitched, and she took a small step closer, instinctively leaning into his touch. She seemed confused, but the way her eyes softened and her lips parted slightly told Rykan she was curious, maybe even longing for a deeper connection.

"Will you just kiss her already?" Kadin interjected. "We don't have all day for this romantic nonsense."

Rykan rolled his eyes before leaning in, giving her enough leeway to turn away if she didn't want him to kiss her.

"I've never kissed anyone like this before," Selaina said softly, her voice trembling.

Rykan smiled gently. "Neither have I."

With his thumb still resting on her lips, he leaned in and gently pressed his lips to hers. The kiss lingered, tender and filled with unspoken promises. He reluctantly pulled back.

"I could never forget that," he whispered as his eyes met hers.

Kadin applauded mockingly, prompting Ysadora and Garrick to join in with amused smiles. The moment felt both tender and bittersweet, a small island of intimacy amid the looming chaos.

Selaina took a deep breath, her voice steady but filled with emotion. "Goodbye, everyone," she said, her eyes meeting each of theirs in turn. "Thank you for everything you've done. I hope our paths cross again someday, in a world where the circumstances are kinder."

They bade her farewell, stepping back to give her space. An eerie silence fell over the clearing, broken only by the rustle of leaves and the distant call of a night bird. Darian stood apart, his shoulders heaving, a pained expression twisting his features. His eyes, glassy with unshed tears, moved to Selaina.

He had known Selaina longer than any person in the group, so it was understandable he would want to give her a personal goodbye. When she reached out to embrace him, Darian pushed past her, hurrying toward the Wishing Stone, his movements desperate and unsteady.

"Darian, what are you doing?" Selaina's voice cracked as she caught hold of the back of his tunic.

Before Rykan could react, Darian pulled a knife from his belt and held it beneath Selaina's chin. She froze as he moved behind her, the blade drawing a thin red line across her cheek as his unsteady hand slipped.

"Release her, Darian!" Myrradin commanded, his voice like thunder as he and the others moved closer. "Or your next breath will be your last!"

Darian's voice was a hoarse whisper. "If she dies, so does your wish," he said, edging closer to the Stone and dragging Selaina with him. "I don't want to do this, but I have to. I understand now—Bellaria wanted me to come on this journey to bring her back."

Myrradin stepped forward, his voice stern. "Darian, think of what you're risking. We need the Stone to save the world, not just one soul."

But Darian's eyes were wild with grief. "Without her, the world is an empty place," he cried out, as blood trickled from his blade where it pressed against Selaina's throat.

"Darian, this isn't you. Think about what Bellaria would want. Would she want this for you? This isn't the way." Selaina's voice was calm, but her eyes were wide with fear.

"You don't understand," Darian choked out, his voice breaking under the weight of his sorrow. "Her memory was all I had left. But now her life is within my reach. I must do this, no matter the cost."

"My staff isn't working in this forest," Ysadora whispered to Myrradin with a tone of frustration. "What about your Aedavaris? Trap him in the shield."

"It may trap them together," said Myrradin. "Or damage the Stone."

Rykan readied his sword, his mind racing, each second stretching into eternity. The surrounding forest closed in, the trees leaning down as if to witness the unfolding nightmare. Memories of his father's death at the hands of Vatreus flashed through his mind, a haunting reminder of his failure to protect the one he loved. Regret gnawed at him, the bitter weight of helplessness still fresh in his heart. But this time, he couldn't let the same fate befall Selaina. He wouldn't stand by and lose her too.

Darian's resolve hardened as he met their gazes, one by one. "I'm sorry, truly, Selaina. For anything else, I would never dream of harming you, but for even a moment more with her, I'd risk the world."

"We all carry our ghosts, Darian. But we must let them rest. We live for those who are still with us." Garrick's voice was soft, resigned.

"In the new time that is created," said Darian, "my actions here will be undone. None of this will matter anymore."

"But the Iron Flood will still exist," said Garrick. "What kind of life would you have?"

"Put the weapon down," said Myrradin with an icy tone. "Or we will be forced to destroy you."

Darian's eyes narrowed, his decision made. "Then you leave me no choice." His grip tightened, and in one swift, desperate motion, he shoved Selaina aside and lunged for the Stone.

Rykan reacted instantly, his blade slicing through the air with the weight of his father's death and the future of Tathara hanging in the balance. If Darian reached the Stone, there would be no undoing the past—no saving his father, no stopping Vatreus or the Iron Flood. Darian collapsed, mere inches from the Stone, his eyes wide with shock and betrayal. Garrick was there in a heartbeat, pulling Darian back, away from the fatal temptation of the Stone.

Garrick laid Darian on the grass, and Ysadora restrained Selaina from rushing to his side.

"He's bleeding!" Selaina cried out, struggling against Ysadora's strong hold. "We have to help him!"

"The wound is …" Garrick said, his voice faltering as he looked up at Selaina, his expression heavy with sorrow. "It's too late for that."

"Let me bleed," Darian muttered, his voice barely above a whisper, his gaze lost in a distant sorrow. "I was prepared to bring her back or die trying. I'm sorry it had to come to this. You deserved a better companion than me."

"Darian, no," Selaina sobbed, her voice thick with tears. "One mistake doesn't define you. You're still one of us."

From a short distance, Rykan watched, his sword in hand, trying to resist the need to protect. He couldn't fathom Selaina's compassion. Darian had just threatened her life, yet here she was, pleading for his.

Darian looked at Selaina, his eyes filled with regret. "I was too weak to let her go, too weak to be who I needed to be," he confessed, his voice cracking.

"I forgive you, Darian," Selaina whispered, reaching out to touch him, "and when I use the Wishing Stone, we'll erase this, all of it."

"I hope you're right." Darian's voice faded, his life ebbing away. "I hope … you can …"

As Darian's final breaths faded into silence, Selaina bowed her head, tears tracing silent paths down her cheeks. Rykan placed a comforting hand on her shoulder, his own heart heavy with the weight of what had transpired.

"Did you have to kill him? Was there no other way?" Selaina's voice trembled, laden with grief and conflict.

Rykan's hand fell away as he grappled with her questioning gaze. "I … I was trying to protect you … and the Stone," he stammered, the burden of his decision pressing down upon him.

Myrradin stepped closer, his voice steady yet sympathetic. "Rykan saved us all. There are moments where we are forced to make harrowing decisions. Rykan acted to preserve the future we are all striving toward."

"His actions were pure," Ysadora added gently. "Once you prevent Vatreus from receiving the power, Elysia and Darian will be restored."

Garrick nodded in agreement, a somber expression on his face. "Had Darian used the Stone, we would have lost everything."

Selaina wiped a tear from her cheek, nodding slowly. "I understand. It's just … this is all so much. I don't know how to handle it," she said, barely getting the words out.

Myrradin offered her a small, encouraging smile. "The Stone awaits, Selaina. When you are ready."

Taking a deep breath, Selaina wiped the blood from her chin and approached the Wishing Stone. Myrradin leaned in, his voice quiet and soothing as he guided her thoughts toward the powerful memory needed to activate the Stone. On her other side, Ysadora whispered encouragement, painting a vivid picture of Selaina's mother and a vision—a woman, two men, and a child, journeying together in a ridgeback-drawn carriage.

CHAPTER 32

Ysadora's voice changed from an audible sound to a whispering thought in Selaina's mind, guiding her through a vision only she could see.

"Now," Myrradin instructed, his voice cutting through the ethereal vision, "place your hands on the Stone."

As Selaina reached out, her fingers touched the cool surface of the Wishing Stone. It pulsed with life, its crystalline structure alive with swirling hues of violet and blue interspersed with bright white sparks that danced like the life cycle of stars from birth to death in the blink of an eye.

"Keep your focus on that event," said Myrradin. "Only that location in space and time. If you attempt to look beyond that, you may get lost in the infinite."

Ysadora continued to describe the scene in vivid detail as the energy from the Stone enveloped Selaina. Violet light surrounded her, and incomprehensible visions swirled around her. Countless people, animals, and objects appeared at every stage of their life spans, creating a surreal panorama. Places she had never been folded in on themselves repeatedly, forming a continuously shifting pathway of existence.

As she moved forward, Selaina glimpsed multiple visions of the same people, their images layered and intertwined. The overlapping figures fanned out in increasingly intricate patterns, their forms bending and morphing into shapes more and more complex as they approached her. Each shape revealed itself to be composed of even smaller, detailed forms, surrounded by tiny, shimmering dots.

Shades of events never seen or heard of played out around her. She saw the world burning in blue-flamed destruction. Selaina witnessed a man touching the Wishing Stone as the fire abated. Many men pulling a giant metal door to cover the vacuous cave in the side of a mountain. Many more hands touching the Wishing Stone, over and over again.

The scene overwhelmed Selaina, a continuous flow of life and time converging into a single, mesmerizing spectacle. She felt as if she were walking through the very fabric of reality, each step taking her deeper into the heart of the Stone's profound energy. The air hummed with power, and the boundary between the physical and the mystical blurred, making her question the nature of existence itself.

She saw a man with striking white hair—a Lith like her—assisting a young Lith woman from a carriage. She wondered if it could be the same man from the portrait her mother kept locked in a drawer. The rugged mountain path contrasted sharply with the woman's elegant attire, designed to shimmer like silver under any light, its ruffled sleeves fluttering gently in the mountain breeze. The woman placed a protective hand over her rounded belly. A surreal feeling washed over Selaina as she realized she was observing her own mother, pregnant with her, from an outsider's perspective.

Beside them, the carriage driver helped a young boy with Lith features but dark hair, his face partly bandaged and his breathing labored, down from the carriage. The group approached a massive metal gate embedded in the mountain. Intricate patterns that pulsed with a faint, otherworldy glow etched the ancient and imposing gate.

Selaina watched the Lith man speak in hushed tones to the driver, his eyes scanning the surroundings with a mixture of caution and determination. Her mother, Thessalia, despite her delicate condition, exuded a calm strength, her hand never leaving her belly, as if to shield Selaina from the world outside. The boy, wincing with every step, clung to the driver, his eyes wide with fear and pain.

"Not far now," the driver assured, leading them toward a hidden bend at the gate's base. He stepped aside, letting the white-haired Lith man pick the boy up and carry him closer to the gate.

"What do I do?" the Lith man asked with fear in his voice.

"Call to him," instructed the driver. "Let him know why you've come."

The Lith man beckoned Thessalia to join him by the gate. She complied, tenderly brushing her hand through the boy's dark hair as she approached. The boy's breathing was shallow, each breath a struggle.

"Hello," the Lith man began, his voice steady but filled with an underlying plea. "We have come seeking your wisdom. We've heard tales of your remarkable abilities."

"Our son is dying," Thessalia added, her voice breaking as she knelt by the gate. "We implore you, we beg you, please heal him."

Selaina's heart raced as the realization struck her—this boy, her mother's son, was Vatreus? The future tyrant who would slay thousands, obsessed with domination of Galanor. If true, then this Lith man must be her father, and Vatreus her brother—a thought too grievous to bear.

Overwhelmed, Selaina yearned to escape, to return to her simpler life before these revelations, before this nightmare. She pondered making a different wish, one where she could warn her mother and Jeth about the strange man in the forest. Perhaps they would have been prepared for the assault. Maybe her mother would never have been kidnapped and Jeth wouldn't have been killed. Perhaps she could forget all of this and return to her simple life in the forest, like waking up from a bad dream.

A voice, deep and resonating, vibrated through the ground, interrupting her thoughts. "You seek to draw from my power, yet offer nothing in return."

"What could we possibly offer you?" the Lith man asked, desperately.

"OPEN THIS GATE!" boomed the voice, which seemed to echo across time. "RELEASE ME FROM THIS PRISON!"

Startled, Thessalia, the driver, and the Lith man retreated in haste, their faces pale with fear. The ground trembled under the weight of the command, the air thick with a palpable sense of ancient power.

After a brief pause, the Lith man gathered his courage and returned to the gate, his voice shaky but resolute. "How do I open it?" he called out, his eyes searching the massive structure for any sign of a mechanism.

"Bring me a sacrifice," the voice demanded. "Flesh, blood, and bone. Provide this, and I will lend my power for the boy to live another year."

"Just one year?" The Lith man faltered, his voice laced with despair. "Isn't there anything else I could offer? His time is short."

"That is my price," said the voice, unyielding. "For every sacrifice, I will grant enough power for the boy to live another year."

Faced with an unthinkable choice, the Lith man hesitated, then solemnly set the boy down and walked him over to Thessalia. She took the boy's hand before turning her eyes to the man.

"The price is too high, Lucianis. We will find another way."

Lucianis, Selaina's father, walked back to the carriage as Thessalia followed with the boy. The carriage driver rushed to him.

"I was unaware he would demand such a sacrifice. Let me take you back. You owe nothing for this journey."

Ignoring the offer, Lucianis seized the driver's coat. The driver resisted, planting his feet firmly on the ground, but Lucianis's desperation fueled his strength, allowing him to pull the unwilling driver closer to the ominous gate.

"Lucianis!" Selaina's mother cried out in anguish.

After shoving the driver toward the shadowy gap at the gate's base, Lucianis recoiled when a giant clawed hand, shrouded in night-black with pulses of blue energy, snatched the driver, pulling him under the small opening in the gate. The man's screams echoed, abruptly silenced by the grotesque sounds of crunching bones and tearing flesh.

Lucianis took the boy from a stunned Thessalia, lifting him high above his head. A beam of blue light surged from beneath the gate, enveloping the boy in its radiant glow. His eyes flickered open, now blazing with a fiery blue intensity.

Selaina's breath caught in her throat as the stark reality of Vatreus's origins unfolded before her. It was too late to alter this past, yet as she spun around, the surroundings morphed, stretching into an endless plateau of repetitive gates, each echoing different moments of the same tragic scene.

In this kaleidoscopic nightmare, she noticed variations where Vatreus had not yet been empowered. A chance to rewrite history was still within reach. Selaina moved toward another vision, feeling herself split into countless iterations, each aligned with a different gate.

In each vision of the gate, the scene played out in different increments of time. In most of them, Vatreus had not yet received the power. She could still change it. All she had to do was move to a different facet of the Stone.

At the end of this surreal procession, one iteration of Selaina turned, locking eyes with the next. This cascade of mutual recognition rippled toward her. The Selaina immediately in front of her turned, staring back at her.

Sight beyond seeing, whispered her own voice. *Look into my eyes and see the future we forged with the Wishing Stone.*

Their gazes locked and Selaina had a vision. A brilliant light obliterated everything around her. Time and possibilities fused into a singular, stark reality. She beheld a city, orderly and lifeless, where people moved in rigid lines—some hauling wood, others drawing water. Fields were tended and seeds planted with mechanical precision. No laughter, no chatter, disturbed the oppressive silence. Guards patrolled the lines, their whips ready, overseeing the toiling figures of something that more resembled an ant colony than a human city.

Selaina's vision adjusted, and she could see the faces of the people—expressionless, their eyes void of hope or spirit. They moved with the same mechanical precision, their individuality stripped away, leaving only shells of their former selves. This was the cost of trying to change what was meant to be. Order reigned, but it had stripped the world of its soul. What if, by trying to escape her fate, she would only set into motion a different tragedy? Would the price always be too high?

In the distance, a castle loomed like a beacon, its walls sparkling as if carved from crystals, each facet shimmering with radiant colors. This majestic yet foreboding structure stood as a stark contrast to the lifeless order of the city below, an imposing symbol of the power that now dominated this world.

Selaina walked toward the castle. She followed her multiple selves inside, passing through an entrance guarded by rows of soldiers, their bodies rigid in salute.

The throne room lay beyond a grand archway, its design intricate, with vaulted ceilings reaching toward an opalescent sky. The air felt thick with a forced serenity. Velvet rugs softened her steps as she ascended the stairs to where a man sat on a high, golden throne, surrounded by attendants. Two women meticulously trimmed his hair, while others attended to his feet. He nonchalantly ate from a silver tray, discarding it with a clatter once his appetite was sated. Immediately, another tray appeared, this one bearing an extravagant dessert.

A pair of men stood by, reading from a scroll—their voices flat as they recounted regional reports.

"The Northern Uprising has been effectively quelled," one attendant read aloud, his voice echoing in the vast throne room. "Rebel leaders have been apprehended, and peace has been restored under the new management protocols."

The other attendant continued, "In the eastern sectors, cities have been successfully reconfigured to enhance work efficiency. Productivity has increased by 17 per cent. Food distribution is now fully optimized, ensuring all citizens are adequately nourished."

He then added, "Reproductive management is progressing as planned. Genetic selection protocols are in place to optimize breeding for task-specific traits. Workers are being engineered for enhanced endurance and cognitive function, matching labor demands in agricultural and technological sectors. "Expansion of population control measures is scheduled for the next quarter to ensure optimal workforce alignment," he concluded, his voice devoid of emotion as he detailed the engineered future of their society.

Selaina edged closer to the throne, her gaze fixed on the ruler. The crown on his head gleamed, his beard perfectly groomed, and his eyes burned with an unsettling blue intensity. A shock ran through her when she recognized Myrradin, the emperor of Galanor.

Disoriented and dismayed, Selaina fled the throne room, the castle's oppressive orderliness clashing with the chaos of her thoughts. Outside, the realm stretched into countless iterations, each pathway a corridor to a different possibility.

Running from the castle, Selaina chased the fleeting glimpses of herself—each a different version, a different possibility—as the environment stretched back into endless facets of time. Shadows of her own choices and their ripple effects swirled around her, dizzying and surreal.

Your destiny is ahead of you. Claim it. Her own voice, distant but unmistakable, echoed through her thoughts.

Sometimes, the true power lies not in altering fate, but in embracing it. Elysia's words resonated in her mind, more vivid and closer than ever before. She could almost feel Elysia's steady hand on her wrist, anchoring her in this chaotic storm of choices.

But there was another voice too—her own, weaving between time and possibility, whispering a haunting refrain: *Make the choice I failed to see. Claim your destiny.*

The world spun around her, a kaleidoscope of time and decisions. Selaina's heart pounded with the weight of realization—this future, born of her attempt to stop Vatreus, had unleashed a new and darker tyranny. Myrradin's cold, calculated control would hold the world in its grip. Was this the price of changing fate? Was this the future she had wrought?

The realization clawed at her. This world—this bleak, oppressive order—was worse than the one she had left behind. She felt the crushing weight of responsibility bearing down on her. She owed it to Elysia, to Darian, to Jeth, her mother … even to Rykan, who still longed to bring back his father. Myrradin had told her the Wishing Stone could only be used once. Then, it would vanish, lost to the distant future. If she hesitated, if she faltered now, the chance to set things right would be gone forever.

Jeth's words came rushing back to her, his voice warm and steady, even in her memory. *True strength lies not in seeking to change the river's course, but in becoming the water itself.*

And then, a familiar voice—older, wiser, filled with knowledge—whispered in her mind: *Water yearns for form, bending to the shape of anything that dares hold it. So too does destiny—it needs a vessel, waiting for the one who dares to bear its weight.*

The last remaining destinies of Ethyllion, the voices urged, *someday, they must be claimed. That time is now.*

Suddenly, Selaina found herself standing back at the gate—the very place where all of this had begun. She turned, her breath caught in her throat. There, standing behind her, was herself—another version of her, with confusion in her eyes, mirroring the uncertainty she felt.

The moment of decision was upon her. Countless lives—past, present, and future—balanced precariously on her next move.

It was time to make her choice.

CHAPTER 33

RYKAN'S GAZE LOCKED onto the Wishing Stone as a surge of light erupted from within, casting ghostly shadows around the forest before dying down to an ominous dullness. The Stone, now a lifeless husk, seemed to mock their hopes with its silent darkness.

Myrradin's face contorted with horror, his eyes wide and unblinking. A sharp intake of breath was the only sound before the clearing erupted into chaos. The others exchanged uneasy glances, whispers of fear and confusion weaving through the air. The Stone's energy was not meant to fade out—the Stone itself was supposed to vanish, reappearing centuries later.

But now, it sat there, an epitome of their failed endeavors. Myrradin's horror swiftly morphed into seething rage, aging his face with sudden wrinkles etched deep by despair. The luminescent lines and shapes in the grass stretching out from the base of the Stone dimmed to a faint glow.

Selaina stepped back, her hands falling from the surface of the Stone. A new light kindled in her eyes—a fierce determination Rykan had never seen before. The innocence had faded, replaced by a confident resolve.

As Myrradin advanced, his voice thunderous, she stood her ground. "What have you done!" he shouted. "The Stone should have vanished into the future!"

Her reply was calm yet carried conviction. "I made the only choice that was left to make."

"Choice? There was no choice! You were to follow orders! You have squandered our last hope!" Myrradin's words cut through the

air, sharp and merciless. "The lives of Elysia and Darian have been utterly lost now!"

The group stood stunned, the gravity of Myrradin's accusation beginning to warp their expressions. Rykan waited, his trust in Selaina shaken but intact. Deep in his soul, he knew she must have a profound reason for her actions.

"You used us!" Selaina's retort shattered the tense silence, her voice rising in defiance. "You only aimed to thwart Vatreus to—"

"Silence!" Myrradin's command was a palpable force, encapsulating Selaina within the aura of his Aedavaris.

Her words were cut off, her frustration visible when she realized he had muted her inside the shield, her voice stolen by his magic.

"What was she about to reveal, Myrradin?" Ysadora's demand cut through the tension, her eyes narrowed in suspicion.

"Leave her silenced!" Myrradin snapped, his eyes dark pits of wrath. "Let her suffocate as her air dwindles. It's no more than she deserves."

Selaina's hands pressed against the shimmering barrier, her eyes wide with anger. She mouthed words no one could hear, her pleas and protests trapped within the confines of the Aedavaris.

"Release her!" Rykan commanded.

Ysadora took a step forward, speaking firmly. "This is madness, Myrradin. We need to know what she was going to say. You can't just—"

"She betrayed us!" Myrradin interrupted with a harsh growl as he focused his shield. "She brought this upon herself. And now she must face the consequences."

Rykan and the others exchanged uneasy glances, the weight of Myrradin's fury pressing down on them.

"I demand to hear her side." Kadin's firm voice joined the chorus.

Selaina, trapped within the shimmering aura, stretched out her hands, and to Rykan's shock, her eyes began to burn with an intense blue flame— something he had never seen in her before. She had never wielded such power, and yet, with a focused intensity that seemed almost foreign, she shattered her magical confines with a resounding crack.

The Aedavaris exploded in a shower of light, knocking Myrradin backward onto the ground, his face full of surprise and fear. Where had this power come from? How had she suddenly become capable of such a feat?

Selaina's movements were swift, her bow in hand, an arrow nocked and aimed straight at Myrradin's heart as he rose to his feet.

"I saw the future you created," she declared, her voice penetrating. "With Vatreus thwarted, you made your own vile bargain with Azragal!"

Myrradin slowly and painfully rose to his feet, Ysadora offering no assistance.

"She's telling the truth isn't she, Myrradin?" Ysadora's voice cut through the still air, her question echoing off the perfectly aligned trees.

"I warned you not to look beyond the time and space of the event!" Myrradin shouted at Selaina before turning to appeal to Rykan and the others. "She's lost her mind now."

"The only one who has lost their mind is you, Myrradin," said Garrick.

"Why did you neglect to mention this?" Ysadora's eyes bore into Myrradin, demanding an answer he could no longer evade.

Myrradin's face displayed a brief moment of desperation. "I didn't tell you because you wouldn't understand," he replied, his voice strained. "For years, I searched for the iron gate, but when I found it, the bargain had already been struck."

"What did you intend to do?" Ysadora pressed, her tone sharp with accusation. "What was all this for?"

"He was seated upon a golden throne," Selaina continued, her eyes locked on Myrradin, "controlling everything. He used the power of order to rob everyone of their own will. He had turned everyone into obedient servants under his rule."

Myrradin's response was laced with a chilling tone. "None of you can even comprehend the fate that is coming to Galanor!" he roared. "And now you have ruined the best chance we had of stopping it!"

"What happened to the Stone, Selaina?" Garrick asked, with an urgency to his voice. "Can we still get Elysia back?"

"The Stone is too dangerous for anyone to wield," Selaina replied, as she eyed each of them. "We are not meant to write our own history, to manipulate the destinies of Ethyllion, to change them. Those who did so in the past are responsible for the mess we're in now. I made the choice no one else has been willing to make, to become Ethyllion's vessel."

"She bears the mark!" Ysadora exclaimed, pointing to Selaina's forehead. The mark of three blue dots in the points of a triangle appeared vividly against her skin, shimmering as if reflecting some supernatural light. "She is Zhal Evurah!" Ysadora's eyes widened in awe as she took a step back, almost reverent in her realization.

Rykan stepped closer, he observed the mark, recognizing it as the mark of the three Sky Serpents that herald the Whisper Beyond the Stars.

"That's where you got such power! You absorbed the destinies inside the Stone, the last remaining destinies of Ethyllion," Ysadora noted, a new hope sounding in her voice. "All is not lost, Selaina can lead us to victory!"

"She's a fool who has doomed you all," Myrradin spat, his form beginning to shimmer and dissolve. "Forever stranded in Wekenwild."

The air around him vibrated with an unseen tension, his skin fragmenting into millions of tiny particles, each shimmering like a speck of dust caught in sunlight. In a moment, his solid form dispersed, transforming into a swirling vortex of wind. The transformation was seamless. His body became a gust that spiraled upward, carrying with it the raw energy of a tempest. Selaina released her arrow as the whirlwind swarmed through the trees, rustling leaves and bending branches until it moved out of sight.

"What was that?" Kadin wondered aloud in awe and fear.

"A Windwraith …" Ysadora stared at the trees where Myrradin had last been seen. "Another secret he kept from me." Her hands tightened around her staff.

"Myrradin is a Windwraith?" Kadin asked. "He could have easily killed us all."

"He left us here to die," Garrick stated grimly. "You were supposed to use the Wishing Stone. That was our only way out of Wekenwild."

"We don't need the Wishing Stone, I can see the way through now," Selaina assured them.

The forest around them seemed to whisper, the leaves rustling with secrets.

Ysadora trailed closely behind Selaina, weaving through the ancient trees that appeared to part for them. Garrick and Kadin exchanged hesitant glances, their uncertainty clear in the slow gathering of their belongings. Rykan, however, broke into a broad grin, the thrill of the unknown sparking in his eyes as he hastily adjusted the straps of his pack. Yet, beneath that excitement, a shadow of conflict lingered in his mind.

If Selaina had used the Wishing Stone, time would have rewritten itself. His father might be alive again, in a world reshaped by Myrradin's cold tyranny. The thought tugged at his heart, bittersweet and heavy. He had dreamed of undoing the pain of his father's death, of seeing him once more. But at what cost?

His gaze shifted to Selaina, who walked ahead with purpose. If she had changed fate, he might never have met her. The bond they had forged, the battles fought side by side, all of it could have been erased. A world with his father but without Selaina felt like a hollow victory.

With a few quick strides, he caught up to her, the weight on his heart easing as he fell into step beside her. So much remained to be done. Tathara needed to be retaken. He needed to make sure his mother was safe. And he knew Selaina would continue the search for her own mother. As he looked ahead to the challenges they still faced, Rykan found himself oddly grateful for this moment, for this uncertain future, and for the path they still walked together.

ACKNOWLEDGMENTS

I would like to begin by expressing my deepest gratitude to God for the strength, guidance, and inspiration that made the completion of this book possible. His blessings have been the foundation of this journey.

To my family, who have been my unwavering pillars of support and encouragement, thank you for standing by me at every turn. Your belief in me has fueled my perseverance and driven me to push through challenges.

To my friends, I'm truly grateful for your constant support, your kind words, and your invaluable feedback. Your presence in my life has enriched me in more ways than I can fully express.

A special thanks to Emily Katzenberger, whose steadfast support and encouragement as an editor played a pivotal role in bringing this book to life. Her thoughtful insights and unshakeable belief in my abilities pushed me to pursue excellence and ensure this book reached its fullest potential. Emily, your inspiration and motivation have been a guiding light.

A heartfelt thank you to Annie Percik, whose keen eye as an editor helped refine the manuscript. Her attention to detail, especially in catching small yet significant logical flaws, ensured that the story was as polished and coherent as possible.

I'd also like to thank Danny Raye for her encouraging support and helpful beta reading. Her feedback was invaluable in shaping the story.

Finally, to everyone who has contributed, whether through encouragement, insight, or support, your help has meant more to me than words can express.

ABOUT THE AUTHOR

Kevin Cox has always been captivated by the mysteries of the universe, using his imagination to explore the unknown. Though he never planned to become a writer, ideas for stories often played in his mind. After writing just one chapter to see if he could do it, he discovered a passion for writing he never knew he had.

Much of Kevin's inspiration comes from growing up in the 80s, immersed in fantasy and science fiction. Ideas often come to him during long drives or while listening to music—especially songs that capture the mood he's trying to create.

Kevin believes that a great story needs strong characters, each with their own struggles and desires to overcome them. He hopes his readers will see their own challenges reflected in these characters and be inspired to find their strengths and always strive to be the best versions of themselves. Themes of friendship and helping others are central to his writing.

Kevin lives in Leesburg, Georgia, where he enjoys playing guitar and video games when he's not writing.

For the latest news and updates on the next book in the *Fates of Galanor* series, follow Kevin on social media or contact him via email.

Email: authorkevincox@gmail.com

Instagram: @kevincoxauthor

Twitter: @authorkevincox

THANKS FOR READING!

If you enjoyed *The Weight of the Wishing Stone*, I would be incredibly grateful if you could take a moment to leave a review on Amazon (or your preferred platform). Your feedback not only helps other readers discover the book but also means the world to me as an author.

Thank you for your support, and I hope you'll join me for the next adventure in *Fates of Galanor*. Book 2 is in the works, and I can't wait to share it with you soon!

Stay Connected!

Want more stories and updates? Join my newsletter and receive a free short story as a thank you for subscribing!

Sign up now at www.authorkevincox.com to get your free story and stay updated on upcoming releases, exclusive content, and special offers.

Thank you again for your support, and I hope to connect with you soon!

KEVIN COX
BEWILDERNESS
BOOK ONE

KEVIN COX
SHADOWSPHERE
BEWILDERNESS
BOOK TWO

KEVIN COX
NEVERSCAPE
BEWILDERNESS
BOOK THREE

KEVIN COX
STORMWAKER
BEWILDERNESS
BOOK FOUR

KEVIN COX
ETERNIUM
BEWILDERNESS
BOOK FIVE

OTHER BOOKS BY KEVIN COX

If you enjoyed *The Weight of the Wishing Stone*, be sure to explore the *Bewilderness* series, a thrilling blend of fantasy, sci-fi, adventure, and mystery. In this series, you'll journey through multiple worlds and encounter alien races while battling against the Shadows, with characters facing challenges that will test their strength and determination.

The *Bewilderness* series includes:

Book One: *Bewilderness*

Book Two: *Shadowsphere*

Book Three: *Neverscape*

Book Four: *Stormwaker*

Book Five: *Eternium*

Available on Amazon:

https://www.amazon.com/dp/B09J3Z9J2F

Copyright © 2024-2025 by Kevin Cox